PRAISE FOR IAN HAMILTON AN

D0460088

## PRAISE FOR *THE WATER RAT OF WANCHAI*
### WINNER OF THE ARTHUR ELLIS AWARD FOR BEST FIRST NOVEL

"Ian Hamilton's *The Water Rat of Wanchai* is a smart, action-packed thriller of the first order, and Ava Lee, a gay Asian-Canadian forensics accountant with a razor-sharp mind and highly developed martial arts skills, is a protagonist to be reckoned with. We were impressed by Hamilton's tight plotting; his well-rendered settings, from the glitz of Bangkok to the grit of Guyana; and his ability to portray a wide range of sharply individualized characters in clean but sophisticated prose." — Judges' Citation, Arthur Ellis Award for Best First Novel

"Ava Lee is tough, fearless, quirky, and resourceful, and she has more — well, you know — than a dozen male detectives I can think of... Hamilton has created a true original in Ava Lee." — Linwood Barclay, author of *No Time for Goodbye*

"If the other novels [in the series] are half as good as this debut by Ian Hamilton, then readers are going to celebrate. Hamilton has created a marvellous character in Ava Lee... This is a terrific story that's certain to be on the Arthur Ellis Best First Novel list." — *Globe and Mail*

"[Ava Lee's] lethal knowledge...torques up her sex appeal to the approximate level of a female lead in a Quentin Tarantino film." — *National Post*

"The heroine in *The Water Rat of Wanchai* by Ian Hamilton sounds too good to be true, but the heroics work better that way...formidable...The story breezes along with something close to total clarity...Ava is unbeatable at just about everything. Just wait for her to roll out her bak mei against the bad guys. She's perfect. She's fast." — *Toronto Star*

CALGARY PUBLIC LIBRARY

DEC    2017

"Imagine a book about a forensic accountant that has tension, suspense, and action... When the central character looks like Lucy Liu, kicks like Jackie Chan, and has a travel budget like Donald Trump, the story is anything but boring. *The Water Rat of Wanchai* is such a beast... I look forward to the next one, *The Disciple of Las Vegas*."
— *Montreal Gazette*

"[A] tomb-raiding Dragon Lady Lisbeth, *sans* tattoo and face metal."
— *Winnipeg Free Press*

"An enjoyable romp with a feisty, ingenious heroine whose lethal martial arts skills are as formidable as her keen mind." — *Publishers Weekly*

"Readers will discern in Ava undertones of Lisbeth Salander, the ferocious protagonist of the late Stieg Larsson's crime novels... She, too, is essentially a loner, and small, and physically brutal... There are suggestions in *The Water Rat of Wanchai* of deeper complexities waiting to be more fully revealed. Plus there's pleasure, both for Ava and readers, in the puzzle itself: in figuring out where money has gone, how to get it back, and which humans, helpful or malevolent, are to be dealt with where, and in what ways, in the process... Irresistible."
— Joan Barfoot, *London Free Press*

"*The Water Rat of Wanchai* delivers on all fronts... feels like the beginning of a crime-fighting saga... A great story told with colour, energy, and unexpected punch." — *Hamilton Spectator*

"The best series fiction leaves readers immersed in a world that is both familiar and fresh. Seeds planted early bear fruit later on, creating a rich forest that blooms across a number of books... [Hamilton] creates a terrific atmosphere of suspense..." — *Quill & Quire*

"The book is an absolute page-turner... Hamilton's knack for writing snappy dialogue is evident... I recommend getting in on the ground floor with this character, because for Ava Lee, the sky's the limit."
— *Inside Halton*

"A fascinating story of a hunt for stolen millions. And the hunter, Ava Lee, is a compelling heroine: tough, smart, and resourceful."
— Meg Gardiner, author of *The Nightmare Thief*

"Few heroines are as feisty as *The Girl with the Dragon Tattoo*'s Lisbeth Salander, but Ian Hamilton's Ava Lee could give her a run for her money... Gripping... [Ava is] smart, gutsy, and resourceful."
— *Stylist UK*

"With Ava Lee comes a new star in the world of crime-thrillers... Hamilton has produced a suspenseful and gripping novel featuring a woman who is not afraid of anything... Captivating and hard to put down." — *dapd/sda*

"Thrillers don't always have to be Scandinavian to work. Ava Lee is a wonderful Chinese-Canadian investigator who uses unconventional methods of investigation in a mysterious Eastern setting." — *Elle* (Germany)

"Ava has flair, charm, and sex appeal... *The Water Rat of Wanchai* is a successful first book in a series, which will definitely have you longing for more." — *Sonntag-Express*

"Hamilton is in the process of writing six books and film rights have already been sold. If the other cases are similar to this first one, Ava Lee is sure to quickly shake up Germany's thriller business."
— *Handelsblatt*

"Brilliantly researched and incredibly exciting!" — *Bücher*

"Page-turning till the end of the book!... Ava Lee is the upcoming crime star." — *dpa*

"Exciting thriller debut with an astonishing end." — *Westdeutsche Zeitung*

"Seldom does one get a thriller about white-collar crime, with an intelligent, independent lesbian and Asian protagonist. It's also rare to find a book with such interesting and exotic settings...Readers will find great amusement in Ava's unconventional ways and will certainly enjoy accompanying her on her travels." — *Literaturkurier*

## PRAISE FOR *THE DISCIPLE OF LAS VEGAS*
### FINALIST, BARRY AWARD FOR BEST ORIGINAL TRADE PAPERBACK

"I started to read *The Disciple of Las Vegas* at around ten at night. And I did something I have only done with two other books (Cormac McCarthy's *The Road* and Douglas Coupland's *Player One*): I read the novel in one sitting. Ava Lee is too cool. She wonderfully straddles two worlds and two identities. She does some dastardly things and still remains our hero thanks to the charm Ian Hamilton has given her on the printed page. It would take a female George Clooney to portray her in a film. The action and plot move quickly and with power. Wow. A punch to the ear, indeed." — J. J. Lee, author of *The Measure of a Man*

"I loved *The Water Rat of Wanchai,* the first novel featuring Ava Lee. Now, Ava and Uncle make a return that's even better...Simply irresistible." — Margaret Cannon, *Globe and Mail*

"This is slick, fast-moving escapism reminiscent of Ian Fleming, with more to come in what shapes up as a high-energy, high-concept series." — *Booklist*

"Fast paced...Enough personal depth to lift this thriller above solely action-oriented fare." — *Publishers Weekly*

"Lee is a hugely original creation, and Hamilton packs his adventure with interesting facts and plenty of action." — *Irish Independent*

"Hamilton makes each page crackle with the kind of energy that could easily jump to the movie screen...This riveting read will keep you up late at night." — *Penthouse*

"Hamilton gives his reader plenty to think about...Entertaining."
— *Kitchener-Waterloo Record*

## PRAISE FOR *THE WILD BEASTS OF WUHAN*
### LAMBDA LITERARY AWARD FINALIST: LESBIAN MYSTERY

"Smart and savvy Ava Lee returns in this slick mystery set in the rarefied world of high art...[A] great caper tale. Hamilton has great fun chasing villains and tossing clues about. *The Wild Beasts of Wuhan* is the best Ava Lee novel yet, and promises more and better to come."
— Margaret Cannon, *Globe and Mail*

"One of my favourite new mystery series, perfect escapism."
— *National Post*

"As a mystery lover, I'm devouring each book as it comes out...What I love in the novels: The constant travel, the high-stakes negotiation, and Ava's willingness to go into battle against formidable opponents, using only her martial arts skills to defend herself...If you want a great read and an education in high-level business dealings, Ian Hamilton is an author to watch." — *Toronto Star*

"Fast-paced and very entertaining." — *Montreal Gazette*

"Ava Lee is definitely a winner." — *Saskatoon Star Phoenix*

"*The Wild Beasts of Wuhan* is an entertaining dip into potentially fatal worlds of artistic skulduggery." — *Sudbury Star*

"Hamilton uses Ava's investigations as comprehensive and intriguing mechanisms for plot and character development." — *Quill & Quire*

"You haven't seen cold and calculating until you've double-crossed this number cruncher. Another strong entry from Arthur Ellis Award–winner Hamilton." — *Booklist*

"An intelligent kick-ass heroine anchors Canadian author Hamilton's excellent third novel featuring forensic accountant Ava Lee...Clearly conversant with the art world, Hamilton makes the intricacies of forgery as interesting as a Ponzi scheme." — *Publishers Weekly,* *Starred Review*

"A lively series about Ava Lee, a sexy forensic financial investigator." — *Tampa Bay Times*

"This book is miles from the ordinary. The main character, Ava Lee is 'the whole package.'" — *Minneapolis Star Tribune*

"A strong heroine is challenged to discover the details of an intercontinental art scheme. Although Hamilton's star Ava Lee is technically a forensic accountant, she's more badass private investigator than desk jockey." — *Kirkus Reviews*

## PRAISE FOR *THE RED POLE OF MACAU*

"Ava Lee returns as one of crime fiction's most intriguing characters. *The Red Pole of Macau* is the best page-turner of the season from the hottest writer in the business!" — John Lawrence Reynolds, author of *Beach Strip*

"Ava Lee, that wily, wonderful hunter of nasty business brutes, is back in her best adventure ever...If you haven't yet discovered Ava Lee, start here." — *Globe and Mail*

"The best in the series so far." — *London Free Press*

"Ava [Lee] is a character we all could use at one time or another. Failing that, we follow her in her best adventure yet." — *Hamilton Spectator*

"A romp of a story with a terrific heroine." — *Saskatoon Star Phoenix*

"Fast-paced...The action unfolds like a well-oiled action-flick."
— *Kitchener-Waterloo Record*

"A change of pace for our girl [Ava Lee]...Suspenseful." — *Toronto Star*

"Hamilton packs tremendous potential in his heroine...A refreshingly relevant series. This reader will happily pay House of Anansi for the fifth instalment." — *Canadian Literature*

## PRAISE FOR *THE SCOTTISH BANKER OF SURABAYA*

"Hamilton deepens Ava's character, and imbues her with greater mettle and emotional fire, to the extent that book five is his best, most memorable, to date." — *National Post*

"In today's crowded mystery market, it's no easy feat coming up with a protagonist who stands out from the pack. But Ian Hamilton has made a great job of it with his Ava Lee books. Young, stylish, Chinese-Canadian, lesbian, and a brilliant forensic accountant, Ava is as complex a character as you could want...[A] highly addictive series... Hamilton knows how to keep the pages turning. He eases us into the seemingly tame world of white-collar crime, then raises the stakes, bringing the action to its peak with an intensity and violence that's stomach-churning. His Ava Lee is a winner and a welcome addition to the world of strong female avengers." — *NOW Magazine*

"Most of the series' success rests in Hamilton's tight plotting, attention to detail, and complex powerhouse of a heroine: strong but vulnerable, capable but not impervious...With their tight plotting and crackerjack heroine, Hamilton's novels are the sort of crowd-pleasing, narrative-focused fiction we find all too rarely in this country." — *Quill & Quire*

"Ava is such a cool character, intelligent, Chinese-Canadian, unconventional, and original...Irresistible." — *Owen Sound Sun Times*

## PRAISE FOR *THE TWO SISTERS OF BORNEO*
### NATIONAL BESTSELLER

"There are plenty of surprises waiting for Ava, and for the reader, all uncovered with great satisfaction." — *National Post*

"Ian Hamilton's great new Ava Lee mystery has the same wow factor as its five predecessors. The plot is complex and fast-paced, the writing tight, and its protagonist is one of the most interesting female avengers to come along in a while." — *NOW Magazine* (NNNN)

"The appeal of the Ava Lee series owes much to her brand name lifestyle; it stirs pleasantly giddy emotions to encounter such a devotedly elegant heroine. But, better still, the detailing of financial shenanigans is done in such clear language that even readers who have trouble balancing their bank books can appreciate the way conmen set out to fleece unsuspecting victims." — *Toronto Star*

"Hamilton has a unique gift for concocting sizzling thrillers." — *Edmonton Journal*

"Hamilton has this formula down to an art, but he manages to avoid cliché and his ability to evoke a place keeps the series fresh." — *Globe and Mail*

"From her introduction in *The Water Rat of Wanchai*, Ava Lee has stood as a stylish, street-smart leading lady whose resourcefulness and creativity have helped her to uncover criminal activity in everything from illegal online gambling rings to international art heists. In Hamilton's newest installment to the series, readers accompany Ava on great adventures and to interesting locales, roaming from Hong Kong to the Netherlands to Borneo. The pulse-pounding, fast-paced narrative is chocked full of divergent plot twists and intriguing personalities that make it a popular escapist summer read. The captivating female sleuth does not disappoint as she circles the globe on a quest to uncover an unusually intriguing investment fiasco involving fraud, deception and violence." — *ExpressMilwaukee.com*

"Ava may be the most chic figure in crime fiction." — *Hamilton Spectator*

"The series as a whole is as good as the modern thriller genre gets." — *The Cord*

## PRAISE FOR *THE KING OF SHANGHAI*

"The only thing scarier than being ripped off for a few million bucks is being the guy who took it and having Ava Lee on your tail. If Hamilton's kick-ass forensic accountant has your number, it's up." — Linwood Barclay

"One of Ian Hamilton's best." — *Globe and Mail*

"Brilliant, sexy, and formidably martial arts-trained forensic accountant Ava Lee is back in her seventh adventure (after *The Two Sisters of Borneo*)... Ever since his dazzling surprise debut with *The Water Rat of Wanchai*, Hamilton has propelled Ava along through the series with expanded storytelling and nuanced character development: there's always something new to discover about Ava. Fast-paced suspense, exotic locales, and a rich cast of characters (some, like Ava's driver, Sonny, are both dangerous and lovable) make for yet another hugely entertaining hit." — *Publishers Weekly*, *Starred review*

"A luxurious sense of place... Hamilton's knack for creating fascinating detail will keep readers hooked... Good fun for those who like to combine crime fiction with armchair travelling." — *Booklist*

"Ava would be a sure thing to whip everybody, Putin included, at the negotiating table." — *Toronto Star*

"After six novels starring Chinese-Canadian Ava Lee and her perilously thrilling exploits, best-selling Canadian author Ian Hamilton has jolted his creation out of what wasn't even yet a rut and hurled her abruptly into a new circumstance, with fresh ambitions." — *London Free Press*

"It's a measure of Hamilton's quality as a thriller writer that he compels your attention even before he starts ratcheting up the suspense."
— *Regina Leader Post*

"An unputdownable book that I would highly recommend for all."
— *Words of Mystery*

"Ava is as powerful and brilliant as ever." — *Literary Treats*

## PRAISE FOR *THE PRINCELING OF NANJING*
### CANADIAN BESTSELLER
### A KOBO BEST BOOK OF THE YEAR

"The reader is offered plenty of Ava in full flower as the Chinese-Canadian glamour puss who happens to be gay, whip smart, and unafraid of whatever dangers come her way." — *Toronto Star*

"Hamilton's Chinese-Canadian heroine is one of a kind... [An] exotic thriller that also offers a fascinating inside look at fiscal misconduct in China... As a unique series character, Ava Lee's become indispensable." — *Calgary Herald*

"Ava Lee has a new business, a new look, and, most important, a new Triad boss to appreciate her particular financial talents... We know that Ava will come up with a plan and Hamilton will come up with a twist." — *Globe and Mail*

"Like the best series writers — Ian Rankin and Peter Robinson come to mind — Hamilton manages to... keep the Ava Lee books fresh... A compulsive read, a page-turner of the old school... *The Princeling of Nanjing* is a welcome return of an old favourite, and bodes well for future books." — *Quill & Quire*

"Hamilton uses his people and plot to examine Chinese class and power structures that open opportunities for massive depravities and corruptions." — *London Free Press*

"As usual with a Hamilton-Lee novel, matters take a decided twist as the plot unrolls." — *Owen Sound Times*

"One of those grip-tight novels that makes one read 'just one more chapter' and you discover it's 3 a.m. The novel is built on complicated webs artfully woven into clear, magnetic storytelling. Author Ian Hamilton delivers the intrigue within complex and relentless webs in high style and once again proves that everyone, once in their lives, needs an Ava Lee at their backs." — *Canadian Mystery Reviews*

"The best of the Ava Lee series to date…*Princeling* features several chapters of pure, unadulterated financial sleuthing, which both gave me some nerdy feels and tickled my puzzle-loving mind." — *Literary Treats*

"*The Princeling of Nanjing* was another addition to the Ava Lee series that did not disappoint." — *Words of Mystery*

## PRAISE FOR *THE COUTURIER OF MILAN*
### CANADIAN BESTSELLER

"The latest in the excellent series starring Ava Lee, businesswoman extraordinaire, *The Couturier of Milan* is another winner for Ian Hamilton…The novel is a hoot. At a point where most crime series start to run out of steam, Ava Lee just keeps rolling on." — *Globe and Mail*

"In Ava Lee, Ian Hamilton has created a crime fighter who breaks the mould with every new book (and, frankly, with every new chapter)." — *CBC Books*

"The pleasure in following Ava's clever plans for countering the bad guys remains as ever a persuasive attraction." — *Toronto Star*

"Fashionably fierce forensics…But Hamilton has built around Ava Lee an award-winning series that absorbs intriguing aspects of both Asian and Canadian cultures." — *London Free Press*

# THE
# IMAM
# OF
# TAWI-TAWI

# THE
# IMAM
# OF
# TAWI-TAWI

## AN AVA LEE NOVEL
## THE TRIAD YEARS

## IAN HAMILTON

SPIDERLINE

Copyright © 2018 Ian Hamilton

Published in Canada in 2018 and the USA in 2018
by House of Anansi Press Inc.
www.houseofanansi.com

All rights reserved. No part of this publication may be reproduced or
transmitted in any form or by any means, electronic or mechanical,
including photocopying, recording, or any information storage and
retrieval system, without permission in writing from the publisher.

House of Anansi Press is committed to protecting our natural environment.
As part of our efforts, the interior of this book is printed on paper that
contains 100% post-consumer recycled fibres, is acid-free, and is processed
chlorine-free.

This is a work of fiction. Names, characters, businesses, organizations,
places, and events are either a product of the author's imagination or are
used fictitiously. Any resemblance to actual persons, living or dead, is
purely coincidental.

22 21 20 19 18 1 2 3 4 5

Library and Archives Canada Cataloguing in Publication

Hamilton, Ian, 1946–, author
The Imam of Tawi-Tawi / Ian Hamilton.

(An Ava Lee novel: the triad years)
Issued in print and electronic formats.
ISBN 978-1-4870-0274-9 (softcover). — ISBN 978-1-4870-0275-6 (EPUB). —
ISBN 978-1-4870-0276-3 (Kindle)

I. Title.  II. Series: Hamilton, Ian, 1946– .  Ava Lee novel.

PS8615.A4423I43 2018          C813'.6          C2017-901326-2
                    C2017-901327-0

Library of Congress Control Number: 2017933809

Book design: Alysia Shewchuk

We acknowledge for their financial support of our publishing program
the Canada Council for the Arts, the Ontario Arts Council, and the
Government of Canada through the Canada Book Fund.

Printed and bound in Canada

For Steele Curry, with thanks for his support
and incisive advice.

**AVA LEE WAS IN BED, FLAT ON HER BACK, WITH HER** head propped up by three pillows. She was awake, and her eyes were fixed on a long, lean woman standing naked next to a window that looked out onto Dianchi Lake. The woman stretched her arms above her head, yawned, and turned to Ava.

"I don't want to leave," Pang Fai said. "But I have to get moving."

"Stay."

"There will be more than a hundred people at the pre-shoot party tonight. I have to be there. The director is angry enough that I took the weekend off."

"Surely being one of the biggest movie stars in China gives you some advantages," Ava said.

"I think the opposite is true," Fai said. "I'm expected to set an example for the other cast members, and this director hasn't been shy about making me feel responsible for the ultimate success of the film."

"And how long will the shoot take?"

"We begin early tomorrow morning, and then it's at least

ten weeks of work. We'll start here and then work our way northeast to Beijing — city by city, town by town — for about twenty-seven hundred kilometres."

"I think it's ridiculous to drag you and the whole crew from place to place like that."

"He's a fiend for authenticity," Fai said. "The whole idea is to have one lonely, brave woman duplicating at least part of Mao's Long March. It's a challenging role. I play a farmer's wife who's brave — or foolish — enough to protest. I'm supposed to be a symbol representing the spirit of the march, but in reality showing how Mao's Great Leap Forward betrayed his original ideals and brought unimaginable suffering to ordinary Chinese people. Mao may have wanted to accelerate agrarian reform, but his policies dispossessed farmers, brought on catastrophic food shortages, and caused the deaths of millions."

Ava smiled. The women were staying at the Intercontinental Hotel on the outskirts of Kunming, in Yunnan province, which was almost three thousand kilometres to the southwest of Beijing. They had arrived from Hong Kong, where they had spent the previous two days. During their time together in Kunming, they had left the room only three times — for lunch and dinner in the Shang Tao Restaurant and for late-night drinks in the Butterfly Bar.

They had known each other for months but had been lovers for only four days. The experience was proving to be momentous for both of them.

Over the years, Ava had had a series of flings before meeting Maria Gonzalez, a Colombian woman living in Toronto, with whom she'd had a relationship that lasted several years. Maria had ended it just as Fai came into Ava's life. Ava had thought she loved Maria, but now, after these few days with Fai, she was beginning to wonder if she'd ever experienced real love before.

"I could meet up with you on the road here and there," Ava said.

"No, I don't want you to," Fai said. Being gay in China was still considered unacceptable, and public knowledge of Fai's sexuality would destroy her career. It was a burden that Ava, Hong Kong–born but Canadian-raised, could barely comprehend but knew to be true.

She feigned pain and pulled the duvet over her head.

Fai rushed to the bed, pulled back the duvet, and crawled in beside her. She nuzzled Ava's neck. "I'm going to miss you, more than I've ever missed anyone," she whispered. "No one but you and me will know that the misery I portray in this role is because you're not with me. When the film is done, I want to go away with you for weeks, or months, or for however long you can put up with me."

"Would you consider coming to Toronto? I have a condo in the centre of the city. There are lots of designer shops and every type of restaurant, including Chinese, within walking distance. And we can be ourselves without you having to worry about how people will react," Ava said. "I also don't think you'd have to worry about being recognized — my neighbourhood is not that Chinese."

"I think my ego can handle not being recognized."

Ava reached down and gently lifted Fai's chin. She wasn't wearing any makeup and her hair was slightly dishevelled, but she was the most mesmerizing woman Ava had ever been with. The slightly square chin, strong cheekbones, well-defined lips, and proud nose were in almost perfect proportion. And then there were her eyes. They were large, almost Western, and had triggered gossip about who her parents really were. But it wasn't their size that Ava found remarkable; it was the way they pulled her in. In many ways, her eyes reminded Ava of Uncle, her former partner, her mentor, and — in every way imaginable, except for blood-line — her grandfather. She had always thought that Uncle communicated with the world through his eyes rather than with words or physical mannerisms. Now, she felt connected in the same way to Fai.

"When do you really have to leave?" Ava said.

"Now." Fai sighed.

Ava slid her hand down Fai's body until it rested between her legs. "I can't convince you to stay?"

"You probably could, but if we start again, how will we stop? I don't want to leave here feeling guilty."

Ava kissed her on the forehead. Fai rolled off the bed and reached for her underwear, which lay on a chair. As Ava watched her dress, her phone rang. She picked it up and saw that the incoming number had the Philippines country code.

"Shit, I forgot about this," she said.

"What is it?" Fai said.

"I think Uncle Chang Wang from Manila is calling. I don't know if you remember, but he phoned me in Hong Kong. I put him off then and told him to call me tonight." Ava pressed the answer button. "This is Ava."

"Good evening, this is Chang. I hope this time my call isn't inconvenient."

"No, I was expecting to hear from you. Is Mr. Ordonez there as well?"

"Tommy is in Singapore on business, so it's just me."

Tommy Ordonez was the richest man in the Philippines. Chang Wang was his second-in-command. Despite his name, Ordonez was Chinese. He had been born Chu Guang in Qingdao and moved to the Philippines as a young man. In an effort to blend into the different society — and to avoid periodic outbursts of xenophobia — he had changed his name. It was such a common practice in the Philippines that there was even a word for it. Chinese immigrants who adopted Filipino names were called Chinoys, a play on "Pinoy," Filipinos' informal term for themselves.

"I've always enjoyed our conversations, with or without Tommy," Ava said.

"That's a very diplomatic remark. It reminds me of something that Uncle would say."

He was referring to Chow Tung, Ava's former partner. Chow and Chang were both from Wuhan, in Hubei province, and had known each other since they were boys. After leaving China, they had stayed in touch for more than fifty years and helped each other innumerable times. The last occasion had been a few years before, when the Ordonez organization hired Ava and Uncle to recover stolen money. They had successfully returned close to fifty million dollars.

"I can't begin to list the things I learned from Uncle," she said.

"I miss him," Chang said quietly. "We used to chat most weekends. Some Sunday mornings I pick up the phone to call him and then realize he isn't there anymore."

"I feel that way nearly every day."

"I know how close you two were. He talked about you often. He adored you."

"And I loved him."

Out of the corner of her eye, Ava saw that Fai was now dressed and putting her makeup bag into the small suitcase she'd brought with her. Ava reached under the pillow and pulled out a black Giordano T-shirt that she slipped over her head. "Uncle, excuse me for just a moment. Don't go away. I'll be right back," she said, sliding out of bed and placing the phone on the bedside table.

She walked over to Fai and hugged her so tightly she could feel their hearts beating.

"I want you to call me every day," Fai said. "You can text and email me too, but I want to hear your voice. The best times are before eight in the morning and after six in the evening."

"I will," Ava said. "This is going to be a long ten weeks."

"But when it's over, I don't have any other immediate commitments, and I'm not going to let my agent make any."

"I'm determined to get you to Toronto. I know you'll love it."

"I'll love anywhere as long as I'm with you."

"And I feel the same way. But still, you'll enjoy the freedom we can have there."

Fai nodded, but Ava saw doubt in her eyes. *How can you explain freedom*, she wondered, *to someone who's never truly experienced it?*

"You'd better go back to your friend on the phone," Fai said.

"I'll call you in the morning."

"Please don't forget," Fai said.

Ava waited until the door closed before picking up the phone again. "Sorry, Uncle."

"That's not necessary. I realize this is rather an imposition on my part."

"Except I don't know what it is you're imposing."

"As I said to you the other night, we have a problem here in the Philippines that we need some help with."

"But I don't do debt collection work anymore. I'm partners in an investment business with May Ling Wong."

"Does she still live in Wuhan, and are she and Changxing still married?"

"Yes."

"I've known them for many years, although I haven't had any contact with them recently. She is very capable and I'm sure an ideal business partner."

"That's been my experience," Ava said. "She's also a good friend."

"As someone who doesn't have any family, I place enormous value on friendship. I was fortunate to have Uncle for so many years."

Ava didn't doubt Chang's sincerity, but she suspected he was stalling as he searched for a way to circumvent her less-than-enthusiastic reaction to his request for help. "And you still have Tommy."

"We're not friends in the way I was with Uncle," Chang said. "We have different tastes and personalities, and outside of the office we never socialize. Inside the business, though, we trust and support each other, and think almost as one mind. For example, when I mentioned to Tommy that I wanted to involve you in our problem, he leapt at the suggestion."

"Perhaps I didn't make it clear enough. I'm not only not in the old business, I have absolutely no interest in or intention of returning to it."

"This has nothing to do with debt collection."

"Then I'm confused, because I can't think of any other talents I have that could be of use to you and Tommy."

"I could spend several minutes repeating what Tommy and I have said about your abilities, but my experience with you leads me to believe you wouldn't welcome that kind of flattery. Tommy also suggested that we offer you money, but I told him — aside from the fact that you're a wealthy young woman — this isn't the kind of problem you can put a price on," Chang said. "So I guess what it comes down to is I'm asking you to help us as a personal favour — the kind that Uncle and I did for each other over the years."

*God, he's smooth*, Ava thought. Despite her cynicism, her curiosity was aroused, and she couldn't dismiss his request for a favour out of hand. "Uncle, you have my interest," she finally said. "What kind of problem can't you put a price on?"

"On the surface — and truthfully this is Tommy's main concern — we believe one of our most successful businesses could be at risk. And there are larger issues, Ava, that could have an impact not just on us but on many other people, in the Philippines and beyond."

"And what do you imagine I could possibly do to prevent whatever it is you're alluding to?"

"I allude, as you call it, because we lack hard information. We have suspicions but we need to confirm them. We need to determine whether we actually have a problem," Chang said. "And if we do have one, then we need to develop a strategy to deal with it. But that all starts with having facts. We need someone we trust totally to confirm some things we've been told and to gather as much additional information as possible. As Tommy and I remember very well, you have an extraordinary talent for getting to the truth. The truth is what we're after, and we think you're the person who can find it for us."

"What is this potential problem?"

Chang hesitated. She thought she heard ice clinking in a glass and wondered if he was drinking. "Ava, I would like that explanation to take place in Manila," he said. "I know this will sound vague and maybe even conspiratorial, but I'm not comfortable explaining it to you over the phone. First, it's very complicated and I'm not as well-informed as some other people I'd like you to talk to. Second, this isn't something that can be explained in half an hour or even several hours. I believe you should meet and take the measure of the people who've related at least part of their suspicions to us."

"And you have no one in the Philippines you can turn to?"

"Absolutely not. As I said, this is about trust, and the number of people who Tommy and I truly trust we can count on one hand. Of those, only one lives in Manila, and he's the first person we want you to talk to."

"Uncle, I really don't know what to say. I have other responsibilities now."

"Give us one day," he said quickly. "Get on a plane tomorrow and come to Manila for one meeting. If you decide to go back to Toronto or Hong Kong or wherever after that, the issue will never be mentioned again and we'll still be grateful for your time."

"I'm expected in Shanghai tomorrow for a business review that's scheduled to last several days."

"Postpone it," Chang said. "Please, Ava."

The word "please" startled her. It wasn't something she could remember Chang or Tommy Ordonez ever uttering. Not only was it out of character, in her mind it was an acknowledgement that she was their equal.

"I can't give you an answer this minute," she said. "I have to think about it, and I also want to talk to my partners and the people expecting me in Shanghai."

"Of course, do that," he said. "But there is urgency to this matter. Waiting four days to talk to you wasn't easy — more than once I reached for the phone. Can you possibly speak to them tonight?"

"Yes, I can, and I'll call you when I have."

"Thanks. I'll stay up until I hear from you," he said.

"Uncle, you do understand that this doesn't mean I'm leaning towards saying yes?"

"Please, give us that one day, Ava," Chang said. "My belief is that if you do, you'll commit to helping us get to the bottom of this problem."

*He's dangling bait*, she thought. She admired how skillfully he had handled his end of the conversation: he had started it by invoking their connection through Uncle. Then he'd complimented her while insisting that he thought she was above flattery. Finally, he had framed his request as a personal favour. She didn't know why he thought he had the right to ask for one, since he and Ava were hardly friends, but he had anyway, and it had been exactly the right approach. Indeed, it was probably the only approach that had a chance of succeeding with her.

"Let me make some calls," she said.

## 2

**AVA HAD NOT BEEN MISLEADING CHANG WHEN SHE** said she had meetings scheduled in Shanghai, but what she didn't tell him was that she'd already had doubts about attending them.

Ava and her partners, May Ling Wong and Amanda Yee (who was also her sister-in-law through her marriage to Ava's half-brother Michael), owned Three Sisters Investments. One of their largest holdings was in PÖ, a recently formed fashion design company based in Shanghai. PÖ was run by Chi-Tze Song, a Three Sisters employee, and by Gillian Po, who was the sister of Clark Po, the brand's visionary young designer. They had successfully launched the company in Asia the year before, and just a month ago they had introduced the line to fashion buyers and journalists from North America and Europe, at London Fashion Week.

Initially London had been a success, so much so that PÖ attracted the attention of VLG, a Milan-based luxury-brand conglomerate. But when Ava and her partners turned down VLG's bid to buy Three Sisters' shares in the company, the directors of VLG retaliated by attempting to damage

PÖ's reputation in the industry and shut them out of the major Western markets. PÖ fought back, and at a meeting in Macau, VLG had agreed to end the hostilities and help repair PÖ's reputation. The deal was brokered by Ava's friend Xu, the Triad leader in Shanghai and a silent partner in Three Sisters, and by Franco Bianchi, who ran the Camorra Mafia organization in Naples and was a silent partner in VLG.

In the days since Macau, VLG had been true to its word, and the meeting in Shanghai was to lay the groundwork for recontacting key Western markets. Ava was feeling some concern that her presence might inhibit contributions from the people who were actually running the business. She was also wondering why May Ling — who had been in nearby Hong Kong when they negotiated the truce in Macau — had begged off going to Shanghai and instead had returned to Wuhan. She had said there were business issues there that needed her attention, but Ava sensed that something else was in play. She reached for the phone and called her.

When May Ling answered, Ava could barely hear her over the background noise. "I'm in a restaurant. I have to go outside to talk," May said. A moment later the noise died down and she came back on the line. "Where are you?"

"I'm still in Kunming."

"I've been thinking about you all weekend. How did it go with Fai?" May knew Fai from Shanghai and London, where Fai had modelled for PÖ's runway shows. On a more personal level, she had also spent some time with her and Ava in the bar of the Hong Kong Mandarin Oriental Hotel, on the night that Ava and Fai became lovers. She had long been privy to Ava's sexual orientation, and now she was aware of Fai's and the emergence of their relationship.

"It was wonderful."

"How wonderful?"

"May, I'm not going to talk about my sex life."

"My problem is that I don't have a sex life to talk about."

"Well, good friends though we are, I still don't want you living vicariously through mine."

May laughed. "Is that what you're calling to tell me?"

"No. I've been thinking about Shanghai and whether I'm really needed at the PÖ meetings."

"What's caused you to ask that?"

"Something else has come up and I'm wondering what I should do about it," Ava said. "I was also thinking about your return to Wuhan. I know you said it was because you're busy, but I keep thinking there might be some other reason."

May didn't respond right away, and in that hesitation Ava knew immediately that her instincts had been correct.

"I didn't think it was a good idea for me to go to Shanghai," May said carefully. "Amanda and Chi-Tze have the hands-on responsibility for Three Sisters' concerns in that business, and Clark and Gillian are one hundred percent dedicated to it. I felt they should be left to go at it on their own. I know they're all young, but they're also very smart and committed, and they won't learn how to run and grow a business with me looking over their shoulders. They need to make their own decisions and know that they're trusted to do it."

"Why didn't you tell me how you felt before you left Hong Kong?"

"I didn't think it was my place to suggest that you go to Shanghai or not. And truthfully, I wasn't sure whether my reasoning applies to you in the same way. You're closer in age to them and you have a different set of relationships.

I'm like their mother; you're a slightly older sister. And let's not forget, you're the one who actually saved the business."

"May, we're equal partners. What applies to you should apply to me."

"I didn't want to impose my opinion on you about how we should operate, because that's all it is — an opinion. If pushed, I could probably even make an argument for our being there, but in this case I felt it was best to back off. We've given Amanda and Chi-Tze lots of responsibility, and there are times when they should be allowed to exercise their authority completely. I thought this was one of those times."

"I do wish you'd discussed this with me beforehand," Ava said. "I'm still learning how to work with a team. I've spent too many years operating on my own."

"Next time I'll speak up."

"Thanks. What's strange is that I was having the same kind of thoughts, but I didn't know how to express them."

"Does that mean you've decided not to go to Shanghai?"

"I have now. I'll call Amanda to let her know."

"I think it's the right decision, and I'm really glad you were considering it before talking to me. I'm sure Amanda and the others will understand," May said. "So what will you do instead? Spend more time with Fai?"

"She starts shooting tomorrow. She's going to be completely tied up for weeks," Ava said. "But I've been invited to Manila. In fact, that's the other reason I wanted to talk to you."

"Who do you know in Manila?"

"Chang Wang and Tommy Ordonez. Chang called me a few minutes ago. He said he knows you and Changxing very well. Is that true?"

"It is. In fact, Changxing is a partner with them in a Chinese cigarette factory. I've only met them socially and have never done any business with them directly. Why did our names come up in your conversation?"

"I mentioned that you're my partner," Ava said. "He had called to ask me to help him and Ordonez with a problem they have. I told him I'm not in the debt collection business anymore, and that you and I have our own investment company. He was very complimentary about you."

"Knowing him, I'm sure you're exaggerating about the compliments," May said. "What did he say when you told him you aren't in the old business?"

"He told me their problem has nothing to do with that. He asked me to go to Manila tomorrow for a meeting, and he made it clear that if I accept, he'll consider it a personal favour. He asked me to commit to one day, but with all the flying involved, it will most certainly be two days, if not more."

"What's the problem?"

"He told me it's serious but wouldn't give any details over the phone. He said he wants me to get those directly from the sources," Ava said. "The thing is, I've never known him to overstate anything, and he was quite insistent, though in the politest way imaginable. He even said 'please' several times."

"The Sledgehammer said 'please'? That's a first," May said. "He usually just curses and makes loud threats."

"I've heard that about him but I've never experienced it," Ava said. "He has never been anything but courteous towards me. But then Uncle and I did save him and Ordonez fifty million dollars, and considerable embarrassment."

"I remember hearing about that. I was told that Chang and Uncle were lifelong friends, which also speaks well for him."

"But May, I don't know what to do. Now that Shanghai is off the table, I have the time, but I don't know if I'm willing to take on someone else's problems."

"Chang and Ordonez have to be the most powerful business combination in the Philippines," May said.

"I think that's true."

"I also have to say that I'm intrigued by the manner of Chang's request," May said. "He and Ordonez obviously have tremendous respect for you. Having them indebted to you could be very good for our business in the Philippines and here in China. Chang still has deep financial roots in Hubei and Wuhan, and Ordonez has made some substantial investments in and around Qingdao."

"Are you telling me I should go to Manila?"

"No, but there might be some benefit for us if you did."

"It could also turn negative if I went and then decided not to help or couldn't help with whatever problem they have," Ava said. "I need to think about this a bit more."

"I'm sure whatever decision you make about Manila will be the right one. You know Chang better than I do."

"I'll let you know as soon as I've made up my mind."

After they said their goodbyes, Ava sat quietly and thought about Chang. How well did she actually know him? She'd met him in person twice, both occasions related to the recovery job she was doing for him and Ordonez, and both times with Uncle by her side. He had come to Uncle's funeral and they may have exchanged words, but she had no specific memory of that, or of anything else that day except for the shock of meeting Xu for the first time.

She hadn't even known Xu existed until a few days before, when had he sent some of his Shanghai Triad crew to Borneo and saved her life. He had appeared at her side as she was walking behind Uncle's casket to the graveyard in Fanling, and after the burial he walked back with her to the funeral home. On the way there, he told her that Uncle had been mentoring him for years, and that one of Uncle's last wishes was for the two of them to forge a relationship. Despite her initial doubts they had done exactly that, and now she considered him the most important man in her life, her *ge ge* — big brother.

Would Xu know Chang? she wondered. He must, she reasoned. His father, like Chang, was from Wuhan and had been a lifelong friend of Uncle's. But had Chang and Xu's father stayed in contact? Ava reached for the phone and called Shanghai.

"*Wei*," a woman's voice replied.

"Auntie Grace, it's Ava."

"Hello, my dear, how are you? Xu said you will be visiting Shanghai in the next day or so. I know he's meeting you for dinner, but will you be coming to the house?"

"I've had to change my plans," Ava said to Xu's elderly housekeeper, who had once been his nanny. "That's one reason I'm calling. Is Xu available to chat?"

"He's sitting outside by the pond with a glass of whisky and his cigarettes," she said, disapproval in her voice. "I'll take the phone to him."

There was silence, then Ava heard a door opening and Auntie Grace say, "A call for you. And don't shake your head — it's Ava."

"*Mei mei*," he said a few seconds later. "Are you in Shanghai already?"

"I'm still in Kunming and I've decided not to go to Shanghai.

May and I have just talked, and we feel it's better for Amanda and Chi-Tze to manage the meetings with the Pos."

"Things are still on track?"

"Absolutely. VLG has followed through on all of the commitments they made."

"That's good to hear. And even though you don't think you're needed at the meetings, you do know that you don't need a reason to come to Shanghai. Come and stay here for a few days. Auntie Grace would be thrilled."

"As tempting as that is, I have another offer that I'm considering, and I want to discuss it with you," she said.

"Offer?"

"Yes. Do you know Chang Wang?"

"For more than thirty years. He and my father were friends and I've met him many times."

"Was he a member of the Heaven and Earth Society?" she said, referring to the formal name the Triads used for their organization.

"I've heard that he took the thirty-six oaths, but I don't believe he was ever active. Why do you ask?"

"I was just wondering, given his association with Uncle and your father."

"I assume he's the person who made you the offer?"

"Yes. He phoned to ask me to go to Manila to look into a problem he and Tommy Ordonez have," Ava said.

"What kind of problem?"

Ava related her conversation with Chang, including his reluctance to give her any details.

"He's consistent — the most close-mouthed person I've ever met," Xu said when Ava finished. "Information is power and power gives you control. That's how he and Ordonez have always operated. If they can't completely control a project, they're usually not interested in it."

"This is a problem, not a project."

"That won't change the way they think and act."

"You sound as if you've had some unpleasant experiences with him... with them."

"My father tried to do some business deals with them, but nothing was ever finalized. There was always that problem of who had control. And then, of course, their idea of a fair profit split was ninety-nine percent for them and one for us."

"Why did your father bother?"

"On a personal level, he and Chang were close. They grew up together with Uncle in Wuhan. They escaped China together and they helped each other over the years. The main problem with doing business with him is Ordonez. On his own, Chang can be reasonable. But when he's with Tommy, he takes on Tommy's personality."

"I saw some of that when I was chasing money that had been stolen from them," Ava said. "When Chang was alone with Uncle, he was more considerate, almost gentle."

"He had tremendous respect for Uncle, and from the sound of what you're telling me, it's a respect he may have transferred to you."

"I don't know how you can make that inference."

"He may be closed-mouthed, but when he does talk, he doesn't dissemble. When he said that he and Ordonez trust you, I'm sure he meant it."

"Except he doesn't trust me enough to tell me specifically why he wants me to go to Manila."

"He told you enough to tempt you, though, didn't he."

"He did, and May thinks that if I take it on and it works

out, it could help our business prospects in the Philippines and in China."

"They're heavily invested in both places, and you can't overestimate their *guanxi*, their influence, especially in the Philippines. May's correct that having them on your side and owing you favours could open many doors for you. Their *guanxi* is the benefit you want, rather than any attempts at a business partnership."

"Is it substantial enough to justify my going to Manila?"

"I think so," Xu said, and then he paused. "But Ava, I don't recommend that you go unless Chang is more forthcoming up front. Remember what I said about information, power, and control. You need to let him know that if you go, it will be on your terms and not his. As a first step, I think you should demand more information."

"I like that idea, although I have to say they already know I work on my own terms. We butted heads a few times when I did that job for them. They know they can't push me around."

"Then you already have the advantage."

## 3

**AFTER HER CONVERSATION WITH XU, AVA THOUGHT** about calling Amanda, and then she decided there was no point in putting off Chang.

"Ava, I'm so pleased to hear back from you so quickly," he said.

"I've rearranged my schedule," she said. "So I can come to Manila if I decide to."

"If you decide to...You still haven't made a decision?"

"No. Before I do, I want more information about the problem you're facing."

He paused. "I explained to you that I don't want to do that over the phone. It's best done here in person."

"You mentioned that it would be someone other than you who would be briefing me. Who is it?"

"The name wouldn't mean anything to you."

"Uncle Chang, in case I'm not being clear, let me be very specific. You need to tell me a lot more than you have, or I'm not coming to Manila. And I apologize if you think I'm being rude."

"Your candour is appreciated."

"Appreciated enough to have it returned?"

He hesitated long enough that Ava began thinking about where she would go when she left Kunming. Hong Kong? Toronto?

"His name is Miguel Ramirez," Chang said. "He's a Philippine senator, and he's our partner in a business that we think might be at risk. I'm sure if you go online you'll find a substantial amount of information about him, but nothing about our business partnership. We all thought it best to keep his involvement private."

"I'll do a search, and thank you for disclosing his relationship with you," Ava said. "Now this business, this problem — is it in Manila?"

"The business and the potential problem are not directly connected. As I told you, this is a complicated matter that goes far beyond our normal commercial concerns. The senator can outline it in detail."

"But you haven't answered my question. Is the problem in Manila?"

"That is very difficult to answer."

"Uncle Chang—"

"Ava, don't be annoyed," he said quickly. "I'm not being evasive. I'm just trying to accurately represent the potential complexity of this problem. While the simple answer to your question is that it has its source in Tawi-Tawi, its impact could be far more widespread."

"Where, or what, is Tawi-Tawi?" she asked. "I've never heard of it."

"It's the southernmost island in the Philippines."

"I thought that was Mindanao."

"Mindanao is a large region with a lot of islands. Tawi-Tawi is one of them."

"And what is your problem in Tawi-Tawi?"

"Zakat College."

"What?"

"More properly, the Zakat College of Tawi-Tawi."

"That's a strange name for a college."

"The word *zakat* is Arabic. I'm not entirely sure what it means."

"Are you telling me that the college is Islamic?" Ava asked.

"That's what we've been told."

"And what else?"

"We've been told there are things going on inside the college that could be disruptive."

"To whom?"

"The entire southern region of the Philippines could be affected, and if it is, our business might be crippled."

"How could a college impact the region, and your business?"

"You need to talk to Ramirez," he repeated. "He's the one who brought these concerns to us, and he's the one who really understands their ramifications."

"This already sounds like it's far removed from my expertise."

"You're making an assumption that you should resist until you talk to Ramirez," he said. "I promise you, Ramirez is by far the best equipped to explain everything. You will find that he is an intelligent and thoughtful man."

"Is that all you can tell me?"

"It's all I feel qualified to say."

Ava drew a long, slow breath. Chang had been only slightly more forthcoming, but she sensed that his reluctance wasn't just stonewalling, that it might have some justification. The question was, had he told her enough to convince her to go to the Philippines? She thought of the last time she had seen him. It was in the Old Manila restaurant in the Peninsula Hotel, and she and Uncle had just agreed to take on the collection job. Chang had become quite emotional when they told him; he'd expected them to decline. What had impressed Ava was how calm and considerate he'd been as he waited for their anticipated rejection. She could feel the same kind of restraint on the other end of the phone line. *What would Uncle want me to do?* she asked herself.

"I'll try to get to Manila tomorrow," she said. "I'm not sure about flight connections from here, but I'll check as soon as I hang up."

"I would send the company jet to get you, but Tommy has it in Singapore and he is going to the U.K. from there," he said. "We'll pay for your flight, of course, first class. Do you have a hotel preference? I remember the last time you were here you stayed at the Peninsula. Shall I reserve a suite for you there?"

"Yes, thank you."

"I'll see that it's done, and when you've booked your flight, let me know the details. I'll have to make arrangements at Aquino Airport for your arrival and pickup."

"I'll call you the moment the flight is booked."

"Thank you," he said after a slight hesitation.

"Was there something else you wanted to say?" she asked.

"No."

"Then I'll talk to you in due course." She ended the call and sat back in the chair. *What have I just committed to?* she thought.

## 4

**SHE SAT DOWN AT THE ROOM DESK, TOOK A BLACK** Moleskine notebook from her bag, and opened it to the last page. She wrote *Chang Wang* across the top and then jotted down *Tawi-Tawi, Zakat College,* and *Miguel Ramirez*. She then began to make a list of questions that came to her as she mentally reviewed her talk with Chang.

When she worked with Uncle, she had kept a notebook for every job they undertook. In it she recorded names, numbers, and thoughts and generally tracked the progress of the investigation. When the job was done, she stored the notebook in a safety deposit box at a bank branch in Toronto. It was a habit that she hadn't broken. The front part of this notebook was filled with details of the conflict with VLG. Her friends found it amusing that she still insisted on writing things down the old-fashioned way. Her response was that the act of writing, of creating a permanent record, helped her remember and process details in a way that using an electronic device couldn't.

The list of questions grew until it almost filled the left-hand column of the page. Ava felt increasingly apprehensive about the commitment she'd made. She reached for the phone.

She spoke to Amanda first. The news that Ava would be going to Manila to help an old friend of Uncle's instead of going to Shanghai elicited some disappointment but no objections, which made Ava realize that May Ling had probably assessed the situation more accurately than she had.

May Ling was next on her list, and she was immediately and enthusiastically supportive of her decision. "The fact that you're going there at all should create some obligation in return," May said.

"I'm not going in with the expectation of getting repaid sometime down the road."

"Of course not, but it wouldn't hurt if that was one of the results."

Ava was about to caution her about prejudging the outcome but bit her tongue. One of the many things she loved about May was her practicality.

Xu was her last call. He was quiet while she related her conversation with Chang. "He must really need you," he said finally.

"Well, he certainly thinks he does. I just don't want to disappoint him."

"Ava, whatever help I can provide, I will. Don't hesitate to ask," he said.

She smiled. With May and Xu, she never had to worry about having her back covered.

After she ended her call to Xu, she opened her laptop. It had been sitting on the desk, ignored, all weekend. She had begun to search for flights when she was struck by hunger pangs. She reached for the room service menu, quickly ordered, and then returned to the computer.

Getting from Kunming to Manila was harder than she'd expected. There were no direct flights; the quickest, simplest route was to Hong Kong on China Eastern Airlines and then a Cathay Pacific flight to Manila that didn't arrive until eight o'clock in the evening. She checked her other options, but that was the best one. She reserved first-class seats on both flights and then phoned Chang.

"There's nothing earlier?" he said when she gave him her schedule.

"That's the best I can do."

"All right, we'll make it work. I'll get back to you with details from this end."

She leaned back in the chair and sighed. She needed to prepare for the meeting, and that meant getting some information on the Zakat College of Tawi-Tawi. She found some general information online about Tawi-Tawi and a couple of colleges on the island, but none with the name Zakat. She looked up the word.

"*Zakat* — an obligatory payment made annually under Islamic law as almsgiving for the relief of the poor," read one definition. "The mandatory charitable process for Muslims to spiritually purify their annual earnings," read another. The literal translation of the word was "that which purifies."

The doorbell sounded before she could delve much deeper. She let in the room service attendant and stood by as she set up the table for dinner. She had been hungry when she ordered, but now she felt ravenous as the hot and sour soup and beef with fried noodles and XO sauce were laid out on the table. She opened the half-bottle of Pinot Grigio she'd ordered and then dug into the food.

The soup portion was big enough for two and loaded with shrimp and scallops. The noodles were piled high on a large plate. The slivers of beef almost melted on her tongue, and the XO sauce gave the dish a spicy kick. Almost unawares, Ava finished the half-bottle of wine. She took a smaller bottle from the room bar and made it last until she'd polished off her meal.

*I'll need to exercise tomorrow,* she thought as she stood up from the table. She liked to run and managed to do ten kilometres three or four times a week. If she was stressed she ran more often, and the runs were longer and harder. She also practiced bak mei, a centuries-old martial art that was taught one-on-one and had very few disciples because of its physical and mental demands. She had started training when she was in her teens and didn't become proficient until she was in her mid-twenties. It wasn't a pretty martial art. It was designed to inflict damage by attacking the most vulnerable areas — eyes, nose, ears, nerve endings — of an opponent's body. During her days working as a debt collector with Uncle, she'd been attacked more times than she could remember by men wielding guns, knives, tire irons, or their own fists. Bak mei had saved her more than once.

She groaned. *I'll go for a long run and maybe a bak mei workout tomorrow,* she promised herself. She was five foot three and had weighed about 115 pounds since she turned twenty. Her slim physique was partly genetic, but she knew the exercise made a difference. Uncle used to joke that she ate more than any man he knew; he said one day she would wake up weighing two hundred pounds.

She sat down at the desk with the intention of doing more research on Tawi-Tawi. Just as she opened up a website, her phone sounded and she saw Uncle Chang's number on the screen.

"Ava, Ramirez will see you at his home. He lives on Flame Tree Road in Forbes Park, which is in the Makati district."

She'd been to Makati, the commercial centre of Manila, and she knew Forbes Park was a wealthy residential district next to it. She tried to calculate when she might arrive at the house on Flame Tree Road. She was familiar enough with Aquino Airport to know that clearing Customs could be tortuous at any hour and that traffic in the city could be equally slow. Even if her flight arrived on schedule at eight, she figured she'd be doing well if she reached Flame Tree Road by ten.

"It could be late by the time I get there," she said.

"We're making arrangements with Immigration Services to have you escorted through Customs and Immigration, and he's sending a driver to meet you. He also doesn't care what time you get to the house."

"Will you be there?"

"No. I don't want to interfere. Ramirez is the man you need to listen to, but we can talk afterwards."

"Sounds good," she said.

After ending the call, Ava was overcome by a yawn so powerful it made her shiver. She had spent the weekend running on sexual adrenalin, surviving on less than eight hours of sleep in total. Now the combination of wine, the dinner, and Fai's departure came crashing in on her.

*Tawi-Tawi and Miguel Ramirez will still be there in the morning,* she thought as she fell face down on the bed.

## 5

**WHEN AVA WOKE, THE EARLY SPRING SUN WAS STREAM-**
ing through the window. She looked at the empty side of
the bed and imagined Fai there, stretched out with one
arm flung across Ava's body. She glanced at the bedside
clock and saw that it was eight-fifteen. Fai had said to call
before eight, but Ava phoned her anyway and left a message: "I miss you."

She walked over to the window and looked out onto
Dianchi Lake. The water shimmered in the light cast by the
sun, which was suspended in a clear blue sky. Ava had been
spending so much time in Shanghai that she had forgotten
the sky could actually be blue rather than perpetually grey.
The Kunming air was fresh and almost crisp, the tempera-
ture hovering around fifteen degrees Celsius. She felt a surge
of energy and immediately thought about going for a run.
She still had to research Ramirez and Tawi-Tawi, but she
could do that while she was waiting for her flight. She calcu-
lated when she'd have to be back at the hotel to get ready to
leave for the airport, and figured she had just enough time
to get in a ten-kilometre run.

She went to the bathroom to brush her teeth and splash cold water on her face, downed a quick coffee, threw on her running gear, and headed downstairs. She asked the concierge if there was a running path around the lake. He told her all she had to do was follow the signs. The hotel wasn't far from the lake, and when she eventually reached it, she found a wide promenade that was surprisingly uncrowded. In her experience, public and open spaces in most Chinese cities were usually crammed with people from dawn until late at night. She ran north, her pace gradually increasing until she felt some strain, then slowed and reversed course.

Ava felt herself relax, and her mind moved away from the process of running. She thought about Pang Fai and found herself grinning like a lovestruck teenager. Then Chang Wang and the trip to Manila entered her mind and the smile disappeared. She wasn't entirely comfortable with the decision she'd made, but she would see her commitment through. Her hope was that her meeting with Ramirez would be expeditious and she could leave Manila the next day.

Ava showered as soon as she got back to the hotel, did a quick check of her emails and phone messages, and got ready for the trip. She was conservative when it came to clothes. For casual wear she preferred black Giordano T-shirts and Adidas training pants and jackets. When she wasn't promoting PÖ, her work wardrobe consisted of slacks and skirts in neutral colours and an array of cotton and linen button-down shirts from Brooks Brothers. Ava thought they presented a professional image, the kind of clothes that a female accountant would wear. For the trip to Manila, she chose a white button-down shirt and black slacks.

She left the hotel shortly after eleven. It was a forty-five-kilometre drive to Kunming Changshui Airport, and she didn't want to risk getting stuck in traffic. By twelve-thirty she was sitting at a computer terminal in the China Eastern Airlines international lounge and entering "Senator Miguel Ramirez" into a search engine.

Unlike Zakat College, there wasn't any shortage of information about the senator. If anything there was a surfeit, the result of a long career in public service and the fact that the Philippines had an incredibly large and vibrant media industry. Ava counted multiple stories from five daily newspapers in Manila alone.

Ramirez came from a humble beginning, which wasn't that common among high-level Philippine politicians, most of whom were the beneficiaries of family dynasties. He was born in Roxas City on Panay Island, the son of two schoolteachers. He graduated from the University of the Philippines with a degree in agriculture and went to work for the Cooper Pineapple Company of Hawaii, becoming vice-president for Southeast Asia while still in his thirties. He had been a supporter of Benigno Aquino, the main leader of those opposed to Ferdinand Marcos.

Marcos had been the Philippine president for more than twenty years, and for much of that time he used martial law to govern as a dictator. For four years Aquino led the opposition from his temporary home in the United States, but in 1983 he returned to the Philippines to challenge Marcos directly. Minutes after his plane landed, he was assassinated on the tarmac. Following Aquino's assassination, Ramirez transferred his support to Aquino's wife, Corazon. Three years later, Corazon defeated Marcos in an election. When she became president, she appointed Miguel Ramirez minister of agriculture.

Ramirez served under Aquino for the six years of her single term. When Fidel Ramos was voted in as the new president of the Philippines, he retained his position as minister of agriculture. But three years into that appointment, things started to get messy.

Depending on their editorial policies, political alliances, and penchant for sensationalism, the spin the various media put on Ramirez varied, but on one thing they all agreed: it was remarkable that a man born into a lower-middle-income family, who had been a salaried employee at Cooper and made a modest amount as a government minister, had somehow managed to accumulate what was estimated to be more than US$70 million. Charges of corruption, specifically of taking bribes, were levelled by various members of the legislature, and there were cries for a public enquiry. Ramirez's claim — that he had simply gotten lucky in the stock market — was dismissed as far-fetched, and an enquiry was launched.

But before the enquiry began, there was a scheduled election for twelve seats in the country's twenty-four-seat Senate. Senators did not run in or represent specific regions. The election was country-wide, and the top twelve candidates would win seats. Ramirez resigned his position in the cabinet and ran. By some estimates he spent $5 million on his campaign, making it the most costly in Philippine history. One of his most prominent friends was Tommy Ordonez, who publicly endorsed Ramirez and was identified by various media as one of his key financial backers. The money was well spent; Ramirez finished second and won a seat in the Senate. The position paid only a modest salary, but a more important reward accompanied it: as a senator he was immune from prosecution, a protection his cabinet position didn't provide.

*There's some dirt under your fingernails, but not enough to have scared off the electorate or your friends,* Ava thought as she read accounts of the election.

After the election, the enquiry was cancelled and the questions about Ramirez's wealth faded. When he was mentioned in the media, it was usually in reference to his political role as a senator — a position that carried with it very real power. Not only did every national law and treaty have to be approved by the Senate before being passed on to the president for final signature, it was the only institution in the country that could impeach the president.

Ava noted that Ramirez's role in the Senate wasn't restricted to matters of general concern. He also had long-standing involvement with two key committees. One of them was, not surprisingly, agriculture. But he was also vice-chair of the committee that oversaw the National Intelligence Coordinating Agency. Since his first election he had been on both committees, and he was now serving his second six-year term as a senator. According to the law, she read, he could serve only two terms. She did a quick calculation and saw that his second term would end in less than two years. She wondered if he was worried that the old corruption charges would resurface when his immunity privileges lapsed.

Curiously absent from nearly all of the stories was information about Ramirez's private life. A wife was mentioned but never named, and there was no hint of any children. If he had hobbies, they were kept out of the public eye. And the only social functions he attended were those directly related to Senate business.

Ava reached into her bag, pulled out her Moleskine notebook, and made notes on Ramirez. Just as she finished and was about to research Tawi-Tawi, she heard the boarding announcement for her flight.

The plane left ten minutes late. Ava hoped they would make up the time en route, because she had a tight connection in Hong Kong for the flight to Manila. She took out her notebook to review the information she'd gathered about Ramirez, and then just as quickly put it away. She knew the basics and she'd be seeing him soon enough. Instead she scanned the in-flight entertainment system and found a Pang Fai film among a group of classic movies. It was one she'd made at the beginning of her career, when she and the director, Lau Lau, were still a team. Ava was about to select it and then stopped. Did she really want to see a different, younger version of her lover? She had a sudden image in her mind of Fai sprawled naked across the bed, and another of Fai hugging her at the door before she left for the film shoot. Those memories were still warm and she didn't want to cool them. She opted for *A Better Tomorrow*, an early Chow Yun-fat gangster movie directed by the legendary John Woo.

It was past four o'clock when the plane began its descent over the South China Sea into Chek Lap Kok airport. Ava loved the approach over the open water, carpeted by an armada of vessels of all sizes and types going in and out of one of the world's busiest harbours. Normally she would have been gazing out the window during the landing, but the film had captured her imagination. Despite her concern about landing on time to make her connection, she was hoping she'd be able to see it through to the end.

China Eastern and Cathay Pacific Airlines were both located in Terminal 1, but Ava still had to go through in-transit passport control and baggage screening. By the time she got to her gate, the flight to Manila was already boarding. She walked past the long, snaking line of economy passengers to the first-class entry point. A few minutes later she was drinking champagne and checking the entertainment listings to see if she could finish the Woo film. No such luck, but *The Grandmaster* was listed. It was the story of Ip Man, the famous Wing Chun master who had trained Bruce Lee. Tony Leung Chiu-wai played the lead alongside the luminous Zhang Ziyi, who had shot to fame after starring in Ang Lee's *Crouching Tiger, Hidden Dragon*. Ava felt almost guilty about watching director Wong Kar-wai's first martial arts film. She knew she should be thinking about Chang Wang and Senator Miguel Ramirez, but her mind wasn't fully locked in.

They landed on time at Ninoy Aquino International Airport. On her previous trip to the Philippines, Tommy Ordonez had sent a government official to meet them at the gate; he had led them past the lines of people waiting to clear Customs and Immigration, personally stamped their passports at an empty booth, and then took them to a waiting limousine. Ava didn't know what to expect on this trip, but when she got off the plane, she saw a man in a dark suit holding a card with her name on it, and a uniformed man standing next to him.

"I'm Ava Lee," she said to the man.

"I'm Rodrigo. Mr. Chang sent me to drive you to Senator

Ramirez's home," he said, and then turned to the officer. "This is Inspector Arroyo. He will look after your needs in the airport."

"Did you check any bags?" Arroyo asked.

"No."

"Then may I see your passport?"

Ava took it from her bag and passed it to him. He opened it, pulled a stamp from his shirt pocket, pressed it onto a page, and handed the passport back to her.

"Welcome to the Philippines," he said. "There's a back route we can use to avoid the crowds at Immigration and in the baggage area. It's a bit longer walk."

"It will feel good to stretch my legs," she said.

"I'll take your bags," Rodrigo said, reaching for them.

"Just this one," Ava said, letting go of her Shanghai Tang Double Happiness bag.

After leading them through a maze of corridors and offices, Inspector Arroyo opened a door that took them outside the terminal. "Your car is about fifty metres down there on the right," Arroyo said. Rodrigo handed him a thick white envelope.

The area was crowded with people waiting for buses and taxis. Rodrigo wasn't especially large, but he was forceful and made good progress through the crowd. Ava tucked in behind him, staying as close as she could. "The car is across the street, in the indoor parking garage reserved for VIPs," he said as he stopped at a pedestrian crossing that led to the garage entrance. She followed him across the street.

Rodrigo pressed a key fob as soon as they stepped inside the garage. She saw the front lights of a black BMW come on, and another press opened the trunk. He opened the back door for her, and Ava was soon nestled in the soft leather interior of the luxurious 7 Series model.

"Mr. Chang asked me to call him when you arrived," Rodrigo said as he climbed into the driver's seat. He took a phone from his shirt pocket and hit speed dial. "Ms. Lee is with me," he said a few seconds later. Then he listened, turned, and passed the phone to her.

"Welcome to Manila, and thank you for coming," Chang said.

"Thank you for making the arrangements at the airport."

"It's something we do only for very special guests."

"Uncle, I'm here now. You don't need to flatter me."

"It's the furthest thing from flattery," he said. "Now, do you want Rodrigo to take you directly to see the senator, or would you rather check in at the hotel first?"

"I'd rather meet Ramirez."

"Very well, I'll tell him to take you directly there. In good traffic it should take about half an hour."

"We're moving well so far."

"I imagine you're still at the airport and in the restricted traffic area. The moment you reach the main street, it may change."

Ava saw a bank of rear lights in the near distance. "I think I see what you mean," she said.

"I'll call the senator and let him know you're on the way. I would appreciate it if you phone me after the meeting."

"I'll do that."

"Thank you. Please pass the phone back to Rodrigo so I can tell him what the plan is."

A moment later, Rodrigo put down the phone and focused on the road ahead, which was jam-packed with jeepneys, buses, taxis, cars, and motorcycles.

"This isn't so bad," Rodrigo said several times during the first forty-five minutes of crawling. "In the morning and evening rush hours — we call them 'crash hours' — it would have taken twice as long to get this far."

It wasn't until she saw the first signs for Forbes Park that Ava believed they were making any progress at all. She knew of the neighbourhood. It was the wealthiest in Manila and one of the richest in Asia. The car went past the Manila Polo Club and turned right and then left onto Flame Tree Road. Despite everything she knew about Forbes Park, she found herself gawking at the huge houses, some the size of hotels, and all of them walled and gated. "Quite the street," she said.

"There's more money here than in the entire province I come from," Rodrigo said.

He made a slight right turn and brought the car to a halt in front of a steel gate between three-metre-high brick walls. He opened the window, leaned out, and said, "Eight, six, five, four" into the intercom. After a ten-second wait, the gate started to open. Rodrigo drove through, wound his way around a circular driveway, and parked the car in front of the double doors of a sprawling one-storey brick house. The house was partially floodlit, and Ava saw that it had a red tile roof and enormous windows on either side of the doors. It looked welcoming rather than imposing.

"I'll wait for you," Rodrigo said. "Mr. Chang wants me to drive you to the Peninsula when you and the senator have concluded your business."

"Thank you," Ava said as she stepped out of the car. She took a moment to look at the house and then heard a noise behind her. She turned to see two heavily armed security guards leaning against the brick wall. She hadn't seen them from the car, but their presence didn't surprise her. Security was important in the Philippines. Banks, malls, hotels, and private residences often hired armed guards. She turned again when she heard the front door open. A tall, slender man wearing a white *barong* nodded at her and said, "Come in."

Ava held out her hand when she reached the door. Ramirez shook it almost cautiously. When she stepped into the house, she felt the rush of air conditioning.

"Thank you for coming," he said.

She knew from his website that he was sixty. His hair was thick and black, with a few streaks of grey above the ears, and his skin was taut and nearly wrinkle-free. He had an air of reserve and sophistication. *He's the kind of man who makes you conscious of your use of language and grammar,* Ava thought.

"Chang Wang can be persuasive," she said.

"I am very aware of that," he said, and smiled. "Come, we'll go to the back patio to talk."

She followed him across a white marble floor, past a grand piano, heavily upholstered furniture, wooden coffee and end tables with elaborately carved legs, and a series of original oil paintings of landscapes. The glass-enclosed patio was furnished with two separate sets of bamboo sofas and chairs. A bottle of water, a bucket of ice, and two glasses sat on a coffee table between two of the chairs. Ramirez motioned for her to sit.

"You have a beautiful home," she said.

"I worked for it."

"I'm sure that makes it all the more satisfying," she said, taken aback by his brusque response.

"My name is Ramirez, not Lopez or Marcos or Aquino or Cojuangco. I wasn't born into a dynasty that secured my political and financial future."

"Maybe you're beginning to build your own dynasty."

"I have no children and no family worth mentioning." He pointed to the water. "Is this all right or would you prefer something else?"

"It's fine."

Ramirez poured two glasses and then sat back with his hands folded on his chest. He looked across the table at her, his eyes half-closed as if he were sleepy. "You aren't at all what I expected," he said.

"Pardon?"

"Chang Wang said that he and Tommy Ordonez have tremendous respect for you. He said you have done some remarkable things for them," Ramirez said. "I have known both those men for more than twenty years. They are people who demand respect and rarely extend it. I find it hard to imagine what you could have done to generate so much admiration."

"It wasn't something I did alone, but even if it were, I'm not at liberty to discuss it," she said. "I was led to believe that Uncle Chang gave you some idea of what we did."

"Only in the most general way, and I apologize if I sound rude. It's just that I'm a bit surprised," he said. "Chang didn't tell me much about you personally, and he certainly didn't mention how young you are. I expected someone closer to middle age, a wealthy businesswoman in a Chanel suit with coiffed hair."

"I'm older than I look," she said. "There is no business relationship between them and me, and my reason for being here is Chang's request that I do him a favour."

"I know," Ramirez said. "But I have to say that if the request to meet with you hadn't come directly from Chang Wang and hadn't been as forceful as it was, I would have been reluctant to even chat with you on the phone."

"Why?" Ava said.

"I didn't expect that they would take the information I gave them to an outside party so quickly," he said. "I thought they would use someone from inside their organization."

"But here I am," Ava said. She took a sip of water, then leaned back in the chair and crossed her legs.

"Yes, here you are." He nodded, looked thoughtful, and then leaned forward. "Tell me, Ms. Lee, what do you know about growing pineapples?"

## 6

**AVA SHIFTED UNCOMFORTABLY IN HER SEAT. "I KNOW** nothing about growing pineapples. Why don't you explain it to me."

"Pineapples aren't difficult to grow," Ramirez said. "They don't need much water. They don't need a lot of soil, because they don't have a large root system. They like heat and there can never be too much sun for them. You can, of course, regulate their supply of water and other nutrients and you can improve the quality of the soil, but they'll grow even if you do none of those things."

"From what I've read, you were certainly in the business long enough to know."

"I'm still in it," he said. "I'm a silent partner in several very large plantations on Mindanao."

"I understand you're in partnership with the Ordonez organization."

"That's right."

"But why silent?"

"It would have raised some ill-informed questions if it had been known that the minister of agriculture was an investor in those plantations — and that a current senator is a major shareholder."

"What specifically would be the problem?"

"Not many products are grown in this country without subsidies or other forms of government assistance. The plantations got only their fair share, but still, how would it have looked?"

"I can understand how public perception could be skewed. Have your plantations done well?"

"The Philippines is now one of the world's main exporters of pineapples, and Mindanao represents ninety percent of the production. Our plantations are among the most productive in Mindanao. Their combined output makes us by far the leading exporting company, and we're very profitable."

"I see," Ava said, at a loss as to where the conversation was going.

"Like I said, pineapples are easy to grow. It takes eighteen to twenty months to get a first crop, and after that it's every fifteen months like clockwork. The challenge is to find the labour. Unlike many other fruits and vegetables, pineapple production doesn't lend itself to automation. You need human labour, and there is a direct correlation between the amount of work you invest and the eventual volume of pineapples you produce. Fortunately, Mindanao has a large labour pool that we've able to tap into."

"At reasonable rates, I assume."

"We pay what the law requires."

"Of course."

"But even then, the plantations aren't without labour disputes and other external challenges."

"You said you're profitable, so obviously you've overcome the challenges."

"Not entirely on our own. We required some assistance."

"From whom?" she asked.

Ramirez paused and then reached for the bottle of water. He topped up her glass, did the same for his own, and took several sips before placing the glass back on the table. "We were helped by the Muslim Brotherhood of Mindanao."

"I don't know them."

"Then I presume you also don't know that much about our country's struggles in that region."

"I understand that there is a large Muslim population in the southern Philippines that wanted to separate. I also know there was terrorist activity, but I thought things had calmed down."

"The word 'large' is relative. Our country has a population of close to one hundred million, and eighty-six percent of it is Roman Catholic. There are about four million Muslims, but they're nearly all in the south. The entire Mindanao region is twenty percent Muslim, but there are four provinces within the region — Sulu, Basilan, Maguindanao, and Tawi-Tawi — where Muslims form the majority," Ramirez said. "The Muslims have been living in that region for more than five hundred years and have been fighting for the right to govern themselves for every one of those years, until 1989. They fought everyone who tried to control them — the Spanish, the Americans, the Japanese, and, most lately, us.

"We finally reached a peace settlement when the first government I was part of — Corazon Aquino's — passed into law the Autonomous Region in Muslim Mindanao Act. It gave the Muslims considerable independence and self-government but kept them inside the bigger Philippine tent."

"So it's calmer now?" Ava said.

"Yes, though it hasn't stopped all the agitation and extremism. There are still organizations — Abu Sayyaf, Jemaah Islamiyah, the New People's Army, the Moro Islamic Liberation Front — that want more or even complete independence. But they're much smaller and relatively insignificant compared to the Brotherhood. During the most difficult years in the south, the Brotherhood was our largest, smartest, and most determined opponent. Getting them onside made the autonomy agreement possible. Without them as part of the solution, it would never have happened."

"You sound as if you respect them."

"That's because I do. They fought us with dedication and perseverance. They didn't kill innocent civilians. They didn't kidnap Westerners, hold them ransom, and then murder them like Abu Sayyaf did, and still does. When our government finally tried to reach an accommodation in the south, they were the main negotiators on the other side. During that process I met some of their leaders and we got to know each other. In fact, I became friends with some of them."

"I don't quite understand what this has to do with the pineapple business," Ava said.

"Given the proper set of conditions, the business is highly profitable. Tommy and Chang wanted to get into it and came to me for advice. I told them I thought Mindanao had the right mix of labour, climate, and land to become a major growing area. We agreed to try to nurture the industry there, but we didn't start until the agreement on autonomy was reached. It would have been too dangerous before that, and even after, there were still issues." He reached for his water, finished it, and poured a third glassful. "We had workers who thought they deserved a larger wage and called numerous wildcat strikes. Truck drivers were offloading and selling our goods ten or twenty kilometres from the plantations. There were people who couldn't accept the deal with the government and who burned private property as a way of making a political point."

"Are those problems still ongoing?"

"No, we managed to resolve them," he said. "Most of our workers, like many people who live in the region, were members of the Brotherhood. I contacted the leaders I'd come to know and asked them for their help. I told them we needed labour peace, no more logistical problems, and real security. I convinced them that successful plantations would be beneficial for their membership and for the region, which is the poorest in the entire country. They agreed to co-operate with us."

"Did you pay them?"

"Better than that, we made them partners in the business. We gave them a minority stake, of course, but enough for them to care that we became profitable," Ramirez said. "Other businesses in the area took note and did the same thing. Now just about every successful large-scale business in Mindanao has the Muslim Brotherhood as a partner."

"It sounds like a cozy relationship."

"As long as it lasts."

"Is it threatened?"

"The Brotherhood likes the current status quo. They have considerable influence with the Mindanao regional government and hold senior positions in it. Their central organization is accumulating funds from the profit-sharing. Their members have steady employment. They are growing in strength and numbers," Ramirez said. "But in their line of business — the revolution business — nothing is permanent. They could decide one day that they're strong enough to make another play for complete independence. New leaders could adopt different objectives and tactics. And then, of course, there's always the large, dark cloud that is Manila."

"Manila?"

"We have a new president."

"Yes. I've read about him."

"He's a Christian from Davao City on Mindanao, and he's not pro-Muslim — in fact, it could be argued that he's the opposite. That wouldn't matter so much if he hadn't been erratic and impulsive in the past, when it came to directing the local police force. The way they operated there was to shoot first and ask questions later. There are expectations that his style won't change, and that makes him potentially dangerous at the national level," Ramirez said. "But even if he is stable, many of my political colleagues in the Senate and the House of Representatives would rip up the Muslim Mindanao Act if given half a chance, and the military are dying to unleash their dogs on the region.

"The politicians don't remember how bad things were before Aquino took the action she did. Mindanao was a true war zone. We were fighting against a well-equipped army and hundreds of people were dying. Now all we have are occasional kidnappings, but the politicians use those few instances as proof that the region is still lawless and out of control — a direct result of granting it autonomy. It's true there are still terrorist groups in the south, but they're like flies on a bull compared to what we had before. The military just want to flex their muscles and are desperate to find any kind of provocation. One of my fears is that this new president won't need much of an excuse to turn them loose."

"Senator, as interesting as all this is, I'm not sure what it has to do with what was described to me as a problem at the Zakat College of Tawi-Tawi," Ava said.

"I want you to understand the Brotherhood and my connection to them. I also thought it was important to give you some knowledge of the political landscape in which they operate."

"But why?"

"Well, simply put, if you want to find out what's going on at Zakat College, you're going to have to talk to the Brotherhood, and I didn't want you to do that in a vacuum," he said. "Please remember what I told you: they like the status quo. They're nervous about anything that might bring instability to the region."

"Are you suggesting the college might do that?"

"Yes."

"Uncle Chang said it was Islamic."

"There are many forms of Islamic education. I'm not an expert, and neither is Chang."

"But what did your friends at the Brotherhood tell you about the school? Why did both you and Uncle Chang tell me it has the potential to be disruptive — which I take to mean destructive?"

"Those questions are best answered by the Brotherhood. My preference, as I explained to Chang, is for you to talk to them directly," he said. "He agrees with me that it is the most sensible approach. I can assure you that the Brotherhood will be forthcoming, because they are as obliged to me as I am to Chang Wang and Tommy Ordonez. I consider them to be our partners and our staunch allies."

Ava looked across the table at him. His face was impassive but his body had tensed. "This is getting absurd," she said. "Chang Wang wanted me to talk to you, and now you want to hand me off to the Brotherhood."

He shook his head. "I apologize for our lack of clarity. Everything I've been told and have passed on to Tommy and Chang is at best second-hand, and it might be third- or fourth-hand information. I've asked the Brotherhood to arrange for you to meet the main sources. We want you to hear their stories, directly from them, and for you to assess their reliability. Then we need to confirm or prove false what they're telling us. Chang told me that you're the only person he and Tommy Ordonez trust to do that."

Ava sighed, feeling a mixture of frustration and growing anger. "It's lovely to be so trusted, but right now that means nothing to me. What I want is to be told why I should even consider meeting with the Brotherhood. So unless you can give me a reason that I think has merit, I'm going to be on the first plane back to Hong Kong."

Ramirez turned away from her, fixing his gaze on the patio windows, which looked out on a floodlit garden. "I've been getting around to that. It's just a difficult thing to say out loud," he said softly, and again lapsed into silence.

"Senator?" she said.

He turned towards her. His eyes were hooded and his mouth tightly drawn. "We've been told that the college in Tawi-Tawi is training terrorists."

## 7

AVA LOWERED HER HEAD. SHE TOOK A MOMENT TO absorb what Ramirez had just told her, then reached for her water and drained it.

"I'm not quite sure I heard you correctly," she finally said, pouring herself another glass.

"That was my first reaction," Ramirez said. "But that's exactly what we've been told, and we have to find out if it's true."

"I can understand your shock, but why haven't you gone to the appropriate authorities here in the Philippines? I'm sure they're well equipped to do surveillance, and there can't be any doubt they'd have an interest."

"Which authorities? The intelligence service of the armed forces? The National Bureau of Investigation? The Philippine National Police intelligence service? We have so many, and when they're not fighting each other, they're leaking stories to the media."

"I read that you're on the oversight committee for intelligence. Couldn't you have gone to them?"

"I am vice-chair of the Senate committee that oversees the

National Intelligence Coordinating Agency. All that means
is that I get to watch the chaos from a front-row seat. There
is no coordination and there isn't much intelligence attached
to the agency or my committee. Besides, if I went to anyone
in the agency, I have no doubt that my colleagues on the
Senate committee would be briefed immediately. After that
it wouldn't take more than a few minutes for the information to become public, which would result in disaster in one
way or another."

"Why do you think it would be a disaster?"

"It would give our security organizations, the police, and
the military the excuse they've been looking for to go after
Muslims in the south," he said. "Have you heard of SAF, the
Special Action Force?"

"No."

"It's like Detachment 88 in Indonesia."

"Excuse me, but I also haven't heard of Detachment 88,"
Ava said.

"It's an elite anti-terrorist unit that was formed in 2002 in
Indonesia after the Bali bombings. It's financed and trained
by the Americans, and it has earned a reputation for going
beyond the law, torturing and even executing suspects and
then boasting about it. The SAF is modelled after British
SWAT teams. It hasn't been quite as brazenly public about
killing terrorists or suspected terrorists as Detachment 88,
but they have the firepower and they're itching to use it. I am
one hundred percent sure they're who our security people
would turn to if I went to them now with these rumours
we've heard about the college," he said.

He added, almost mournfully, "I promise you, they'd attack
it with full force. And if there was even a hint of resistance,

there would be very few survivors. And don't think the retribution would end with the college. The politicians would use the issue to undermine the Brotherhood and other peaceful and co-operative Muslim organizations. Then, I suspect, the military would jump at the opportunity to broaden their activities in the south. They'd find some way to link the Brotherhood to the college and then they'd go after them. It would destabilize the entire region, both politically and economically."

"And have a harmful impact on some large pineapple plantations?"

"We don't deny we're worried about that," he said. "But — and I'm not speaking for Chang here — it isn't my primary motivation. I want peace to continue in the south, for a great many political and humanitarian reasons. The people who live within the Autonomous Region are the most impoverished in the entire country. Any resumption of hostilities would result in economic devastation. The fact that I have a personal interest in the outcome doesn't make my reasoning, or my objective, wrong."

"What is your objective?"

"I want to maintain stability in the south. But to achieve that, we need to find out what's going on at Zakat College, and if something is going on, who's behind it. Once we have that information, we can make an informed decision about how to proceed."

"Just so I'm absolutely clear, you don't trust your own national security agencies to do this?"

"Not at this stage. And depending on what you find, maybe never."

"You'll have to pardon me, Senator, but I do find your approach quite unorthodox and confusing."

"I agree. But I've made my position clear about the trustworthiness of our security forces, and the confusion will persist until we get some hard information," he said. "All we have now are accounts from two young men who work at the college. They went to their local imam five days ago with a tale about terrorist training, but they didn't provide any details or substantiation. They insisted that their identities be protected. The imam, who is a member of the Brotherhood, relayed their information to senior Brotherhood officials. They passed it on to me and I talked to Chang Wang."

"How long has this college been open?"

"About a year."

"What does it purport to teach?"

"All we've been told is that they're training terrorists."

"How many terrorists are supposedly being trained?"

"The young men didn't supply those details."

"And they're being trained to attack whom?"

"Again, for now, we lack details."

"For now?"

"The imam has persuaded the young men to be more forthcoming and to talk directly with the Brotherhood. They're scheduled to meet tomorrow morning near Bongao, the capital of Tawi-Tawi," Ramirez said. "Our hope is that you will join them to question the young men and help us arrive at a real understanding of the goings-on at Zakat College."

"How long have you known about this meeting?"

"It wasn't confirmed until this morning."

"It sounds like it's been in the works for longer than that."

"The Brotherhood has been pressing the imam for several days, but the meeting didn't appear to be a possibility until yesterday."

Ava shook her head, irritated that Chang hadn't mentioned a word about Bongao when he called her in Kunming, or after she'd arrived in Manila. "Why is it necessary that I be there? Surely the Brotherhood can handle the interview by themselves."

"I tried to make that point to Chang Wang, but without any success," Ramirez said. "He isn't the most trusting man and he doesn't know the Brotherhood as well as I do. There's a lot at stake. He made it clear that he wants his set of eyes and ears at any meeting that takes place."

Ava didn't disagree with Ramirez's description of Chang's attitude, but it still irked her. "Let's say that I do go to Bongao," she said. "What if those young men repeat their story about terrorists and provide us with details that I find believable? What then? Don't you still have the same dilemma around your security forces?"

"We need facts, and until we have them it's premature to speculate about what our best course of action might be."

"What other course could possibly be open to you?"

"That might depend on who those terrorists are and what they intend to do. It's possible that their activities extend well beyond the Philippines. If that's the case, we might be able to interest and involve other governments."

"Who fits that bill?"

Ramirez turned his gaze back to the floodlit garden, and she could see his uncertainty. "It could be anyone or no one," he said, waving his hand almost dismissively. "We need facts. Please help us get them, and then we can decide."

"And you want me to do this alongside the Brotherhood? Do they know that I might be going to Bongao, or have you kept them in the dark about me?"

"They know about you, and believe me, they'll welcome your assistance."

"I assume that's because they know Chang has insisted on my participation, and that I'll go there with the full backing of him and Tommy Ordonez."

"You have my full support and backing as well," Ramirez said.

"If I do go," Ava said, "how will this work? What arrangements, however tentatively, have already been made?"

"I'm not entirely sure."

"What do you mean?"

"The commander of the Brotherhood is named Yasin Juhar, but everyone calls him Juhar; I doubt many people know his given name. The single name is a carryover from the days when he was leading the fight against us, positioning himself as the Philippine Che Guevara. I thought it was an affectation, but it earned him recognition and respect. He is now, without any doubt, the best-known and most powerful man in the region. I've known him personally for years, and I trust him completely. He's been working with the imam to facilitate the meeting, but he won't be present for it. His deputy, Omar Wahab — he's usually just called Wahab — will be representing the Brotherhood.

"As it currently stands, the plan is for you to fly to Bongao early tomorrow morning. There isn't a direct flight from Manila, so you'll have to go through Zamboanga City. Wahab will meet you there and accompany you to Bongao. I haven't been briefed on what the specific plans are once you reach Tawi-Tawi. I imagine Wahab will fill in those details when he meets you at the airport."

"From your tone, I'm assuming that my flight reservations have already been made."

"We are holding seats for you on flights for tomorrow morning. Regrettably, it will necessitate an early start."

"How early?"

"The plane from Manila leaves at four a.m. and connects with a six-thirty flight in Zamboanga City."

"Good god."

"I realize it's all a bit rushed, but only one flight a day goes to Bongao. If you aren't on it we'll lose an entire day, and maybe risk those young men changing their minds about talking to us." He looked at his watch. "It's already getting late. If you're willing to go and you want to get any rest tonight, we should think about getting you to your hotel."

Ava sat back in her chair. "I can't deny that you've got me interested, but the way you and Uncle Chang went about this comes close to infuriating me."

"I apologize, for both of us."

"I'm wondering what else I haven't been told."

"I assure you that you now know everything we know. My only regret is that it's so little," he said.

Ava turned her head and gazed out the window as she thought through everything she'd just been told. Ramirez seemed sincere enough, but then, he was a politician. If he was misinformed or lying to her or exaggerating, she would be wasting at least one day travelling to the southern tip of the Philippines. But even if he was misinformed or lying, she would still earn a favour from Uncle Chang and Tommy Ordonez. If Ramirez was telling the truth, how bad could the consequences be? She didn't know, but she realized she couldn't risk saying no to him.

"Okay, I'll go," she said sharply. "But I have some conditions."

"Such as?"

"Your friends at the Brotherhood have to be completely open with me. I want all the access they have and I want to hear everything they hear. No secret meetings. No behind-my-back briefings."

"That's the way it will be."

"And I want to be involved in any discussions about what's to be done with the information we uncover."

"I'm not sure —" Ramirez began, and then stopped when he saw Ava stiffen.

"If I'm not to be part of that process, then I'm not prepared to provide you with the information that will fuel it," she said. "Call Uncle Chang if you need his permission to agree to that condition."

Ramirez nodded, and then reached into his shirt pocket and pulled out a business card. "Here, take this. It has my personal email and phone number on it. I'll be available to you twenty-four hours a day until we conclude this business."

"So that's a yes to my involvement?"

"It is."

Ava stood up. "Then I guess I should get to the hotel as soon as possible."

"I'll walk you to the door."

As they retraced their steps, Ramirez lagged a pace behind her. When she looked back at him, she thought she saw a combination of concern and reluctance in his face.

"Is something wrong?" she asked.

He stopped at the door, his hand resting on the handle. "I know this might be unnecessary, but I don't feel right about your going to Tawi-Tawi without warning you not to get any ideas about wandering around on your own," he said. "The island is one of the last real hotbeds of terrorism in our country. The Abu Sayyaf group is as active and militant as ever. There are only about four hundred members, but they make up in viciousness what they lack in numbers. Their specialty is kidnapping for ransom, and they often target foreigners by staking out the airport, the harbour, and the resorts. So if for any reason Wahab isn't at the airport in Zamboanga to accompany you to Tawi-Tawi, don't go. I don't want to have to explain to Chang Wang that something unfortunate has happened to you. After all the complimentary things he's said about you, I don't think he would be the least bit understanding."

*As if I didn't have enough to worry about*, Ava thought.

## 8

**THE PENINSULA HOTEL WAS ON AYALA AVENUE IN** Makati, no more than a ten-minute drive from Forbes Park. She remembered staying there when she worked on the Tommy Ordonez job. From the outside, the hotel's Georgian façade made it look like the headquarters of an old and very profitable bank. Inside, it was art deco in design and completely modern in function.

Chang had reserved a premier suite for her with a garden view that was rather wasted at eleven-thirty at night. Her second disappointment was that the Old Manila restaurant closed at eleven. She had mouth-watering memories of an Irish rib-eye beefsteak topped with seared foie gras. She thought about ordering it from room service, but it wasn't an option, so instead she ordered a BLT with french fries. Then she phoned Chang.

"*Wei*," he answered.

"Uncle Chang, it's Ava," she said. "You asked me to call after my meeting with Ramirez, but I figure you must have heard from him by now, so I'm not sure what more I can add."

"Yes, he did phone me," he said. "And thank you for agreeing to go to Bongao."

"I wish you'd told me about Bongao. You had the chance and you didn't."

He hesitated, and she knew that her abrupt tone had caught him off guard. "I apologize. I could make the excuse that it wasn't confirmed, but the truth is I was worried that you might be reluctant to come to the Philippines if you knew we wanted you to go to Bongao. And when you arrived, I thought it best for Ramirez to tell you, after he'd explained the political and economic realities of Mindanao and the other southern islands."

"He was long and strong on context and short on detail," Ava said.

"That is unfortunately the position in which we find ourselves. Hopefully you and the officials from the Brotherhood can remedy that lack of detail."

It was Ava's turned to pause, before saying very deliberately, "Uncle, do you remember how I operated when I took on that job for you and Tommy?"

"I'm not sure what point you're making."

"When I worked on an assignment, I didn't brief clients as I went along. I communicated with them only on an absolutely need-to-know basis," she said. "I know you're not strictly a client, but don't expect me to contact you or the senator with every little detail I uncover. The people from the Brotherhood can do as they like, but that's how I operate."

"I have no interest in the process or the methods you employ, only in the conclusion you reach," he said. "So I won't expect to hear from you until there is something definitive to report. But I do have to tell you that Ramirez can be very helpful. He has many contacts inside and outside the government. You shouldn't hesitate to use him, to make demands of him."

"I'll keep that in mind."

"And now would you like your flight details?"

"Please."

Ava wrote as he spoke. The flight to Zamboanga was very early, as Ramirez had said. She was booked on a late afternoon return flight that arrived in Manila mid-evening.

"There's only one flight in and one flight out of Bongao every day. If you have to stay over, you should keep that in mind. The flights are never full, though, so you shouldn't have a problem getting out of there," Chang said.

"Hopefully one day will be enough, but I'll take an overnight bag just in case," she said.

"Good luck, Ava, and thank you again for making this effort."

She put down the phone and sat back in the chair. She couldn't remember a time when she'd felt less enthusiastic about taking on a job of any kind. She opened her notebook and began to record her perceptions of Ramirez and the stories he'd told her. After she wrote *They're training terrorists at the college*, she underlined it, and as she did, she felt her interest spike. Could it be true? Ramirez hadn't been certain, only alarmed at the possibility that it might be. Then she thought about the timeline he'd given her and other questions came tumbling forth. He said the college had been open for a year, for example, but how could it train terrorists for that long without it becoming known?

The doorbell rang, and five minutes later she was devouring the sandwich and fries, at the same time pondering how best to spend the few hours she had before leaving for the airport. She considered showering and then decided she'd be better served by getting all the sleep she could. She undressed, threw on a T-shirt, and climbed into the luxurious king-size bed.

She quickly gave up any attempt to sleep. Her mind kept replaying her meeting with Ramirez. The more she thought about it, the more she realized that she knew virtually nothing about the southern Philippines, other than what she'd been told by him. And how much of that could she believe? She got out of bed, went to the desk, opened her computer, and entered "Tawi-Tawi" into a search engine.

It was indeed the southernmost island in the Philippines and a separate province of the Autonomous Region in Muslim Mindanao. It was surrounded by the Sulu Sea and shared ocean borders with the Malaysian state of Sabah and the Indonesian province of North Kalimantan, both of which were on the island of Borneo. It had a population of about four hundred thousand, ninety-six percent of whom were Muslim. And, as Ramirez had said, it still had active terrorist groups, Abu Sayyaf being the largest.

She typed in "Abu Sayyaf" and quickly realized that Ramirez hadn't been exaggerating. Since the 1990s the organization had been fighting for control of the Sulu Archipelago, of which Tawi-Tawi was a major part, for the purpose of establishing an Islamic state. They had targeted and killed soldiers, priests, journalists, and foreign tourists, a strategy they still employed. The group had external ties. *Abu sayyaf* translated to "bearer of the sword"; it was the name of a mujahedeen commander in Afghanistan who had fought the Soviets in the 1980s. In addition to their Afghani connections, several Abu Sayyaf commanders had recently pledged allegiance to the Islamic State. *Are they active in Bongao?* she wondered as she entered that name. If they were, there was no mention of them. In fact, all the descriptions of Bongao painted it as a pleasant city of about eighty thousand people with a lot of government offices, a couple of colleges — Zakat not among them — and a new two-storey mall.

She closed that page and entered "Yasin Juhar." There wasn't a lot of information, but what she could find confirmed what Ramirez had told her. Juhar had been leading the Muslim Brotherhood for more than thirty years, first in combat and now in government. She read some recent newspaper articles and ascertained that nothing of any real importance seemed to happen in Mindanao without his involvement and, she assumed, his approval.

She checked the time. She'd figured she would leave the hotel at around two a.m., and it was already past one. She decided to shower and have some coffee, in the hope that the combination would keep her awake and alert until she got on the first plane.

## 9

**AVA LEFT THE PENINSULA DRESSED IN BLACK LINEN**
slacks and a blue button-down cotton shirt. There was virtually no traffic on Ayala Avenue, and her taxi got her to Aquino Airport in less than fifteen minutes. She checked in, cleared security, and joined one other person in the business-class lounge of Cebu Pacific. She drank coffee and watched CNN until it was time to board.

The moment the flight took off, she reclined her seat, slipped on an eye mask, put in earplugs, and fell soundly asleep. She woke reluctantly, prompted by a flight attendant who was gently shaking her arm.

Only three other people were waiting at the boarding gate for the flight to Bongao. She sat in an orange plastic chair and waited. By six o'clock she was beginning to wonder if Wahab was going to show. Then she saw a short man in blue jeans and a black short-sleeved shirt scanning the departures area. He was sturdy, with a fleshy face and a thick handlebar moustache. He caught her eye and waved in her general direction. She stood up and waved back.

"I'm Wahab," he said when he reached her. "Sorry for

being a bit late, but on the way I had to drop off my children at my mother's home."

"It's been an early start to the day for all of us," Ava said.

"I know. I told Senator Ramirez that it's ridiculous to send you here, but he insisted. You could have stayed in Manila and let us handle it. It would have the same result," he said.

"Maybe that's true, but I'm not here because of or for the senator," Ava said. "There are other people who have an interest in this. I'm here on their behalf."

He shrugged and looked at the gate, where people were beginning to form a line.

Ava noticed he was carrying a small travel bag and pointed to it. "Are we staying over in Tawi-Tawi?"

"I shouldn't think so, but is it a problem if we do?"

"No, I have my things with me," she said, noticing cigarette on his breath.

"Did you book a return flight?" he asked.

"I have one at four."

"That should work."

Before she could ask why, she was interrupted by the boarding announcement. Wahab smiled awkwardly at her, turned, and headed for the gate. Ava was starting to get irritated by his manner.

They both had aisle seats but were separated by ten rows. The plane was an Airbus 319 that could hold more than a hundred passengers. There were fewer than twenty on board, and both she and Wahab had a row to themselves. She considered sitting next to him and then thought, *Let him make that decision.* She took out her Moleskine and began to reread her notes. They held her attention for only a few minutes before her eyes began to close. She put the notebook on the seat next to her, let her head fall back, and closed her eyes.

She woke as the plane began its descent. Ava looked at her watch. They'd been in the air for twenty minutes of what was only a thirty-minute flight. The pilot announced their approach to Tawi-Tawi's Sanga-Sanga Airport in an almost singsong manner.

She walked down the steps of the plane onto the runway and waited for Wahab. There was a scattering of white clouds overhead, but they didn't offer any protection from the blinding sun. The sky was a shockingly brilliant blue. She couldn't remember the last time she had seen a sky that colour. The tarmac shimmered in the heat like a desert mirage, and soon she was wiping the sweat off her brow.

Wahab was one of the last people to get off the plane. "You didn't have to wait for me," he said. "It's too hot out here in the open."

They walked towards the small one-storey terminal, which was bordered by a row of trees blooming with yellow flowers. Ava breathed in deeply. "That's such a beautiful scent," she said.

"It's ylang-ylang. We call it the perfume tree," Wahab said.

"Another double name."

"What?"

"Nothing," she said.

As soon as they entered the arrivals hall, a thin young man wearing a New York Yankees baseball cap, a white T-shirt, skin-tight jeans, and Nike high-tops rushed towards them. "Good morning, sir," he said to Wahab, bowing deeply.

"Hi, Saham. Is everything arranged?" Wahab said.

The young man stepped to one side and looked in the direction from which he'd come. "The imam can explain that better than I can," he said, motioning at a short, stout man wearing a white *thawb* and a black *taqiyah* who was walking laboriously towards them.

The imam bowed his head ever so slightly when he reached them. Wahab did the same and then turned to Ava. "This is Imam Sharif," he said. "He is the person who contacted us about the college."

"Pleased to meet you," Ava said.

The imam's eyes moved back and forth between Ava and Wahab. Then he began to speak to Wahab in what Ava recognized as Tagalog, the native tongue of the Philippines. Wahab replied in the same language. Ava had no idea what was being said, but she did catch her name and those of Ramirez and Ordonez.

"Is there a problem?" Ava asked when their conversation paused.

"No. The imam just wasn't expecting me to bring a woman."

"He does understand the circumstances?"

"Now he does. I explained to him that you're working for one of our partners and that you're an expert at gathering and assessing information."

"Is that what Ramirez told you?"

"Yes."

"So why did you say earlier that it's a waste of time for me to come?"

"Because I'm quite good at it myself."

"I'm sure you are."

"But now that you're here, we need to show solidarity."

"I couldn't agree more."

Saham led the way out of the terminal with Ava by his side and Wahab and Sharif trailing them. They crossed the roadway, entered an outdoor parking lot, and turned right. About twenty metres away, another young man jumped out of the driver's seat of a black Honda SUV and opened all the doors. He was dressed almost identically to his colleague, except he wasn't wearing a baseball cap. Ava could hear the air conditioning going full blast and gratefully slid into the back seat. Wahab joined her, leaving the front seats for the imam and Saham, who took the driver's seat. The young man who'd been sitting in the car left without an explanation.

Ava looked out the window as they drove towards the city. She noted the looming presence of a mountain covered in trees and a magnificent whitewashed building overlooking the harbour and bay. Wahab noticed her interest and pointed to the mountain. "That's Bud Bongao," he said. "At 340 metres, it's the highest mountain in Tawi-Tawi. There are three Muslim shrines at its peak, and many pilgrims go there."

"And the building?"

"That's Tawi-Tawi's Provincial Capitol building. It's modelled after the Taj Mahal."

The city was mainly low-lying, and aside from the miniature Taj, the tallest buildings they passed were mosques, their minarets decorating the skyline. The car made a right and they were now skirting the city, moving away from the mountain. They turned right again, and what Ava assumed was the Sulu Sea filled the view ahead. The road narrowed and the asphalt became dirt; houses became less frequent and red tiled roofs gave way to thatched.

They turned right once again and the Honda came to an abrupt stop in a dirt courtyard in front of a long, narrow wooden building painted pink and white. A canvas sheet that said MARIA'S HOTEL AND RESTAURANT hung on the side of the building. Ava estimated they were about a hundred metres from the sea, with several clusters of small huts between them and the water.

"You can leave your carry-on here," Wahab said to Ava, and then turned to Saham. "Turn off the car while you're waiting. If you get warm, sit in the shade."

He and Sharif got out of the car and she followed them into the building, carrying her Chanel bag. It was dark inside. All the blinds were drawn, and two giant ceiling fans were slowly churning warm air. "Over here, sirs," a voice said.

They walked to the left, past a small reception desk and into a room with ten or twelve wooden tables. Two young men sat at the table farthest from the entrance. They were wearing identical blue short-sleeved cotton shirts with "Zakat" stitched in large letters above the pocket. They stood and bowed. One had long hair parted down the middle; the other's was closely cropped. They both had thin, scraggly beards. *They look like teenagers*, Ava thought.

"Sit," Wahab said to them with an impatient wave of his hand.

They did as he asked. The table was long enough to accommodate eight people, and the young men sat side by side with what looked like glasses of lemonade in front of them. The imam sat with them. Ava and Wahab slid onto a bench facing them.

"Do you want something to drink?" Wahab asked her and the imam.

"Black coffee would be perfect," she said, while the imam shook his head.

Wahab raised his hand and held it in the air until a short, wiry woman arrived at the table. "Two black coffees," he said.

He waited until she left before he said, "Imam, will you introduce these men?"

"This is Ben," the imam said in English, indicating the one with cropped hair. "And this is Alcem. They're cousins."

"My name is Wahab, and this is a colleague, Ava Lee," Wahab said to them.

"Wahab is deputy commander of our Muslim Brotherhood," the imam continued. "He has flown all the way from Mindanao to speak to you. The woman is a friend of a friend of the Brotherhood. I expect you to show her every courtesy."

Wahab nodded at them. "We flew here for the sole purpose of speaking to the two of you. The imam has relayed to us what you said to him about the college. We found it disturbing, so we asked to speak directly with you to hear it in your own words. He said you are prepared to answer questions and to be completely open and honest with us. Is this the case?"

The two young men glanced anxiously at each other.

"They will tell you everything they know," the imam said.

"Yes, we'll tell you everything we know," Ben said.

"Good. As the imam said, Ms. Lee is completely trusted by men who are good friends of the Brotherhood, and we trust her in turn. She has the first questions for you."

Ava was stunned by the way Wahab had abruptly turned the meeting over to her. Her first thought was whether he had some ulterior motive. But when she saw the young men and the imam looking attentively at her, she asked an obvious first question: "I was told you work at the college. Looking at your shirts, can I assume that you still do?"

"We do," Alcem said.

"What kind of work?"

"We are cleaners."

"How long have you been there?"

"Nine months. We started three months after it opened."

"How did you get the jobs?"

"One of our cousins is a cook there," Ben said. "He told us there were job openings and we applied."

"Did either of you have cleaning experience?"

"No, but the work is simple enough."

"The fact that we are Muslims helped," Alcem said.

Wahab glared at him. "But your bosses at the college aren't Brotherhood, are they."

"No, sir," Ben said quickly.

"How many students are at the school?" Ava asked.

"Right now there are about sixty," Alcem said.

"Right now? There were more or less before?"

"The students attend only for three months. The classes keep changing."

"So in nine months you've seen how many students?"

Alcem glanced at Ben and the two of them began to count on their fingers. "Well, when we first got to the school, it was the last month for one class. Then there were two more full classes. And now we're starting the last month for another class," Alcem said. "I guess we've seen more than two hundred students."

"Are all those students Filipino?"

"There were hardly any Filipinos."

Ava couldn't hide her surprise. "Then where were they from?"

"The world."

"The world is a big place."

"We met people from Saudi Arabia, Kuwait, Australia, Turkey, Syria, England, Belgium, and Palestine — from all over, really."

"How did you find out their home countries?"

Alcem leaned forward with his hands clenched. "We were told by the bosses not to speak to the students, but you can't help hearing things. And when they talked to us, it was impolite not to answer. Besides, they knew we were Muslims and we were about the same age, so we had things in common. We talked about all kinds of things, including where they were from."

"So most of the students were young?"

"Yes, in their early to mid-twenties."

"All men?"

"Yes."

"So you have all these young men coming from all over the world to attend a college in Bongao — to do what?"

"To study the Koran with Imam Tariq al-Bashir."

"Who is Tariq al-Bashir?"

"The imam who runs the college."

"They told this to Imam Sharif when they first spoke to him," Wahab interrupted. "He and his local colleagues have never heard of a man by that name. The Brotherhood searched for information on him throughout the Philippines and found not a trace — no history, no background."

"How hard did you look?"

"We used every means we could. We believe he must be a foreigner, but the senator had one of his staff run Bashir's name through customs and immigration records and he came up with nothing."

That was one more thing the senator hadn't told her, Ava thought. "With students from so many countries, what language did the imam use to teach?" she asked them.

"Some Arabic, but mainly English," Alcem said.

"How well does he speak English?"

"He hardly has any accent. He sounds American or Canadian."

"How would you know that — I mean, apart from watching television?"

"I lived in Canada for two years," Alcem said.

"Didn't you find it odd for an imam to have an accent like that?"

He shook his head. "Islam is the world's religion. There are imams everywhere."

"That's true enough," Ava said. "But do you think all the students understood English?"

"They seemed to."

"Then tell me, why would an English-speaking imam go to one of the most isolated parts of the Philippines to teach the Koran to foreign students in English?"

Imam Sharif leaned across the table and almost hissed at Ava, "He is promoting jihad."

"I know that's what Ben and Alcem have told you, but did they give you any real details?" Ava said.

"No. That's why they're here."

"Yes, it is," she said, hoping he would realize that his interruption had disturbed her line of questioning. "And now I'd

like to continue by asking Ben and Alcem if they actually
heard this imam preach jihad or were just told about it."

Ben glanced sideways at Imam Sharif. "Tell us everything," Sharif said.

"Well, every day after the morning prayer, the students
gather and the imam instructs them from the Koran," Ben
said, his eyes cast downward and his voice a monotone, as
if reciting words he'd memorized. "He tells them that our
religion is under attack from the Jews and the Christians and
that it is God's will that we defend ourselves from the defilers."

"He talks for hours," Alcem added. "His voice is powerful."

"Do you mean that his message is powerful?" Ava said.

He nodded.

"Was it powerful enough to tempt you to join al-Bashir's
jihad?"

Ben glanced at Alcem. "We talked about it, but we thought
it was wrong."

"If you thought it was wrong, why didn't you see your
imam sooner? Why did you wait for so many months?"

"We both left high school five years ago," Ben said. "This
is the first real job either of us has ever had. We are finally
able to help our families and to start thinking about some
kind of future. We don't want to lose our jobs."

"That's true what the boy says — about the jobs, I mean,"
Sharif said. "It's very difficult for young men on this island."

"We were also scared to say anything," Alcem said.

"Why?" Ava said.

"Security."

"What does that mean?"

"The college is like an armed camp. It's surrounded by
a fence with razor wire. No one can get in or out without

going past security and without being searched," Alcem said. "Most of the security people aren't local, and they're tough. The guy who heads it up meets with every new employee and tells them the rules, and the number one rule is never talk about the college."

"So why did you?"

Alcem looked at Ben and then across the table at Wahab. "Because some students were talking about killing people in Manila," he said.

"Killing who?" Wahab said.

"They were told to target Jews. They are planning to bomb two synagogues."

"When?" Wahab asked, his voice becoming strained.

"In May, at the same time as the other attacks."

"Attacks in the Philippines?"

"No. Manila is the only place in the Philippines we heard them talk about."

"Then where else are these attacks supposed to take place?" Ava asked.

"Mainly in the U.S.," Alcem said.

"And who's being targeted there?"

"Mostly Jews."

Ava tried to speak, but she stopped when she couldn't find the words.

## 10

**AVA EXCUSED HERSELF TO GO TO THE BATHROOM. SHE** splashed cold water on her face, looked at her reflection the mirror, splashed more water, and looked into the mirror again. *What am I doing here?* she thought. "Get hold of yourself," she said to the pale, drawn face in the mirror. "All you're doing is gathering information."

The four men at the table looked at her anxiously when she returned. A fresh cup of coffee had been set at her place. She sat down, took a healthy swallow, and said, "Okay, I'm ready to hear the rest of this."

"Where do you want them to start?" Wahab asked.

"Bombs. Alcem mentioned bombs," Ava said.

"They teach the students how to make them and show them how to detonate them at the back of the college property—" Alcem said.

"But not right away," Ben interrupted.

"No, that's true," Alcem said. "They have to make the commitment before they're taught."

"A commitment to jihad?" she said.

Alcem nodded. "The students at the college don't do

anything for the first three or four weeks except study the Koran and listen to the imam talk about jihad. The same message is repeated over and over again, until their heads are full and there isn't room for anything else. Then, towards the end of that time, the imam and his assistants meet with the students one-on-one. After the meeting, each student has to decide whether or not to commit to jihad. If they do, they stay at the school and continue their training. If they don't, they're sent back to where they came from."

"How do you know about this?"

"The students talk about it among themselves. The group there now is the fourth we've seen, and they've gone through the same interview process as all the others."

"And the students actually talk about this in front of you and Ben?"

"They're so used to seeing us, we've become like the walls or the floor — just part of the building. No one cares what they say when we're around."

"So, counting this new group, you've seen about two hundred students who were given the choice between jihad and leaving?"

"That sounds about right."

"How many refused to commit and left?"

"Maybe ten."

"From each group?"

"No. In total."

"I think that most of the students were committed even before they got to the school," Ben said. "They knew why they were there. Any complaints we heard were about things moving too slowly, or about their electronic devices being taken away from them."

Ava thought about taking out her notebook but held back, not wanting to do anything that might inhibit the boys. "You mentioned assistants. How many does the imam have?"

"Seven or eight. I'm not sure," Alcem said. "They keep separate from the students when they're not teaching, and they never talk to us."

"What do they teach?"

"Bomb making, shooting, other stuff."

"Other stuff?"

Alcem shrugged. "They tell them how to stay hidden and how to plan and execute attacks."

"Did you say earlier that they not only make but actually detonate bombs at the college?"

"It's a very large property, without any close neighbours. They go to the back, near a clump of trees, and set the bombs off there."

"How do you know this?"

"We heard the bombs going off and guns being fired."

"And they do this for a couple of months?" Ava said.

"For about a month, because for the last few weeks, after the final commitment, the focus is on where they're going. They meet in small groups and sometimes one-on-one with the assistants, to familiarize themselves with where they're being sent."

"What is this final commitment? Is it different from the one you just explained?" she asked.

"Yeah. It's their second and last chance to leave the college and return home. They're given the chance to leave after they've been told where they're scheduled to be sent and which cell they will be assigned to."

"Did any of them leave?" Ava said.

"Over the nine months, only a handful, maybe three or four."

"And you're saying that the students talked openly in front of you about where they were going?"

"For a few days that's all anyone talked about."

"You mentioned destinations and cells as if they are separate. What did you mean?"

"In the last group, I know of at least five students who said they were going to Miami, but they were joining different cells," Alcem said.

Ava felt her sense of foreboding return. "Did they mention why they were being sent to Miami?"

"They said there are a lot of Jews there."

Ava's foreboding began to take on physical dimensions, her stomach knotting.

"They were being sent all over the U.S.," Ben said. "I knew as many who were going to New York City."

"Because there are a lot of Jews in New York?"

"I think so."

"And to different cells?"

"I'm not sure, but one was bragging that he was joining a cell that would bring down Times Square."

"What other American cities were mentioned?" she asked.

"Chicago, Los Angeles, Las Vegas, Boston, Dallas...and more."

"They weren't just being sent to the U.S.," Alcem said. "We also heard them mention Palestine, Jordan, and Lebanon."

"All countries that border Israel," Ava said.

"Yes, they said it would be easy to attack Israel from those places."

"I don't know how easy it is to get in and out of countries

like Jordan, but the United States is very difficult to get into for anyone, let alone young, single Muslim men." She shook her head. "Did any of them have an idea how they were going to get into the U.S.?"

"They were told that an organization called the Zakat Foundation would make all the arrangements, and there wouldn't be any problems."

"So no one had details about how they would be travelling?"

"No."

"Were these suicide missions?" she said, her throat constricting.

Alcem and Ben looked towards the imam. "Tell the lady what you think," he said.

"No one ever used the word 'suicide,'" Alcem said.

"But did they expect to die?"

"If that was Allah's will."

Ava took a deep breath and closed her eyes. When she opened them, she said, "The last group of students, the ones who left a month ago, how did they leave the college?"

"What do you mean?"

"Did they go by bus, by car, in groups, separately? How was it done?"

"We don't know," Alcem said. "We weren't at the college when they left. In fact, all the local staff were given two days off. The students were there when we left and they were gone when we came back."

Ava drained her coffee and sat back, trying to remember what else Wahab had said before she went to the bathroom. "May," she said suddenly. "You mentioned attacks that are scheduled for the month of May. What else do you know about that?"

"According to the boys, all the students who've gone over-seas are in place and waiting. The plan is for a massive, coor-dinated attack to take place two months from now."

"In May?"

"That's the month."

"And what do you mean by 'coordinated'?"

"They will all strike at the same time and on the same day."

"What date? What time?"

"They didn't know, or at least they didn't mention it in front of us."

Ava leaned forward, looking Ben and Alcem straight in the eyes. "You don't have any idea at all? You can't remember a single reference to a specific day?"

They shook their heads.

She sat back. "This is terrifying. Even if only a tenth of the students make it into the United States and the other countries, the impact could be horrendous."

She looked across the table at the imam, Alcem, and Ben, and saw blank faces. Wahab was silent. The boys lowered their eyes, avoiding her gaze.

Imam Sharif shifted in his chair and said, "Do you have any more questions? The boys have to be at work in about half an hour. We can continue this conversation when they're gone."

"Will they be available if we have to speak to them again?"

"Yes," said Sharif. "They understand there is no going back now, only forward."

## 11

**NO ONE SPOKE AGAIN UNTIL BEN AND ALCEM HAD LEFT** the coffee shop, and then it was Ava who asked the first and most obvious question. "Do the two of you really believe those boys?"

"I do. They may not have come forth as quickly as they should have, but now that they have — and at some personal risk — I think they're speaking the truth," Sharif said firmly.

"Me too," Wahab said.

"Do you think they're telling us the entire truth? Could they be embellishing? Could they be holding things back? Could they have misinterpreted what they saw and heard?"

"Any of those scenarios is possible," Sharif said.

"You say that so calmly," Ava said. "Did you know what they were going to tell us? Had you heard it before?"

"No, and while I may sound calm, I'm extremely disturbed," Sharif said. "It doesn't take much imagination to realize that if even half of what they've told us is true, the consequences for our local Muslim community, for Tawi-Tawi, the entire Mindanao region, and the Brotherhood would be terrible."

"What about the people these terrorists have supposedly targeted?" Ava said. "Don't you have any concerns about their safety, their welfare?"

"Of course I do," Sharif said. "But my first concern always is the people I live among."

Ava closed her eyes. Uncle used to say that self-preservation was the strongest and most basic of all human instincts. She wondered if Wahab shared the imam's sentiments, but decided that asking him wouldn't serve any purpose. Instead she said, "I assume that you share the imam's and Senator Ramirez's opinion that the various government, military, and security forces in Manila would use the college as an excuse to reassert their authority."

"They would threaten our religious freedom, subjugate us politically, and destroy whatever economic gains we've been able to make," Wahab said harshly. "This college is the excuse they've been waiting for, and maybe even praying for."

"The senator told me he's determined not to let it come to that," Ava said.

"How is that possible?"

"Preventing those attacks would be a great place to start."

"How would he do that?"

"I have no idea. All I know is that we need to gather a lot more information, so that we can confirm what we've been told, add whatever we can to it, and then pass everything along to the senator, so that whatever he does is based on facts."

"We don't have enough now?"

"All we have is the story the boys told us," she said.

"What more do we need?" Wahab said.

"I'll answer that question in a minute," Ava said. "First,

I want to know if it is your intention to share what we just heard."

"Of course."

"With whom?"

"Juhar is the head of the Brotherhood, and he needs to know what's happening."

"How many other people in the Brotherhood know why you were coming here?"

"None."

"So just you, Juhar, and Senator Ramirez were privy to the information that the imam initially provided?"

"Yes."

Ava looked at Imam Sharif. "What about you? Did you tell anyone else, and is there anyone you have to tell?"

"No."

"Good. The last thing we want is to tip off the people at the college that someone has an interest in them," she said, and then turned back to Wahab. "I understand why it's necessary for you to brief Juhar, but when you do, I think you have to stress that we need time to confirm what we've been told, and that it's premature to expand the list of people who know. Luckily, if the May timetable the boys mentioned is accurate, we have a bit of time."

"What if it isn't accurate?" Wahab said.

"Have there been any terrorist attacks, here in the Philippines or anywhere else, in the past six to nine months that can be traced back to Tawi-Tawi, Bongao, or the college?"

"None that I know of."

"More than a hundred students have already gone through the college and have been sent God knows where, and there haven't been any reports of attacks. That leads me to believe that the boys could be correct about the timing."

"Okay, let's assume they are," Wahab said. "Where does that leave us?"

"As I said earlier, we need to gather more information, starting with finding out all we can about this college and Tariq al-Bashir. Then we have to figure out who the young men were who went to the school and where the hell they are now."

"How are we going to collect that information?"

"I'm not sure exactly. Give me some time to think about it."

"But you've done this kind of thing before."

"I have never, ever been involved in anything that resembles what we could be looking at here."

"I mean information gathering and getting to the truth."

"Yes, I have."

He nodded and rose from his seat. "I have to phone Juhar, and Imam Sharif has obligations in Bongao. I'll walk him to the car and have Saham drive him back to the city. I'll make my call outside."

"Before the imam leaves, I'd like to ask him if he's ever been to the college," Ava said.

"Why?" Wahab said.

"I would find it odd if you had no curiosity about a new Islamic college on your home island."

"Once. I saw it once, a month or so after it opened," Sharif said. "I was curious about it and had one of my people drive me there. It is in an isolated area that can be accessed only by a dirt track. As the boys said, it is a compound surrounded by high fences with double rolls of razor wire. As for the rest of it, I don't know. I got a glimpse from afar of the general layout and then had the driver turn around."

"Did you sense anything strange about the college's location, the fences, the wire?"

"No. What I thought was that these were people who valued their privacy. Who was I to invade it?"

## 12

**AVA WATCHED WAHAB AND IMAM SHARIF LEAVE AND**
then reached into her bag and took out her notebook. She
turned to the back, where she'd started making notes
about Zakat College, and under her previous entry wrote:
*INTERVIEW IN TAWI-TAWI.* She then began to record
everything that Ben and Alcem had told them. When that
was done, she looked towards the café entrance. There was
no sign of Wahab. More than fifteen minutes had passed
since he'd left.

She turned to a clean page and forced herself to focus on
the questions that needed to be asked. After ten minutes she'd
filled almost the entire page. She was still writing when she
heard the door open and saw Wahab walking towards her.

"What did Juhar have to say?" she asked.

"He doesn't want to believe it."

"Who does?"

"He made me repeat everything we were told three times
before he finally accepted that it might be possible."

"How did your conversation end?"

"He said we have to do everything possible to find out the

truth, and that the senator and his partners sent you here to direct that effort," he said. "Juhar told me he'd agreed that you would be in charge and that he'd committed the Brotherhood — and me specifically — to providing all the assistance you need."

"Is providing help a problem for you?"

"No."

Ava nodded. "Did you tell Juhar that we want to keep everything as contained as possible?"

"I did, and you don't have to worry about him. I can't think of a single person Juhar would want to share this information with."

"Good."

"Now what? Where do we start?" He pointed at her notebook. "Have you come up with any ideas?"

"The first thing I want to do is see the college."

He flinched. "I don't think that's wise."

"Why not?"

"I wouldn't want them to be able to recognize us."

"How could they? We can just drive past it without stopping. I'm not suggesting we drop in for a visit."

"Is that really necessary?"

"I don't like dealing with the abstract," she said. "I want to see it."

"I'm not sure —"

"Is the car back?"

"Yes."

"Then let's go now."

He settled the bill and led her outside. Saham was sitting on a picnic bench under the shade of a tree, his chin resting on his hand.

"Hey, start the car!" Wahab shouted.

As Ava and Wahab climbed into the back seat, she said, "I'm glad I brought my carry-on. I thought about leaving it at the hotel in Manila, but chances are I'll miss that four-o'clock flight."

"Ms. Lee —"

"My name is Ava. Please call me that."

"Ava, are you telling me that you already have plans for the rest of the day?"

"No. I just have questions that will hopefully lead to answers that will lead to more questions. This kind of information gathering is an unpredictable process, and often laborious and time-consuming."

"Where are we going, sir?" Saham asked.

"Zakat College, but don't stop when we get there. Just drive past it, turn around, and head back this way. Make it look like we're lost." He turned to Ava. "What kind of questions?"

"For starters, how hard did you look for information on Imam al-Bashir?"

"We went online and searched every site we could think of. The imam did the same, and he also made many phone calls to colleagues. This al-Bashir is not Filipino or Moro for sure, or someone would have known of him."

"What does 'Moro' mean? I've heard it a couple of times now."

"It's the Spanish word for 'Muslim,' or at least it's what the Spanish in the Philippines called Muslims."

"You're suggesting that al-Bashir isn't Muslim?"

"No, just that he isn't a local Muslim."

"You said earlier that Ramirez also did some searching."

"He asked a junior staffer to make some enquiries. They found nothing."

"So you think he's from overseas?"

"Well, that's odd as well. Ramirez's staffer ran his name past the immigration department. There is no record of anyone named Tariq al-Bashir entering or leaving the country."

"Maybe that isn't his name."

"That's my thought."

They had been on a dirt road since they left the café, and now the car veered to the right and drove onto a ruttier, narrower path. They slowed to a crawl as Saham tried to avoid the potholes.

"Where are we exactly?" Ava asked.

"About ten kilometres from downtown Bongao. The college is officially within the city limits."

"So to build the college, someone would have to get a building permit from the city?"

"Yes."

"And I'm trying to remember . . . are foreigners allowed to own land in the Philippines?"

"No," Wahab said.

"So who bought the land? Who applied for the building permit? Which company did the construction? Who paid them? There have to be a lawyer, an accountant, and a bank attached to a project of this size. Who are they?"

"Those are a great many questions."

"There are more," Ava said, remembering the list she'd made in her notebook. "How are Alcem and Ben and the other employees paid? How about suppliers? Somewhere there is a bank dispensing money. Whose name is on the account? Who has signing authority? Where does the money originate?"

Wahab shook his head.

"We need to find out. Someone paid for the land and for construction of the college. Someone is paying for its upkeep. Someone is paying for those students to get to the U.S. and elsewhere," Ava said. "Money does not exist in a vacuum. It has to be moved from point to point. It has to have an origin."

"We're nearing the college," Saham said.

Every eye in the car stared straight ahead, none more intently than Ava's. She saw the metal fence first. It had to be five metres high, and the imam was correct about the razor wire. Then the school appeared, and Ava was surprised how plain but ominous looking it was. The one-storey wooden structure was painted a dull brown and didn't have a single window. Above grey steel double doors was a painted sign that simply read ZAKAT. The building was dotted with security cameras.

"It looks more like a medium-security prison than a school," Ava said.

As they drove slowly past the entrance gate, also topped by razor wire, two guards came out of the security hut and stared at them. Wahab rolled down his window. "We took a wrong turn," he shouted. The guards didn't acknowledge him.

Ava could now see that the structure was shaped like a horseshoe, with two wings extending from either end of a long, deeply recessed main building. When they reached the edge of the property, the car stopped and Saham began to execute a U-turn, giving Ava a clear view of the fenceline, which ran for at least two hundred metres towards the back of the property.

"That's a lot of land," Ava said.

"Drive faster," Wahab said to Saham as the guards moved towards the gate.

No one in the car spoke until the school receded from view. Ava started to say something but suddenly felt almost drained. She knew that sign; she needed to get some sleep before her mind shut down. "I didn't sleep at all last night," she said. "I think it would be smart for me to find a hotel and have a nap. Maybe while I'm doing that, you can start finding some answers to my questions."

"I've already been thinking about them," Wahab said.

"And?"

"We have good contacts in the city government. I'll find out who owns the land and who got the building permits," he said.

"That's a good starting point. But if you're successful, don't try to talk to them without me."

"I won't."

"Thanks," she said. "Now, how about finding a hotel."

"There are only two or three in and around Bongao. The one I usually stay at is the Beachside Inn. It has some nice gardens and a view of the Sulu Sea and Bud Bongao. But it isn't fancy."

"I just need it to be clean."

He nodded and then said, "Saham, take us to the Beachside Inn."

They retraced their path all the way to Maria's Restaurant, drove past the cutoff, and continued south. The Sulu Sea appeared sporadically in the distance, but Bongao Mountain was a constant companion. Saham drove for ten minutes past Maria's and then turned off the main road and headed towards the sea. A moment later they pulled up in front of the sprawling complex of whitewashed one-storey buildings that formed the Beachside Inn.

"I'll check you in," Wahab said.

Ava stood outside by the car, surrounded by a massive garden. She liked the wildness of it, and the perfume that she guessed was from ylang-ylang trees. When Wahab reappeared, Saham ran to the trunk to get her Shanghai Tang Double Happiness bag. She took it from him and walked towards Wahab.

"I got you the end unit over there," he said. "It should be quiet, and you'll have a great view of the sea."

She took the key from him. "Thank you. I'll find it," she said, and then looked at her watch. "Give me two hours. Do you have my phone number?"

"The senator gave it to me."

"Then call me about fifteen minutes before you come back to get me." He nodded, and Ava turned and walked towards the unit.

The room was small, plain, and clean. Ava put her bag on the teak coffee table, stripped down to her underwear, pulled back the blanket, and slipped into bed. Despite her fatigue, her mind was still active, turning over the morning's conversations. As it did, that feeling of dread returned, triggered by thoughts of what could happen somewhere, sometime in May, and intensified by the fact that she knew so little. *Don't leap ahead*, she thought. When she worked with Uncle, she had conditioned herself not to think about the conclusions of cases until they presented themselves. Any success was achieved small step by small step, not by overreaching or getting too far ahead of what the facts on hand dictated.

*I need to calm down*, she thought, and began to draw deep breaths, holding them for as long as she could before slowly emptying her lungs. It was a relaxation technique she had learned from her bak mei instructor, Grandmaster Tang. She hadn't reached twenty breaths before she fell into a deep sleep.

She didn't dream, which was unusual, and woke to knocking on a door. She opened her eyes, wondered where she was, and then heard the knocking again. *I'm in Bongao*, she suddenly thought.

She sat up in bed. "Who's there?"

"It's Wahab. I called you twice and you didn't answer. It's been more than two hours, and I was getting worried."

"I'm fine," Ava said. "I'll be there in ten minutes or so."

"Hurry if you can," he said. "We have an appointment with a lawyer in the city in half an hour."

"What lawyer?"

"The one who bought the land, got the permits, and is fronting the college."

## 13

**IT TOOK AVA LESS THAN TEN MINUTES TO WASH, BRUSH** her hair, and throw on the same clothes she'd been wearing that morning. She didn't bother with makeup or perfume, but she did pull her hair back and secure it with her ivory chignon pin. The pin was the first valuable piece of jewellery she'd owned. She'd purchased it in Kowloon with the money she'd made on her first collection job. It was an antique, many hundreds of years old, and the jeweller who'd sold it to her said it had probably been owned by an emperor's wife. She loved that thought, although she didn't entirely believe it. What she did know for sure was that it was her lucky charm, something she'd worn on every job and every special occasion in her life. She knew she was being superstitious, but she was no more or less so than any other Chinese person she'd ever known, which meant that she'd never stop believing that the pin brought her luck.

When she left the room, she saw Wahab standing by the car with a small smile on his face. It was too soon for smiles, she thought, but she didn't want to be discouraging. "I'm sorry for sleeping so late," she said. "I was more tired than I realized."

"I just called the lawyer. He's not going anywhere or scheduling any other meetings."

"That's good. Who is this guy?"

"His name is Jaafar. He runs a one-man firm that handles mainly commercial and real estate transactions."

"How did you find out it was him?"

"He owns the land. He applied for the building permits," he said. "Everything is in the city records. I feel silly that we didn't think to look there ourselves."

"Do you know him?"

"Yes, and he knows who we are."

"Does he know why we want to talk to him?"

"He might have some suspicions, but we didn't say anything specific."

"What did you tell him?"

"I didn't talk to him. Juhar did," Wahab said. "We wanted to guarantee that he would be co-operative."

"He knows Juhar?"

"Everyone in Mindanao who is anyone — or wants to be anyone — knows Juhar."

"That's what I read. I just wanted to confirm it," she said as she got into the car.

They quickly reached the outskirts of the city and worked their way through light traffic, past the new shopping mall she'd read about online and into a district lined with three- and four-storey office buildings among restaurants and stores. The car came to a halt in front of a grey stucco building.

"Stay close," Wahab said to Saham. "I'll call you when we're ready to leave."

Ava followed Wahab into the building. There was no

elevator, but he turned right as soon as they reached the lobby and walked towards a single wooden door. It had a brass plate with JAAFAR LAW OFFICES on it. He opened the door and stood to one side to let her pass. As soon as they stepped inside, a bulky man wearing a short-sleeved white shirt and grey slacks with red suspenders rushed towards them.

"Mr. Wahab and Ms. Lee, so pleased to meet you," he said.

"Thank you for shuffling around your schedule for us," Ava said.

"Mr. Juhar said it was an urgent matter, but he really didn't have to. I would give any request from him the highest priority."

"Then shall we sit and talk?" Wahab said.

"This way," Jaafar said, motioning towards an open door that led into a small boardroom.

They sat down at a round table. "Can I offer you something to drink? Soda, coffee, tea, water?"

"Nothing for me," Wahab said.

"I'll have a black coffee," Ava said.

Jaafar got up and went to the door. "Two black coffees," he said loudly.

When he sat down again, he placed his hands rather primly on the table, interlocking his fingers. "Now, what is this urgent matter that I can help you with?" he said.

"The Zakat College of Tawi-Tawi," Wahab said. "We have questions about it."

Ava saw Jaafar's eyes flicker, and she detected a slight nervous twitch. "They are a client," he said.

"We know."

"I say that because there is the matter of lawyer–client confidentiality."

"Whatever you tell us won't leave this room," Ava said.

Jaafar shifted in his chair and looked at Wahab, his discomfort increasing. Before he could speak, a young woman appeared in the doorway with a tray. He stood, went to her, and took the tray. Ava smiled; she knew he was using the distraction as a way to gather his composure. She was certain that he had information they would be able to use.

He came back and fussed with putting the cup of coffee in front of her. "I'm quite confused about your objectives where the school is concerned."

"We'll come to that later," Ava said.

"And I'm not privy to how it operates."

"That doesn't matter. My immediate interest lies elsewhere."

Jaafar glanced at Wahab.

"In case Juhar didn't explain things clearly, Ms. Lee is acting on behalf of the Brotherhood and has our full support. We'd like you to answer her questions as if they were coming from us."

Jaafar sat down. "Well, I can't make any promises until I know what she wants."

"As a start, who is Imam Tariq al-Bashir?" Ava asked briskly.

"I don't know. I've never met him and I've been told nothing about him."

"He had nothing to do with construction of the school?"

"No."

"Who did?"

Jaafar hesitated.

"Don't play games," Wahab said.

The lawyer tried to stare at Wahab but quickly backed off. "The Zakat Foundation of Riyadh, Saudi Arabia," he said.

"And who represented the Foundation?" Ava asked.

"Two years ago I was approached by a man named Kassab. He said the Foundation was established to promote international community development and wanted to build a training centre on Tawi-Tawi. He told me they needed a large tract of land somewhere outside the city that could afford some privacy."

"Does Kassab have a first name?"

"Ishak."

"Why did the college need to be outside the city, and why did they want privacy?"

"He said they needed an environment that didn't have any distractions for the students."

"And you believed that?"

"I didn't have any reason to question him. And he was very matter-of-fact and sincere."

"How generous was your fee? Was it more than you normally charge?"

"A bit."

"Which undoubtedly made him seem more sincere."

"That comment wasn't necessary," Jaafar said.

"No, it wasn't, and I apologize," Ava said. "So tell me, what did you do to earn your fee?"

"I looked for sites. Kassab made a couple of trips to look at some I thought might suit the Foundation, and then told me to buy the one they now occupy. As soon as that deal was done, he asked me to get a building permit and to recommend a local construction firm."

"You bought the land and got the permit under your own name?"

"I did."

"Who hired the construction firm?"

"Kassab did. When he met with them, he gave them a set of plans and asked how long it would take to build the complex. They said six to nine months. Kassab told them it had to be finished in six months and he was willing to pay a bonus if they met the deadline," Jaafar said. "I attended all those meetings."

"Who supervised construction?"

"Kassab. He visited the site every month until the job was done."

"How much money was involved in the purchase, the permit, and construction?"

"About 150 million pesos."

"Three million U.S. dollars. I thought it might be more."

"This is the Philippines. And besides, the college wasn't built to be a hotel."

"Mr. Jaafar, did you run any checks on Kassab or the Zakat Foundation?"

"No. As I said, he was sincere, and the Foundation's objective seemed laudable."

"Did he give you an advance on your fee at that first meeting?" Ava said, resisting the urge to jab him again about the value he put on Kassab's sincerity.

"What does that have to do with anything?" Jaafar asked, looking at Wahab.

"Well, if he did, how was it done? Did he give you cash? Arrange a bank wire?" Ava said.

"Once I agreed to take them on as a client, money was wired to my account."

"Which bank?"

"The Planters Co-operative Bank, here in Bongao."

"Do you know where the money originated?"

"A bank in Saudi Arabia."

"Name?"

"SAABD."

"Did the same bank send you the money for the land purchase?"

"Yes, and they also paid the construction company through my account."

"Are you paying the expenses of running the college?"

"No, and I don't know who is. They asked me for a contact name at the Planters Bank. I gave it to them and that's the last time I was in touch with them. I believe they opened their own account there."

"So you don't currently have contact with Kassab or the Foundation?"

"They still pay me a monthly fee for maintaining ownership of the land in my name. It goes into my company account."

"Through this SAABD bank?"

"No, that money comes through a different bank, in Jordan — the Amman Credit Corporation."

"Why did the bank change?"

"I don't know and I didn't ask."

"What name is attached to the Jordanian bank account?"

"The Zakat Foundation, just like the Saudi one."

"Do you have an address for the Amman Credit Corporation or the bank in Saudi Arabia?"

"No, but the bank here should have them."

"Ava, the manager of the Planters Bank is another Brotherhood friend," Wahab said. "We'll call him when we leave here."

"Great," she said. She leaned forward towards Jaafar. "What contact information do you have for Kassab? Phone number, address, email, anything?"

"I had an email address, but after the college opened it was discontinued."

"So what do you do if you have a problem with your fee?"

"I haven't had one."

"But if you did?"

"I'd probably go to the school and talk to the person in charge."

"Do you know who that is?"

"No."

"His name is Tariq al-Bashir."

"I told you, I don't know him."

Ava sat back and looked down at the cup of coffee, which she hadn't touched. "I think we're done here," she said to Wahab. "Let's go and call that bank manager."

"I would appreciate it if you didn't tell him that I told you what I did," Jaafar said.

"And we don't want you to say a word to anyone about this conversation," Wahab said. "It never happened."

"You can count on me."

"It would be better for you to remember that Juhar is counting on you."

## 14

**WAHAB PULLED HIS PHONE FROM HIS POCKET AS THEY** walked into the office lobby. Ava thought he was calling for the car, but instead he said, "I have to speak to Mr. Mutilan. Tell him that Mr. Wahab is calling."

They left the building and stood outside in the shade. A moment later he said, "Mutilan, this is Wahab. Juhar has me working on a project and we might need some help from the bank. I'm a block away. Can I come over?" A few seconds later he said, "Thanks," and then turned to Ava. "Let's go. He'll see us now."

"I'm impressed with your ability to open doors," she said.

"It isn't unlimited. This is Bongao, not General Santos City or Manila."

"Well then, let's maximize your influence here."

The bank was larger than Ava had anticipated. It dominated the middle of a city block and was the only brick building she had seen in Bongao. They walked through revolving glass doors into an airy marble-floored foyer that reminded her of old-style Canadian banks. There were ten counters, all of them staffed, and a long line of customers. At the rear of the bank was a row of offices, the occupants hidden by frosted glass windows and frosted glass doors with names painted on them. Mr. Mutilan had the middle office and what looked like a personal secretary sitting at a desk in front of it. She smiled at Wahab, stood and walked to the glass door, knocked, and opened it. As Ava followed Wahab through the wooden gate that separated the general banking floor from the offices, a small, neat-looking middle-aged man appeared in the office doorway.

"Wahab, good to see you," he said, walking towards them.

"And you, my old friend," Wahab said.

Mutilan looked at Ava. "And this beautiful young woman is with you?" he said.

"Her name is Ava Lee. She's assisting the Brotherhood with the project I mentioned."

"A pleasure," he said to her.

Mutilan couldn't have been taller than five feet five inches. He wore a white silk shirt, a tightly knotted blue Hermès tie, and black leather wingtip shoes. His slicked-back hair curled halfway down his neck.

"Shall we go inside?" Wahab said.

"By all means," Mutilan said. "Before we do, would you like my assistant to get you something to drink?" Both Wahab and Ava shook their heads.

The office was large enough for a massive wooden desk, a couple of credenzas, and an oval conference table in the corner. Mutilan led them to the table.

"This is going to be a confidential discussion," Wahab said as he took a seat.

"I expected as much."

"And I'm going to let Ava ask the questions."

Mutilan looked surprised. He turned his attention to her and his manner suddenly became businesslike. "Ask away."

"Everything we want to know is related to the Zakat College of Tawi-Tawi."

"Ah, the mysterious college."

"Why do you say that?"

"I don't have any other customers I've never met putting millions of pesos through their account."

"We just left Mr. Jaafar. I promised him we wouldn't bring his name into this conversation, but I don't see how we can keep it out. I'm sure you can keep a confidence," she said pointedly.

"Of course. What did Jaafar say that he doesn't want repeated?"

"He told us the money to buy the land and build the college went through his account."

"That's true."

"But now he believes that the college or some other organization attached to it has opened its own account here at the bank, and he says that he has nothing to do with it."

"That's true."

"In whose name is the new bank account?"

"The Zakat College of Tawi-Tawi."

"What individual names are attached to it?" Ava asked.

"The money comes through the Amman Credit Corporation in Amman, Jordan, from an account held by the Zakat Foundation. The signing authority is a Fileeb al-Touma and the instructions we receive are in his name. I've never met or spoken to him. He communicates with us by email, and only when changes are to be made to the payroll."

"I'm surprised you can remember all that."

"I take pride in being thorough and on top of things. This arrangement is out of the ordinary for us, and I've kept myself briefed."

"So you find it strange?"

"A bit odd, perhaps, but we're not lending them money and we don't think they're laundering money. So, as long as the bank isn't at risk and nothing illegal is apparent, they can conduct their business any way they want."

"What is the account used for?"

"Payroll and expenses."

"How many people on the payroll?"

"I'd have to check, but I think it's somewhere around thirty."

"Do you know them all?"

"Not personally, but I do know they all seem to be local, because we make direct deposits for them."

"So no foreign employees?"

"Not that I know of," he said. "But we're only paying the kitchen, security, and maintenance staff. I don't know about anyone else who's working there."

"We were told that some of the security people aren't local," Ava said.

"That may be the case, but if they aren't, I don't think we're paying them. As I said, I can connect every name on that list to a local source."

Ava paused and then said, "Jaafar claimed he is also being paid through this bank in Jordan."

"He receives a monthly payment from the Foundation, but nothing even close to what he was getting when he was buying the land and paying construction companies."

"And the money for the land and construction came from Saudi Arabia, not Jordan?"

"Correct."

"But all the payments originated with this Zakat Foundation?"

"Yes."

"So they have bank accounts in Jordan and Saudia Arabia."

"That seems to be the case."

"Can I have the bank addresses and other contact information?"

"I'll get them before you leave."

"How much money goes through the Zakat account on a monthly basis?"

"A million pesos, give or take, and I know that Jaafar is getting about two hundred thousand."

"Have you ever seen the name Tariq al-Bashir on any payroll?"

"I'd have to check, but I can't remember it offhand."

"Could I get a copy of the payroll?" Ava said.

He glanced at Wahab, who gave him a slight nod. "Sure," Mutilan said.

"Now, you said that the money was being used for payroll. Is that all?"

"No, we also make the necessary disbursements for taxes and various supplies like food."

"How about for travel?"

"What do you mean?"

"I'm told that after students finish their courses at the college, they are sent to the U.S. and other countries to complete their training. That's an expensive undertaking. When you factor in the money they'd need to get visas, it would have to cost at least a thousand U.S. dollars for each of about 150 students," Ava said, stressing the last number.

"We've never paid out money to any travel company, airline, or visa consultant that I'm aware of."

"Could you double-check?"

"Sure."

"Can we wait here while you get that and the other information I requested?" Ava said.

"Of course you can," he said. "It won't take long to pull together."

As soon as he left the office, Ava reached for her phone and found Miguel Ramirez's number. His phone rang three times and went to voicemail. "Senator, this is Ava Lee," she said. "I need to talk to you. I'm in Bongao with Wahab. I'll be here overnight but I expect I'll be flying back to Manila tomorrow. In the meantime, there's something I need you to do, so please call me."

Wahab looked at his watch. "What else do you want to do in Bongao?"

"Unless there's something startling in the information I get from the bank, I think I'm just about finished."

"How long will it take you to figure that out?"

"If Mutilan goes over it with me, maybe ten or fifteen minutes."

"If that's the case and we hurry, we might be able to catch the late afternoon flight out of here today."

"My bag is at the inn."

"We can pick it up on the way. We only need to get to the airport five minutes before departure."

"Can I get a flight tonight from Zamboanga to Manila?"

"Yes."

"Then let's do it."

Wahab nodded. Then he went silent and looked thoughtful.

"Is everything okay?" she asked.

"I was just wondering why you want to talk to the senator."

"Does it matter?"

"Juhar will want to know."

"I don't like having to provide explanations for everything I do."

"That doesn't mean that I don't have to."

Ava looked away from him towards the door. *He has been incredibly co-operative and effective*, she thought. "You mentioned that the senator had a staffer check to see if there was any record of Tariq al-Bashir arriving in the Philippines. I want him to do the same for Ishak Kassab and Fileeb al-Touma, and also to see if there are any details on their departure from the islands."

"What details?"

"When you land in the Philippines, you have to fill out an arrival card. It contains not only your name and passport number but also your home address and your destination in the Philippines. When you leave, you fill out a departure card that contains the same information, plus your departing flight number and foreign destination."

"I've never left the Philippines," he said.

Ava glanced at him, not certain whether he was being serious. His face was impassive. "Now you know what to expect when you do," she said.

Wahab grunted, sat back in his chair, and closed his eyes as if he was contemplating that possibility. Ava kept her eyes locked on the door.

Mutilan appeared ten minutes later with two files in his hand. Fifteen minutes after that, Wahab and Ava left the bank. Mutilan had confirmed everything he'd told her about the payroll and other expenses, and now she had the addresses of the banks in Riyadh and Amman. Her only problem was that she didn't know what she could do with that information.

## 15

**THEY MADE THE FLIGHT TO ZAMBOANGA WITH FIFTEEN**
minutes to spare. This time Wahab sat next to her, but
their conversation was sporadic and strained. Ava didn't
know what was going through his head and didn't want to
ask. For her part, things were muddled. She knew it would
take time to filter and process everything she'd been told.
Normally she was more certain about what path her enquiries should take, but this was so different in size, reach,
complexity, and possible consequences that she was struggling to figure out where to start. One thing she did feel
certain about was that there was virtually no chance of
containing knowledge of the information they'd gathered
within the current handful of people. She hadn't wanted
to say that to Wahab when he asked her why she wanted
to talk to Senator Ramirez.

She had two hours in Zamboanga between flights. Wahab
offered to stay with her, but she was anxious to get to work
and declined politely. She turned on her phone while they
walked into the terminal. Ramirez hadn't returned her call.
She found herself getting annoyed.

"You'll stay in touch with me?" Wahab said before he left the airport. "We should think of ourselves as partners in this."

"I'll let you know if I need any more assistance or if I find something I think will have an impact on the Brotherhood," she said. He hesitated, and she knew he wanted more assurance. "I promise," she said. He nodded, then reluctantly turned away and left.

Ava found a coffee shop where she could occupy a table for four. She took out her notebook and the files that Mutilan had given her and began recording the data. She had hardly started when a waitress arrived. Ava was about to order a cup of coffee when she realized she hadn't eaten all day.

"What's your specialty?" she asked.

"Fried chicken."

Ava smiled — chicken was the unofficial national food of the Philippines. She ordered some and a coffee.

Then she returned to her notebook. Once she had finished writing down what was actually known, she looked at the questions she'd jotted earlier in the day and crossed some of them off. Most of them, though, remained untouched. Of those, the ones that taunted her most were who was Tariq al-Bashir and, if he wasn't from the Philippines, how and when did he arrive in the country? Then she began to add questions and, as she did, she saw the challenges mount. None was more daunting than trying to figure out how to get information from the banks in Saudi Arabia and Jordan.

The waitress came to the table with the coffee and food. The fried chicken dinner consisted of two golden brown legs and a side of mashed potatoes. Ava closed the notebook and files, put them to one side, and dug in. The chicken was lightly breaded and fresh and moist. She started to eat the first leg with a knife and fork, then picked it up with her fingers like every other customer. She was halfway through the second piece when her phone rang. She thought about ignoring the call until she saw Ramirez's number.

"Ava Lee."

"This is Miguel Ramirez. I apologize for not getting back to you sooner, but I was in a committee meeting when you called, and then Juhar phoned."

"He briefed you on our meeting this morning with the young men in Bongao?"

"He did. He's alarmed, and so am I."

*So much for Juhar not sharing the information*, she thought. Then she realized that he wouldn't have thought her request would extend to the senator. "That's a natural reaction if everything we've been told is true."

"You doubt that it is? Juhar indicated that both you and Wahab found the young men to be believable."

"We still need to verify their story."

"I'm encouraged that you think it might not be true."

"I didn't say that," Ava said quickly.

"Then what are you saying?"

"Actually, I'm trying to say as little as possible," she said. "I don't want to give you or Chang Wang information on a piecemeal basis. I want to chase this thing as fast and as far as I can go. When I'm done, I'll give you as complete a package as I can put together. I only hope it's enough."

"Then why did you call me? I assumed it was to brief me."

"No. I need your help."

"Where are you?"

"In Zamboanga, on the way back to Manila."

"You finished in Bongao so quickly?"

"I got everything I needed there. If I have to go back, I will. If I need more help from the Brotherhood, I'll ask. But it seems to me I'm already past the point where the Brotherhood will be that helpful."

"But you think I can be?"

"Is that reluctance or doubt that I hear in your voice?" she said.

"A bit of both."

"What I want isn't that complicated," she said. "I was told that you had a staff member check with the immigration bureau on the comings and goings of Tariq al-Bashir."

"That's true. And they found nothing in the records."

"Did you explain to the staffer why you made the request?"

"No. She isn't aware of what's going on in Bongao."

"How strong are her contacts in the department?"

"Very."

"No worries about awkward questions or gossip, or worse?"

"None whatsoever. Elisha has worked for me for five years and is entirely loyal and trustworthy. Her contact is a first cousin on her mother's side. The family is tightly knit."

"In that case, I'd like you to ask her to run similar checks on two other people for me."

"I don't think I want to do that," Ramirez said.

"Why not?"

"I think that my playing go-between — the middle man — would be inefficient," he said quickly. "I would much prefer if you spoke to her directly."

"Will you instruct her to co-operate with me?"

"Of course, and I'll make it clear that I expect her to do absolutely everything you ask… within reason, of course."

"I guess that would work."

"Then I'll call her as soon as we hang up and pass along your phone number. Knowing Elisha, she'll be prompt about reaching out to you."

"What's her family name?"

"Gill," Ramirez said. "Her grandfather was an American who married a Filipina. Her cousin has the same mixed heritage."

Ava looked at the time. "I'll be boarding in about an hour."

"I'm sure you'll hear from her by then."

"Senator, there is one other thing," Ava said slowly. "We discovered that the money that built the school originated in Saudi Arabia, and that the money supporting the running of the school comes from a bank in Jordan. I'm not the least bit sure that I'll be able to find out anything else about those bank accounts and who operates them, without outside assistance."

"Saudi Arabia and Jordan?"

"Yes."

"That's disconcerting," he said carefully.

"What is? The money sources or the fact that I may need outside help."

"Both, but obviously for different reasons."

"We can't change the fact of where the money originated. If I talk to someone outside, you can be assured that it will be done with maximum caution," she said. "Besides, I'm not telling you that I'm going to do that right now, but given the complexity of what we may be looking at, I have to believe it's a question of when and not if."

"And when you say 'outside,' what do you mean?"

"I don't know yet."

"After everything you've learned today, I'm sure you understand the sensitivities involved," he said. "And Ms. Lee, regardless of who you speak to, you have to keep my name and the Muslim Brotherhood out of the discussion."

"Senator, it would never have occurred to me to use your name, or the Brotherhood's. But I have to say you seem anxious to keep those sensitivities, as you call them, at arm's length. Is that why you want me to deal directly with Elisha Gill?"

Ramirez became quiet, and Ava wondered if she'd insulted him. She didn't care if she had. She was starting to feel that this was a man who liked pulling strings, and her strings weren't for pulling.

"In my profession," he finally said, "there is a necessity for what I call 'deniability.' It wouldn't be prudent, for example, for me to be officially linked with the Muslim Brotherhood. And my colleagues on the Senate oversight committee — not to mention the security people we oversee — would be more than unhappy if they knew I had information about the goings-on at the college and had withheld it from them."

"So what am I, your Chinese wall?"

"Are you being sarcastic or do you mean the traditional definition?"

"Traditionally, but only in the most cynical definition. You want a wall but you wouldn't object if notes were slid over or under it."

"I have been candid with you," he said. "Ms. Lee, I am a politician. Sometimes I forget that, but not for very long. It is the nature of the beast. I am being as honest as I can; when I tell you I need deniability to provide at least a semblance of cover if this thing explodes, that is the political truth. And

I have to add that Chang Wang and Tommy Ordonez would both completely support my position, since we are bound together in myriad ways."

"I understand the point you're making, but it doesn't mean I'm comfortable with it."

"Who is comfortable with any part of this situation? What we thought might be a problem is now more of a certainty, and its magnitude is frightening. We all have to do the best we can over the short term. I assure you that I will step up to the plate when the time is right. For now, please keep gathering information."

"That's my intent, but I have to repeat that I want to do it in my own way and report when I see fit."

"I have no issue with your approach," he said. "And look, when I speak to Elisha, I will be very specific that what transpires between the two of you is not my business, until you decide it is. Will that give you some level of assurance that I won't be interfering?"

Ava sighed. "Have her call me."

"Leave your phone on," Ramirez said.

Ava pushed her chicken dinner to one side and put the notebook in front of her with the phone next to it. The conversation with Ramirez had ruined her appetite. She'd now spoken to him twice, and both times she'd felt he was trying to manipulate her. *Screw him*, she thought as she checked the time. It was still very early in the morning in Toronto, a bit too soon to call her friend Johnny Yan at the Toronto Commonwealth Bank.

Yan and Ava had been at York University together and were part of a group of about twenty Chinese-Canadian accounting students who had become friends. In typical

Chinese fashion, they'd also agreed to help each other progress in their careers. Countless favours had been exchanged among them, and Ava and Yan's relationship had been especially mutually beneficial. His position at the bank allowed him to make enquiries and gather information from other banks and businesses that outsiders would have found difficult, if not impossible, to acquire. Ava had used his ability to get access to help her on several jobs. In return she had directed several large chunks of business to the bank, letting it be known that Johnny was the reason the bank was getting it. If anyone could find out about the bank accounts in Jordan and Saudi Arabia, she was betting it would be Johnny. As she was contemplating the best time to contact him, her phone rang.

"This is Elisha Gill. I'm trying to reach Ava Lee."

"This is Ava."

"Senator Ramirez asked me to call and stressed that there is some urgency to the matter." Ava noticed she had traces of an American accent.

"What else did he stress?"

"He said that I'm to give you all the help I can, and that whatever you and I discuss is between the two of us and he doesn't want me reporting back to him."

"Are you okay with that?"

"I find it a bit strange," Elisha said slowly, "but I agreed to it."

"You aren't going to be asked to do anything illegal, or at least nothing that you haven't done already."

"And what is it that I've done?"

"The senator told me you have a cousin who works for the government."

"Yes, her name is Zoey Walsh. She's a departmental director at the Bureau of Immigration."

"The senator said you asked her to run a check on Imam Tariq al-Bashir's comings and goings from the Philippines."

"I did. She found nothing."

"How good is her access?"

"She has access to every record in the system. If al-Bashir had entered the Philippines under his own name, she would have found him. She looked at entries from every airport in the country and nearly every seaport."

"What if I want her to look for two other people?"

"I can't imagine that would be a problem."

"What if it were two hundred people?"

"Are you serious?" Elisha said.

"I'm just trying to understand the system's limitations."

"It has none that I'm aware of. It was updated a year ago and is as modern as any in Asia. If you arrived in or left the Philippines legally, all your data will be in it."

"And you said your cousin has complete access?"

"She does."

"Did she ask why you wanted the data on al-Bashir?"

"No, and if she had, I wouldn't have been able to tell her, because I didn't know."

"The senator didn't give you any idea?" Ava asked.

"None whatsoever."

"Do you expect me to?"

"Only if you think it's necessary."

Ava looked down at her notepad. "Do you have a pen handy?"

"I have pen and paper."

"I need you to ask your cousin to check on the arrivals and departures of these two people: Ishak Kassab and

Fileeb al-Touma," Ava said, and then spelled each name. "I believe Kassab is from Saudi Arabia, and al-Touma could be Jordanian."

"How soon do you want the information?"

"Can you get it tonight?"

"I don't think that's likely. Zoey's probably left the office by now."

"Then first thing tomorrow morning."

"I'll do the best I can."

"Thanks, Elisha. Call me at this number when you have the information."

Ava ended the call, made a note of Zoey Walsh's name, and picked up the phone again. Wahab answered on the first ring.

"So soon?" he said.

"Sorry. I was thinking about the meeting with the boys this morning, and something occurred to me. I need you to talk to them right away," Ava said.

"What do you want from them?"

"I need dates. For example, when did the last batch of students leave the college and when did the new group arrive? And then ask them to go back as far as they can remember to come up with dates for the other groups that have arrived and left since they've been working at the college. I don't expect them to be precise — even a rough estimate could be helpful. They can use their days off as a guide."

"When do you want this information?"

"By tomorrow morning at the latest."

"I'll do what I can."

*That isn't good enough*, Ava almost said, and then swallowed the words. "Thanks. I'll be waiting."

## 16

**THE FLIGHT TO MANILA DEPARTED TEN MINUTES LATE;** after an hour and forty minutes it landed at just past ten o'clock. With only a carry-on bag and no Customs and Immigration to deal with, Ava quickly exited Aquino Airport, got into a taxi, and then sat in traffic for close to an hour. But the time on the plane and in the cab wasn't wasted. Although it was a domestic flight, the plane from Zamboanga had arrival and departure cards on board, and Ava was able to confirm what she thought she remembered about the information that had to be entered.

The landing card was one of the most detailed she'd ever seen. It requested basic data such as name, birthdate, country of birth, citizenship, passport number and date and place of issue, airport of origin, and flight number. It also asked for the home address of the traveller and a destination address in the Philippines, including street, town, and province. The departure card wasn't quite as detailed, but it required the same basic personal data plus a flight number and a destination. If Elisha Gill was correct about the efficiency of the Bureau of Immigration, and if Kassab and al-Touma were in the system, Ava would soon know a lot more about them and their whereabouts.

She reached the Peninsula Hotel at a quarter after eleven — again too late for the restaurant. She checked in and got exactly the same room she'd barely used the night before. It occurred to her that everything else about her time in the Philippines had undergone a seismic change within the past twenty-four hours.

She showered, pulled on a clean T-shirt and underwear, and sat at the room desk. She turned on her computer and, while it booted, checked her phone. She'd missed one call from a Chinese number, and the caller had left a message.

"This is Fai. I just finished the second day of shooting, and it went well. I miss you and I love you."

Ava hit the Return Call button and seconds later was put through to voicemail. She swore and then said, "I love you too. I'll call in the morning."

She returned to the computer and opened her email. There were several messages from Amanda with updates about the meeting in Shanghai. She scanned them for any hint of a problem with the Italians' commitment, but it seemed that the PÖ team was getting a positive reception in the market. She replied to the last one. Glad things are going well. I'm caught up in a complicated situation that's going to be demanding of my time, so for now don't bother updating me unless there's an issue you want me to deal with. I'll be in touch as soon as I resolve matters here. Love, Ava.

She then glanced at her other email and, when she saw nothing of any importance, switched to a search engine. She entered "Ishak Kassab" and linked the name to "Zakat

Foundation" and "Zakat College." There were no hits. She did the same for "Fileeb al-Touma," with the same result. She then linked their names to the banks in Saudi Arabia and Jordan. The banks were well established and there was a lot of information about them, but there were no connections to the foundation or the college. She changed search engines and repeated the process. Again no hits. She stared at the screen in disbelief. These men had to exist somewhere. The Foundation had opened bank accounts in Jordan and Saudi Arabia and had been funnelling money to the Philippines for a year. How did they manage to remain so far below the radar? It was time to reach out to Johnny Yan.

He answered his office phone on the second ring, with a brisk "Yan."

"It's Ava. Are you free to talk?"

He paused. "Wait five minutes and then call my cell."

*That was strange*, she thought. She wasn't surprised that he wanted her to call his cell, but his manner had been uncharacteristically brusque. She waited for ten minutes before doing as he'd asked. When he answered, she could hear traffic in the background.

"Are you outside the building?"

"I'm taking a smoke break," he said. "Where are you this time?"

"Manila."

"You're always somewhere other than Toronto when you call me."

"That was the nature of my old business."

"And now?"

"I guess it's the nature of my life." She laughed.

"Are you phoning me for some help?"

"I am. There's a bank in Saudi Arabia and another in Jordan —"

"Ava, I can't do it."

"What?"

"That last project — the one involving the holdings of that family in China — caused a lot of problems," he said.

"It was the Tsai family of Nanjing, and the information you provided helped put an end to their massive corruption."

"Even if that's true, the blowback here was so strong that even people two and three levels up were ducking for cover."

"Were you affected directly in any way?"

"No, I'm still in the same job, but I have a feeling I'm being watched. And I think my chances for promotion have stalled," he said. "Felix Lau wasn't so lucky."

Felix was Johnny's friend and his main contact in the international branch of the bank. All the enquiries made of international banks for Ava's benefit had been initiated by Felix. "Oh no, what happened to him?"

"He was taken off the international desk and moved to domestic consumer banking. It's the same pay grade but it's boring as hell, and there's not much of a future in it."

"And you're sure they moved him because of the Tsai enquiries?"

"Ava, he was grilled a couple of times about them. For a while he thought he was going to lose his job. I have to say he's got balls. He kept both our names out of it, although mine did pop up somewhere in the electronic trail."

"Were you questioned?"

"Briefly, but like I said, I think I'm still being watched."

"I'm so sorry. I had no idea."

"It isn't your fault, and when all is said and done, we were on the side of the good guys."

"Is there anything I can do for you or for Felix?"

"I think it's best if we just leave things as they are for now."

"Johnny, please know that you can call me anytime you need help. And please pass along that same message to Felix."

"I'll let him know," he said. "Now I should get going."

When the line went dead, Ava put down the phone with a sinking feeling. She hated being the cause of her friends' difficulties. She wished she could have said more to Johnny and could do more for him and Felix. Then, she thought, a bit selfishly, there was the problem of losing the access they provided to foreign banks. What the hell would she do now?

In the past she'd contacted banks directly, either by phone or electronically, and tried to bluff her way into getting the information she wanted. But her successes were hit-and-miss, and the downside of missing was that the banks would often alert the party she was interested in. Alerting the college or whoever was financing it wasn't a risk she wanted to take. That left using a third party as her best option. But whom could she trust — and who trusted her enough — to do it?

The first name that came to mind was May Ling, but when Ava thought about asking her to help, the associated complications began to accumulate. She couldn't expect May to use one of her companies to make an approach without clearing it with her husband and partner, Changxing. The same complications would probably arise if she asked May to go through one of her banks. Besides, how would banks in the Middle East react to a request from a Chinese bank in Wuhan?

Then she thought of Burgess and Bowlby, the Hong Kong law firm that represented Three Sisters' interests in Asia. She had involved them when she went after the Tsai family, and they'd been terrific, but everything they did had drawn on their wealth of experience and contacts in China. Ava wasn't sure they would have any expertise or contacts in the Middle East. She also didn't feel like answering the multitude of questions that any approach to Brenda Burgess would unleash.

"Shit," Ava said, and reached for the phone to call Shanghai.

"Hi, Ava. Where are you? Still in the Philippines?" Xu said.

"I'm in my room at the Peninsula Hotel in Manila."

"And how's it going with Chang and his mysterious problem?"

"It isn't mysterious anymore, and that's not a good thing," she said. "Do you have time to listen?"

"How much time are you talking about?"

"It could take a while."

"I'm supposed to meet friends for a late drink. Give me a moment while I reschedule it."

"You don't have to do that."

"From the tone of your voice, it sounds like you're into some heavy stuff."

"That's actually true."

"So give me a minute."

He was gone for several minutes, but that gave Ava time to start organizing her thoughts. Her decision to call Xu had been spontaneous, and now that she had, telling him what she'd stumbled into seemed completely natural.

"Okay, I'm back," he said. "You have all the time you need."

She drew a deep breath and began to speak calmly and concisely. She had no idea how long it took to describe and explain the details of her conversation with Chang Wang, her meeting with Ramirez, the trip to Tawi-Tawi, and her encounters with Wahab, Imam Sharif, Ben, Alcem, the lawyer Jaafar, and the banker Mutilan, but it was long enough that twice she had to drink water to relieve her dry mouth and throat.

Xu listened silently until she began to talk about her problem with accessing the banks in Saudi Arabia and Jordan. "Ava, are you asking me if I can help get information from them?" he interrupted.

"I guess I am."

"Even if I could, I don't know if I would," he said. "Do you know how crazy everything you've told me sounds?"

"That's the world we live in now."

"It isn't my world, and it shouldn't be yours."

"You're lucky to live in Shanghai."

"Which is where you should have come instead of going to the Philippines."

"It's a bit late for that now," Ava said, surprised but not displeased by his protective attitude.

"What does Chang have to say about what you've found out? I find it hard to understand how he can expect you to manage this for him."

"I haven't told him anything about today, although I expect Senator Ramirez has," she said. "In any event, all I'm doing is gathering information."

"The problem is that you're gathering information about people who'd rather stay in the dark. If they find out you're prying into their affairs, you can't expect them to react passively."

"Xu, you know how careful I am. I'm not about to run off half-cocked."

"But you're not doing this alone. There are other people involved."

"Yes, and it's in their self-interest to be as close-mouthed as possible."

"I can understand why the Brotherhood would want to keep things quiet, but do you trust the politician?"

"He's a business partner of Chang and Ordonez in the pineapple plantations. I figure they must have a couple of hundred million U.S. dollars at risk. They'll want to protect that at all costs, and to do that they have to keep the region stable and protect the Brotherhood. So yes, I trust him."

"Even though you do, and even if the Brotherhood is as discreet as you say, where does that leave you?"

"I don't know. The immediate challenge I have is those damn banks in Jordan and Saudi Arabia. I need someone who can help me get the information I want from them."

"I can't help you there, and I don't know anyone who can," he said. "But it seems to me that if the senator is correct about the unreliability of Philippine security services, you should consider getting in touch with the people who could be most directly affected by the situation in Tawi-Tawi."

"The Americans?"

"Precisely."

"I don't know anyone I could contact. Do you?"

"Ava, in my business I try to avoid those kinds of people, not get to know them," Xu said. "I can't even think of an intermediary I'd feel comfortable using."

"Actually, now that you mention an intermediary...I might have one," she said.

"Someone you can really trust?"

"I won't have a sense of that until I talk to him — assuming that I can," Ava said. "He might not be in the same job, and even if he is, he knows me by another name. And he might not remember me that fondly."

"That doesn't sound like a recipe for trust."

"Maybe not, but he's the only person I can come up with right now. Don't worry, I'll mull it over before I do anything."

"I'm still worried," Xu said. "I'd feel better if I knew you had some protection. Do you want me to send Suen or some of my other men to the Philippines?"

"No, that's not necessary."

"Have you thought of bringing over Sonny?"

"Sonny doesn't function very well outside of Hong Kong and some parts of China," Ava said. Sonny Kwok had been Uncle's long-time bodyguard and chauffeur, and she had inherited him when Uncle died. Technically he was her employee, and he devoted all his time to her whenever she was in Hong Kong. When she wasn't there, he drove for Amanda and Ava's father, Marcus, and her half-brother Michael.

"Well, if you're going to insist on doing this alone, be careful. And if you need anything, call me."

"I will, I promise," she said.

Xu had probably been correct when he said the best route to the information she wanted was through the Americans. But could she go to them without violating the trust that the Brotherhood and Chang had placed in her? It might work, she thought, if she properly structured an arrangement with them. Besides, even Ramirez had intimated that sooner or later the Americans might be their fallback, and this wasn't a time to be tentative. In her mind it wasn't a question of whether she should be trying to get American assistance; it was a matter of whether Ryan Poirier would agree to act as the conduit.

The last time she had met Poirier, he was running Canadian Security Intelligence Service operations in Jakarta. At least she assumed he was running them, because he certainly acted that way. Through a complicated chain of events, she had found herself forced to work with him at the conclusion of a massive theft investigation that she and Uncle had pursued from Toronto to Vietnam and finally to Surabaya in Indonesia. With Poirier's hands-on assistance, which included the bloody involvement of an elite Indonesian army unit whose help he'd enlisted, Ava had managed to recover thirty million dollars for their clients. Poirier and the Indonesians got the credit for busting an international money-laundering scheme operated by the 'Ndrangheta — a brutal Italian mob — and also managed to pocket close to forty million dollars for their governments to split.

Poirier's attitude towards Ava before and during the Surabaya raid had been suspicious. Several times he had made it clear that he didn't trust her, and even when events transpired exactly as she had predicted, his attitude didn't change. Her last memory was of him abruptly closing a car door before driving away without so much as a thank-you or a goodbye.

If she'd told Xu that story, she knew he would not have taken seriously the idea of her using Poirier as the intermediary. But to her mind, the opposite was true. She had gone to Poirier with a story about the 'Ndrangheta that was almost preposterous. Moreover, she had made contact with him through a tenuous connection in Ottawa, who in turn had been introduced to her through a Mountie in Guyana who'd met her only twice, and both times briefly. Yet he had heard her out, asked a number of hard but fair questions, and then fully committed to the project and delivered everything he said he would.

Admittedly she had been a bit nervous after his less than polite departure at the Surabaya airport, because he and the Indonesians had all the money. All she had was his promise that he would wire thirty million to Uncle's bank in Kowloon. It would have been easy for him not to send anything and then make up some story about illicit funds. She would have no recourse if they sent nothing, and she was sure Poirier understood that. But the money was sent in full and on time, and with that act he earned her respect and trust. However, the question wasn't how she felt about him; it was how he felt about her.

One of her biggest problems was that he didn't know her as Ava Lee. She had used the name Jennie Kwong and had backed up the deceit with a Hong Kong passport. How would he react when she told him the truth? *I won't know unless I tell him*, she thought.

She tried to remember where she had stored his contact information and began searching through her phone and emails. After ten minutes she gave up, frustrated, and went to the website of the Canadian embassy in Jakarta. She entered Ryan Poirier's name. To her surprise, a photo appeared on her screen, and there was Poirier's lean face, long chin, and red hair. He was officially an assistant commercial officer and evidently still stationed in Indonesia.

## 17

**SHE HAD NO IDEA WHAT TIME SHE FELL ASLEEP. IT WAS** well after midnight when she gave up searching for Kassab and al-Touma, and she was exhausted when she finally went to bed. But her mind kept turning, and not even doing bak mei exercises in her head could shut it down. Finally, in the middle of an imagined conversation with Ryan Poirier, trying to explain why the woman he knew as Jennie Kwong was really Ava Lee, she nodded off.

She woke to the sound of her phone. She grabbed it from the bedside table and glanced at the incoming number. "Wahab," she said, answering as she pulled herself erect.

"Is it too early to call?" he said.

"No," Ava said.

"I talked to Alcem last night, and he and Ben phoned me a few minutes ago with that information you wanted."

"Let me get a pen," Ava said, swinging her legs over the side of the bed. She walked to the desk, sat down, and opened her notebook. "Go ahead."

"Okay, the boys had two days off on February second and third. A group of students was there when they left and gone when they returned. They said the new class arrived on their first day back, so that would be February fourth."

"Excellent."

"Now, working back from those dates, they don't have specific records of their days off, but they insist that the college operates on a tight three-month schedule. So if you go back three months from February fourth, we should have the approximate date for when the previous class arrived. And so on and so on."

"It sounds kind of harmless when you say it like that."

"Pardon?"

"Sorry, I was just thinking aloud — 'and so on' sounds so harmless."

"I meant it to," Wahab said. "When Juhar and I talk about this problem, we both — subconsciously, I guess — use the most neutral, passive words. It makes it easier to stay calm."

"I understand," Ava said.

"Ava," Wahab said carefully, "speaking of Juhar, he is wondering why you want to know those dates."

"We need to locate as many of the students who have left the college as we can. Knowing when they arrived might help us identify them, and once we identify them, we might be able to find out when and how they left and where they went."

"How are you going to do that?" he asked, his voice rising.

"I'm not putting out a public appeal or going to the armed forces intelligence service," she said. "I have some sources I hope to use that come recommended by Senator Ramirez."

"Oh."

"Now look, I have to go. I'll be in touch when things become clearer," she said, and then hung up before he had a chance to ask more questions that she didn't want to answer.

She had written the February dates in her notebook. Now she worked back three months to November, and then back again and again. It wasn't precise but it provided a starting point, which was more than she'd had before.

She rose from the desk and went to the bathroom to get water for the in-room coffee machine. As the coffee began to brew, her phone sounded and she saw Elisha Gill's name on the screen.

"Good morning, Elisha," Ava said. "What do you have for me?"

"I have nothing."

"You haven't spoken to Zoey yet?"

"I talked to her last night and she ran the names through the system first thing this morning. She came up empty. I asked her to run them one more time. She did and got the same result."

"So absolutely nothing on Kassab or al-Touma? Was every legal point of arrival and departure part of the search?"

"They were."

"That's so odd."

"Is there anything else you'd like me to do?"

"Yes, but it's a big project that would involve Zoey even more," Ava said. "The senator emphasized that you and Zoey are close. Is that true?"

"We're cousins but we're as close as sisters. There isn't much we wouldn't do for each other."

"And she obviously shares your lack of curiosity."

"You're referring to the fact that neither of us seems to care why you want this information?"

"Yes."

"Senator Ramirez operates on an absolute need-to-know basis. Thus far he hasn't chosen to share what he's doing with you, and I have no problem with that. As for Zoey, so far she's extended me the same respect."

"What I want you to do might test your capacity for not asking questions."

"Why don't you tell me what you want, and I'll tell you if it does."

"Okay, for starters I want to know how many foreign visitors entered the Philippines between February first and February fourth of this year and named Tawi-Tawi Island, the city of Bongao, or a local college called Zakat as a final destination on their landing card."

Elisha paused and then said, "You're right. I'd like to have some idea of why you want that information, and I think Zoey will as well."

"It's related to a security matter that the senator is investigating. He's asked me to help on an unofficial basis."

"Is that true?"

"It is, but it's too soon to start sharing details. We're in information-gathering mode, and knowing who went to Tawi-Tawi will be an important start," Ava said. "Does that satisfy you? Will it satisfy her?"

"For now, I think so," Elisha said. "But tell me, do you want to know how many went in total or who they actually were?"

"I want to know who they were."

"That is a big project."

"That's only the start of it," Ava said. "Then I want Zoey to go back to November fourth and capture the same data for the two weeks on either side of that date. And I want her to go back to August fourth and do the same, and then do it one more time for May fourth."

"You could be talking about thousands of people."

"I doubt that," Ava said. "We're talking about visitors from overseas only, and I can't believe that Tawi-Tawi is a prime destination. Besides, I know that the only way to fly into Tawi-Tawi is through Bongao, and there are at best only a handful of flights a day and only one from a major airport — Zamboanga. I took that flight yesterday. There were about twenty people at most on the plane, and they all looked Filipino."

"Are there any other criteria you want her to apply?"

Ava hesitated. "The three keywords she should be entering are 'Tawi-Tawi,' 'Bongao,' and 'Zakat College.' Any one of those or any combination of them is what I'm looking for."

"This could take some time."

"We don't have that luxury. Please ask her to work as quickly as she can."

"I'll do my best," Elisha said. "How do you want the information transmitted to you when she gets it?"

"Is it possible to get printed copies of the landing cards?"

"I'll make the request. If she can do printed copies, how do you want me to get them to you?"

"I'm staying in Manila, at the Peninsula Hotel. We can meet here or somewhere close."

"The hotel is fine."

Ava ended the call, feeling confused. She had hoped for some sighting of Kassab or al-Touma. She made a note to ask Wahab about the frequency of sea travel between Bongao and the cities in Indonesia and Malaysian Borneo that faced it, only hours away, across the Sulu Sea. If someone wanted to enter or leave the Philippines as anonymously as possible, it seemed to her that going by sea afforded the best opportunity, from a country that was completely surrounded by water.

She checked the time. Jakarta was one hour behind Manila, and by her reckoning the Canadian embassy should be open for business. She phoned the general number, expecting an automated answer and voice prompts. Instead she got a real person. "I'd like to speak to Mr. Ryan Poirier," Ava said.

"I will need to confirm that he's in the office today," a woman said. "Who can I say is trying to reach him?"

"Jennie Kwong. Please remind him that we last met in Surabaya," Ava said.

"Just one moment, please."

The one moment turned into several. Ava was anticipating rejection when the woman came back on the line and said, "I'll put you through."

"This is a surprise," Poirier said.

"I wasn't sure that you'd remember me," Ava said.

"How the hell could I not?"

"It was a brief encounter."

"Perhaps more memorable because of the brevity," he said. "And now you're calling again, except this time you aren't going through our colleagues in Ottawa."

"What I'm calling about doesn't have any direct connection to or impact on Canada."

"Then why am I so fortunate to be the recipient of your attention?"

"It's quite complicated. But before I get into it, there's something I need to clarify," Ava said slowly. "My name is not actually Jennie Kwong. It's Ava Lee."

"I know," Poirier said.

"You do?"

"When we were in Surabaya, I thought your behaviour was a bit strange, so after our little adventure I tracked down the RCMP sergeant in Guyana you used to open doors for you in Ottawa."

"Marc Lafontaine?"

"Yes, and you'll be pleased to know he was reluctant to talk about you until I applied the right kind of pressure."

"Pressure?"

"The RCMP are very respectful of their chain of command, and I used it," Poirier said. "Interestingly, once Lafontaine started talking about you, I could hardly get him to stop. Evidently you cut quite a swath when you were in Guyana. Some local bad guy named Robbins still curses every time your name is mentioned."

"I was in the debt collection business. It took me to strange places and put me in contact with people who were...well, people who were different."

"Like in Surabaya."

"Exactly."

"You used the past tense about your job. Have you changed professions?"

"Yes. I've gone into the investment business with some partners. It's much tamer."

"Yet here you are, calling me about something you describe as being quite complicated."

"I didn't phone you about an investment," Ava said, suddenly not sure that she was doing the right thing.

"I didn't think you were, but I'm not good at guessing," Poirier said.

She drew a deep breath. "How good are your contacts in the Middle East?"

"Why?"

"I need to get information about some bank accounts in Saudi Arabia and Jordan."

"Why?"

"And I need to be put in touch with someone in the CIA who has some clout and who you trust to keep a confidence."

"Is that all?"

"Yes."

"You aren't asking too much, are you."

"I apologize if it sounds insane, but there are significant reasons for my requests."

"I'm waiting to hear what they are."

"It isn't anything I can discuss over the phone," Ava said. "It needs to be done in person. Can you come to me?"

"Where are you?"

"I'm in Manila."

"Why didn't you call our embassy there?"

"I don't know anyone here, and what I want to talk about doesn't lend itself to a cold call."

"But your presence in the Philippines is related to the problem you want to discuss?"

"Yes. But the ramifications could be on a much broader scale, especially in the United States."

"What ramifications?"

"I told you, I don't want to discuss it over the phone. I'm hopeful that since you know something of my background, you'll know that I'm not given to exaggerating or overreacting."

"What aren't you exaggerating?"

"Something that has the potential to make Surabaya look like a kindergarten playground."

Poirier paused and then said, "Ms. Lee, you do know that it's a four-hour flight from Jakarta to Manila?"

"Yes, and I wouldn't ask you to come here if I didn't think it was necessary and worth your time."

"What does my time matter if I can't help you?" he said. "What if I don't know anyone in the CIA who meets your criteria? What if I have no bank contacts in the Middle East?"

"Then you'll tell me that and you'll stay in Jakarta, and I'll move on to Plan B."

"Do you actually have a Plan B?"

"Not yet, but I've never failed to find one."

"I don't know why, but I have trouble disbelieving you," Poirier said. "You're a master of the art of persuasion."

"Only because the cause I'm representing is based on reality."

"Just give me a minute," Poirier said suddenly.

Ava immediately felt uneasy. She had no idea what kind of communications technology Poirier had at his disposal. Was it possible he was tracking her call, trying to pinpoint her location? The last thing she wanted was unwelcome visitors showing up at the Peninsula. The minute turned into two and three, and her unease grew.

She was contemplating hanging up when she heard a woman's voice in the background, and then Poirier came back on the line. "I've got a flight booked into Manila that will land at 5:45 tonight," he said. "Where do you want to meet?"

"I'm staying at the Peninsula Hotel."

"Under which name?"

"Ava Lee," she said, smiling.

"I'll come directly to the hotel."

"Does this mean you can help me with the banks?"

"Possibly."

"And you have an American you trust?"

"I have an American, and he's in Manila," Poirier said. "If I think your concerns have any validity, I'll bring the two of you together. Then you can make your own decision about whether he's trustworthy or not."

## 18

**AVA SAT QUIETLY AT THE DESK AND REPLAYED HER CON-**versation with Ryan Poirier. Her main concern was whether she'd overhyped the situation. She didn't like exaggeration, and as much as she was convinced that Alcem and Ben were telling the truth, she was also aware — and almost desperate to believe — that what they had heard and seen was a selective sample. It was possible that nothing as calamitous as they feared was going to happen. The problem was that she couldn't operate under that assumption; her experience was that if you expected the worst, you were seldom disappointed.

She looked at the time. The morning was drifting by and a day of waiting stretched out in front of her. She thought about going for a run and decided she couldn't handle the pollution or the pedestrian traffic. The hotel, though, had a fitness centre on the ground floor. She wasn't a fan of treadmills, but it was her only option if she wanted a workout. She called the concierge and was told there were ten treadmills available. *That will have to do*, she thought, and then noticed the number for the spa. Allocating time for a one-hour run and a half-hour cool-down, she booked a massage.

The fitness centre was almost deserted. That didn't surprise her. Generally Asians didn't share the Western mania for hard physical exercise. May Ling and Amanda, for example, never lifted anything heavier than a wineglass, and hurrying in high heels was the extent of their aerobic workouts. They couldn't understand Ava's need to run, even if she told them it was as much a way of cleansing her mind as her body.

She programmed the treadmill for a one-hour twelve-kilometre run that had several gradations. For the first five minutes she was conscious only of her body, but then gradually the physical effort became incidental and she found herself thinking about Ryan Poirier, Elisha Gill, and Miguel Ramirez. But when she was finished, things seemed just as confusing as when she'd started.

The spa was next to the fitness centre, and again Ava seemed to be one of only a few customers. After showering and slipping into a bathrobe, she sat in an upholstered chair, sipped jasmine tea, and contemplated her massage options. She chose an hour and fifteen minutes of *hilot*, which was described as a traditional Philippine massage involving heated banana leaves and a blend of virgin coconut and organic lemongrass oils. If nothing else, she thought, she'd smell good.

"I'll have a medium-strength massage," Ava said, when the thin, middle-aged masseuse asked for her preference. It started slowly, with hot banana leaves covering her body. Then the oils were worked into her skin and she was wrapped in new leaves. After fifteen minutes Ava was beginning to regret her choice, as it seemed to be more relaxation treatment than massage. Then the masseuse's fingers gripped her shoulder muscles and she yelped. For an hour the woman's steely fingers kneaded her body, every muscle and joint. Ava groaned several times; when she did, the woman backed off for a few seconds to let the pain subside and then attacked the muscles again.

The woman finished with a gentle rubdown and left Ava on the table for a few minutes. She flexed her muscles but could hardly feel them. Her body had the consistency of a marshmallow, albeit one that had an aroma of coconut and lemongrass. When the woman returned, she helped Ava down from the table and led her to the shower.

Ava left the spa wearing a clean T-shirt and her Adidas training pants. She hadn't brought her phone with her, so she thought about going back to the room to change her clothes, check her messages, and then have a late lunch. But as she walked past the Old Manila restaurant, she saw a sign that said it closed at two-thirty. She took an immediate right and went inside.

Despite its name, the restaurant was thoroughly modern. Ava felt slightly out of place sitting at a table with a white linen tablecloth and an elegant oak chair. The service was impeccable, and within ten minutes she was sipping a white French burgundy and dipping into a shrimp bisque. She briefly considered an Australian wagyu steak but was drawn irresistibly to the Irish prime rib-eye topped with seared foie gras. She knew the meal would cancel out any good she'd gotten from her workout, but it tasted so heavenly that she decided it was worth it.

She was the last diner to leave the restaurant. She realized that between the fitness centre, the spa, and Old Manila, she'd spent more than four hours away from her phone and computer, and for most of that time she hadn't thought about

Tawi-Tawi. She was still feeling rather mellow when she got back to her room. That changed the second she picked up her phone and saw a text message from Elisha Gill that had arrived only a few minutes before. Call me. I don't know what to do, it read.

"What's the problem?" Ava asked when Elisha answered her phone.

"I'm standing outside the immigration bureau with two shopping bags filled with copies of landing cards."

"How many cards?"

"Between two and three thousand."

"That was quick work," Ava said, surprised at the number.

"I told you it was an efficient system."

"Yes, you did," Ava said. "Now I guess we're going to be the inefficient part of this process."

"What do you mean?"

"Do you have any plans for this afternoon?"

"Not if there's something you want me to do. The senator made it clear that you're to have priority."

"Then bring the cards to my hotel. We have to go through them one by one."

"What are we looking for?"

"I'll tell you when you get here," Ava said, and gave her the room number.

She hadn't expected quite that many hits, but obviously the more there were, the greater the chance of identifying the people who'd made their way to Zakat College. Now she needed to get organized. There was a large, round table near the window with a vase of flowers on it. She removed the vase, turning the table into a clear workspace. Then she grabbed her notebook and started listing criteria in order to prioritize the search. She had barely finished when she heard a sharp knock at the door. When she opened it, she saw a sturdy young woman wearing black slacks and a blue blouse. She was dark-skinned, with deep brown eyes and short black hair.

Ava looked down at the shopping bags in her hands. "Elisha?"

"Yes."

"I didn't expect you so soon," Ava said.

"The bureau is only a ten-minute walk from here."

"Well, it's nice to meet you, and it was kind of you to come," Ava said. "Put the bags over there by the table." She stood to one side so Elisha could pass and then followed her to the table.

"How are the cards organized?" Ava asked.

"They're not. They've just been bundled into sets of two hundred and put into these envelopes," Elisha said, pulling one from a bag.

"Even so, I'm amazed that your cousin was able to do this without attracting any attention."

"All she did was input and correlate the dates and key-words you gave me and press Enter."

"Still…"

"As I told you, she's a senior director in the bureau, but she also has a lot of personal influence. Her father is one of the most prominent corporate lawyers in the city, and her mother, like mine, is a member of the Quirino family. Being part of a Spanish establishment family is a bit like being royalty. Not many people are likely to question her."

"Well, however she did it, I'm grateful," Ava said. "Now why don't you empty that first envelope and we can get started."

"What are we looking for?" Elisha asked as she slid the landing cards onto the table.

Ava hesitated. "There are some activities going on in Tawi-Tawi that we need to understand."

"Activities?"

"Training."

"At that Zakat College?"

"Yes."

"What type of training?" Elisha asked as she began stacking the cards. "If you don't want to tell me anything else, that's fine, but I'm sure you'll understand that I am curious. You should also know that I have top secret security clearance. All of the senator's staff are required to have it."

*What the hell*, Ava thought, tired of sliding around the issue. "We've been told that there might be terrorist training being conducted on Tawi-Tawi. If that's true, we need to identify the trainees."

"If it's true?"

"We don't know for certain."

Elisha nodded and then said calmly, "Given the names I was asked to look into, I thought it might be something like that. And I think Zoey may have reached that conclusion herself, although she didn't say anything directly."

"The senator didn't say anything to you?" Ava said, pleased by her matter-of-fact reaction.

"No, but that's typical of him," Elisha said, taking a seat. "How do you want to start with these cards?"

"We'll go after the low-hanging fruit first," Ava said. "We need to separate out all the cards that specifically give Zakat College, or any variation of that name, as a destination. Once we've done that, we will group them by those approximate dates I gave you."

"That sounds easy enough," Elisha said.

There were thirteen envelopes, but one was only half full. Ava estimated that they had about 2,500 copies of landing cards to wade through. She started with a sense of anticipation, but the first envelope yielded only one person who was bound for Zakat College. Ava placed the card next to her on the table as the beginning of what she hoped would be a pile. The next four envelopes were only marginally better than the first, and Ava began to feel discouraged. Her mood changed when they opened the sixth, in which ten Zakat students identified themselves. None of the remaining envelopes had as many, but Ava's stack grew steadily higher. When they had finished examining the contents of the last envelope, she counted the cards she'd set aside. Seventy-six people had declared that they were headed for Zakat College.

Ava split her stack in two and handed half to Elisha. "Let's group them by date."

Ten minutes later they had four stacks of approximately equal size. Ava took the one with arrivals from the February just past and put it aside. The other three stacks she put on the floor by her feet.

"That was the easy part," Ava said. "Now we're going to have to go back through the rest of these cards in more detail." She glanced at her notebook. "What we're looking for are men between the ages of eighteen and thirty who were heading for Tawi-Tawi or Bongao. Look for names that aren't distinctly Western, East Asian, or Filipino."

"What about country of origin?"

"That's less important than their age and a name that has roots in places such as the Middle East or South Asia."

Elisha glanced at her. "I'm already alarmed that we've found so many people going to that college."

"There should be more, and we need to find out who they are."

"This is very hard to believe."

"I don't disagree, but it's what we're dealing with," Ava said. "I think we should winnow down the number of cards by eliminating all the women first. Then anyone over thirty-five. Finally, we can get rid of all the people who obviously don't meet the criteria. That should leave us with a more workable number to examine."

The process went more smoothly than Ava had anticipated, and they quickly found themselves with less than two hundred cards. They went over them together, their major focus the family name. If there was any doubt about a name's origin, the card was kept. When they were finished, they had discarded another fifty cards. Then they sorted the remainder by date, again leaving aside the block of students who had arrived in February. Ava looked at what was left.

"Combined with the people who were clearly going to Zakat College, this total is more than what I was led to believe," she said. "But it's better to be safe."

"Safe? How are we going to confirm who is who?"

"You're going to have to pay your cousin another visit, and what we want her to do this time will be even more demanding," Ava said. "We've been told that the trainees were at the college for three months — that's why I wanted the arrivals searched over those three-month periods — and then were sent to various foreign destinations. There should be records on file of their departures: when they left and where they were headed. We need Zoey to find that information for each of them."

"She would have to input every name and passport number individually."

"I know it's a lot to ask, especially unofficially."

"This time she might ask some questions. How much can I tell her? "

"Senator Ramirez was most complimentary about your trustworthiness, which is why I've been willing to share things with you," Ava said. "How do you feel about Zoey?"

"She'd never break a confidence."

"Then tell her whatever you decide is necessary," Ava said.

"That would be everything you've told me."

"Okay. The decision is yours. All I care about right now is that she gets us the information we need."

Elisha looked at her watch. "I'll call her now. I might be able to catch her before she leaves the office."

"I'll give you some privacy while you do that," Ava said.

Ava went into the bathroom and closed the door. She could hear Elisha's voice but the words were indistinct. When silence fell, Ava re-entered the suite to find Elisha putting the cards back into the envelopes.

"Zoey was in a meeting when I called. She's not sure how much longer it's going to last, but she told me she'll make some time for me if I go over."

"So you didn't have a chance to explain what's going on?"

"No, not over the phone, but I said it was urgent and I'd fill her in when I got there," Elisha said. "My worry is that we won't be able to do these searches until tomorrow."

"It won't be a crisis if we have to wait an extra half day," Ava said.

"I know that logically, but as I was talking to her, I started to panic. I kept thinking about what will happen when we locate all these people."

"That won't be our decision," Ava said. "We're simply gathering information. When we have enough to pass on, someone else with more authority will decide what's next."

"This is still really scary shit," Elisha said, shaking her head.

"Try not to think of it in those terms. Right now it's all supposition. Who knows, when they left, instead of going to some foreign country, they may all have gone home."

"Do you really believe that's possible?"

"I don't know, but it's easier if you think that maybe it is."

( 19 )

**AFTER ELISHA HAD LEFT THE SUITE, AVA BUNDLED ALL**
the cards, except those for the February student arrivals, and
put them in a closet. She then sat at the table with the stack
of February cards in front of her and began to leaf through
them. She could picture young men sitting on a plane with
the tray tables lowered, carefully printing their names and
passport numbers. She wondered what they were thinking
as they wrote in their home addresses. Nostalgia? A sense
of loss? Relief to be away? She stopped at a card with the
name BARRY FAWAZ printed on it in almost childish block
letters. He was from London and twenty years old, and he
had listed ZAKAT MUSLIM COLLEGE, BONGAO as his destination. What had been running through his mind? Excitement?
Adventure? Martyrdom?

She reread them, making notes about home countries.
Pakistan, England, Belgium, Syria, Algeria, Palestine,
Australia, Germany, the Netherlands, Saudi Arabia, Turkey,
Kuwait, and France all had more than one entry. How had
Zakat College found them, or how had they found the college?
How broad was the college's reach, and what was its pitch?

Who paid for the trip? Where did their families think they had gone? How depressing it was, she thought, all that time, intelligence, energy, emotion, and money wasted on hate.

She restacked the cards, pushed them to one side, stood up, and went to the window. It was dark outside, and she realized that it was already past seven o'clock. Poirier should have landed, and with any luck he was on his way to the hotel. She was still dressed in her training pants and T-shirt, and that was no way to meet him.

Fifteen minutes later she emerged from the bathroom in a pink shirt, black pencil skirt, and black pumps. She had fastened the shirt cuffs with the jade links she'd bought in Beijing many years ago, and secured her hair with her ivory chignon pin. Then she put on black mascara and a touch of red lipstick.

She sat at the table, looked down at her notebook, and then looked out the window at the Makati skyline. She began to imagine the conversation she would have with Ryan Poirier. She knew what she wanted to tell him and how she wanted to proceed. What she didn't know was how patient he was prepared to be and how willing he was to take her information at face value. In Surabaya he had been quick to assert his authority, despite a disbelieving attitude. She wasn't about to cede control this time, and she didn't have the patience or the time for skepticism. He would either buy in or he wouldn't, and if he didn't, then she would find a Plan B.

Her phone rang. She watched it for a few seconds, certain it was him. "Ava Lee," she finally said.

"Ava, it's Elisha."

"Are you with Zoey? Is there a problem?"

"I'm at her office but I'm about to leave. She just came out of the meeting to tell me it's going to go on for a few more hours. We've agreed to get together early tomorrow morning."

"That's fine. And thanks for making the effort tonight."

"We'll be on it first thing," Elisha said. "I'll call as soon as we're done."

Despite knowing beforehand that the meeting could run late, Ava felt a touch of disappointment. It would have been ideal to have actual names, dates, and destinations to put in front of Poirier. She returned to the notebook, trying to focus on the questions she needed answered and anticipating what he would want to know. She circled the names of the banks in Riyadh and Amman. Fileeb al-Touma might control the flow of funds from Jordan to Bongao, but she wanted to know who had opened the original accounts and where those deposits had come from.

The phone sounded. She had been so locked into her thoughts that it startled her. "Yes?"

"I've checked into the hotel," Poirier said.

"The Peninsula?"

"Don't sound surprised. I thought it made the most sense."

"Of course it does."

"Where do you want to meet?"

"Are you hungry?"

"No."

"Then let's meet in the lobby. The bar has some corner tables and alcoves that provide some privacy."

"What's it called?"

"The 'Bar.' And I spent part of the afternoon in the 'Spa.' The Peninsula doesn't feel the need to be grandiose when it comes to names."

"Five minutes?"

"See you there."

Ava sat quietly for a couple of minutes, then put a couple of landing cards in her notebook and slipped the book, her phone, and a pen into her bag before heading out the door. When she exited the elevator in the lobby, she looked in the direction of the Bar and saw a man with a mop of red hair standing at the entrance.

"Mr. Poirier," she said, walking towards him.

He turned and looked at her. When she first met him, she had thought that at five foot nine he was too small to be in the RCMP, and in his slim designer jeans and green silk shirt, he also looked too hip. He was still in designer jeans, but now he was wearing a rust-brown Paul Smith T-shirt.

"Call me Ryan," he said, extending a hand. His hair was a bit longer than she remembered. The blazing blue eyes were the same.

"Thank you so much for coming," she said. "And call me Ava."

"They're clearing off a table for us in the far corner," he said. They stood awkwardly for a moment, and then the hostess returned with a big smile. "This way," she said.

They had a corner alcove and the tables on either side of them were empty. A server appeared just as they began to settle into seats directly across from one another.

"A glass of white wine — something French and dry," Ava said.

"A San Miguel pale ale," he said.

Ava opened her notebook and smiled at him tentatively.

"Before you begin, I have a confession to make," he said.

"What?" she said, immediately on guard.

"Before I left Jakarta, I called my friend at the American embassy here in Manila. I wanted to make sure he's in the city and I thought it would be wise to have him on standby. He was and he is."

"What did you tell him?"

"What could I tell him? I said I was coming to Manila to talk about a project that might have some interest for him, but that I didn't have any details."

"That's all?"

"No. I said I'd call him either tonight or tomorrow to let him know whether my lead panned out or not."

"What's his name?"

"Does that matter?"

"Not really, and there isn't much chance I'd recognize it anyway. I don't move in your circles."

Poirier pursed his lips and gave a little shrug. "In the event that you do get the chance to meet him, his name is Alasdair Dulles," he said. "He's smart, focused, and creative and has been known to bend the rules. Actually, that's why he's in Manila. He was running a larger operation, in Bangkok, but ran into some bullshit political problems. They've parked him here until things settle down."

"Is he a Dulles Dulles?"

"You know of Allen Dulles?"

"I took some American history. He was an important diplomat and the first civilian director of the CIA."

"Alasdair isn't related to him...unless, of course, being coy about it can be of some use."

"And what kind of problems did he have?"

"Like I said, it was bullshit."

"I'd still like to know."

The server arrived with their drinks. The conversation stalled as she poured Poirier's beer.

"Isn't it premature to talk about Alasdair?" he said after the server left.

"Not really," Ava said. "If he's your go-to guy, then I can't imagine he won't get involved."

"The information you have is that good?"

"Sadly, I think it is."

"I'm here to listen."

Ava sipped the wine, her eyes almost unconsciously darting around the room to see if anyone nearby seemed to be listening. "There are some conditions that I need to explain first," she said.

Poirier leaned forward. "There was no mention of conditions when you asked me to come here. If there were, I might have stayed in Jakarta."

"They aren't in the form of demands. You can think of them as requests."

"Concerning?"

"The main sources of the information I have. They'd like to be non-existent, or at least to have the lowest possible profile."

"Will you tell me who they are?"

"Yes, and I think that Dulles will have to know as well, but I'd like you to keep it between yourselves — or limited to as few people as possible — until we know exactly what we're dealing with."

"Who is it in particular you don't want plugged in?"

"The Philippine government, especially its intelligence services."

"And why would your sources be so sensitive about their involvement?"

"They don't have much faith in the intelligence services' ability to perform," Ava said. "It's also fair to say that they're afraid of repercussions."

"Who are these sources?"

Ava looked across the table at him. He was calm enough, much as he had been in Surabaya, even when guns were going off all around them. She didn't think of him, then or now, as a man who would panic or who was given to knee-jerk reactions.

"The Muslim Brotherhood of Mindanao," she said.

"That is a significant name," he said carefully. "But how on earth are you connected to them?"

"I came here as a favour for a friend. That led me to Senator Miguel Ramirez. He put me in touch with the Brotherhood."

"I know of Ramirez. He's a power player here," Poirier said. "What's the connection between your friend and him?"

"Business."

"What kind?"

"It's irrelevant. What matters is that Ramirez and my friend, Chang Wang, and Tommy Ordonez are in it together. One thing led to another."

"You're involved with that crew? How did that come to happen?"

"It isn't worth getting into," Ava said. "The point I'm making is that I came here with no other intention than doing a favour for Chang, and in the process I fell into this situation."

"About which I'm still waiting to hear."

"You obviously know something about Mindanao."

"I do."

"How about Tawi-Tawi, and Bongao?"

"I know they're heavily populated with Muslims and have active terrorist groups."

"Well, now it seems that a college called Zakat on the outskirts of Bongao has become a training centre for would-be terrorists."

"Would-be?" he said, his face impassive.

"Would-be insofar as they haven't yet attacked anyone or any place we know about. But they appear to have plans to do exactly that in a massive, coordinated manner sometime in May."

Poirier had both hands wrapped around his beer glass, and it looked to Ava as if he was squeezing it. "How many would-be's do you think there are?" he said.

"Right now we know of about 150 students who have gone through the school," she said. "We've been told that they've been sent overseas to join existing cells."

"Sent where?"

"Mainly to the United States, but also to countries surrounding Israel."

"Where in the U.S.?"

"Major cities."

"And who or what are the targets?"

"I've been told that the focus is on the Jewish population."

"Fuck," he said, closing his eyes. When he opened them again, they were hooded and his face was drawn. "And the source of this information is the Muslim Brotherhood?"

"Yes, both directly and indirectly. They've already helped confirm some of the things I've been told."

"So you believe this is real?"

"As real as that planeload of money I believed was being flown into Surabaya."

"Even if that's true, I have a lot of questions."

"I expected that you would."

"And I don't see any purpose in asking them twice or hav-ing you answer them twice," he said. "I think I should phone Alasdair Dulles and ask him to join us."

"I think you should too," Ava said.

## 20

**POIRIER LEFT THE BAR TO CALL DULLES. WHEN HE DIDN'T** return after five minutes, Ava began to feel nervous. By the time the five minutes had turned into twenty, she was angry.

When he finally appeared, he looked flustered and his face was flushed. "I'm so sorry, Ava," he said, when he reached the table. "I had to wait until they pulled Dulles out of a meeting."

"So you reached him?" she said, feeling her anger dissipate.

"He's on his way," he replied, glancing at the doorway. "He works nearby."

"How did he react?"

"He's a cool customer, but I think I rattled him a touch."

"It's good that you have so much credibility."

"I'm not so sure it was mine. The instant I told him that Ramirez is involved and that Tommy Ordonez owed you a favour, your value as a source skyrocketed."

"This has nothing to do with me directly," Ava said. "I'm a bystander who's been dropped into this."

"You can explain that to Alasdair, because he's here," Poirier said, nodding towards the doorway.

Ava had never met a CIA agent. Her mental image was

constructed from novels and films, and it was a conflicting one, flitting between dumpy intellectual and hip action hero. At first glance, Alasdair Dulles didn't appear to fit either stereotype. He was close to six feet tall and lean and rangy. He wore sharply creased slim grey slacks and a white Lacoste polo shirt. The shirt was tight, showing off a taut abdomen and muscular arms. His face was almost square, with a wide forehead and a broad chin. His nose and mouth might have looked large on a smaller face, but on his they were perfectly proportioned. His hair was light brown and short. As he came closer to them, Ava noticed that he was freshly shaven. *This is a man who cares about his appearance*, she thought. In her mind, that was a good thing. Uncle believed that how you presented yourself to the world was a reflection of your inner being. He had been meticulous in his dress and manner. Dulles met that standard.

Dulles stopped just short of the table and stared at her. Ava met his gaze. His eyes were blue, like Poirier's, but lacked the French Canadian's sparkle. They were a darker blue and seemed to be imbued with a hint of sadness. He had fine lines under his eyes, and Ava noticed that the skin around his jaw was just starting to sag. He was forty-five, she guessed, maybe fifty.

"It's always good to see you, Ryan, even on an unexpected occasion like this," Dulles said.

Poirier slid out from behind the table. The two men shook hands so vigorously that it looked as if they were closing a business deal.

"This is Ava Lee," Poirier said, turning towards her.

"Ah, the mysterious Ms. Lee," Dulles said, his voice surprisingly gritty.

"That's the second time I've been called that tonight," she said. "There is absolutely nothing mysterious about me, and I prefer being called Ava."

"As you like," Dulles said.

"Is it okay to talk here, or would you rather find a less public place?" Poirier asked.

"We seem to have the Bar pretty much to ourselves," Dulles said. "It will do."

They joined Ava at the table, sitting across from her. The server wasted no time making an appearance. Poirier ordered a second San Miguel beer and Dulles a Red Horse. Ava still had half of her wine left and decided that was enough for the evening.

"Tell me, how do you know Miguel Ramirez and Tommy Ordonez?" Dulles asked as soon as the server was gone.

"Does that matter?" she said.

"It might. It's one thing to use their names if they're simply acquaintances, but it's another thing entirely to be able to call upon them for assistance or, God forbid, protection."

"Do you know of Chang Wang?"

"Ordonez's second-in-command of everything, the man they call the Hammer?"

"I call him Uncle," Ava said. "If I phoned him now and said, 'Uncle, I need to speak to Tommy Ordonez within half an hour, and I want Miguel Ramirez to meet me at the Peninsula Hotel this evening,' both would happen."

"I see," Dulles said.

"More to your point, my former partner was a man of considerable influence. He and Chang were close from child-hood, and he helped Chang and Ordonez in their climb to success. A few years ago, Ordonez had a problem that involved his family. He reached out to my partner, who in turn brought me into the picture. We saved Ordonez a lot of money, but more important, we helped him save face," Ava said. "There isn't much that I could ask of Ordonez and Chang that they wouldn't do for me."

"Former partner?"

"He died a couple of years ago, of cancer. He was in his eighties. I still miss him...He was like a grandfather to me."

"I'm sorry," Dulles said. "But Ramirez — where does he fit into all this?"

"He, Chang, and Ordonez are partners in a business that's based in Mindanao. There are things going on in the region that they think threaten stability, and thus their business."

"The college in Bongao?"

"Yes.

"So here we are," Dulles said as the server placed their drinks on the table.

"Where do you want Ava to start?" Poirier asked.

"At the beginning."

"That's fine with me, but I should tell you that I don't like to rush things," Ava said.

"Take all the time you want, and don't skip a detail, no matter how minor you think it is," Dulles said.

Ava took a small sip of wine, then drew a deep breath and began. "I was in China when I received a phone call from Chang Wang asking me to do a favour for him and Tommy Ordonez..." Half an hour later she finished the wine and asked for a glass of water. Half an hour after that the water was gone and she had finished explaining why she'd made the phone call to Ryan Poirier. She waited for her glass to be refilled before telling them about her afternoon's work with Elisha. Then she sat back and looked across the table at Poirier and Dulles.

She had spoken as deliberately as she could, consciously being completely factual, not drawing conclusions or implying motives, and keeping her emotions and any hint of drama out of the recital. They had listened intently, not saying a single word. A few times she thought she saw doubt in their eyes, but she didn't react to it.

"Incredible," Dulles finally said, and then turned to Poirier. "What do you think of this?"

"I hadn't heard any of the details until now. Now that I have, I'm not sure 'incredible' does it justice." He looked at Ava. "Do you really believe everything you've been told?"

"I don't want to."

"But you do?"

"Yes, I do, but that doesn't mean it's all true," she said. "There are things we need to confirm."

"That's an understatement," Dulles said.

"Perhaps, but I don't like the feeling of being overwhelmed by anything. I've found that if I focus on component parts, the whole eventually becomes manageable."

"Ryan told me that you've been involved in some shady escapades in the past."

"I'm a forensic accountant by training, and I was a debt collector. There isn't anything that isn't shady about that profession, especially when — as in our case — the debts ran into the many millions and our customers preferred privacy. So I know a thing or two about conducting an investigation and about money trails."

"But you obviously don't know enough, or you wouldn't be bringing us into this so quickly."

"I know what I've found. I know what I can do. I also know what I can't do. You, or someone like you, were going to get dragged into this sooner or later. I need help, so I thought sooner was better."

"And if we take the information you've given us, say 'Thank you very much,' and then go off on our own?"

"You're not that stupid."

"Pardon?" Dulles said.

"I have the full co-operation and trust of the Brotherhood and Senator Ramirez and his staff. I wouldn't count on those being transferable. I also have investigative skills that could prove useful," Ava said. "My thinking — my reason for contacting Ryan — is that if we quietly and collectively gather information, we'll end up in a better place. I mean, where does your scenario lead? You don't work in a vacuum in this country, and almost certainly the Philippine intelligence services will be alerted that something is going on. That's the Brotherhood's biggest fear — not that the intelligence services find out, but that they find out prematurely. If they do, you can't count on their showing any restraint.

"Never mind the impact on Mindanao and the Brotherhood. On a narrower scale, they would go after the college, and then what? We lose the chance to identify who's financing and running the college and the foundation. We make it that much more difficult to identify and locate the students who've been sent overseas. And worse, we cause whoever is behind the college to panic and move that date in May up to early April. Right now we have time on our side, because they don't know we're looking into them. Let's not throw away that advantage."

"Have you ever been involved in politics?" Dulles asked.

"No."

"You should think about it for your next career."

"I don't lie well enough."

"That's a problem we share." He looked at Poirier. "Would you agree that she makes sense?"

"I would."

"But for the record, Ava, if I did take the information and run, it wouldn't end up in tomorrow's CIA wash. I'm part of a special operations unit that's not required to report through normal channels. I'm quite adept at keeping information contained."

"I felt obliged to represent the Brotherhood's reservations."

"I understand, and I don't think they're unfounded or misplaced," Dulles said. "The question is, if we agree to follow your advice, how do we proceed?"

"We haven't been able to find out anything about Fileeb al-Touma, Ishak Kassab, or Imam Tariq al-Bashir. We'd like your help."

"We'll do what we can."

"What is the Zakat Foundation? Who founded it? Who runs it? Does it have an aim?"

"I've already made a mental note of that. We'll work on it."

"And then there are the Zakat Foundation bank accounts in Jordan and Saudi Arabia. Who opened them? Who controls them? Where does the money originate?"

Dulles looked at Poirier. "It might be better if those enquiries came from your side. How are your contacts with the Mukhabarat and the Mabahith?"

"Good enough," Poirier said.

"Who are you talking about?" Ava said.

"The Mukhabarat is the Jordanian secret service, and the Mabahith is the Saudi version," Poirier said. "And don't look so worried. You aren't the only person who collects and exchanges favours."

"I get it."

"Well, it looks like we've been given our assignments," Dulles said. "What does that leave you with?"

"The departure cards."

"Speaking of which, I'd like copies of them."

"Why?" Ava said quickly.

"You said they contain names and passport numbers and possible destinations?"

"They do."

"I'll input them into our system. If anyone listed on them has landed in the U.S., we should be able to identify when and where."

"I'll ask Elisha to run an extra set."

"Thanks," Dulles said, glancing at his watch. "As I remember, there's a five-hour time difference between here and Riyadh. If I leave now, I might be able to start a local search for the Zakat Foundation."

"How do you want to handle communications from now on?" Poirier asked.

"I'm working out of an office near the embassy, but since Ava is stressing security, it's a not a good place for us to meet. Everything I do there is scrutinized," Dulles said. "Do you mind being the middle man?"

"Not at all, but Ava might be the better choice. She's the one linked to the Brotherhood."

"Are you okay with that?" Dulles said.

"I guess so," she said.

"Okay, that's it, then. We'll run everything through Ava and she'll make sure everyone is in the loop."

"I have to say that working with the CIA is a bit strange," she said.

"There isn't anything about this project that isn't strange." Dulles stood up. "Let's hope that it's just a false alarm, a product of the active imaginations of two young men in Bongao."

*There's not a chance it is*, Ava thought. "What's the best way for me to get hold of you?" she said.

"You can use the email address on my card or, better still, call me at the number on the back," Dulles said, passing her his business card.

"And here's my contact information," Ava said.

"Thanks," he said, and paused. "There is one other thing I need to say to you. I operate with a reasonable amount of autonomy and I can keep this project tightly contained for now. But if we are able to confirm everything you've been told, you must expect that others will be very quickly brought into the picture."

"As long as that happens because of facts and as long as I'm given some notice, I can't object."

"Then, until we talk again," Dulles said.

"He's different," Ava said, as she and Poirier watched Dulles leave the bar.

"What he is is reliable."

"Then why is he in Manila until 'things settle down' — I think that's the phrase you used earlier?"

"He ran a special operations unit out of Bangkok that encompasses Thailand, Laos, Cambodia, Myanmar, and northern Malaysia."

"Drugs?"

"Yes."

"So what happened?"

"He worked closely with the Thai military and placed quite a bit of trust in them. When a new president was elected about six months ago, the military came to him and said that the president wanted to wage war against the local drug kingpins. They asked him for the names of the three biggest and swore that's where it would end. He gave them the three names. The military arrested them, tortured them, and came up with more names, which led to more names, and so on and so on. By the time it ended, they had executed more than three thousand people they were convinced were connected to the drug trade. As it turned out, a few of the dead were CIA or DEA agents, or their paid informants. Alasdair is not loved in Thailand right now."

"And he's the guy you chose to involve in this?"

"I've always been able to count on him. What else can I say, except to add that he's in need of redemption."

"Who isn't?"

## 21

**RYAN POIRIER STAYED TO REVIEW THE BANK INFORMA-**
tion and make sure he had the names correct. "I'm going to
get started on this right away, and I'll be surprised if Alasdair
doesn't spend the rest of the evening working things through
from his end," he said.

"So you think it went well?" Ava asked.

"From your viewpoint, I don't see how it could have gone
any better."

They left the Bar together and headed towards the elevator. Ava paused as they passed the entrance to Old Manila.
"I need something to eat and the restaurant's still open. Do
you want to join me?" she asked.

"No, but thank you," he said.

"Then I'll hear from you later or, most probably, tomorrow?"

"I would expect tomorrow," he said. "Have a good night."

The restaurant was fifteen minutes from closing, and
the staff didn't seem particularly pleased to see her. "Is the
kitchen still open?" Ava asked.

"I think so," the hostess said without enthusiasm.

"All I want is a salad. Can they manage that?"

"Of course," she said.

After a Caesar salad with shrimp and another glass of wine, Ava went back to her room. She showered, put on a clean T-shirt and underwear, and sat at the desk. There were no emails marked "urgent" from either May Ling or Amanda, and no others that seemed to demand her attention. She checked her phone in case she'd missed a call, and when she saw there were none, she headed for bed. She plugged the charger into the wall and placed the phone, its volume set at the highest level, on the bedside table.

She lay on her side with her back to the phone. Her mind was still churning, and despite what had arguably been a day of progress, her dominating mood was anxiety, especially when she thought about the scope of what she'd been dragged into. Her priority, she told herself, was to find out what she could and simply pass the information along.

She was just turning over when the phone rang. She stared at it, uncertain who could be calling. "Yes?" she said.

"It's Ryan. I've just finished speaking to Alasdair, and we have some news."

"So fast?" she said, sitting up.

"Looking into people's lives is what we do for a living, and since 9/11 we've all become better at it," he said. "Everything moves so damn quickly there are times I wish it would slow down, but this isn't one of them."

"What do you have?"

"We've managed to confirm that someone named Fileeb al-Touma opened the Zakat bank accounts in both Saudi Arabia and Jordan," he said. "We haven't been able to get any real details about him or locate him — or anyone named Kassab or Tariq al-Bashir — in any of our systems, and our friends overseas can't find them either. We're assuming the names are bogus, but al-Touma's paperwork had to be first-rate for him to open those accounts, so we're most likely dealing with professionals."

"Is there an address attached to the accounts?"

"Yes, both have the same Riyadh address. It's already been checked and it's an empty office with a sign on the door that reads 'Zakat Foundation' and a phone that no one answers. It was too late to speak to people working in the adjacent offices, but the Mabahith will do that tomorrow. Who knows, al-Touma might have made an appearance there."

"Are both accounts active?"

"The Saudi one was opened first. The banker in Bongao was correct when he said the money used to fund the school's construction came from it, but it's now basically dormant and has only about ten thousand dollars in it. The Jordanian account was opened just over a year ago, and it's the active one. There have been monthly wire transactions to the Philippines, which you already knew about, but the account has also been accumulating a tidy balance. There's almost a million dollars in it."

Ava slid from the bed and went to the desk. She opened her notebook. "Ryan, can we get a detailed list from the Jordanian bank of all the transactions attached to that account?"

"We'll have it tomorrow."

"That's great, and does that include deposits?"

"Yes, but that's where things get a bit strange," he said. "We were told that all the deposits have been made in cash and all of them made by al-Touma. He seems to go to the bank at least once a week."

"Didn't the bank find that many large cash deposits odd?"

"Evidently not, and the bank in Riyadh didn't either, because he did the same thing there."

"And there are no restrictions on the size of cash deposits in either country?"

"If there are, he's obeyed them, or else someone is turning a blind eye."

"So where does this leave us?"

"In a lot better shape than we were a few hours ago," Poirier said.

"Well, at least we know that the foundation and the bank accounts aren't figments of someone's imagination."

"If we have the slightest bit of luck, we'll know a lot more than that," he said. "Alasdair has made arrangements, with the Mukhabarat's assistance, to interview bank staff tomorrow. We've also been given permission to review the bank's closed-circuit camera records. Al-Touma made those deposits himself, and they're all time-stamped. We'll get a look at him and so will the Mukhabarat. If we can't identify him that way, then we'll post someone at the bank and wait for him to show up."

"As anxious as I am for you to get your hands on him, I'm just as eager to look at the bank records."

"Why?"

"I want to know who paid the travel costs for the students they brought to the Philippines, and who paid what to whom to get them out of the country," she said. "And if they've got all those people in place in the U.S. and elsewhere, who's supporting them financially?"

"If we can answer half of those questions, then tomorrow promises to be more of the same."

"I'd like to thank you," Ava said suddenly.

"For what?"

"Trusting me enough for you to come here, and for bringing Alasdair Dulles into play. I don't know what I would have done if you hadn't said yes, and looking at what you've accomplished in just a few hours leaves me feeling breathless and almost inadequate."

"Shit, we wouldn't be here in the first place without you and that web of contacts you have," Poirier said. "And let me be clear: we both want you to stay involved. Coming from Dulles, that's quite the compliment — he typically hates amateurs. Truthfully, he doesn't have much respect for most of his professional colleagues either."

"Did you tell him about Surabaya?"

"I did, in detail, but it was your briefing tonight in the bar that impressed him."

The compliment surprised her, and she felt herself blush. "I'll talk to you tomorrow" was all she could finally think of to say.

"Ava, you might not be talking to me so much from now on," he said carefully. "This has a major and immediate impact on the Americans. Alasdair will assume the major role while I fade into the background. In fact, I'm heading back to Jakarta in the morning. Knowing Alasdair, he'll keep me informed, so that's not an issue. But I want to make it clear that I'll be available to you anytime, anywhere. We Canadians have to stick together."

"If he's going to take over, why did he let you make all those contacts in Jordan?"

"That's Alasdair being cautious. He wanted to confirm that what you told us has some basis in fact," Poirier said. "If the information was shit, his name wouldn't be part of the conversation. If it's gold, he steps into the picture."

"That would bother me, but it doesn't seem to bother you."

"It isn't personal; it's the nature of our business," he said. "And I can tell you honestly that in the past he's done the same for me."

## 22

SHE SLEPT FOR ONLY SIX HOURS, BUT IT WAS A DEEP, sound sleep without dreams or interruptions, and when she woke she felt an immediate surge of energy. She rolled over, looked at the bedside clock, and saw that it was ten to seven. She smiled as she reached for her phone.

"*Wei*," Pang Fai said.

"It's me," Ava said.

"Finally. I was getting annoyed that we kept missing each other."

"My project here has had me keeping crazy hours."

"And this movie is just making me crazy," Fai said. "We're only a few days into it and already the crew is fed up about having to tear down and set up every day. This was one of those ideas that sound good in principle and turn out to be absolute crap."

"Is there anything you can do to improve the situation?"

"It might help if I shot the director, but then there would still be the guy from the Chinese Film Syndicate to deal with."

"What does he do?"

"Everything and nothing — the syndicate approved the script and put up the money. The guy who's here was sent to make sure we don't change the story and don't go over budget."

"One day you're going to have to explain to me how that process works."

"I'd rather walk on hot coals," Fai said with a laugh.

"You know, I could be wrapped up here in a week or so. My offer to meet you somewhere still stands."

"I'd love to see you, but it isn't a good idea. I don't have any real privacy, and I don't want to have to pretend that we're just friends."

"Then we'll stay in touch by phone and text," Ava said, realizing she was making Fai uncomfortable.

"Yes. Every day from now on, okay?"

"Every day."

"I love you."

"I love you too," Ava said.

She sat quietly on the edge of the bed and thought about the different lives she and Fai led. It wasn't just what they did for a living or the people who surrounded them. There was a cultural divide that Ava was only beginning to understand. She had been raised in what Westerners would consider Chinese culture, but having grown up in Canada, she didn't have to worry about what people thought or said. The only people she needed to make happy were her family and friends, and even then it was her choice to do so or not. Fai worked in a system that demanded respect and had the means to punish those who resisted. *I need to get her to Canada*, Ava thought.

She made a coffee and then sat at the desk. She scanned her emails half-heartedly. Again there weren't any that caught her attention, and her mind floated back to Pang Fai. Their conversation hadn't depressed her. On the contrary, it had only stiffened her resolve to help Fai get out of China as soon as possible.

She put on her running gear and headed downstairs to the fitness centre. It was almost nine o'clock by the time she came back, showered, and got dressed. She wondered how Dulles was doing but didn't want to seem too pushy by calling him. She didn't have the same reluctance when it came to Elisha Gill.

"Are you with your cousin?" Ava asked when Elisha answered.

"I'm at her office. We've been here since seven."

"How is it going?"

"I don't want to talk about it until we're completely done. We'll need another twenty minutes or so."

"Will you phone me?"

"I'd rather come to the hotel with what we have."

"Are you okay?" Ava asked, sensing some discomfort in Elisha's voice.

"I'll see you at the hotel."

*What was that about?* Ava thought. Then she realized she hadn't asked Elisha to make a second set of cards for Dulles. She decided it could wait until she saw her.

She made another coffee and this time settled in at the computer and went through her inbox more thoroughly. She was just finishing an email to May Ling about another expansion request from Suki Chan, their partner in a Shanghai-based warehouse and logistics company, when the doorbell rang. "Be right there," she shouted, and a few seconds later hit the Send button.

Ava walked quickly to the door and opened it. Elisha stood with her head lowered. When she looked up, Ava hardly recognized the pale, drawn face. "What happened to you?" she said.

Elisha was clutching her handbag and a paper shopping bag against her chest. Ava motioned for her to come into the room. She followed her to the table they had occupied the day before. "Did something happen at the bureau? Did someone object to what you were doing? Was there a confrontation?"

"No, nothing like that."

"Then what?"

"We ran the passports through the system. We ran all of them, every name and number. We came up with only seven people who had left the Philippines."

"You're not serious."

"Seven. And according to the records, six of them left the country about a month after arriving, and one left after two months."

"This makes no sense at all," Ava said. "Was the program working properly? Were the entries confirmed? Were all the possible points of departure included?"

"After we got the first negative results, Zoey input test data and confirmed that the system was working as it should. Then we double-checked our input and got the same response. And her search was system-wide. It covered every airport and harbour where the bureau has immigration staff, and you obviously can't leave the islands any other way than by sea or air."

"This is the last thing I was expecting."

"Me too. I'm in shock," Elisha said. "Even Zoey was upset. She offered to rerun the numbers tonight when she has some spare time, but I told her I don't see the value in that."

Ava dropped into a chair at the table. "How easy is it to leave the Philippines without clearing Immigration?"

"That's the first question I asked her, and evidently it isn't that difficult, particularly if you go by sea. There's more than thirty thousand kilometres of coastline and God knows how many ports."

"Let's assume, then, that they did leave by sea," Ava said, grasping at the only straw she had. "Where is the most likely place they would go?"

"Zoey pointed out that Bongao is only 240 kilometres from Tawau, a city in Sabah."

"I've been to Sabah. It's a Malaysian province on the island of Borneo."

"Yes, and she also mentioned a city called Tarakan. It's on Borneo as well, but on the Indonesian side, and about three hundred kilometres from Bongao."

"It takes only a day-long trip to land in Malaysia or Indonesia," Ava said. "It's feasible that they went there and then connected to flights to North America."

"One thing that Zoey is confident about is that they didn't leave the Philippines by air. Even if they used private aircraft, they'd have to file detailed flight plans before leaving our airspace, and private airstrips are closely monitored."

Ava shook her head. "We're going to have to come at this from other angles."

"What do you mean?"

"Does Zoey have any good contacts in the Malaysian and Indonesian immigration services?"

"I'm sure she must. There's quite a bit of regional coordination."

"Can she ask them for some assistance? We need to know if any of these people cleared Immigration in Malaysia or Indonesia over the past twelve months."

Elisha took the stack of landing cards from the bag and placed them on the table. "That's quite a bit to ask of them."

"Then pick ten at random. If any of them pop up, we'll have a reason to pursue the rest."

"What excuse can she use?"

"Let her figure that out."

"And are those cities large enough to warrant having immigration services?"

"Just a second," Ava said. She went to her computer and entered "Tarakan" and then "Tawau."

"Tarakan has a population of about two hundred thousand, and Tawau is only a bit smaller. I'm sure they'll have immigration staff in both places," she said.

"Okay, I'll ask Zoey."

"Now, could you give me what you have on the seven people who did leave?"

Elisha reached into the bag, took out a manila folder, and slid it across the table. Ava opened it and quickly read the immigration records of seven men aged twenty to twenty-seven, all with Middle Eastern family names. Their home addresses were in Belgium, the Netherlands, Syria, Lebanon, and Australia; two were from England. Everyone but the Australian had flown back to his home country after a stay of about a month. The Australian had left the Philippines after two months.

"What are you thinking?" Elisha asked.

"This confirms what I was told about the students being given the option to leave, and that's a good thing."

"So my morning wasn't entirely wasted?"

"I'm sorry if I gave you the impression that I thought it was," Ava said. "It isn't your or Zoey's fault that the Zakat students left the country illegally. But given what we think they're up to, it's logical that they did."

Elisha leafed through the card copies in front of her and extracted ten. "I'll take these to Zoey."

"You can leave the rest with me," Ava said.

## 23

**IT TOOK A WHILE FOR AVA TO GATHER HERSELF** together after Elisha left the suite. The news about the landing cards had stunned her, and it had taken all her willpower to stay calm. But the moment the door closed behind Elisha, she felt a sense of helplessness wash over her.

She sat at the table and stared blankly at the pile of cards. *Now what the hell will I do?* she thought. *And how stupid am I going to look to Poirier and Dulles? I virtually guaranteed that I would be able to confirm names and have some idea of where everyone had gone. Now I'm almost back at square one in terms of being able to positively identify students.*

She picked up the manila folder. *But I've got these,* she thought. She leafed through the cards of the students who had left the school early and separated out the one with the name Jason Said on it. He was the Australian who had left the college after two months, presumably after he was asked to make the second commitment. If that was true, then he would have some knowledge of what the students were being asked to commit to.

She checked the date of his departure, worked back two

months, and then went through the other cards to find similar arrival dates. When she finished, she had more than fifty cards in a stack. Surely he had known some of them well enough to be able to verify that they were at the college with him. *This gives me something positive to talk about with Dulles*, she thought. *And maybe Zoey will get lucky with the Malaysians and Indonesians. And maybe Wahab can help in Bongao.* She picked up the phone.

"This is Wahab," he said.

"It's Ava. Is this a good time for me to call?"

"Sure."

"I have something I want you to do for me," she said. "It doesn't appear that the students who left the college used normal commercial transport. There's no record of them leaving from any of the airports. We think it's possible they went to either Malaysia or Indonesia by sea. Do you have any contacts at the port in Bongao?"

"We have some."

"See what you can find out."

"You think they may have chartered a boat?"

"Something like that."

"I'll send a man to the port today to make some enquiries."

"Thanks."

"Is that all?"

"For now."

"How is it going on your end?"

"It's far too soon to tell. Give me a couple more days and I may have something to report."

"Don't forget about us."

Ava put down the phone, reached into her bag, and pulled out the business card Alasdair Dulles had given her the night before. She called his number and he answered immediately.

"Good morning," he said. "I was just speaking to Ryan, and he told me that you and he talked last night."

"Yes, he told me about the banks and Fileeb al-Touma."

"There's nothing new to add just yet. It's still very early in Jordan, and I imagine it will be a couple of hours before we can do anything else."

"That's not why I'm calling," Ava said. "I have a large number of arrival cards for the students we think have left the Philippines for the U.S. and the Middle East. You said you want copies to run through your system to see if any of them applied for a visa or actually landed."

"You said 'arrival cards.' Don't you mean departure cards?"

"There's a bit of a problem there."

"I'm listening," he said.

She put the best spin on it that she could. Dulles listened, and when she finished, he said, "So you have the Brotherhood making enquiries in Bongao and your contact at the immigration bureau checking with Malaysia and Indonesia?"

"Yes. And I'm reasonably sure that the cards I have are those of students. They will give you names and passport numbers."

"But none of it is certain?"

"No, it's a best guess."

"That's unfortunate."

"There's another lead I want to follow that could give us some certainty."

"And that is?"

"How strong are your contacts in Australia?" she asked.

"That entirely depends on what your needs are."

"We didn't come up completely dry in terms of departure

cards. We found seven, but they belong to students who I think left the college early, six of them after one month and the seventh after two. The one who left after two months is an Australian named Jason Said. I'm sure he was at the college, because his landing card lists it as his destination. He has a Sydney address on that landing card and Sydney as his destination on his departure card. I'd like to locate him and talk to him," she said. "If he was at the college for two months, then he reached the final commitment stage. That means he might have been briefed on some attack plans and might have some information on foreign cells. At the very least he can tell us how he was recruited, verify many of the things the Brotherhood told us, and give us insight into this imam Tariq al-Bashir."

"Speaking of the imam, I still haven't been able to find a single reference to him, and I've looked everywhere."

"Yes, Ryan mentioned that he thought it might be a pseudonym," she said, disappointed at his non-reaction to her suggestion about interviewing Said.

"I think it's important that we find out who he is and who he's connected to."

"Of course. We've all been trying."

"My point is that if we can't find an information trail that leads us to him, we need to use a physical one," Dulles said. "You said the Brotherhood has people working at the college?"

"Yes, Ben and Alcem. They're cleaners."

"I'd like you to ask them to get something belonging to al-Bashir that might help us identify him."

"You're looking for DNA?"

"No, that takes too long, it isn't as reliable as television makes out, and the existing DNA databases are very small," he said. "I'd much rather have something with fingerprints on it, like a comb, a hairbrush, a toothbrush, a pen, spoon, or fork — anything they can get their hands on that they're reasonably sure he touched. We can do a fingerprint analysis in a few days from here."

"I'll talk to my contact at the Brotherhood," she said.

"Great. Now, as for Australia, give me the address of this Jason Said. I'll make some calls."

"I want to talk to him myself," she said.

"I wasn't suggesting anything else," he said. "But we should make sure he's actually where you think he is, and I'll need to bring my Australian colleagues on board before we go."

"We?"

"That's something you should probably start getting used to."

"I'm fine with that, as long as it works both ways."

"Agreed," he said. "Now, when are you going to get me those landing cards, so I can see if any of the students tried to get into the U.S.?"

"I'll bring the cards to you. Where is your office?"

"From the Peninsula, we're the largest building on the right side of Roxas Boulevard, about half a mile before the American embassy. Any taxi driver should know it. There's a Mercury Drug store and a Jollibee restaurant on the ground floor. We're listed as the Global Trading Company, on the tenth floor, but the elevator will take you only as far as the eighth. You'll have to call me from the lobby when you arrive."

"Then I'll see you in about an hour, if traffic is as bad as it normally is."

She put down the phone and then thought about Wahab. How would he react to another request? Maybe she should tell him she'd met with the Americans. But what would that generate except perhaps some mistrust and, more assuredly, a lot of questions? *He has to trust me*, she thought and reached for the phone.

"I'm surprised to hear from you so soon. Did something happen?" he said.

"No, but I was thinking about the imam. It's crazy that we don't know more about him."

"We've tried."

"I know. And I looked everywhere I could think of and found nothing as well, but we can't leave it at that."

"What are you suggesting?"

"As I remember, Ben and Alcem are cleaners at the college."

"That's true."

"Does the imam have his own bathroom?"

"Yes, they told me he did."

"Then could you please ask them to get something that has the imam's fingerprints? A brush, a comb, a book cover — anything at all."

"That could be risky."

"Well, I think we're at a point where some risks have to be taken, and I don't think a missing brush will set off panic alarms," she said. "Wahab, it's important that we find out who this man is."

"I'll talk to the boys," he said slowly.

"Thank you. And if they can get something, make sure they handle it with care. They should probably bag it and then you can arrange to fly it to me here in Manila. We can get the fingerprints analyzed in a matter of a few days."

"How would you organize that?" he said.

"I have some friends who can help."

"Which friends?"

"Some people I trust," Ava said carefully. "You needn't worry. They won't ask why I want the prints analyzed."

"Even if they don't, I have to say the idea makes me nervous."

"You'll feel better once we know who the imam is, and this is one way of accomplishing it," Ava said. "Call me the instant the boys have something, so I can make arrangements on this end. I won't do anything until I hear from you."

"I think I'd better talk to Juhar about this."

"Do that, but please don't drag it out," she said. "The sooner we can get a fix on the imam, the better it will be for all of us."

"I don't disagree, but I still think I should talk to Juhar."

"Do what you think you need to."

She ended the call with mixed feelings about how she'd handled it. She hadn't misled him but she had shaded the truth. She hadn't lied, though, at least not overtly. *If the boys do come through for us and we get a match for the fingerprints, that's when I'll tell him everything,* she thought as she left the suite.

## 24

**IT TOOK HER CLOSE TO TWO HOURS TO MAKE THE TRIP** to Dulles's office. "God, this traffic is terrible," she said at one point. The city had no subway and no elevated trains; all it had were roads that were clogged by cars, motorbikes, more than fifty thousand jeepneys, and thousands of pubs — small buses called public utility vehicles.

When the taxi finally reached the nondescript ten-storey brown brick building, she was relieved to be out of the traffic and to stretch her body. She walked into a white tiled lobby with the drugstore on one side and the restaurant on the other. Ava checked the building directory and saw that the tenth floor was indeed occupied by the Global Trading Company. She phoned Dulles.

"I'm in the lobby," she said when he answered.

"When you're facing the elevators, get into the one on your right. I'll stay on the line until you do."

"Traffic was horrendous," she said, as she watched both elevators descend.

"It always is."

"I'm getting into the elevator now," she said as it arrived.

"Okay. I've unlocked the button for the tenth floor."

When she reached the floor, he was waiting for her in an enclosed foyer with one door. "Hey," he said. He entered the security code and opened the door. They walked down a hall lined with closed doors to one at the far end that was open.

She handed him the paper bag. "The cards are in here," she said. The office was plainly furnished, with a desk, a grey metal filing cabinet, and two faded leather chairs.

"I'll have someone start on these this afternoon," he said. "Grab a chair. It's been one hell of an interesting morning."

"Australia?"

"We'll get to that later," he said, sitting behind the desk.

Ava sat down across from him. "The bank? Fileeb al-Touma?"

"Our friends in the Mukhabarat were far more aggressive than we anticipated. They got bank employees out of bed in the middle of the night for questioning and they started reviewing the CCTV tapes right away," he said. "We now have an understanding of how the money was moved, and they were able to identify al-Touma from the tapes." He spoke calmly but Ava detected more than a hint of satisfaction in his manner.

"Who is he, this al-Touma?" she said.

"His name is Omar Obeidat. He's forty-five years old and, until twenty-four months ago, he was a member of the Mukhabarat."

"That's ridiculous," Ava said.

"I know it sounds far-fetched but they assure me he was, and at a middle-management level. He told them he was leaving to take a senior position at a security company. They hadn't heard from him, or about him, since he left."

"Did you tell them why you were trying to find out who he is?"

"Not in detail, but I'm sure they have some idea. Without any prompting, they told me that they remember him as a man who was moderate in most things — except in his dislike for extremists."

"Is that a cover?"

"Likely."

"Have they spoken to him?"

"No. They haven't found him yet. He's not living in Jordan under either of those names. They have an email address he uses to communicate with the bank, and they've asked the bank to invite him for a meeting. If he shows up, the Mukhabarat will detain him."

"What about bank records?"

Dulles reached into the top right-hand drawer of his desk. "Here's your copy," he said, passing her an inch-thick wad of printouts. "Every deposit and withdrawal is detailed."

Ava scanned the first few pages. "Lots of deposits, and always in nice round numbers," she said. "Were they all in cash, as we were told?"

"So it seems. And one of the bank employees remembered something distinctive: at least some of the cash bundles had strips with the name 'Paradise Casino, Beirut,' on them."

"Is there such a place?"

"Indeed there is."

"So he was using the casino to launder money?"

"We don't know, but we intend to find out. One of my people will be paying the casino a visit later today, with some colleagues from the Lebanese Internal Security Forces."

"This is fantastic," Ava said.

"It's a start. I hope by the time we land in Australia we'll know more."

"So that's on too?" she said.

"I've booked flights for this evening. We arrive early tomorrow morning and we'll be met by Phil Johnson, who works with me, and a friend of his from Australian national security. The ANS ran a check on Jason Said and he's on their watch list as a low-level risk. They told us he lives with his parents at the address you provided."

"Will Johnson take us to see Said?"

"Yes, but we have to involve the ANS. It's smart to do that for several reasons, especially if Said refuses to talk to us."

"They can bring pressure to bear?"

"They can detain him for up to fourteen days without laying charges if they suspect he's associated in any way with a terrorist threat."

"How much proof do they need?"

"None. Suspicion is enough, and I assured Phil that we can provide adequate information if it's needed," he said. "In the meantime, the ANS is putting Said under immediate surveillance to make sure they know where he is when we arrive."

"What time is our flight?"

"Five after eight on Qantas. We get into Sydney at seven a.m."

"I guess I'd better go back to the Peninsula and pack," she said. "Given the way traffic was today, I've no idea how long it will take to get there and then to the airport."

"I'll meet you at the gate, or in the Qantas lounge if you're early," Dulles said. "Here's your flight confirmation number." Ava took the sheet of paper from him and stood up to leave.

"Just a minute — did you get a chance to talk to the Brotherhood about the fingerprints?" he asked.

She took her phone from her purse and looked at the log. There were no calls from Wahab. "They're working on it. What do you want them to do if they come up with something while we're in Australia?"

"My assistant's name is Susan Crawford and she's been partially briefed. If they do get something, we'll arrange for her to hook up with them. It would be best if they could fly it to Manila."

"Does she know who the Brotherhood are?"

"Yes, but not precisely what we're doing with them."

"Have you told Ryan everything that's going on?"

"His Jordan connections have been a big help and we'll keep him in the loop, but he and I agreed that you and I should be managing this from now on," he said, confirming what Poirier had told her the night before. "Is that a problem for you?"

"No, just as long as I'm not unilaterally sidelined and you continue to respect my desire to shield the Brotherhood."

"You should have no worries about that," he said. "And don't worry about Ryan either. If we're successful, he'll get his share of the credit."

"And if we're not?"

"Failure can't be part of our thought process."

## 25

AVA GAVE HERSELF FIVE HOURS TO GET BACK TO THE hotel, pack, check out, and travel to Aquino International Airport. It took another hour to check in and clear Immigration and Security. By the time she got to the Qantas lounge, it was almost seven o'clock.

Dulles was already there, sitting on a couch with his carry-on by his feet and a glass of beer in his hand. He waved at her and she went to join him.

"I forgot to thank you earlier for buying my ticket, and what a nice surprise to see that it's in business class," she said.

He looked up at her and smiled. "I'm senior enough to get a few perks," he said. "Do you want something to drink?"

She was about to say yes when her phone rang. She saw Wahab's number and hesitated. When she hadn't heard from him during the day, she assumed that Juhar had said it was okay for Ben and Alcem to collect some of al-Bashir's possessions. Now she felt a twinge of doubt, and she was also slightly uncomfortable about talking to him while sitting next to Dulles. So far she'd managed to keep them separated, and this was, psychologically at least, one step towards bringing them together. *I need to know*, she thought, and hit the Talk button.

"Wahab," she said, and just as she did, a very loud pre-boarding announcement came over the speakers in the lounge.

"Where are you?" he said.

"I'm at Aquino Airport," she said, certain he'd heard the boarding call. "I'm flying to Australia tonight. I've managed to locate a student who left the college after two months and I'm going to talk to him. He should be able to fill in some details."

"Has he agreed to meet with you?"

"Not yet, but he will."

"What makes you so sure?"

"This isn't the time to talk about that, but what I will do is call you the moment I'm finished with him," she said. "Now, what's going on with you?"

"Two things. First, we asked questions at the harbour in Bongao. No one knows anything about a boat chartered by the college, or about a charter boat that can hold more than ten people at a time," he said. "Next, Juhar has agreed that the boys should collect whatever they can for you. Ben and Alcem aren't working today but they have the early shift tomorrow morning. If they do get something, he wants them to leave the college right away, before the imam notices anything is missing."

"Thanks for asking about the charters, and thank Juhar, Ben, and Alcem. Let's just hope the boys get lucky."

"But Ava, if you're in Australia, what do we do with what they get?"

"Call me as soon as the boys leave the college and we'll talk about it then. Sydney is three hours ahead of the Philippines, so the time difference won't matter."

"When will you be back?"

"I'm not sure. Maybe tomorrow, but probably the day after."

"I'd feel better about this if you were here."

"It can't be helped. We need to find out what this young Australian knows."

"Okay," he said.

"Then we'll talk tomorrow," she said, ending the call before he could ask another question.

"The Brotherhood?" Dulles asked, looking up at her.

"Yes."

"You haven't told them that you've brought us into this?"

"No, it would only make them nervous, and my fear is that they'd stop working with me."

"What was the call about?"

"They were confirming that they're going to try to acquire something with Tariq al-Bashir's fingerprints on it."

"Good."

"But if they do and I'm not in Manila, I'm going to have to tell them about your involvement — or make them wait until I get back and can receive the samples myself."

"Time is not our ally," Dulles said. "I think events are likely to unfold quickly, and as they do, more and more people will be brought into this situation and any hopes of maintaining control will disappear."

"What makes you think events will unfold so quickly?" she said. "Has something happened that I don't know about?"

"From a negative viewpoint — and one that really concerns me — we put the data you pulled from the Philippine immigration bureau into our system and came up absolutely empty. There isn't a single record of any one of those students even attempting to enter the United States."

"What does that mean?"

"I wish I knew. It would be nice to believe that your contacts misconstrued what they heard and saw at the college. But when you consider the trouble the group took to set up the banking situation and hide the identities of everyone involved, I don't think that's probable."

"So what then?"

"I don't know. Maybe Jason Said or Omar Obeidat can shed some light. We've tracked Obeidat to Beirut. We figured that if he's getting all the money from the casino, he should be flying from Amman or Riyadh to Beirut on a regular basis. But when we checked his travel patterns, we discovered the reverse — all his flights originated in Beirut. We're trying to find a home address, and eventually we will," Dulles said.

"How about the casino operators?"

"We'll be meeting with the management in a few hours."

"The management or the owners?"

"We don't have a name to attach to ownership just yet; all we have is a numbered company registered in Liechtenstein. The company has a bank account, but thus far the bank officials are invoking local law and refusing to divulge who owns or can sign on the account. We'll lean on the casino managers, though, and hopefully they'll be more co-operative."

Dulles drained his beer and then shook his head. "The billion-dollar question is, where are the students? Is the U.S. really their major target or do they have others? Are they waiting in the Philippines before going overseas? Have they found a way to get past our border security? Hopefully Said can help answer some of those questions. If he can't, then we'd better get our hands on Obeidat, or pray that your Brotherhood friends give us what we need to identify the imam."

## 26

**THE BUSINESS-CLASS SECTION WAS FULL. AVA WAS**
seated two rows behind and three seats over from Dulles.
She was tired, and her head was a whirling mass of questions
and conjecture. The sense of helplessness and the nagging
fear she'd felt earlier were also threatening to return. She
knew she needed to shut down her mind.

She had a glass of complimentary champagne and, as
soon as cabin service started, she downed a glass of white
wine, quickly followed by another, and then a cognac. She
scanned the entertainment system for anything that might
divert her attention, but most of the films were recent
Hollywood schlock. She reclined the seat, put on an eye
mask, inserted earplugs, wrapped herself in a blanket, and
tried to visualize her bak mei exercises. She focused on the
Tiger, whose spirit epitomized the martial art, and began to
mentally bring together all of its elements. She imagined she
was at Grandmaster Tang's house and he was her opponent.
Back and forth they went, intercepting and checking each
other's strikes. Twice she blocked his phoenix-eye fist, and
the second time she used his energy against him, slipping

inside his guard to deliver her own fist to his throat, stopping half an inch short. Grandmaster Tang took a step back and bowed in recognition of her success. She bowed in return. *Again?* he said. *Yes, Grandmaster,* she said, drifting into sleep.

It was an eight-hour flight to Sydney, and Ava slept for six of them. The cabin attendant woke her when they were about an hour away, which gave her just enough time to freshen up in the bathroom and have a couple of cups of coffee.

When they reached the gate, Dulles exited ahead of her but waited just inside the ramp. He had his phone in his hand. "I'm trying to get service," he said.

Ava pulled her phone from her bag and turned it on. After a minute she said, "I don't have anything either."

"Let's go. I imagine it will be better when we're inside the main terminal."

They walked side by side, Ava barely reaching Dulles's shoulder. He walked quickly, his long strides carrying them past fellow passengers. She took two steps to every one of his but had no difficulty keeping up.

They were the first from their flight to reach immigration services. In less than ten minutes their passports were stamped and they'd been waved through Customs.

"Hey, Allie," a distinctly American voice said when they entered the arrivals hall. A short, portly, balding man in baggy khakis and a white short-sleeved shirt stepped towards them.

"Phil, it's great to see you. You haven't changed a bit," Dulles said.

"Neither have you. You still look like a goddamn GQ cover model."

After they shook hands, Johnson turned and motioned to a tall, trim middle-aged man wearing grey slacks and a pale blue cotton shirt. "Alasdair, this is Manfred Pinson. He's our host for the day, or for however long we need him."

"This is very good of you," Dulles said, extending his hand.

"Phil has been outstandingly co-operative since his arrival in Sydney, and I'm happy to oblige in return," Pinson said with a vigorous handshake.

Ava was standing several feet behind Dulles while all this was going on, and neither Johnson nor Pinson paid her the slightest attention.

"There's someone you have to meet," Dulles said. Ava took a couple of steps forward and smiled. "Gentlemen, this is Ava Lee. Phil, I know I mentioned her to you, but I wasn't sure if you'd told Manfred that Ava would be with me and will be a key player today."

"Indeed, he did," Pinson said, extending his hand.

"It's nice to meet you," Johnson said.

They were about to leave when Dulles said, "Just a minute." He looked at his phone. "I need to look after something first. Excuse me while I do." To Ava's surprise he walked towards a bank of seats about twenty metres away and sat down.

"How long have you two known each other?" Ava asked Johnson. In that instant she felt very much like her mother, who couldn't abide silence and was known for starting conversations with complete strangers.

"We met in Hong Kong at a regional meeting in 1997, just before the Brits turned over the island and territories to the PRC," he said, his eyes on Dulles. "As it turned out, he's from just outside Albany, in upstate New York, and my family farm is about fifty miles from his place. So we had geography in common — and bachelorhood. We've both moved around since then. We lost touch for a while when he was shipped to London and I was lost in the Langley maze, but we reconnected when we both got back to Asia. He's been a good friend. You never have to worry about your back when Alasdair's around."

Ava wondered if that last remark was intended for her, and how much detail Dulles had passed along to Johnson about their reason for being in Sydney. She wasn't about to ask. She was forming a question about what Hong Kong was like in 1997 when her phone vibrated and she saw that she had voicemail. She entered the access code and put the phone to her ear.

"Ava, this is Elisha. I want you to know that Zoey has already heard back from her colleagues in Indonesia and Malaysia. None of those ten students landed there. So I'm assuming those are dead ends. I'm sorry we can't be of more help. Call me if you need anything else."

"Shit," she said.

"Bad news?" Johnson said.

"Moderately."

"Here comes Alasdair," Pinson said.

Dulles strode towards them with purpose, his face blank. "Sorry about that," he said.

Pinson led the way, with Johnson at his heels. Dulles lagged a bit, and Ava sensed that he wanted her to do the same. When there were about five metres between them and the two men, he said, "I was speaking to Beirut. There's been a development that's going to need our attention, but I don't want to talk about it in front of Pinson. Once we're finished with Said, we'll figure out what to do."

Ava's immediate reaction was to ask a question, but Dulles had already sped up and was closing in on Pinson and Johnson. When she caught up to him, she said, "And I've heard from Manila. They checked with Indonesia and Malaysia, and neither country has any record of the students."

"Shit," he said.

"Exactly."

They left the terminal and walked into the bright morning sunlight. A white Holden Commodore was parked at the curb with an ON POLICE DUTY sign on the driver's-side dashboard. Pinson hit the key fob and the trunk opened. Ava and Dulles put their carry-ons into it and then climbed into the back seat.

"Do you still know where Said is?" Dulles said to Pinson.

"He's at his parents' house in Lakemba." Pinson looked at his watch. "He's most likely still in bed. He was up half the night on his computer."

"Where's Lakemba?"

"It's a Sydney suburb about a twenty-minute drive from here. It has a large Muslim population, mainly of Lebanese origin."

"What's the split between Shia and Sunni among Lakemba residents?"

"About fifty-fifty, but the Sunnis, especially those linked to Wahhabism — like your boy — cause us most of the problems. Last week we stopped two men from Lakemba from getting on a plane to join Daesh in Iraq."

"I've certainly heard of Wahhabism, but I don't know that much about it," Ava said.

"It's at the core of most of the fanatical Islamist groups in the world today," Pinson said.

"A cult? A sect?"

"Those terms don't come close to describing it. It has its own ideology: a blend of hatred towards everyone who isn't Sunni and an anti-modern romanticism. The combination fuels rage, particularly in these young men. We've been trying for months to shut down a madrassa in Lakemba — financed by money from Saudi Arabia — that preaches it, but the government won't let us do it. A breach of civil liberties, they say."

"Did Jason Said go there?"

"We don't know, but it's a reasonable assumption. The two men who were on their way to join Daesh certainly did."

"Daesh and ISIL are connected, aren't they?" Ava asked.

Johnson nodded. "In Arabic Daesh means 'al-Dawla al-Islamiya al-Iraq al-Sham,' and that translates to 'Islamic State of Iraq and the Levant' in English, or ISIL."

"Your Arabic has improved," Dulles said to him.

"Manfred makes me look like a beginner. The first time I referred to ISIL as Daesh and then tried to show off a bit with my Arabic, he informed me that *Daesh* can also sound like *daes*, which translates into 'one who crushes something underfoot.' And it can also sound like *dahes*, which means 'someone who sows discord.'"

"I am hopeless with languages. I spent all these years in Thailand and I can barely say hello and goodbye," Dulles said. "Ava, how about you?"

"I speak fluent Cantonese and Mandarin, but I can hardly take credit for it — that's how I was raised. I can't remember not being able to speak both them and English. They were interchangeable."

"Traffic isn't too bad," Pinson said as they left the airport.

"What's your plan for handling Said?" Johnson asked.

"We need to talk to him, that's all," Dulles said.

"Yes, but at the house or do you want to take him into custody?"

"We'll start at the house. If he stonewalls us, what are the options?"

"We can take him into preventive custody and hold him for up to fourteen days in isolation," Pinson said. "Most of them act brave when we take them in, but after a few days, when they realize that no lawyer, family member, or friend can help, they start to break down."

"We don't have time to wait for that to happen," Dulles said.

Pinson glanced sideways at Johnson, and Ava could see concern on his face.

"Manfred, we're not going to rough him up or do anything that would break Australian laws," Dulles said quickly. "We're just going to have to be especially persuasive. I've been told by a mutual acquaintance of Ava's that that's one of her many talents."

Ava stiffened. The acquaintance was obviously Poirier. What else had he told Dulles?

"I wasn't thinking anything different," Pinson said.

"How old is this Jason Said?" Johnson asked.

"He's twenty," Dulles said.

"They get them young here," Pinson said.

"They get them young everywhere. What makes this one interesting is that he walked away and came home."

"Walked away from what?"

"I can't discuss that," Dulles said.

"Alasdair, if he represents any kind of threat—"

"We'd tell you, but we don't think he does," Dulles said. "If that opinion changes, you can count on our letting you know."

Ava saw a sign that read LAKEMBA, and a few moments later Pinson eased the car onto a street lined with shops. It wasn't eight a.m. yet, but all the stores were open for business and the sidewalks were crowded with people. They drove past an IGA advertising halal meat, a Masri Brothers kitchenware store, a Boutique Al-Houda, and a halal meat shop. About a kilometre along, Pinson turned left and entered the outskirts of a residential area. The stores disappeared, replaced by bungalows, split-levels, and the occasional two-storey home. The houses were well maintained and almost uniformly fronted by bushes, flowerbeds, and lawns.

"The family lives at the end of the street," Pinson said. "The father is a foreman at a well-established construction company. The mother has never worked outside the home. There's an older brother who's an elementary school teacher."

About thirty metres ahead Ava saw a parked white Commodore with two men inside. "Those are my men," Pinson said. He stopped his car alongside the vehicle and the man closest to them rolled down his window. Pinson did the same. "The father and brother have gone to work," the man said.

The Said home was a two-storey brick house with a terrace on the upper floor that faced the street. Ava could see a woman in a housecoat hanging shirts on a drying rack on the terrace. Pinson parked his car in front of the Commodore and looked up at the woman. When she went inside, he waited for a minute and then said, "Let's go."

The four of them walked up the gravel path. Ava wondered what the woman would think when she opened the door and saw them standing there. Pinson pressed the doorbell. When there wasn't a response, he pushed it again. The door finally opened a crack and the woman peered out from under a chain. "Yes?" she said, her face confused and fearful.

"My name is Manfred Pinson and I'm an officer with the Australian National Security Agency," he said, holding up his badge. "We're here to speak with your son, Jason Said."

"He's not here," she said.

Pinson looked down at her and drew a deep breath. "Mrs. Said, we know Jason is here. You need to understand that we're not here to arrest him; we just need to speak to him. But if you persist in denying that he's at home, we'll have no other choice than to enter your residence forcefully. And if we have to do that, things will not go well for Jason."

She closed her eyes and her chin dropped to her chest.

"I promise you, Mrs. Said, if you open the door, it will go much better for you and Jason," Pinson said.

She looked up at Pinson. He arched his eyebrows and gave her the slightest smile. Her hand reached up and the chain fell away. Ava and the three men stepped inside.

"Is he still sleeping?" Pinson asked.

She nodded.

"Wake him please, and try not to alarm him. We want to have a talk with him, nothing more. Do you want me to come with you?"

"I know how to talk to my own son," she said.

They stood in the hallway and watched her slowly climb the stairs. "Do you think this is wise?" Johnson asked.

"She'll bring him down. She's a Lakemba mum. She'll do anything, whatever it takes, to keep her son out of trouble, and she knows we could be trouble. And he'll listen to her. Their mothers are the only people — aside from their imams — that some of these guys listen to."

"I don't want to give her more than five minutes," Johnson said.

They waited closer to ten, and Ava could feel Johnson becoming increasingly agitated. She was starting to get anxious herself when Mrs. Said reappeared. Behind her was a young man in a black T-shirt and jeans. He looked down at them with disdain.

"Where do you want to do this?" Pinson asked Dulles.

"Anywhere we can have privacy," Dulles said.

"The kitchen?"

"Sure."

Pinson waited until the woman and her son reached the bottom of the stairs. Then he said, "Mrs. Said, Agent Dulles and Ms. Lee here will be speaking privately to Jason in the kitchen. Why don't you sit with us in the living room."

"Is there any point in my objecting?" she said.

"No."

Jason Said emerged from behind his mother and Ava had her first good look at him. He was skinny, about five foot nine, and his hair was shaved into a wide mohawk. He had a thin moustache and a weak attempt at a beard. His puffy eyes glared at them.

"Where's the kitchen?" Dulles asked.

"Over there." Mrs. Said pointed to the left. "There's still coffee in the pot if you want any."

"Thanks, I'd love some," Ava said. The others shook their heads.

"Let's go," Dulles said to Jason.

The kitchen was small, with a round wooden table and four chairs. Ava poured a coffee, turned to Jason, and said, "Do you want something to drink?"

"I'd like some water," he said, but remained standing until Dulles and Ava were seated. Dulles didn't take his eyes off Said while the young man filled a glass, drank half, refilled it, and then joined them at the table.

"Do you know why we're here?" Dulles asked.

"No."

"Is that because you have zero idea or too many things to choose from?"

"Zero idea."

"I'm American and my colleague here is Canadian, but we work closely with Australian national security, which is why Agent Pinson is here."

"I've never been to America or Canada, and I've never done anything that should interest either of you."

"It interests us that you went to the Philippines and that until two months ago you were attending Zakat College in Tawi-Tawi."

"What's it to you?"

"That depends entirely on what you tell us about your time there."

"There's nothing to tell."

"That's not true," Ava said.

He looked at her as if he were noticing her for the first time. "I've got fuck all to tell."

Dulles leaned forward, placing his hand on Said's knee. He didn't apply any pressure but Said recoiled anyway. "Jason, there are two ways we can do this. The easy way is for us to ask you questions and for you to answer them honestly. If that's the way it plays out, we'll leave when we're finished and we won't tell anyone what you said. There will be no charges, no record that we met — nothing.

"On the other hand, if you decide to be foolish and not co-operate, then, at our request, Agent Pinson will take you into custody and you'll be held in isolation for at least fourteen days. You can expect to be interrogated by people who are much less accommodating than us. Everything you say will be on the record. And if you've done anything illegal, or even thought about doing anything illegal, you can expect that they'll find out and you can expect charges to be laid."

Said tried to look at Dulles but his eyes wandered.

"Jason," Ava said gently, "they will find something to pin on you even if you haven't done anything. You know how they operate. They'll grab your computer and get into your hard drive, and once that happens an innocent web search will be interpreted as something far more sinister and illegal."

"They are all so full of bullshit," he said.

"Maybe they are, but that doesn't discount the power they have and the damage they can do to you and your entire family," she said.

He nodded.

"Look, we're not expecting you to tell us your life story. Why don't we start with me asking a few basic questions and see where that leads," Ava said. "Our interest is in the Philippines. We don't care what you did before you got there or what your plans are now...unless, of course, they still involve Zakat College."

He didn't react. There were two ways for her interpret that, and she decided to assume it was positive.

"You're a Sunni, correct?" she said.

"You know that already," he said after a slight hesitation.

Ava knew more than that. She now knew he would talk to her. She glanced at Dulles, not sure if she had overstepped her bounds.

"Go ahead, he's all yours," he said.

## 27

**OVER THE YEARS AVA HAD DEVELOPED A SENSE OF** what motivated people to open up to her. In her old business it had often been coercion, sometimes physical. But she rarely took that route until she'd exhausted other, more reasonable options. The problem she'd faced was that many of the people she was dealing with were the opposite of reasonable. However, her experience and instincts told her that Said was going to be co-operative. Now it was up to her to ask the right questions and maintain the right tone.

"And the other students at the college were also Sunni?"

"Yes."

"And Imam Tariq al-Bashir?"

"Yes."

"Was he Wahhabi?"

"Yes."

"We were told that he has a foreign accent. Do you know where he's from?"

He shrugged.

Ava hesitated. She realized she might have pushed him

on the imam too soon. "We're curious about how you discovered Zakat College," she said.

"I found it online."

"We looked for it there and found no references."

"It was through a ghost website."

"What does that mean?"

"Now you see it, now you don't."

"I'm not very technical. Can you explain that to me?"

"You'll be looking at a website and another will appear for maybe a few seconds or even minutes, urging you to visit another website in half an hour. When you log in to that one, it might direct you to another. And so on, until you reach the ultimate destination."

"What was that final website?"

He reached for his glass of water.

"I don't care what you were searching for or why you were doing it," Ava said. "All I care about is where you ended up."

"I wanted to join the holy war," he said. "I wanted to help establish a true Islamic state."

"And that was the college's objective?"

He shook his head, rose from the chair, and walked to the kitchen window. As he gazed out at the back garden, she saw his shoulders slump and knew he felt conflicted.

"What was the name of the final website, the one that led you to the college?" she asked again.

"Five fourteen forty-eight," he mumbled.

"Was that expressed in numbers or words?"

"Numbers."

"How long did it take you to find it, for you to get there?"

"Months. After I found it the first time it disappeared, and I couldn't locate it again until three months later."

"Then what did you do?"

"I applied to Zakat College."

"Just like that?"

"No. I was directed to other websites and asked to supply all kinds of personal information. They were obviously checking on me."

"And you met their criteria," she said.

"Yeah."

"What did you think you were signing up for?"

"I told you already," he said.

"You could have joined a holy war without going to a college in the Philippines. You could have gone directly to Syria or Iraq."

"I didn't know how to get there from here."

*He's just a boy*, Ava thought. *He lives at home in Lakemba where his mother makes his meals and does his laundry. Of course he didn't know how to get to Syria or Iraq. He's a dreamer, and he would have kept on dreaming if someone hadn't taken him under their wing.*

"By my calculation, you flew to the Philippines four months ago."

"That's about right."

"Did you book your own flight?"

"Yeah."

"Who paid for the airfare?"

"I did, but they reimbursed me when I arrived in Tawi-Tawi."

"Did they give you any special instructions about how to travel or what to put on your landing card, or anything at all about the trip?"

"No, they just told me to send my itinerary when my flight

was booked and that they'd arrange for me to be picked up at the airport."

"Emailed to what address?"

"It wasn't email, it was regular mail."

"That was clever. Ghost websites and snail mail — an unlikely combination," Ava said, catching Dulles's eye. She turned back to Jason. "When you left Sydney, did you tell your parents where you were going?"

"I didn't tell them anything, not even that I was leaving. None of us were supposed to tell our families about the college," he said. "I wrote to them when I got to Tawi-Tawi and told them not to worry."

"Postal mail again?"

"Yeah, and with no return address. Not that it mattered. They told me they never got the letter anyway."

"So they must have been especially pleased when you came home and they knew you were safe."

"My mother cried for two days."

"Who can blame her? She must have been worried sick about you," Ava said.

He broke his gaze from the window and turned towards her with a pained look on his face.

"How many other students were at the college when you got there?" she asked, trying to temper his emotions.

"More than fifty. I was one of the last to arrive."

"From what I've seen from the records, you were a mixed bunch."

"What do you mean? We were all Sunni."

"I meant in terms of nationality."

"We didn't think like that. Where we came from didn't matter. We were all brothers, there to help form and be part of a new state. The imam stressed that every day. He said that for us to succeed, we had to have the same sense of unity that the world's Jews do, but we had to apply it in an even more dedicated way. He said that Israel wouldn't exist if all the other Jews in the world didn't support it."

"He spoke admiringly about the Jewish people?"

"No, he hates the Jews and he hates Israel. He said they are our most important enemy, but if we want to bring them down, we need to understand them and the power they exercise in the Middle East and the rest of the world." He said it matter-of-factly, without any passion.

"My understanding is that the imam spoke to the students every morning after prayer," she said.

"That was the schedule."

"I was told he preached jihad."

"He said there had to be a holy war."

"There is one now, is there not? Was he advocating that you join ISIL, Daesh? Was he recruiting for them?"

"He said they are misdirected, although he didn't say that at first," he said. "For the first weeks we were at the college, he talked about jihad in general terms, and about how the Koran endorses and encourages the defence of Islam. He said it was our duty. He said it would be our blessing. He said it would guarantee our entry into heaven."

"And you all believed him?"

"Nearly all of us believed that before we got there."

"Of course you did," she said. "But still, the imam waited for four weeks before he asked you to formally commit to jihad?"

"He did, and we were ready, and everyone did commit."

"I'm told that a few didn't."

"In my class there was one. He was allowed to leave."

"Did he say why?"

"It was a private conversation between him and one of the imam's assistants. None of us spoke to him after. He was just gone."

"What was his name?"

"I don't remember."

"Okay," Ava said. "Why don't you tell me now what you did after you all made that first commitment."

"We learned to make bombs. We learned to assemble, arm, and fire all kinds of weapons," he said. "And then were taught how, when, and where to detonate bombs with maximum effect and how best to kill with the weapons."

"Was there talk about suicide bombings and attacks?"

"No, it was exactly the opposite. The imam said the longer we stayed in the war, the more likely our victory would be."

## 28

**AVA GOT HERSELF ANOTHER COFFEE, BRUSHING PAST**
Jason as she did. He hadn't left his position near the window
and avoided looking at her. When she sat at the table again,
she changed seats so she could have a better view of his face.

"Tell me more about the imam," she said.

"Like what?" he said, suddenly defensive.

"What does he look like? Is he tall, short, fat, thin?"

"Medium height, medium build, black hair and beard."

"Does he wear traditional clothing?"

"Of course."

"How about his assistants?"

"They all wore a *thawb* except when we were building
and exploding bombs. For that they'd change into jeans and
shirts."

"The imam too?"

"He never had anything to do with the bombs or weapons."

"Did he ever leave the college while you were there?"

"Not that I saw."

"And his assistants?"

"The same, I think."

"Where did you eat?"

"There's a cafeteria."

"Did he eat with you?"

"No, he and his assistants had a private dining room, and they lived in a separate wing of the college."

"So you didn't see the imam often."

"At prayers and the morning lectures. For the rest of the time he kept to himself."

"Was there anything striking about him? Did he have any facial features or habits or mannerisms that stood out?"

He hesitated. "His voice," he finally said.

"What about it?"

"It was different."

"How?"

"He spoke softly, so quietly that even when he was using a microphone, you had to strain to hear him," he said. "One of the other students — he was English and had studied communications at university — said it was a technique, a way of forcing us to concentrate on what he was saying. Whatever it was, it worked. He could be mesmerizing."

"Is 'mesmerizing' your word for him?"

"No, the English student's, but I thought it fitted," he said.

"I heard that the imam has an accent that isn't Middle Eastern or Filipino, or Australian, for that matter."

He nodded. "No one in the class could identify it. Some thought he was American or Canadian, or maybe a foreigner who'd been educated in North America."

"No one asked?"

"You didn't ask questions of or about the imam, or his assistants."

"But they asked them of you, correct?"

"What are you driving at?"

"Well, you told me you were asked if you would commit to jihad. I'm sure that, before that happened, you were questioned about your faith and your level of devotion."

"That's true."

"And then after you went through weapons training, you were asked to make another commitment, a final commitment."

"How do you know that?" he asked.

"You aren't the only person we're speaking to," she said.

"I was the only person from my class who left the college then."

"Yes, but there were other classes and other students, and some of them left too."

"I wouldn't know anything about that."

"I wouldn't expect you to," she said. "What I'm interested in knowing is how this final commitment was presented to you and why you responded the way you did."

His face contorted. "I wanted to say yes to them."

"Say yes to whom?"

"I met with two of the assistants in an office in their wing. It was just the three of us. I know that's how they did it with everyone — two assistants and one student in a private meeting. They told me that my work had been outstanding and that I'd been selected to take part in a very special project."

"Where?"

"Miami, Florida."

"You were to go there by yourself?"

"They said they have several cells already in place there, and that if I agreed to go, I'd be assigned to one of them."

"How many people in the cell?"

"They didn't tell me."

"Did they tell you about the project?" she asked.

"Yes. They said there's an American Jewish Congress conference scheduled to start there on May fourteenth. Two separate cells are going to orchestrate an attack during the opening ceremony. They said there will be thousands of wealthy and influential Jews assembled in that one place, and they asked if I could imagine how much damage thirty *ghazi* could inflict in such a confined space with unlimited firepower."

"*Ghazi?*"

"Warriors."

"So that means there are presumably fifteen people in each cell."

"I guess so. I never took the time to think of it that way."

"And the date May fourteenth was specifically mentioned?"

"It was."

"And you said no to them, just like that?"

"No, I thought about it for two days before I told them."

"What was there to think about?"

"One of the assistants started talking about that day — about May fourteenth — as a day of reckoning. He said they have thousands of warriors in place in the U.S., France, and England, and in countries surrounding Israel, ready to strike. He said they are going to obliterate the Jews — the Jews who matter, the wealthy Jews who keep Israel strong. He said that if we bring them down, Israel will follow."

"What was your objection to that?" she said.

He lowered his head and said, almost regretfully, "I know too many Jewish people who have been good to me and my family. The construction company my father works for is owned by Mr. Loeb. My father says we wouldn't have a decent life in this country without his generosity. And not only us. He sponsored my father's brother and his family, and one more Lebanese family I know of. My father mentions him in his prayers. He and his wife have been guests in our home. He loaned my brother, with no interest, the money he needed to go to teacher's college. How could I kill a man — any man — just because he is Jewish? What if he was related to Mr. Loeb?"

"Did you mention Mr. Loeb to the assistants?"

"No."

"What reason did you give for not making the final commitment?"

"I said I want to fight for the creation of a homeland in the Middle East. I said I want to be a *ghazi*, a soldier, but I have no interest in killing civilians in Miami."

"Did they argue with you?"

"No."

"They just let you leave?"

"No. They offered me a different assignment in New York City, but it was more of the same — an attack on the Bank of Israel. I said no."

"Were they angry?"

"More confused, and a bit annoyed."

"At any time, Jason, did they tell you how they planned to get you and the other students into the United States and those other countries?"

"They seemed to take it for granted that they could. It didn't get so far with me that they went into detail, but some of the other students were already talking about what they would do when they got to places like New York."

"So you said no to them and you made it stick."

"I did, and then they told me I had to leave the college within an hour and that I wasn't to talk to any other student," he said. "They gave me the money to buy a plane ticket home."

"It was that simple?"

"I wish it was," he said. "They told me that they know where I live and where my family works and lives, and that if I speak to anyone about the college, they will kill us all."

"And here you are talking to me," Ava said gently.

"I'm not entirely stupid," he said. "You found me. You obviously know a lot about the college. This can't end well for them."

"No, I don't think it will," Dulles said.

"What about me?"

"Have you been completely honest?" Dulles said.

"I have."

"I don't doubt you. If nothing changes our mind on that, then what I said to you at the beginning of our conversation still holds. What was said here will remain between us and I'll tell Mr. Pinson that you've been entirely co-operative."

"I told you the absolute truth."

"There is one thing I'd like to ask," Dulles said. "What specific reason did the imam give to justify his determination to attack Jews?"

"He said they're godless."

"That's all?"

"Godless parasites, and that the world won't have any peace until they've been completely eradicated."

## 29

**MRS. SAID LOOKED TERRIFIED WHEN AVA, DULLES, AND** her son entered the living room.

"We've finished our interview with your son," Dulles said. "He'll be staying home with you."

She brushed tears from her eyes.

"You have every reason to be proud of him," Dulles said. "He's obviously been raised in a fine household."

"Are we finished?" Pinson asked.

"Yes, that's it. We have everything we need for now. Jason has been co-operative," Dulles said, and then turned towards the young man. "Please don't take any trips in the immediate future. We'll need to know where you are in case we need to speak to you again. And please don't make phone calls to any of your acquaintances in the Philippines."

They thanked Mrs. Said for her co-operation and left the house. When they reached the car, Dulles said to Pinson, "I can't thank you enough for this."

"My pleasure," he said.

Then Dulles turned to Ava. "You were fantastic in there.

If you ever need a job, let me know. Good interrogators are hard to find."

"I hardly consider it an interrogation," she said. "He's just a scared, confused kid."

"That's why you were so damn effective. When we spoke to Chang about you, he said one of your strengths is your ability to get all kinds of people to trust you."

"You spoke to Chang?"

"I know you said you knew him, but in our business we can't take anything at face value," Dulles said. "But don't sound so worried; he doesn't know we're working together. We didn't speak to him directly. We had a third party, a businessman, call him. I hope that doesn't offend you."

"What if it does?"

"There's nothing we can do about it now and we're both in too deep. But I promise you, no more due diligence."

Johnson stood by the front passenger door of the Commodore. "So what now?" he asked.

Dulles looked at his watch. "It's going on nine-thirty here, which means it's one-thirty in the morning in Lebanon. Can Manfred take us to your office, Phil? I have a man in Beirut waiting for me to call him."

"No problem," Pinson said.

The four of them got into the car. They fell silent, and Ava took advantage of the quiet to close her eyes, rest her head against the back of the seat, and replay in her mind the conversation with Jason Said. Did she believe him? There was no other question that mattered. She thought about what Ben and Alcem had told them and knew there were no discrepancies between their story and Said's. In fact, the only reason she had to question Said's tale was its enormity.

If he was correct, he would have joined a cell in Miami that had about fifteen people in it. She guessed that 150 students had gone through the college. If each had joined a cell of a similar size, how many terrorists were waiting for May 14? More than two thousand. The number made her tremble.

"Are you okay?" Dulles asked.

"I'm thinking about May fourteenth, so no, I'm not okay."

"Me neither, but we'll talk about Lebanon when we get to the office. It may help," he said.

"I don't know if that's possible," she muttered.

Pinson drove for close to half an hour before stopping in front of a looming office tower in a crowded commercial area. Ava and the Americans piled out. After another exchange of thank-yous with Pinson, they went into the lobby and Johnson led them to a bank of elevators. Five minutes later they exited on the forty-eighth floor and walked into the office of the American Center for Pacific Rim Studies.

"They're with me and they don't have to sign in," Johnson said as he led them past a receptionist and then through a door that required a security code.

"I need some privacy, Phil," Dulles said.

"You can use the boardroom," Johnson said. He walked down the hallway and opened a door, motioning for them to go in. "My office is at the end. I'll leave the door open. Come and get me if you need anything."

"Thanks," Dulles said.

"When do you intend to leave Sydney?"

"That depends on the conversations I'm about to have."

"Naturally," Johnson said.

The boardroom was long and narrow. Ten seats surrounded an old wooden table. Dulles took the chair at the end. Ava sat in the one on his right. "Did you tell Phil Johnson anything about why we're here?" she asked.

"Are you asking if I mentioned the college?"

"Yes."

"It wasn't necessary."

"And he's not curious?"

"I'm sure he is, but he knows better than to ask questions."

"I'm not quite so disciplined," Ava said. "What the hell is going on in Lebanon?"

"We're about to find out in more detail," he said, taking his phone from his pocket. "Bobby Delvano, one of our people in Beirut, was the person I was speaking to at the airport. He was at the Paradise Casino earlier with some people from the Lebanese security forces, and they spoke to the manager. Our man is known to the manager only as Fileeb al-Touma, and he's a valued customer, what they refer to in that business as a whale — a gambler who plays for huge stakes. The story is that al-Touma plays blackjack in the private high-limit room for ten thousand dollars a hand. The manager maintains that he's been winning consistently for two years."

"He's been making large weekly deposits. I know enough about gambling and blackjack odds to know that it's impossible to win that often and that much."

"Bobby and I agree with you, but it isn't an opinion the casino manager shares."

"What other information have you got out of him?"

"That's another problem. The manager is reluctant to tell us anything beyond the fact that al-Touma is a regular and highly prized customer," Dulles said. "How someone can win millions from a casino and still be considered a prized customer is a bit of mystery, but then I'm not in that business."

"They'll have complete financial records related to his buy-ins and cash-outs, and they'll have filmed all of his play."

"I know, but he's not prepared to make any of that available to us. He said they're a private business and those are private records."

"Can't the Lebanese security forces help? Can't they lean on the owner?"

"Let's find out, because that's exactly what we asked them to do," Dulles said. He hit a number on his phone and placed the device on the table.

"Delvano."

"Bobby, it's Alasdair. I have you on speakerphone and Ava Lee is with me. She's the woman who I told you is helping me on this project."

"Hello, Ava," Delvano said.

"Hello."

"Well, what do we have?" Dulles said.

"Until a few hours ago, one very frightened manager. The Lebanese boys here did a number on him. To give him some credit, he didn't budge on revealing much more about al-Touma. He said that had to come from the owners, and when we pressed him on the ownership, he coughed up two local names. They've just left the casino."

"Who are they?"

"Two quite ordinary businessmen."

"Does the service know anything about them? Are they connected to any Muslim organizations?"

"Alasdair, they're both Christians. They're Maronites, a branch of the Catholic Church."

"What the hell?"

"They claim they have nothing to do with running the

casino. They said all those decisions are made by the operator, Pinetree Gaming," he said. "And when I pushed them on al-Touma, they told me the same thing. They said they obviously know of him but that I have to talk to Pinetree."

"Bobby, the casino is owned by a numbered company in Liechtenstein. They must have shares in it."

"They readily admitted that they do, but the actual operations of the casino are contracted out to Pinetree. They have zero day-to-day involvement."

"We'll come back to Pinetree in a minute," Dulles said. "Tell me, why did they set up the casino as a numbered company in the first place?"

"It wasn't their decision. They were asked to invest in the business by a mutual friend, and they said they owed him some favours and obliged. He established the structure and controls everything."

"Who is this friend?"

Delvano hesitated and then said, "Tom Allison."

Dulles leaned forward until his mouth was directly over the phone. "Are you fucking with me?"

"Only if they're fucking with me, and I don't think they are. We did some research on Pinetree Gaming. It's an Atlanta-based and relatively small-time casino owner and operator. It was bought three years ago by the Harvest Group, and of course the principal shareholder and controlling partner in Harvest is Tom Allison."

"God help us."

"I don't think you're being ironic, but I wouldn't blame you if you were," Delvano said. "And now it gets even stranger. I phoned Pinetree, explained who I am, and told them that we need information on a Fileeb al-Touma who gambles at the Paradise Casino in Beirut. They informed me that he's a preferred customer on a very exclusive list, and that access to any information on the list has to be approved by their ownership, the Harvest Group."

"Who in the Harvest Group did they have to talk to?"

"They didn't give me a name. When I pressed them, they said if I provide the details I want they'll pass the request along and get back to me."

"That's bullshit."

"I know, so I went one step further. I called the Harvest Group head office in Dallas and asked to speak to Tom Allison. I figured I might be able to shake things up by doing that."

"What happened?

"Nothing. They took my name and number and said some-one would call."

"I know Allison," Dulles said.

"Who doesn't?"

"I mean I've actually met him," Dulles said. "When I was in London acting as commercial attaché, he approached the office for help in securing U.K. government contracts for some equipment company he owned. We had lunch and a couple of dinners together. They eventually did land some contracts, and he sent me a thank-you note and an expensive bottle of Scotch."

"Maybe you should be the one to call him," Delvano said.

"I think I should."

"Do you want the office number?"

Dulles looked at his watch and did a quick calculation. "The office will be closed now. Besides, I think I still have his cellphone number and personal email address in my Rolodex."

"Who keeps a Rolodex anymore?"

"I do. They're hard to lose and not that easy to steal."

"Well, good luck with that," Delvano said. "Now what is it you want me to do here, besides keep trying to find al-Touma?"

"Tell the casino manager that we're going to get approval from Pinetree to access al-Touma's financial records and any videos they have of him. He should start getting them organized. If he bitches about the videos, tell him we can provide him with the approximate dates when al-Touma was there."

"You're assuming a day or two before he flew to Amman to make deposits?"

"Yes," Dulles said. "And Bobby, can I also assume that the manager and the two owners you met have been told not to contact al-Touma?"

"Absolutely, and quite forcefully."

"Okay. Stay in touch."

He shut off the phone and then pushed the chair back from the table, leaned back, and linked his hands behind his head. "This is bizarre," he said. "Have you heard of Tom Allison in Canada?"

"An American billionaire who made his first fortune in oil and manufacturing, then a second and larger fortune by being the money angel for tens, if not hundreds, of high-tech start-ups, some of which hit it very, very big."

"That's him," he said. "What you neglected to mention — and what made me say 'bizarre' — is that he's also a leading right-wing Republican, a publicly loud fundamentalist Christian, and an ardent defender of Israel and all things Jewish."

"Oh," said Ava.

"That may be the most restrained reaction I've ever heard."

Ava started to reply when her phone rang. She saw Wahab's number and felt her pulse quicken. "Yes?" she said. "Do you have something?"

"We have al-Bashir's hairbrush and toothbrush. Now what do we do?"

"Just a second," Ava said, covering the mouthpiece. "The boys from Bongao have two of the imam's brushes. What should we do with them?" she asked Dulles.

"Have someone fly to Manila and I'll send Susan Crawford to the airport to meet them. She'll be in the arrivals hall. She's tall and blonde and will be holding a sign with the person's name on it. We'll need to know who's coming and the flight details."

Ava returned to Wahab and repeated the instructions.

"I'll send Ben," he said. "Who is Susan Crawford?"

"A friend of mine, someone you can trust."

He hesitated, then said, "As you know, there's only the one flight from Bongao to Zamboanga. He'll get on the next one and then connect to the same flight you took to Manila. If there's any change in those plans, I'll phone. Otherwise, tell Ms. Crawford that Ben will see her at the airport."

"It's being arranged," Ava said to Dulles after hanging up. "Ben will be bringing the brushes to Manila tonight on a Cebu Pacific flight from Zamboanga that lands at eight p.m."

"I'll call Susan," he said.

It took him only a few minutes to brief her, and then he said, "Look at the Rolodex in my office, will you? There should be a cellphone number and email address for Tom Allison. I need them."

"How long will it take to check the fingerprints?" Ava asked while they waited for Crawford.

"The lab is part of the Philippines National Bureau of Investigation. It's first-rate but we don't have any control over it and we aren't always a priority. Susan knows this is important and she'll push them. If she's her typically effective self, I would expect to get results tomorrow night or the day after."

"I don't like to jinx myself," Ava said, "but you know, I have a feeling that things are starting to move in the right direction."

Susan Crawford came on the line before Dulles could respond.

"She just gave me Allison's contact info," Dulles said a moment later. "Now we'll find out if your intuition is correct."

## 30

**DULLES CALLED THE CELL NUMBER CRAWFORD HAD**
given him, listened for a few seconds, and shook his head
in disappointment at Ava. Then he said, "Mr. Allison, this
is Alasdair Dulles calling. I'm not sure if you remember me,
but I was the American commercial attaché in London when
you were trying to land some government contracts. I need
to talk to you on a matter that is of some importance to me
and our government. I'm currently stationed in Manila but
I'm phoning you from Sydney. I think that makes me about
fourteen hours ahead of Dallas. Please call me whenever
you can."

"Are you going to send an email as well?" Ava asked when
he was finished.

"Not yet. I'll wait until tonight."

"What are the chances he'll call back?" she said.

"Slim at best," he said.

"So what now, we just wait?"

"Yes, for a while at least," he said, just as his phone sounded.
They both stared at it.

"It couldn't be possible, could it?" Ava said.

Dulles picked up the phone. "This is Alasdair Dulles." He paused, the phone pressed against his ear. "Tom, thank you so much for calling me back." He smiled at Ava as he put the phone on speaker mode and placed it on the table. Ava leaned in.

"How could I not? You were most obliging when I was in London, and your message was full of mystery," Allison said. He spoke slowly, carefully pronouncing every word. It was an affected style and could easily have sounded stilted and artificial, but with Allison's deep bass voice, the way he stressed inflections made it sound as if he were speaking a song.

"I'm pleased you said 'mystery,' because I think that describes what I'm involved in."

"I'm slightly flattered but even more confused. Why do you think I might be able to help you with it?"

"Well, it concerns the Paradise Casino in Beirut, which I understand you own part of."

"Alasdair, that casino is part of Pinetree Gaming, a rather small business I rather reluctantly invested in a few years ago. It was at the urging of one of my strategic planners, who was enamoured with the profits being generated by the casinos in Macau. His enthusiasm wasn't warranted."

"But you do know of the casino?"

"Of course."

"How about a man named Fileeb al-Touma? Or Omar Obeidat?

"I've never heard of either of them."

"We're told they're one and the same, and that he's referred to as a whale."

"I know enough about the casino business to know what a whale is, and I also know they come in many sizes."

"This one has evidently won about five million dollars at the Paradise Casino over the past two to three years."

"From what I've been told, we have whales who can win or lose that over a weekend."

"I'm not interested in other whales."

"And what is your interest in this Mr. . . . al-what?"

"Al-Touma."

"So, what has Mr. al-Touma done to warrant so much attention from a commercial attaché with the U.S. government?"

"I'm no longer with the commercial division," Dulles said.

"I thought not," Allison said with a laugh. "In fact, when I met you in London, it was suggested to me that you have additional and strictly non-commercial duties."

"That is the case."

"I understand. You don't need to elaborate."

"Thank you," Dulles said. "So now that we've established who's who, I would like to be completely straightforward with you."

"You shouldn't have called if that wasn't your intention."

"Tom, there are security concerns that have to be respected."

"Alasdair, were you aware that I sit on the president's most influential economic advisory panel?"

"No, I wasn't."

"I was honoured when the president offered me the appointment, but even with his backing, I was still subjected to a substantial vetting process," he said. "Among other things, I had to qualify for one of the highest levels of security clearance."

"That's good to know, but this is a particularly sensitive matter."

"I don't care how sensitive it is. If you're asking for my help, you're going to have to put some faith in me and be more forthcoming," Allison said. "Throwing a name or two at me in conjunction with one of my minor investments doesn't qualify as being forthcoming. It isn't likely to elicit the kind of response you want."

Dulles glanced at Ava. She could see he was struggling with the conversation. "Be blunter," she whispered.

"Tom, I don't know what level of security clearance you have, but whatever it is, it has to be applied," Dulles finally said. "This has to be a conversation between just you and me. No one else can be told about what we discuss."

"I can agree to that."

"In that case, let me tell you that we have reason to believe that this man al-Touma has been using the Paradise Casino to launder money."

"Okay. Assuming you're correct, why isn't that an issue for the Lebanese tax authorities to pursue? Why are you talking to me about security clearance?"

"Because we also believe that the money is being used to fund a terrorist organization."

Allison became quiet, and Ava thought she heard the sound of footsteps on the other end of the line. "Say that again," he finally said.

"We aren't inventing it," Dulles said. "We have a money trail that starts at your casino, winds its way through banks in Riyadh and Amman, and ends up in a bank on one of the most isolated islands in the Philippines, where it is being use to fund a college that is training terrorists."

"How do you know all this? How do you know the money comes from the Paradise?"

"I can't get into that level of detail over the phone."

"And what possible proof can you have that the casino is an active participant in this money-laundering scheme?"

"Truthfully, that is a supposition. We can't confirm or disprove it without your organization's co-operation."

"Which organization? I have interests in many."

"Pinetree, or whoever can give us the information we're looking for."

"I have virtually nothing to do with that company. It's a pimple on our corporate ass."

"That may be the case, but whenever we ask questions, we're directed further up the line. I thought you might be able to break the logjam for us."

"I'll do better than that," Allison said abruptly, his voice rising. "I'll make the enquiries myself. I'll get to the bottom of this."

"As generous an offer as that is, we can't be excluded from the process," Dulles said.

"Where are you exactly? Are you really in Sydney?"

"I am."

"Well, I'm in Hong Kong. Can you meet me here?"

"I guess that's possible."

"When can you come?"

"Today?"

Allison hesitated, and Ava wondered if he was reconsidering the invitation. "Sure, that would work," he finally said. "My schedule is full today, but you won't get here until tonight, and by then I'll make sure I've talked to my people."

"I'm sure we can find a flight."

"I'll make enquiries. By the time you arrive, I'll have some answers for you."

"Where are you staying?"

"The Island Shangri-La in Central."

"I know it."

"You'll be alone?"

"No, I have a colleague, Ava Lee, who'll be coming with me."

"Call me when you land," he said. "I'll leave the entire evening open."

## 31

**PHIL JOHNSON DROVE THEM TO THE AIRPORT. THEY** were on a Cathay Pacific flight that was departing at five after two and would get them into Hong Kong at 9:30 p.m. local time. Ava sensed that, despite Dulles's remark about his lack of curiosity, Johnson was bursting with questions. But all he did was make laughing comments about the short length of their stay. He dropped them off in front of the terminal. "Have a safe journey, and please let me know how this — whatever it is — ends," he said.

They hurried through the terminal, checked in, cleared Immigration and Security, and made it to the gate about five minutes before boarding started. They were seated separately again, and that was fine with Ava. Her head was a jumble, what with Tom Allison now added to the mix of the casino, al-Touma, Jason Said, and Imam Tariq al-Bashir. *Is there no end to this?* she thought.

When they were airborne, she pulled out her notebook and began to write down, in as much detail as she could remember, her conversation with Said and Dulles's with Allison. She filled three pages and then went back over them, underlining points that raised questions or needed clarification. Most of them were related to Allison. Jason Said's recital had the advantage of being familiar, thanks to Ben and Alcem. Still, there were new elements that grabbed her attention, and one was the website that had led him to Zakat College. She couldn't believe that the numbers the website used for its address were random. And as for Allison, why had he returned Dulles's call so quickly, and why was he being so co-operative? Ava knew men with his kind of power and money, and there was no way they would pick up the phone themselves to call someone who was at best a casual acquaintance. But then, she thought, most of the men she knew were Asian. Maybe American billionaires like Allison were different, or maybe it was because he felt — given his connections with the government — an obligation to help however he could.

She considered discussing the website address with Dulles. He was sitting a few rows in front of her, but she saw that his seat was reclined and she guessed he was sleeping. *That's not a bad idea*, she thought, but then dinner service began, and she realized she hadn't eaten all day.

After dinner she located the classic movie channel and watched *High Noon*. She was about halfway through when she remembered Pang Fai's description of the movie she was making. It was also about a person taking on the system. Ava realized how much she missed Fai and wished they were together. As the film ended, Ava drank the rest of her second glass of white wine and then fell asleep, imagining Fai curled up next to her.

They began their descent into Chek Lap Kok Airport before nine. It was odd for her to fly into Hong Kong and not be met at the airport. During her ten years working with Uncle, she'd been there countless times, and with very few exceptions he was always there to greet her, usually sitting in the Kit Kat Koffee House with a racing form on the table and a cigarette in his mouth. Since his death, Sonny had assumed that role and guarded it jealously. But things had been so rushed in Sydney that she hadn't even thought about letting him know she was coming.

She and Dulles turned on their phones as soon as they landed. He listened to a message as they disembarked and then said, "Susan Crawford has the brushes. They're on their way to the lab now."

Ava listened to two voicemails as they walked through the terminal. Fai had called. She had had a good day of shooting and was feeling more optimistic about the film. Wahab was the other caller. He wanted her to know that Ben had landed in Manila and given the brushes to Crawford. He sounded pensive, and Ava could only think how much worse he would feel if he knew who she was travelling with and what they were discovering. But any guilt she felt about not keeping him fully appraised was offset by the knowledge that, thus far, she'd honoured her commitment to provide the Brotherhood with some cover.

"I was thinking we should book rooms at the Shangri-La," Dulles said.

Ava's hotel of choice in Central was the Mandarin Oriental, but she figured she was travelling as a guest of the CIA. "That's fine."

"I'll call from the taxi," he said.

"And you told Allison you'd call him when we landed."

"I'm not as Hong Kong–savvy as you are," he said. "How

long will it take us to clear Customs and Immigration and get to the hotel?"

"Forty-five minutes to an hour."

He looked for Allison's number on his phone and hit it. Seconds later he was shaking his head. "This is Alasdair Dulles. We've arrived in Hong Kong and are just leaving the airport. We should be at the hotel in about an hour."

When they had cleared Customs and Immigration, they walked into the arrivals hall and headed for the taxi stand. It was dark and there was a trace of damp, cold Hong Kong winter in the air. Ava shivered as they waited in line.

"My Hong Kong friends ask me how I can withstand the Canadian winter," Ava said. "They don't believe me when I tell them that I've always felt colder here."

"I feel the same way about winters in upstate New York compared to routine weather in Bangkok. At least in New York I can dress heavily enough for long walks. In Bangkok there's no amount of undressing I can do that makes it comfortable to walk any more than a few hundred yards."

Dulles called the Shangri-La when they left the airport, and by the time they were on the Tsing Ma Bridge, he had two reservations. The journey over the bridge in daylight presented one of Ava's favourite views. Tsing Ma was one of the longest suspension bridges in the world. It spanned the Ma Wan Channel — the route for thousands of ships, boats, and sampans making their way between the South China Sea and Hong Kong's harbour — and provided a spectacular view of the vessels and the sea. When she looked down at the channel at night, the lights from the ships below made it look as if the velvet sky were beneath her.

She was about to comment on it when Dulles said, "I've

been thinking about the address of that website Jason Said mentioned."

"Me too," Ava said. "Those numbers can't be random. They have to have some meaning."

"One that does have meaning is May 14, 1948."

"Which is?"

"The date of Israeli independence."

"Oh shit," Ava said.

"That's only a guess."

"Except it makes perfect sense."

Traffic thickened as they eased their way into Kowloon and towards the Cross-Harbour Tunnel, which would take them to Hong Kong Island and the Central District. It wasn't even remotely close to what non-rush-hour traffic was like in Manila, but it was bad enough that the driver was cursing vehemently in Cantonese.

"Hey, stop that," Ava snapped. "I can understand you. We'll get there when we get there."

The driver turned around and looked at her sheepishly. "Sorry," he said.

For just a second Ava felt like her mother, Jennie Lee, calling out a rude associate in a store or server in a restaurant. "*Momentai*," she said.

"What was that about?" Dulles said.

"Nothing worth mentioning."

It was almost a quarter to eleven by the time they reached the Shangri-La. Once they had checked in, Dulles headed for a lobby phone and asked to be connected to Allison's room. A voice he didn't recognize answered.

"This is Alasdair Dulles. I'm trying to reach Mr. Allison. He's expecting me."

"Come to the Presidential Suite, on the top floor," the voice responded.

"He'll see us now. Do you want to drop off your bag first?" Dulles asked.

"No, let's go," Ava said.

The hotel occupied half of one of the Pacific Place Towers in the Admiralty section of Central. The bottom half of the tower was filled with commercial retailers and the hotel occupied the upper half, all the way up to the fifty-sixth floor. She had been in the hotel before and ridden the glass-lined elevator to the top level. Dulles obviously hadn't. He reacted visibly when they started to pass a painted silk mural that depicted a range of brightly coloured mountains, covered in trees and towering above a river. It seemed to stretch upwards forever.

"It's called *The Great Motherland*," Ava said. "It's sixteen storeys high and it's the largest silk mural in the world."

They exited the elevator and saw a sign for the suite. They headed down the corridor to a set of double doors with buzzers on either side. Dulles pressed the buzzer on the right and the door opened almost at once. The doorway was filled by a massive man in a white shirt that was stretched tight across his chest and shoulders. Wordlessly he stood to one side and they walked past him.

The suite was immense, with a separate kitchen, living room, and dining room. The most striking feature was the floor-to-ceiling window that offered a view of Hong Kong's spectacular skyline, Victoria Harbour, and beyond, to Tsim Sha Tsui on the Kowloon side.

"Mr. Allison will be with you in a minute," the man said. "He'd like you to sit at the dining room table."

The table was long enough to comfortably accommodate twelve chairs. Ava chose a chair that faced the window; Dulles sat next to her. A bottle of water and glasses sat on a tray, and Dulles poured himself a glass. They waited quietly for five, ten, fifteen, twenty minutes while the man, who Ava assumed was a bodyguard, sat on a couch in the living room and watched television with the sound lowered. Once she thought she heard Allison's voice through a closed door that she imagined led to a bedroom. As the minutes passed it became hard to think that Allision wasn't being rude, but Dulles didn't seem as bothered as her. At the half-hour mark she debated asking the bodyguard to knock on the door to remind Allison that they were there. Before she could do or say anything, the door opened and Allison emerged.

Ava knew of him only by name, and any impressions had come from listening to his conversation with Dulles. He had sounded cultured, and the man who walked towards them didn't dispel that image. He was of medium height — she guessed no more than five foot nine —and had a trim build. Everything about him was impeccable, from his full head of carefully coiffed silver hair to what looked like a custom-made grey pinstriped suit, set off by a crisp white shirt, a tightly knotted red Hermès tie, and a pair of brown leather shoes that she was sure had been handmade in London. There wasn't anything about him that looked out of place, and there wasn't a wrinkle where one shouldn't be.

"Sorry for the delay," he said. "I was talking to the office in Dallas."

Dulles stood up to face him. "Thanks for seeing us."

"How could I possibly say no?" Allison said, and then made a right turn past the table and stood in front of the window. "For my money, this is the greatest view on earth. Natural wonders are just that — natural. This harbour would be impressive by itself, I guess, but when you add man's creative element, it takes it to an entirely different level."

When neither Dulles nor Ava responded, Allison swivelled to face them and extended a hand. "You haven't changed much since I saw you in London," he said.

"You haven't either," Dulles said as he shook his hand.

"I'll be seventy next year," Allison said.

"I would never have guessed."

"Good genes, good diet, stress management, and lots of exercise."

"It's an ideal combination."

Allison looked at the table and finally seemed to realize that Ava was sitting there. She stood and offered her hand. "My name is Ava Lee," she said.

"And you're a colleague of Alasdair's?"

"You could say that."

"Ah, more intrigue." Allison smiled. "Now, would either of you like anything else to drink? Or perhaps we can get you something to eat?"

"I'm fine," Ava and Dulles said at the same time.

Allison sat across from them with his hands resting on the table. Ava saw that he was wearing cufflinks that looked like platinum encrusted with rubies.

"Did you check on the status of my security clearance?" he asked Dulles.

"No. I took you at your word."

"I didn't think you fellows took anyone at their word."

"I don't know which fellows you're referring to."

"The CIA fellows."

"We're a very large organization and hardly homogeneous."

"Which branch are you with?"

"I don't think that matters."

"No, I guess it really doesn't. We're all playing our roles on the same team, and by that I mean Team USA," Allison said.

"Precisely."

"My partners in Lebanon, I regret to say, don't share that sense of camaraderie," he said. "I've spoken to them many times today, in fact, so many times that they were getting very annoyed with me."

"But I assume you were ultimately successful."

"That depends on your expectations."

"To begin with, we want to know how Omar Obeidat, operating under the name Fileeb al-Touma — and, incidentally, a former member of the Jordanian security service — managed to extract about five million dollars from your casino over the past two or three years."

"It is inaccurate to refer to it as my casino," Allison said. "I have no involvement with it at all. My partners in Beirut look after our interests."

"That may be true, but we've been told that the day-to-day operations are managed by Pinetree Gaming, and Pinetree is owned by the Harvest Group, which in turned is owned by you."

"And I don't spend ten minutes a month thinking about Pinetree. It's simply an investment I wish I hadn't made."

"Excuse me, but I think we're splitting hairs here," Ava said. "We started this conversation with your saying you've spoken to your partners. What did they tell you?"

Allison looked at her as if surprised she had the nerve to speak. "That's very direct of you," he said.

"That's my style, and I apologize if you find it offensive."

"No, not at all," Allison said. "We should stay on topic, and regardless of who owns or controls what, the topic is the Paradise Casino. And that leads me to a question my partners asked: what makes you so convinced that all this money you're talking about came from there?"

"The cash deposits al-Touma made at the bank came wrapped in Paradise Casino strips," Dulles said.

"Why would he make it that obvious? It could have been a ruse, an attempt to deflect attention away from the real source."

"It's actually more likely that he wanted the bank to see the strips because he wanted them to know where the money came from. The strips connect him to the casino, and when the casino swears that he's one hell of a gambler, al-Touma has his cover story."

"That's another question my partners had. What makes you so sure that he's not a terrific gambler?"

"Mr. Allison, I've spent more time than I care to remember sitting in casinos watching my mother gamble. When I was studying to become an accountant, one of the things I wanted to understand was the economics of casino gambling, so I took it as an elective," Ava said. "No one — and I mean no one — can consistently beat the house for large sums of money. Odds are odds and math is math. Casinos aren't built to give money away."

"And if there's any doubt about that," Dulles said, "we know when al-Touma made his deposits. Between that and getting a fix on flights between Beirut and Amman, we can figure out when he was at the casino. Then we'll get the security footage for those days and see how, when, where, and for how much he gambled, and we'll take a look at how he was paid out."

"That won't be necessary," Allison said.

"Why not?"

"Because this al-Touma did receive the money from the casino. He may have a gambled a little, but that was pretense. Somehow my partners contrived to funnel millions of dollars to this man."

"Did they admit that to you?"

"Yes."

"Then tell me, why didn't you say that ten minutes ago instead of pretending you had no idea what went on?"

"I wanted to see how honest you would be with me."

"Do you mean you wanted to see how much we knew?" Ava said.

Allison shrugged. "When there are conflicting stories, I like to hear both sides before rushing to judgement."

"Where's the conflict?" Dulles asked.

"You implied earlier today that the casino was knowingly financing a terrorist organization. My partners tell me they were being extorted and had no idea what the money was being used for."

"Being extorted how?"

"Several years ago, this al-Touma arranged a meeting through some Lebanese military people with my partners at the casino. He told them he knew about their investment and that he and some Lebanese colleagues were prepared to offer them protection in return for regular payments. Al-Touma implied that the colleagues he was referring to were military and that the protection would be from them."

"And they obviously agreed to pay."

"Of course they did. He said if they didn't, he couldn't guarantee the safety of the casino or their families."

"But it was Pinetree Gaming that was managing the casino," Ava said. "How did your partners arrange to make payments from the casino without Pinetree's knowledge?"

"The partners told the casino's management what was going on and instructed them to keep it quiet."

"And they did? They didn't tell anyone at the office in Atlanta?"

"Evidently not. But you should understand that the management team on the ground is local, and they were sympathetic to my partners' dilemma. And, being local, they took the threats seriously."

"Tom, how well do you know these partners?"

"We're not buddies and we don't socialize, if that's what you're getting at," he said. "But we've done a few deals over the years that worked out okay."

"Why partner with them in the casino?"

"We needed local ownership in order to get a licence."

"So you don't know that much about them on a personal level?"

"What are you really asking?"

"Tom, is it possible that any of your partners could be associated with a militant Islamic group?" Dulles asked.

Allison's face clouded, and then he shook his head and a grin emerged. "They're Christians, for goodness' sake."

"So we were told, but they live in Lebanon, and who knows what forces are at work there," Dulles said. "For example, would any of your partners have any antipathy towards Jews?"

"Certainly not."

"Why are you so sure?"

"I may not know them that well, but over the years we've had discussions and I've never heard either of them say anything or act in any way that could be construed as anti-Semitic — and that is something I'm very sensitive to," he said. "I assume there's a reason for that question that hasn't been shared."

"The terrorist organization that we think has been getting the casino's money appears to be primarily targeting Israel and the Jewish population in the United States."

Allison looked hard at Dulles. "Being targeted is nothing new for Israel."

"This isn't just about Israel. Many of the Jews they've targeted live in the United States. Evidently they believe they can harm Israel by attacking the people who support it."

Allison turned his face away. Ava saw his jaw clench, and both of his hands were now balled tightly into fists. He stood up.

"Excuse me, I'll be back," he said.

## 32

AVA LOOKED AT DULLES AND THEN GLANCED AT THE bodyguard, who was still sitting on the sofa supposedly watching television. She wondered how much he had heard, how much he had understood, how well he had been briefed.

"That was interesting," she said.

Dulles nodded as he poured himself another glass of water.

This time they waited only ten minutes before the door opened and Allison re-emerged. His face glistened in the light and Ava could see damp stains on his collar. "George," he said to the man on the sofa, "bring me a bottle of cognac and three snifters, please."

He rejoined them at the table. His face was tightly drawn, and the overhead lights hit his face in such a way that Ava could see tiny scars around his eyes, the kind left by plastic surgery. He seemed troubled.

"You will have a drink, won't you?" he said. "The cognac is Louis Royer Force 53. I think it's the finest in the world."

"Sure," Dulles said.

"I will as well," said Ava.

"I have to say I need one," Allison said. "This conversation has jolted me."

"Can we continue?" Dulles said. Allison nodded.

"Thank you," Dulles said and leaned towards him. "Tom, do your partners have any contact information for al-Touma? Do they have any way of reaching him if they have to?"

"I don't know. I'll have to ask them."

"Will you?"

"Of course."

George came to the table with an ice bucket, a bottle encased in a pierced metal cylinder, and three crystal snifters on a tray.

"I take my cognac neat. How about you two?" Allison said.

They both nodded. George poured the equivalent of three fingers into each glass. Ava thought the cognac looked like liquid honey.

Allison swirled his around in the glass and said, "Cheers."

Ava took a sip. It was so smooth that it made the cognac she'd had on the plane taste like cheap brandy. "This is superb," she said.

"When do you think you can call your partners?" Dulles said.

"I'll try to reach them later tonight."

"When you do, call me. I don't care what time it is."

"I understand your sense of urgency," Allison said, and then stood and walked to the window with his glass in his hand. He gazed out over the harbour and, with his back still turned to them, said, "Alasdair, I have a few questions for you."

"Feel free to ask them."

"You mentioned that al-Touma was a member of the Jordanian secret service. What makes you think he's not still working for them?"

"We've been in touch with them. He left the service ages ago."

"He could be undercover."

"They would have told us."

"So you think that he's now working for a terrorist organization."

"We do."

"Which one?"

"We don't know yet, but you can be assured that we'll locate al-Touma, and when we do, we'll find out."

"Do you have any hunches?"

"No."

"Don't you find it strange that you were told about this plot in some detail but your sources can't link it to any organization?"

"I hadn't thought about it in that light."

"But you're convinced that your sources, your informants, are reliable?"

"We are, and so far the information they've provided has proven to be accurate."

"Who are these informants?"

"You know I can't tell you that."

"But they were persuasive enough to convince you that some unknown terrorist organization is going to be attacking Israel and American Jews?"

"Yes. The only remotely comforting thing we've learned is that the attacks aren't planned for the immediate future. We think we have time to locate whoever is behind this."

"Do you have any idea how many of them there are? Do you have any clues about where they intend to strike?"

"Tom, I can't get into that level of detail with you."

Ava could see Allison's reflection in the window. His face was tight and his eyes were narrowed. He looked like a man struggling to maintain control.

"I have some other questions for you that are less sensitive," Allison said. "But they are self-serving."

"I think we can handle that."

"Well, did you know that I was one of the three largest donors to the Republican Party last year?"

Dulles glanced at Ava and gave her the slightest smile. "I did read something about that."

"I was also one of the largest individual donors to the president's re-election campaign."

"That isn't a question."

"But you have some idea where I'm heading?"

"I think so."

"Good, because you should also know that I was the founder of Christian Allies of Israel, and over the past twenty years I've donated more than one hundred million dollars to that foundation," he said. "I was also the largest contributor to the Israeli Independent Conservative Party during the last election, and Stephen Weisman, the leader of the party and now prime minister, is a personal friend."

"I knew you had close ties to him."

"Close ties? I bought radio and television stations and newspapers and magazines in Israel for the sole purpose of supporting Weisman and promoting his party. He's keeping Israel safe, and I'll do whatever I can to assist him."

"That's a remarkable commitment on your part."

"I see it more as a fulfillment of my Christian obligation," Allison said. "I believe that the emergence of a Jewish state in the land promised by God to Abraham, Isaac, and Jacob was ordained by God. A unified Israel in the hands of Jews is a prerequisite for the Rapture and for the return of Jesus."

"I respect your beliefs, although I can't pretend to understand them," Dulles said. Allison's shoulders tensed, and Ava wondered if Dulles had offended him.

"Tell me something. How many people know about this threat right now?" Allison said.

"The people in this room and a handful in the Philippines," Dulles said.

"Your colleagues in Beirut?"

"Only in the most general way. I haven't shared details with them."

"And you haven't advised Washington or Langley, or wherever you report to?"

"Not yet, but it is inevitable. We've been in information-gathering mode and it's been a whirlwind. As I said, we've been led to understand that the threat isn't imminent, so we thought it important to confirm what we've been told before raising the alarm."

"Who knows that the casino might have been the source of the money?"

"The same people, here in this room and in Beirut."

Allison spun around, took a step forward, and pointed his index finger at Dulles. His cheeks had turned bright red, and Ava wondered if that was because of anger or the cognac. "Do you have any notion — the slightest idea — how loathsome and destructive it would be to me if it was even hinted that a business I own part of helped fund an Islamic terrorist group?" he said, his voice coarse.

"I understand —"

"You really can't," Allison interrupted. "I have devoted a

good part of my life to defending Israel. All that work and dedication and money would be forgotten. The fact that I knew nothing about what was going on at that damn casino wouldn't matter. I would be a villain to some and a laughingstock to others."

"I don't see why that would necessarily be the end result," Dulles said quietly. "I would certainly make it clear in my communications that we have no reason to believe you were involved in any way and that you've been very co-operative."

Allison took another step forward and almost stood over Dulles. "You could choose not to mention me. You could just name the casino and the local partners."

"That wouldn't be the entire truth."

"Truth? The truth is that my partners were extorted. That needs to be said. Everything else is irrelevant."

"Talk to those partners and get me everything they have on al-Touma, and then we'll see where we sit."

"I'll talk to them," Allison said, "but you must understand that I'm a man who doesn't shrink from adversity."

"I don't know why you would say 'adversity.' I hardly think we represent any kind of challenge or danger to you," Dulles said.

"My name and my reputation are in peril. I'll do whatever I have to do to protect them."

"I would expect you to do nothing less, just as I hope you understand that I have a job to do."

"I'm not going to just sit back and hope all this goes away."

"We should all be so lucky that it goes away," Dulles said.

"I don't count on luck," Allison said, and then walked away. He went into the sitting room, spoke to the bodyguard, and headed for the bedroom. There he stopped at the door and turned to stare at Dulles. "Don't mess with me, Alasdair. I can go so far above your head that I'd seem little more than a speck on the ceiling."

Dulles started to reply, but Allison disappeared into the bedroom before he could speak.

Ava looked at Dulles. "What do we do now?" she said.

## 33

**THEY WAITED, BUT AFTER A FEW MINUTES AVA KNEW** they were wasting their time. Allison wasn't coming back. She was about to say as much to Dulles when the bodyguard spoke. "You two need to go," he said.

He was standing by the sofa, his eyes fixed on them. Ava recognized his body language; she'd seen it often enough, in men who were gearing up for a physical confrontation. "You two need to go," he said again in an accent that Ava thought had its origins in New York or New Jersey. "Mr. Allison is finished with you."

"I don't see any value in hanging around," Ava said.

They walked towards the door. As they passed George, he glared at them and then fell in behind them until they exited the suite. The door slammed shut as soon as they stepped into the hallway.

"Charming," Ava said. "I wonder what Allison said to him."

"Throw the bums out?"

Ava smiled. "It was certainly a strange end to a strange conversation. Do you think Allison will call his partners?"

"I expect so, or maybe I should say I hope so," Dulles said.

"What did you think of him?"

"He's tightly wound, but then a lot of tough, smart people are."

"What about his level of co-operation?"

"Until that closing drama, I think his responses were reasonable, given what you'd just dropped on him," Ava said. "I don't know what more you could expect from him. And if he gets you the al-Touma information, he'll have done everything you want."

"You know, everything he said about his support of Israel is true."

"And that makes his sensitivity about the casino's involvement going public all the more understandable."

They reached the elevator and waited for a car. Dulles appeared lost in thought. Ava turned to him and said, "Are you going to be informing Washington or Langley or wherever about Tawi-Tawi?"

"I should probably have done it by now, but I was holding off until we had some confirmation that this wasn't just another conspiracy theory," he said. "I'm comfortable now that it isn't, so I'm going to make a phone call when I get to my room."

"Do you have to move that fast?"

"I'm sorry, but I think I do. That chat with Allison was the tipping point. I can't trust him not to make some phone calls of his own tonight. If he starts blundering around and my director is questioned, he's not going to be happy about getting caught off guard, and he won't be pleased to hear about this second-hand."

"Do the Philippine security services have to be brought into it?"

"Ava, I'm going to call only one person, and that's Brad Harrison, my boss. I'll explain the sensitivity of the Brotherhood's involvement and their fears about Philippine security. He appreciates that sources have to be protected and he understands there's a vigilante mentality loose in the Philippines right now, so I don't expect him to start making calls to Manila. I'm also going to ask him to let us run with this on our own for another day or two. But that will be his decision, and I won't argue with him if he says no."

"You do know that I haven't told the Brotherhood, Ramirez, or Chang Wang about you."

"Maybe you should."

"I'm not worried how Chang will react, because he knows me and trusts me, but I'm worried about losing the co-operation of the others."

"We still need them."

"I know."

"So don't tell them — not yet, anyway. Wait until I get some kind of direction from Harrison."

The elevator arrived. Dulles's room was on the forty-second floor and Ava's on the forty-first. As they began their descent, she said, "Okay, I'll hold off talking to anyone until I hear from you."

"I think that's best."

"But one more thing: I was thinking about Allison. I wonder whether the agitation and anger he displayed before we left were real or contrived."

"You doubt that it was real?"

"He turned it on in an instant but he was still under control. Those two things don't always go together," Ava said.

"He's a pro."

"Yes, he's smart, tough, rich, and a pro. So how does all the religious hocus-pocus fit with that profile?"

"Are you religious?"

"I'm a lapsed Catholic."

"I'm a lazy Methodist," Dulles said. "I'm not sure which church Allison belongs to specifically, but, as I said, it's fundamentalist, and the attitude he displays towards Israel is common among those groups. He just puts his money where his mouth is — and he's got more money than just about anyone, so he makes a bigger impact. But I think what you're really asking is whether he's sincere."

"That is the question."

"I think he's completely sincere and totally committed."

The elevator came to a stop. "I'll be up early," Ava said.

"Me too. You should assume that we'll be out of here tomorrow and probably heading back to the Philippines."

The curtains in Ava's room were closed when she entered it. She turned on the entrance light and then a desk lamp. She thought about opening her computer, but that just made her feel tired. She sat on the edge of the bed and unpacked her travel bag. It had been a long and exhausting day. They'd made progress, but towards what end she wasn't sure. Knowing how the college got its money and Jason Said's explanation of how it operated were two positives, but it didn't get them any closer to Tariq al-Bashir or identifying where about 150 young men were embedded.

"Fuck," she said. "Why did I let myself get sucked into this?" She closed her eyes and drew deep breaths. There was no point in thinking about it anymore until she heard from Dulles.

In the meantime she needed to look after herself. She

stripped and walked to the bathroom with her toiletries bag in hand. She brushed her teeth and then stepped into the shower. She set the showerhead to a fine mist, and for five minutes she enjoyed the sensation of standing inside a warm, wet cloud. When, wrapped in a Shangri-La bathrobe, she re-entered the bedroom, she climbed straight into bed.

It was still dark when she woke, and at first she thought it was the middle of the night. But the bedside clock read ten minutes after seven. She sat up, not quite sure where she was for a few seconds. Then it registered, and without thinking she reached for the room phone.

"Good morning, baby," Fai answered. "Where are you?"

"I'm in Hong Kong, but I've been running around like mad and I'm about to leave for Manila again."

"And I'm about a hundred kilometres closer to Beijing than I was yesterday morning."

"You know, I saw *High Noon* on one flight, and it reminded me of your film," Ava said, and described the similar theme.

Her cellphone vibrated. She looked at the incoming number and saw that it was Wahab. "Fai, I have a call coming in that I have to take. I love you, and I'll call you tomorrow." She picked up her phone and connected.

"Hi, Wahab. If you're phoning about the brushes, we haven't heard anything yet," she said.

"Ava, they've left the college," he said.

She swung her legs over the side of the bed, walked towards the window, and pulled open the curtains. It was a grey, rainy morning. "I'm not sure I understand," she said.

"They're gone. The imam and all of his assistants, including his own security people. They left the college about an hour ago."

"How do you know?"

"Alcem's cousin, the cook, phoned him. He said they left in three cars and a white van filled with their stuff, including computers. They told the students and staff they were going to General Santos City for a few days to attend a religious conference."

"Is there a conference?"

"I haven't had time to check, but I will."

"What are the students supposed to do while they're gone?"

"I don't know. Study, I guess."

"Well, whether the imam and the others are going to General Santos City or not, they're probably trying to get off the island. Can you send someone to the airport to find out if anyone saw them leave?" she said. "And just in case, have someone check the port as well."

"I'll do that."

"Wahab, is there any security left at the college?"

"Just the local guys. Why do you ask?"

"Do you have good contacts with the local police?"

"We do."

"If I can get to Bongao either late today or first thing tomorrow, can you arrange for your police friends to come with us to the college and get us past security?"

"Why do you want to get into the college?"

"I'd like to see where the imam and the others live and go through whatever they left behind."

"Let me talk to my friend. He's a captain, so I'm sure he can make it happen. All he'll need is some kind of reason, and I'll come up with something."

"Okay, you do that. And stay in touch with me. I'll try to make the flights work from my end."

Ava shook her head. The imam had either gone to the conference in General Santos City or he'd done a flyer. She was almost certain he was on the run, but she didn't want to believe it. She and Dulles should have anticipated it. They should have expected that someone would alert al-Bashir that he was being investigated. How wide had they cast their net? Could Jason Said have called the college? Had Fileeb al-Touma been warned by the bank or the casino or the Lebanese secret service and called his cohorts? What about Tom Allison or someone in the Brotherhood — had they let something slip?

*What a mess*, she thought as she phoned Dulles.

"I haven't heard a word from Allison," he said when he answered.

"Do we have flights booked to Manila?"

"We leave at ten past eleven and get in at one-thirty. I was just about to call to say I'll meet you in the lobby at nine."

"Did you talk to your boss last night?"

"Yes, I did."

"How did it go?"

"We're on our own until the lab results come in or the boys in Beirut find al-Touma. After that, he says, we have to bring in backup and start involving the Philippine security agencies."

"Alasdair, you might have to call him back."

"Why?"

"Things have changed. The imam and his people left the college this morning. They said they were going to General Santos City for a religious conference, but I can't believe it's true. Wahab said they packed a van with their stuff, including computers."

"They've all left?" Dulles said.

"So I'm told."

"Fuck. We didn't need that to happen."

"Someone has to have tipped them off that we're looking at the college."

Dulles paused and then said, "And, unfortunately, we have a healthy list of candidates."

"Whoever it was and whatever they said, it seems to have spooked the imam."

"And now we need to locate him and his crowd. We may have to advise the Philippine government."

"Not yet," Ava said. "Wahab and the Brotherhood are already checking the harbour and the airport. Give them a chance to find out how they left and where they might have gone. Besides, we don't know who al-Bashir and the others really are. How will the Philippine authorities track them down any better than we can?"

"We can't wait forever."

"I know, but I'm also thinking that this gives you and me an opportunity to get into the college. I'd love the chance to go through whatever is there while it's still intact, and Wahab says he can get us in. If you go to the Philippine authorities, the Special Action Force or the National Police Intelligence Section will get called in immediately, and who knows what will be left to look at."

"You said Wahab can get us inside?"

"There's only local security at the college now, and Wahab will have us taken in by a police captain. I can't imagine there will be any resistance."

"That does make some sense, and I can't deny that it's appealing."

"The problem is how to get to Bongao," she said. "As far as I know, there's one commercial flight a day and we've already missed it."

"We can get from here to Manila easily enough," Dulles said. "Maybe I can arrange a private plane from Manila to Bongao. I'll have to make some calls."

"We need to move quickly," she said, and then immediately felt stupid for stating the obvious. "Sorry. You're the last person I should be saying something like that to."

"I'll talk to you as soon as I have things organized," he said.

## 34

**BY EIGHT O'CLOCK AVA WAS DRESSED, PACKED, AND** pacing the room. She hadn't heard from Wahab or Dulles and she was rapidly running out of patience. She went to the window and looked out onto the harbour. The weather was so bad that she could barely see through the veil of fog and rain. She kept checking her watch, and at ten past eight she gave up and called Wahab.

"We could be in Bongao late this afternoon or early evening," she said when he answered. "We're arranging for a private plane to fly us there from Manila."

"Who is 'we'?" Wahab asked.

*Oh god, what have I done?* Ava thought, and then she realized that it was ridiculous to think she could put off telling him any longer. "His name is Alasdair Dulles and he's with the CIA," she said. "He's been working with me for days now. He's been tremendously helpful. He's respected your wish to be kept in the background and he's kept the Philippine security services out of this."

"Did Ramirez arrange for him to be brought in?"

"No, I did it on my own, because it was the only way I

could find out about the banks in the Middle East."

"Does Ramirez know what you've done?"

"No, you're the first person I've told."

"We thought you had involved someone else," Wahab said.

"Is it a problem?"

"Do we have a choice if it is?"

"It's too late to change anything. Besides, you're going to need someone like him on your side. I'm convinced he will not screw you over."

"Then I guess we don't have a problem."

"So can we continue our conversation about the imam leaving the college?"

"Yes," he said.

"Good. Were there any sightings of him or his people at the airport or harbour?"

"No, but one of the people we spoke to said he saw some cars and a white van driving towards the north end of the island. There are a couple of small ports in that area, so I'm going to send someone to ask around there."

"And did you speak to the police captain about getting us into the college?"

"He'll do whatever we want," he said.

"What we want is complete access."

"That won't be a problem."

"Thank you, Wahab, and I mean that. I know this hasn't been easy for you."

"All I need to know is when you'll be arriving."

"I'll call as soon as I have an ETA."

He became quiet, and Ava wondered if he was having second thoughts. Then he said, "Do you think this will be over in another day or two?"

"I can't imagine that much more will happen at the college after today or tomorrow. But we have no idea where the students were sent, and who knows how long it will take for us to find them."

"We can't help with finding the students but we can help here. Let me know when you're arriving," he said, and ended the call.

*Well, that went better than I imagined*, she thought, and decided to press her luck. She called Dulles.

"Hey," he said.

"We're set up to get into the college. The local police will escort us in. Do you have a plane to get us to Bongao?"

"Yep," he said. "Brad just authorized it."

"Did you tell him about al-Bashir?"

"Of course. Has the Brotherhood been able to get a fix on him?"

"Nothing firm, but they think he and his aides drove to the north end of the island. There are ports there. They might also just be lying low for a few days."

"If they do find them, tell them not to initiate contact. We need to have control of that."

"I'll tell Wahab," she said. "I guess, since we're getting a plane, your boss took the news okay?"

"He took it in stride, like he always does. And he obviously agreed with the idea of us going to the college today," Dulles said. "But he also made it clear that this is the last day we'll be doing things on our own."

"I expected that."

"Me too. It's the right move."

"Then why do you sound discouraged?"

"More like frustrated — I haven't been able to reach

Allison. He isn't answering his cell or his room phone, and he's a loose end that I want to tie up."

"Well, we're here in his hotel. Why don't we pay him a visit? We have the time. I'll meet you at the elevator on his floor in about five minutes."

"Yes, let's do that," he said.

She left her room and had to wait several minutes for an elevator. When she reached the penthouse floor, she expected that Dulles would already be there, but there was no sign of him. She watched the elevator floor indicators, her frustration growing over the next five minutes as none stopped at the forty-second floor. Finally one did but then went straight back down to the ground floor. *What's going on?* she thought. She was just about to phone Dulles when she saw an elevator stop at his floor and then proceed upwards. He stepped out, looking flustered.

"You okay?" she said.

"I was talking to Brad Harrison again."

"Did he cancel the plane?"

"No, he wanted me to know that Allison phoned friends in Washington last night, and the impact finally made its way to Brad's ear."

"That's not a surprise."

"I know, but evidently Allison is making it personal. He's accusing me of all kinds of underhanded behaviour. It's bullshit and Brad knows that, but still, he's told me to tread carefully and not give Allison any more reason to complain."

"Do you want us to go back to our rooms?"

"No. We're here and Bobby Delvano still hasn't found al-Touma, so it would be irresponsible not to ask Allison if he talked to his partners or the managers about him."

Ava nodded and they started to walk down the hall. When they reached the double doors of the Presidential Suite, Dulles slid past her and pushed the buzzer. When no one answered, he buzzed again, waited for a few seconds, and then knocked. No sounds came from inside the suite, and they were about to leave when George, the bodyguard, opened the door.

"What do you want?" he said.

"I'd like to speak to Mr. Allison," Dulles said.

"He's not here."

Dulles looked over George's shoulder into the suite. George took a step back, almost encouraging Dulles to get closer, and when he did, the bodyguard's right hand shot out and hit him on the upper chest. Dulles staggered sideways into the doorway and then fell to the floor. As Ava reached out for him, she felt George's hand on her shirt collar. She released Dulles and stood up to face George.

She grabbed the arm that was holding her shirt and dug her fingers into his elbow until they hit the nerve she was looking for. He grunted, his arm dropping uselessly to his side as he blinked at her in surprise. She turned again to help Dulles but was struck on the shoulder. She fell back but managed to steady herself.

"Get the fuck out of here before I really hurt you," George said, looking down at her.

Ava propelled herself forward from her crouching position, her right hand forming the phoenix-eye fist. She drove the middle knuckle of her middle finger into the big man's belly, striking the nerves gathered at the base of his breastbone. He doubled over and staggered two or three steps backwards into the suite. Ava followed him. He glanced up at her and then lashed out again with his good arm. It was an out-of-control swing that she easily avoided. He pulled himself semi-erect and threw another punch. Ava shifted to his right and slammed the phoenix-eye fist into his ear. He fell to the ground with a thud, his good hand covering his ear and his eyes rolling back into his head.

"Stay down," Ava said. "If you try to get up, it will be the last time you do that for a while." She turned and saw Dulles leaning against the doorframe, his mouth hanging open.

"I think if Allison were here this racket would have brought him out. But why don't you check the bedrooms anyway," Ava said.

"Yeah, okay," Dulles said. He walked past them, giving the bodyguard a wide berth. He opened the door to the room that Allison had been in the night before, and then two others. "There's no sign of him," he said.

"Then let's get out of here."

They walked in silence to the elevators. Dulles glanced sideways at her a couple of times and shook his head. When the elevator arrived and they started their descent, he finally spoke. "I don't think this is what Brad Harrison had in mind when he said to tread quietly."

"I thought that applied to you, not me," Ava said.

## 35

**THEY DIDN'T SPEAK DURING THE CAB RIDE TO CHEK LAP**
Kok, or while they waited in the Bridge, Cathay Pacific's
newest business-class lounge. It wasn't a comfortable quiet.
Ava guessed that, like her, Dulles was thinking about where
things stood for him. The problem was that they were in different positions. She remembered what Ryan Poirier had said
about Dulles: he was a man in need of redemption.

They had adjoining seats on the plane. The silence was
finally broken by Ava after they reached cruising altitude.
"Will the way you handled this case cause any problems with
your boss?" she asked.

He glanced at her. "If there's any grief to be had, he isn't
the one who will cause it," he said. "Besides, given that this
is potentially the largest terrorist plot targeting the U.S. in
the past ten years, I think I've managed the situation capa-
bly. It was important, for starters, to confirm what you'd
been told before raising any alarms. I won't be criticized
for being careful. There could be some carping about my
decision not to advise Brad right away and not to advise
the Philippine government at all, but I think my reasons

were sound enough and defensible. Certainly Brad wasn't upset about it. Al-Bashir's vanishing act might generate some second-guessing, but even that could turn into a positive if we get into the college and find something — find anything — that might lead us to the imam and help locate the students who've gone overseas."

"So if there is grief, where will it come from?"

"Tom Allison. But more likely from people connected to him. He's got power and it extends to multiple layers within the government. The agency likes to pretend that it's independent of partisan politics, but Brad is a realist and runs his operations accordingly," he said. "The fact that we trespassed in Allison's suite and that you took out his guard probably won't make Brad's ability to defend me any easier if the shit starts rolling downhill. But — and it's a huge but — if we bring the situation to a successful conclusion, I should be shielded from any criticism by Tom Allison or any of his Washington flunkies."

"I like the way you talk about your boss."

"He's a complicated man, not easy to like but easy to respect. He's been with the agency for decades and has worked all over the world, including Hong Kong and Manila. He's seen it all and nothing seems to surprise him," Dulles said. "And for someone who hadn't spent that much time in Washington until a few years ago, he's become a master at manoeuvring through and around the bureaucratic maze."

"You seem to trust him a great deal."

"I do. I'm quite happy for him to make the decisions about who gets told what, when, and how," he said. "Although I have to tell you, I lobbied him like hell this morning to let me maintain control of this file."

"What did he say?"

"Obviously I'm still running it, but it will be a trickier call for Brad to make when we get our hands on the imam and the Philippine authorities find out about the college. I imagine they'll claim jurisdictional rights, while we'll maintain that because the U.S. is the primary target, we should have control."

"First we have to find the imam, and your man Delvano still has to come up with al-Touma," she said. "I don't mean to sound negative, but in my old business I didn't like to make assumptions. Whenever I did, I always got kicked in the ass."

Dulles shook his head. "There you go again," he said. "Brad asked me about you and I told him I've never met anyone like you. You're a never-ending source of surprises, and every one delivered in the most matter-of-fact way, but with a confidence that seems to say *Wait till you see my next trick.*"

"Even if that's a compliment, I don't think there'll be any more tricks after we get to the college," she said. "No matter what we find — or don't find — I suspect my involvement will end there. Whether it's your government or the Philippines taking over, I'm quite sure they'll want everything contained within an official structure. No one will want anything to do with a freelancer. And truthfully, that's absolutely fine with me."

"Well, we aren't at the college yet, are we," he said. "And unless I'm mistaken, you've just made several assumptions."

"Don't be such a smartass," she said.

He smiled, closed his eyes, and leaned his head against the back of the seat. "I'm going to try to nap," he said. "I want to be well rested when we get to the college."

"Me too," Ava said.

She slept fitfully and was startled when a flight attendant gently touched her arm and told her they were commencing the descent into Ninoy Aquino Airport. She sat up and saw that Dulles was looking at her. "I'm anxious to get on the ground," he said.

"Where do we get that private plane?" she asked groggily.

"At Aquino Airport. They have very good facilities for private planes. They're set apart from the main terminal, so after we clear Customs and Immigration, we won't have to deal with crowds and lineups. Susan Crawford will be waiting for us when we get in. She'll have all the details."

It took them close to an hour to work their way through Customs and Immigration. As soon as they entered the arrivals hall they were greeted by a tall, lean blonde with curly hair and a long, thin face. She looked young; Ava might easily have mistaken her for a junior trainee. But Dulles had told her that, at the age of twenty-eight, Crawford already had a degree in international relations and a law degree from Georgetown University and spoke Spanish, Farsi, and Tagalog fluently.

"The plane is ready to leave," Susan said. "Follow me. I have a limo waiting for us outside."

"What kind of plane is it?" Dulles asked.

"A small business jet, a Cessna Citation something. It should get you to Bongao in a couple of hours."

They left the main terminal, jumped into the limo, and began a laborious drive around the extensive airport grounds to a set of hangars that advertised charter flights. The car drove past the hangars to a two-storey office building. "That's your plane over there," Susan said, pointing to one about fifty metres away on the tarmac. "You'll have to check in with the office first."

Inside the building, Dulles and Ava presented their passports to a man who worked for the charter company. "What would happen if, in mid-flight, we decided we didn't want to go to Bongao but instead wanted to scoot over to Borneo?" Ava asked him.

"The pilot wouldn't take you. If he did, he'd lose his job and our company would run the risk of losing our licence for violating a flight plan."

"That's good to know," Ava said.

"Always testing, aren't you," Dulles said as they left the building.

Susan and the charter company employee walked with them to the plane. "Safe journey," she said.

"Thanks. And you will remember to call us the instant you hear about those fingerprints?" Ava said.

"I called the lab while I was waiting for you, and I'm going to call them every hour on the hour until I get the results," she said. "When I do, you'll get them no more than a minute later, as long as Alasdair's phone is on."

"It'll be on," he said.

Ava stopped on the tarmac near the plane and took out her phone to call Wahab. "We'll be in Bongao about two hours from now," she said. "Is there any more news on the imam?"

"Nothing. I've also checked with General Santos City, and there's no religious conference that we can find."

"I'm not surprised," she sad. "Are things still calm at the college?"

"I think so. At least I haven't heard differently."

"And the police are still willing to help?"

"They'll take us inside. Don't worry about that."

"Okay, then we'll see you at the airport." She turned to Dulles. "No conference in General Santos City. Nothing else has changed."

Ava and Dulles boarded the plane. It had seven seats, and they sat across from each other. "I can't ever remember doing this much flying in such a compressed amount of time," he said.

"When I was in my old business, this was common," Ava said. "We'd take on a job and then go like hell, because once someone got even a sniff that we were onto them, the money could disappear in a flash."

"Ryan said you collected bad debts. Is that correct?"

"Yes."

"And he told me that the first time he met you, you directed him to a plane that was carrying more than eighty million dollars in cash to be laundered."

"That's true."

"How much of that did you get?"

"Thirty million — that was what my clients were owed."

"What was your fee?"

"Thirty percent."

"My god, nine million dollars?"

The plane started its taxi and the conversation quieted. When they were airborne, Ava said, "Thirty percent was standard for what we did. We earned substantially more than ten million on some deals."

"When you did that other job for Tommy Ordonez, how much did he pay you?"

"That would be a breach of client privilege."

Dulles started to say something and then caught himself.

"I'm thinking that you find that rather amusing," she said.

"No, I was actually going to ask how someone gets into that kind of business."

Ava wasn't sure she believed him but let it go. "You fall into it. I mean, there aren't any university accounting courses that specialize in debt collection...Although, now that I think about it, maybe there should be."

"How old are you?"

"Why do you ask that?"

"Curiosity, nothing more."

"I'm thirty-six."

"And how much are you worth?"

"What does that matter?"

"I'm forty-eight and I think I have a net worth of about five hundred thousand dollars."

"You should have chosen a different profession if you wanted big money," Ava said.

"But was it always about the money for you?"

"It was never all, or always, about the money. My partner wouldn't take on clients unless he believed they had been abused or misused. The money was almost incidental to making things right." She smiled. "Mind you, it didn't hurt that some of the amounts involved were large."

"Who was your partner?"

"I called him Uncle — everyone called him Uncle. He was already in his seventies, or maybe even eighties, when we started working together. He became like a grandfather to me."

"What happened if you and Uncle failed?"

"We ate all the costs and we had unhappy clients."

"Was that often?"

"Seldom. So seldom that I can think of only two cases."

"What were they?"

She turned and looked across the aisle at him. "I don't want to talk about them. And I actually don't want to talk about me anymore," she said. "But I would like to know what happened to you in Thailand."

"Did Ryan mention that?"

"He did."

"I screwed up," he said with a shrug. "I trusted some people who I shouldn't have and it turned out to be a disaster. If Brad Harrison and I didn't have a history, it could have ended my career. Instead I was sent to a place where I would be less visible. What's crazy is that if this thing explodes, especially with Tom Allison in the mix, I'll be more visible than ever."

"The setback in Thailand doesn't seem to have made you particularly cautious."

"I only know one way to do this job — full speed ahead. I'm not much good at covering my ass. And I suspect that my lack of paranoia — or, more positively, my tendency to trust my judgement of people's character — is going to get me in trouble again."

"My partner was like that, and it was an attitude I adopted," Ava said, surprised at Dulles's candour. "It actually ran contrary to my training, and maybe even to my nature, but I came to embrace it."

"So here we are, you trusting me and me trusting you and the two of us surrounded by a whole bunch of people who are dying to fuck us over."

"Well, the good news is, if they don't do it by the end of

today, they might not get another opportunity," she said.

He flashed a hint of a smile, turned away, and looked out the window. Ava suspected he'd had enough conversation, and she felt the same way. She pushed her seat back, closed her eyes, and tried to force herself to sleep again, even though she wasn't tired.

The flight took just under two hours, and it was late afternoon when the pilot announced they were starting their approach into Bongao. A few minutes later Ava saw the runway, and in the distance the terminal. They landed with a thump, and after the plane came to a quick stop, it did a sharp turn to the right and parked short of the building. The pilot poked his head through the cockpit door. "We're letting you out here. We're told there are some cars waiting for you."

"Can we leave our bags on the plane?" Ava said. "I'm tired of lugging mine around."

"No problem," he said.

When the plane door opened, Ava saw Wahab standing at the bottom of the steps, next to a tall, thickset man in a blue shirt with braid on the shoulders. Behind them, about twenty metres away, were two black Jeeps, each with a man in an identical blue shirt standing by the driver's-side doors.

"Ava, this is Captain Reyes," Wahab said when she was halfway down the steps.

"I can't thank you enough for your help," she said, extending her hand when she reached them.

"The captain is a good friend to me, Juhar, and the Brotherhood," Wahab said. "And you should know that I told him the truth about our reason for wanting to get into the college."

"He knows about the imam?"

"He does, and about the training we think has been going on there, although I didn't get into numbers."

"And Captain, you're content just to help us? You don't feel a need to investigate yourself?"

"Until there's a crime committed, he'll leave that to us and your American friend, who I also told him about," Wahab said.

"I'm proud to be of whatever assistance I can," Reyes said.

"Getting us into that college might be sufficient," Dulles said from behind Ava.

She stepped to one side so the three men could see each other. Wahab eyed Dulles warily, and to Ava it seemed that the police captain became more restrained.

"This is Alasdair Dulles," she said. "He's with the CIA, and his contacts overseas have helped confirm just about everything Ben and Alcem told us."

"You're alone?" Captain Reyes said.

"Yes, for now," Dulles said.

"I'm not accustomed to seeing American operatives in this region without an entourage of Philippine security personnel."

"Ava asked us to keep them in the dark until we felt secure about our facts. We've done that out of respect for her and for the promise she made to the Brotherhood," Dulles said, looking at Wahab. "I assume you're Wahab?"

"Yes."

"I'm pleased to meet you. I want to say right away that I think the way you've handled this entire situation has been beyond reproach. No matter how it ends, you and the Brotherhood deserve our thanks." The two men shook hands, and Ava could see Wahab starting to relax.

"It's going to be dark soon," Captain Reyes said. "Perhaps we should be on our way to the college."

"We're in your hands," Ava said.

The captain led the way to the Jeeps. As they approached, the two men at the cars stood to attention and saluted. "Wahab and I will lead in one car," Reyes said to Ava and Dulles. "You follow in the other."

"That was a nice bit of politics with Wahab," Ava said as she and Dulles climbed into the back of their Jeep.

"I meant it," he said.

The cars left the airport and followed the same route through the city that Ava had taken on her first trip to Bongao — a trip that seemed an eternity ago. They even followed the roadway that would take them to Maria's Restaurant, but they made a left turn before they got to it. The road had changed from asphalt to dirt, and there were nothing but trees on either side.

"It's isolated enough," Dulles murmured.

The road narrowed to a track, and as the Jeeps negotiated a long, slow bend, Ava saw Zakat College gradually emerge. "There it is," she said.

The lead Jeep stopped in front of the closed gate. Two security guards left a booth and walked tentatively towards it. Both of them were young and wore badly-fitting uniforms. They were obviously local, and they looked uncomfortable when Captain Reyes stepped out of the car and strode over to confront them. "Open the gate," he shouted.

The guards looked at each other, nodded, and then opened it. The others exited the vehicles and the captain led them past the gate towards the main door. It was opened by another security guard. He blinked when he saw the captain and quickly stepped aside.

"I know all these men," Reyes said. "I'm glad they have jobs, but they're hardly qualified to be security guards."

They walked into a large circular foyer. Straight ahead, two double doors lay open, and beyond them Ava saw a plainly decorated room with an empty elevated platform at its centre. She could imagine Imam Tariq al-Bashir sitting cross-legged on it while he preached. There were students sitting on the floor around the platform with books in their hands that she assumed were Korans. Several heads turned in her direction but then just as quickly returned to their books. *Were they expecting us?* she wondered.

She remembered from Ben and Alcem's description that the imam's room was in the wing to their left. "I think we should be looking over there," she said, and headed in that direction, the others quickly trailing behind her.

She reached a long corridor that was lined with closed doors. "This is where the imam and his staff lived. If the doors are locked, can we break through them?" she asked.

"Nothing we're doing here is precisely legal," the captain said. "I don't care what you do."

Dulles walked with her to the first door on the right. He turned the handle and they entered a room that had a single bed, a closet, a small dresser, and a wooden desk and chair. Ava opened the dresser while Dulles looked in the desk. They found nothing. The closet was just as bare.

With Wahab and the captain watching, Ava and Dulles went back and forth along the corridor and into three more rooms. Each was as sparsely furnished and had no indication of ever being occupied. Near the middle of the corridor they entered what seemed to be a communal bathroom. It smelled of bleach. "This has been scrubbed down," Dulles said.

Next to the bathroom was a kitchen with a double sink, cupboards, a stove, a microwave, a fridge, and a long dining table with eight chairs. The fridge was empty and had been cleaned. The sink and counters were spotless. The cupboards had also been emptied. Dulles walked to a door leading to a room next to the kitchen and opened it.

"The recreation room," Ava said, looking over his shoulder. She saw a sofa, easy chairs, a television, and a computer work station without a computer.

"They've taken just about everything," Wahab said.

"At least everything that would help us identify them," Dulles said.

At the end of the corridor they encountered a locked room. Ava looked questioningly at the captain. He nodded, stepped forward, and with three kicks forced it open. It was a larger bedroom than the others. It had the same kind of bed and dresser but its own sofa, easy chair, television, and work station — again with no computer. Ava opened a closed door off to one side into a small bathroom that reeked of bleach.

Back in the corridor, all that was left to open was a rear door that appeared to lead outside the building. Ava opened it, expecting to see open space. Instead she saw what looked like a garage that was big enough to hold about eight cars. Ava couldn't remember seeing it when they had driven by a few days before. The space was empty except for a line of metal bins set on the ground against the far wall, and rows of racks above the bins that she guessed were used for hanging tools, or maybe guns.

"They could have loaded their cars and the van in here, and no one would have seen them or heard them," Dulles said.

They walked to the bins and opened them. One contained bulletproof vests, another was full of shell casings, and two had rolls of wire that Wahab said was used for detonating bombs.

The garage had a dirt floor, and there were tire marks that led to and from a set of tall double doors. As Ava walked towards the garage doors, she saw some marks that didn't look like they had been left by a car or a van. "They had a tractor or some piece of heavy equipment in here," she said.

"Where is it now?" Wahab said.

Dulles opened the garage doors and they stepped outside. The change in the light almost blinded them, as the sun was hovering just above the horizon.

"There's the machine," Wahab said, pointing to the left. It was parked about twenty metres from them, its bright orange paint shimmering in the sun.

"That's not a tractor, it's an earthmover," Captain Reyes said. He walked around the vehicle, inspecting it.

"What do you expect to find?" Ava asked.

"Nothing. I'm just wondering why this machine is here."

Ava looked towards the back of the property, where stands of trees encircled a bare patch of land. "If they've been doing any digging, they were probably doing it over there," she said.

She began to walk towards the area and the others joined her. The grounds were surrounded by a fence that was about three metres high and, like the fence at the front entrance, topped by razor wire. Inside the fenceline were rows of trees that had broad leaves and branches that extended up and away from the trunk like the sticks of a hand-held fan. Ava imagined that anyone standing outside the fence wouldn't be able to see in. The growth was so thick that she guessed the trees would also muffle sound.

"What kind of trees are those?" she asked.

"Traveller's palms," Wahab said.

It took them a few minutes to reach the back of the property, and by that time the sun was on the horizon.

"Someone has been digging here," Captain Reyes said, kicking at some loose golden brown soil with the tip of his shoe.

"We were told they tested bombs and gave lessons on how to use weapons back here," Ava said. "Those trees would have hidden them and reduced the noise."

"This is where they might have deposited the bomb fragments, shells, and other debris," Dulles said.

The captain kicked at the soil again, then took a few stops towards the middle of the patch of ground and did the same. "There's nothing readily visible. We could do a bit of digging but it's going to be dark soon, and with no moon tonight, it will be pitch black back here. I've got some flashlights and shovels in our Jeeps. What do you think, should I get them?"

"We're here now, so you might as well," Dulles said.

"I'll go with you," Wahab said.

The captain and Wahab left, leaving Ava and Dulles staring blankly at the ground. "I was hoping we'd find something," he said.

"I know," she said, sharing his disappointment.

His phone rang. In the silent open space the ring was almost deafening. Dulles answered, listened for several minutes, and then began to smile. "Call me the moment you've finished your first round with him," he said.

"What was that about?" Ava asked.

"It was Delvano. They've got Fileeb al-Touma, a.k.a. Obeidat."

She drew a deep breath. "Thank god we've finally caught a break."

"They caught him at the Beirut airport. He was trying to catch a flight to Paris using another set of false documents, but Lebanese security had alerted the airport police and Immigration."

"Where is he now?"

"He's still at the airport. He'll be transferred to a security detail in a few hours, and then Delvano can have a go at him."

"That's fantastic."

"Well, it's a start."

Ava heard the sound of a car and looked towards the building. One of the Jeeps turned the corner by the garage and started towards them. A moment later, Wahab and the captain climbed out. Reyes took two shovels from the back seat.

"We'll have light for a bit longer, but I've got flashlights if we need them, and I figured we could use the Jeep's head-lights as well," Reyes said.

"I'll take one of those," Dulles said, holding out his hand for a shovel.

He and Reyes walked to the middle of the patch of bare ground. They turned their backs to each other and started to dig in opposite directions. The soil was loose and came away easily. They dug for several minutes, going down about a foot and gradually moving farther away from each other. The captain was the first to stop. "I've found what looks like a shell casing," he said, bending over to retrieve it and then placing it to one side.

Then Dulles found a casing, and he put it next to the captain's. Soon there was a small pile of them, and pieces of what looked like shrapnel. They continued digging, moving towards the outer edges of the patch. Both men were sweating, their shirts wet across their backs and at the armpits. Ava figured they had ten to fifteen minutes of daylight left.

The soil was denser the closer they got to the outer edges, and it took more effort to drive the shovels into the ground. They unearthed more shell casings and metal fragments.

Then suddenly Dulles stopped. He stood still for a few seconds before slowly reaching down. He pulled out something black; from the distance Ava thought it was a strip of leather. Dulles brushed dirt from it and said something to the captain, and the two of them walked over to where Ava and Wahab were standing.

As he drew near, Ava saw that he had a wallet in his hand. When the four of them were together, Dulles handed the wallet to Captain Reyes. He opened it and took out what looked like a driver's licence.

"This seems to belong to Boutros Hadad, age twenty-two, from Birmingham in the U.K.," he said.

## 36

**NO ONE SPOKE. AVA DIDN'T WANT TO GUESS WHAT THE** others were thinking. Her own imagination had taken her to a dark conclusion that she didn't want to voice.

Wahab was the first to speak. "Maybe the wallet fell out of his pocket during one of their exercises," he said.

"I guess that's possible," Reyes said hesitantly.

"We have to do more digging," Dulles said to the captain. "Are you okay with that?"

Reyes nodded. "Yes, but not with these shovels. Let's see if we can get that earthmover started."

They all got into the Jeep and drove back to the college in an uncomfortable silence. Reyes didn't find a key in the earthmover, and a quick search of the garage and al-Bashir's room failed to locate it. "One of the officers who drove us here can jump-start anything," Reyes said. "I'll get him."

The last vestige of the day's sun was peering over the horizon. When Reyes returned a few minutes later with the officer, they were in darkness. Reyes and Wahab turned on the flashlights and illuminated the earthmover's doorless cab. The officer climbed in and motioned for them to come closer as he lay on the floor. He unscrewed a plate below the steering wheel, spent about a minute checking wires, undid two from their connections, and then tied them together. He put his hand on the wheel and pulled himself up onto the driver's seat.

"This should work," he said as he pressed the starter button. The engine sputtered and gradually rumbled to life. He jumped down from the cab. "Do any of you know how to work this machine?"

"I don't have a clue," Dulles said.

"Me neither," said Wahab.

"Can you operate it?" the captain asked him.

"Sure. I spent a summer working with equipment like this," the officer said. "Where am I going with it?"

Wahab swung his flashlight in the direction of the stand of trees. "Over there. We should take both Jeeps, I guess. We'll need all the light we can get."

"I'll get the other one," Reyes said. "I'll meet you at the site."

Ava, Wahab, and Dulles got into the Jeep and, with Dulles driving, slowly made their way to the back of the property, with the earthmover following them. Even with the high beams on, visibility was poor because of the shadows cast by the broad leaves of the palm trees. When they were joined by Reyes and the second Jeep, the combined light created a clear if somewhat haunted-looking view. They got out of the Jeeps and stood at the perimeter of the soil patch. It was like being in a darkened theatre looking up at a brightly lit stage, Ava thought.

"What do you want to do?" the officer asked.

"Make our holes wider and go deeper," Dulles said.

"I shouldn't go straight down," the man said, looking at

Reyes. "It will be more efficient and easier on whatever is in the ground if I scrape across the top and gradually uncover layers."

"Whatever you think is best," the captain said.

The officer drove the machine onto the bare ground and was almost immediately swallowed up in shadow. He manoeuvred it to the left outer edge of Dulles's hole and turned so the light was in front of him. He positioned the earthmover's front-end bucket on the ground, put the machine into reverse, and backed up, taking several inches of soil from the surface with him. He moved the dirt to the far right and deposited it there. Then he drove back to where he'd started and repeated the process.

There was no conversation among the four people watching him. Their attention was riveted on the ground. Progress was almost imperceptible until about half an hour had passed. Ava saw that the original trenches had disappeared and the patch of ground was starting to resemble a large pit. As the ground was laid bare, more shell casings and metal fragments emerged, but nothing else. Ava began to feel a sense of relief, and she could see that the others seemed less tense.

When another fifteen minutes passed without discovering anything new, Ava began to wonder if they should call it off. She was about to make that suggestion to Dulles when his phone rang. He took it from his pocket and receded into the darkness to answer it. Ava tried to eavesdrop, but Dulles was speaking softly and his words were drowned out by the noise from the earthmover.

Then the machine stopped, and as the engine idled she heard Dulles say, "I can't believe it." She turned in his direction, but as she did the officer leaned from the cab and shouted, "Come over here!"

Ava, Wahab, and Reyes walked quickly towards him. He leapt down from the mover and went around the bucket to a spot of ground he'd just uncovered. His body cast a shadow and Ava couldn't see what had caught his attention. Then he moved to the side and pointed. Part of a hand was sticking out of the soil.

The captain shone his flashlight on the protruding object. Then he cast it back and forth around the general area. About two metres from the hand, Ava saw what she thought was a finger. She couldn't tell if it came from the same body. The captain flinched, and she knew he had seen it was well.

"What the hell is going on?" Dulles asked as he came over to join them.

"Body parts," Wahab said, his voice thick with emotion.

"Oh fuck," Dulles said. He stared at the hand for a few seconds, and then he gripped Ava by the elbow. "I have to talk to you for a minute. We need to move away from here."

"This is so awful," she said as they retreated past the Jeeps.

"As bad as it is, it's about to get even more complicated, and maybe worse."

"Your phone call?"

"Yes. It was Susan Crawford. They managed to lift a clean set of prints from the hairbrush."

"They identified al-Bashir?"

Dulles nodded, and even in the darkness Ava could see that his brow was deeply furrowed. "We didn't mention al-Bashir. We just gave them the brushes and asked them to find out what they could. They found Wallace Murdoch," he said.

"Murdoch?"

"I've always known him as Wally."

"You know him?" she said.

"He's ex-agency. He left four years ago for a job in the private sector."

"This is certain? There can't be some kind of mistake?"

"No, there's no mistake. It's him. And it made sense when I heard the name," Dulles said. "His last station was in Jordan. He must know Obeidat—al-Touma."

Ava looked back towards Reyes, Wahab, and the officer. She shivered, felt her body convulse, and fought back a powerful wave of nausea.

"I guess now we know where all those students are," she said.

## 37

**SHE WAS IN SHOCK AND SO WAS DULLES, BUT IT SEEMED** to her they were trying to cope with two different realities. He was trying to comprehend how the man named Murdoch had gone from being a colleague to some kind of pseudo-imam supposedly bent on the destruction of Jews. Ava couldn't turn her mind away from the potential mass grave they'd just unearthed.

They talked over each other at first, but they gradually slowed down and began to listen to what the other had to say. As they did, the realities began to merge, and they found themselves confronting a potential disaster beyond comprehension.

"Are you sure that hand and that finger belong to students?" Dulles asked.

"Who else could it be? And if there are two of them dead in that pit, then there are going to be more," she said. "That wasn't a lost wallet you found."

"We have to stop digging. We're not equipped to do this. A team will have to brought in," he said, almost talking to himself.

"You would know more about that than I do."

"This is like being in a bad dream." He looked at the men still standing by the earthmover. "What did they say?"

"Nothing. They're just numb, like us."

"We can't afford to be numb," Dulles said. "We have to contain this."

"How are we going to do that? That man is a police captain. There are body parts in a pit. This is his province, his jurisdiction. We're hardly in a position to tell him what to do."

"I need to contact Harrison."

"Do what you feel you have to," Ava said. "I'm not sure that I want to be involved in any more of this."

"You may not want to, but you promised the Brotherhood that you'd try to keep them safe from any fallout. This could be even worse than we imagined, especially for them," Dulles said. "All I want is to buy a little time so we can figure out the best way to handle this, for everyone concerned. One way of doing that is to convince the captain not to do anything until we can confirm what's in that pit."

"How long would that take? Days? And how many people would be in that team you'd bring in? Ten, twenty, thirty? There's no way you can keep things quiet and under control for that length of time and with that many people involved."

"If I could get twelve hours — until dawn tomorrow — I'd be satisfied."

"What can you do in twelve hours?"

"Come up with a plan to manage this mess, and that would include keeping the Brotherhood out of the spotlight."

"What about confirming what's in the pit?"

"Have you ever encountered ground-penetrating radar?"

"Of course not."

"It does exactly what the name implies: it can penetrate the soil and tell us how many bodies there are and where they're located. It's a quick and non-intrusive process. There's an operator in Manila we've used several times; he's good, and he knows how to keep his mouth shut. I'll ask Harrison to locate him and get him on a plane to Bongao." Dulles looked at his watch. "With any luck we might get him here by midnight."

"I can't believe we're standing here talking about counting bodies in a pit," she said.

"Ava, please help me with this," Dulles said, reaching for her hand. "The captain will listen to Wahab, and Wahab will listen to you. We all need a little time. It will benefit everyone if we know what we're really dealing with."

She withdrew her hand from his. "Are you confident you can get the radar technician here that fast? Are you sure that dawn deadline will be enough?"

"There are no other choices."

"Okay, then I'll talk to them. But I won't do it again if you fail," she said.

"That's fair enough. But Ava, you can't mention that we've identified the imam."

"You mean I can't mention Murdoch? I can't tell them that he's a former CIA agent?"

"I mean that precisely. There will be a time and place for that, and it isn't for you or me to decide."

"I'm not going to be bound by CIA protocol."

"This has nothing to do with CIA protocol. I don't know of anything that covers a situation like this," he said. "All I know is that we need to establish the facts before saying or doing anything."

"I do understand that this might not be the ideal time to tell them who al-Bashir really is," she said.

"Then wait, please. Wait until it's appropriate."

"Okay, I will. Why don't you go and make your phone calls while I talk to Wahab and Captain Reyes."

"I'll do it from the college. I'll be in the lounge. Join me when you're finished out here."

She watched him walk into the darkness and then started towards the pit. Wahab met her halfway.

"What were you talking about with the American?" he asked.

"What else?" she said, pointing to the pit.

"Captain Reyes wants to call this in. He says we'll need a lot more men," Wahab said. "I asked him to wait until we talked to you."

"That was the smart thing to do," Ava said, relieved that a call hadn't been made already. "We need to take time to confirm what we have here."

"Do you have any doubts?"

"Not really, but I can hope."

"How is it possible? I can't conceive of it. He was an imam!"

"Do you have any other explanation for what we've found? Are there any other candidates?"

"All I can think about is how bad this could be for us. If there are bodies in that pit, Manila won't care that it was Muslims killing other Muslims. It will give the army or the SAF the excuse they want to come in force to Mindanao."

"That's why you need to persuade the captain to do nothing until tomorrow morning. We're trying to fly in some expert from Manila tonight to examine the site with ground-penetrating radar. He'll tell us if there are two bodies or two hundred bodies."

"I pray that it's only two, but my instincts tell me it's more. How could an imam allow this to happen to fellow Muslims?"

"We're all praying for the same thing," Ava said. "But we need time to confirm the truth."

"But even if the captain doesn't call it in, are you sure the American will keep it quiet as well?"

"Yes. It serves his interests."

"I see. Maybe we should speak to Captain Reyes and let him know that. I think he's worried that someone else will report this before he has the chance."

"Okay. But I don't want to go back there," Ava said.

"I'll get him," he said.

"The bodies don't bother you?"

Wahab looked at her with a grim face. "I was in the field and at war against the Philippine government for fifteen years. I've seen a lot of bodies. So has Reyes."

A moment later the two men joined Ava. "Captain, do you know what ground-penetrating radar is?" she said.

"I know of it."

"Our plan is to get an expert to examine the site. Once it's clear what we're dealing with, then we'll know which authorities we need to involve."

"Why wouldn't it be a police matter?"

"Even if it is, are your local men trained to handle something of this magnitude?"

"What magnitude?"

She turned to Wahab. "You didn't tell the captain how many bodies might be in the pit?"

"No, I just said there could be a lot."

"Captain, there could be as many as 150," Ava said.

His face fell, and Ava heard a gasp from the officer who was standing by the earthmover.

"That's a possibility but not a certainty," Wahab said solemnly.

"If it turns out to be true, you'll need an entire team of experts to secure the scene, properly exhume the bodies, and start the appropriate forensic work," Ava said. "I'm assuming that you don't have those resources locally."

"We don't."

"Then all the more reason to wait. It wouldn't look good if you started the process, found out you couldn't handle it, and then had to call in outsiders to pick up the pieces. No one will blame you, though, for being cautious enough to determine the facts before you ask for help."

"How long will this expert take?"

"I'm told that if we can get him here tonight, he'll be finished by dawn."

"I might be prepared to wait until then." Reyes glanced at Wahab. "But what about the American?"

"He'll say nothing."

"Okay. If that's the case, we'll wait."

"Thank you," Ava said. "Now, do we have to stay here or can we go back to the college?"

"It makes no difference to me if you go," Reyes said. "But I'm staying here with my officer."

"I'll go with you," Wahab said to Ava.

"We'll come back the instant we hear about this expert's arrival," Ava said.

Wahab used the flashlight to lead them towards the college. They walked in silence until they were almost at the rear door.

"What if there are only two bodies?" Wahab said.

"You said you were praying for that."

"Yes, but when I was looking at that hand, I found myself struggling with the morality of it. Would the world be a better place if there were two or more than a hundred? If there are two, that means the rest of them are somewhere preparing to kill and be killed. What's worse, the certain death of a hundred or more or the potential death of maybe thousands?"

Ava had no answer.

## 38

**THEY FOUND DULLES SITTING ON THE SOFA IN THE** lounge with his phone pressed to his ear. *Give me five minutes*, he mouthed.

Ava and Wahab wandered back to the main entrance. The other police officer stood at the door talking to one of the security guards. "Have any of the students left the main hall?" Ava asked.

The guard looked at this watch. "They'll be there for about another hour, and then they'll go to their dorms in the other wing," he said.

"Captain Reyes wants you to make sure no one leaves the building," she said to the police officer.

"Yes, ma'am," he said.

Ava looked into the main hall. The students were still sitting with their books resting on their laps. She watched them for several minutes, trying to understand how this studious, seemingly peaceful group of young men could be turned into something so different. Any psychology she knew had been learned from Uncle and her years on the job, and its application was limited to mainly one-on-one dealings. She had no clue about the nuances of mass persuasion. A couple of questions popped into her mind. She thought about asking Wahab but stopped herself — the timing couldn't have been more inappropriate.

"Hey," Dulles said from the wing corridor. "I'm finished."

Ava and Wahab joined him and they walked together back to the lounge.

"What did the captain say?" Dulles asked. "Will he wait?"

"He will," Ava said.

"So you told him about the radar?"

"I did, and he's fine with it."

"Excellent. We should know soon when the technician is going to get here. We should meet him at the airport."

"You've talked to him already?"

"My people did. They're arranging for a private plane," Dulles said. "And Wahab, my thanks for the assistance you've provided."

"Let's hope it wasn't misplaced," Wahab said.

Ava and Dulles sat on the sofa and Wahab took the easy chair. They tried to have a conversation but mostly just stumbled around. Ava had questions for Dulles that she didn't want Wahab to hear, and she was sure they were being as circumspect. Only one subject was on their minds, and nobody wanted to talk about either its possible horrible reality or its ramifications. After some awkward minutes, Wahab turned on the television and found a Philippine variety show.

Dulles's phone rang before the first singer had finished. He looked at the incoming number, listened briefly, and then said, "What's his ETA?" Evidently satisfied with the answer, he ended the call. "The technician's name is Alan Dawson. He'll be here in about three hours."

They watched the variety show, then a quiz show that was mainly about famous Filipino singers and actors, and then a local talent show that originated in Manila but featured amazingly talented young female singers from the provinces. The singers all seemed to come from poor families, and the show's hostess spent countless minutes describing their dire circumstances. Nothing seemed to make her happier than getting the contestants to cry before they had a chance to sing.

"I think we can get going now," Dulles said as the show ended. Led by Wahab's flashlight, they walked back to the pit. Captain Reyes and his officer were sitting in one of the Jeeps. The earthmover was where they'd left it but had been turned off.

"The technician will be arriving at the airport in about half an hour," Dulles said to the captain. "Would you mind taking us there to meet him?"

"I'll be pleased to," Reyes said.

They took one of the Jeeps. The captain drove, Wahab sat in the front passenger seat, and Ava and Dulles sat in the back. When they reached the airport, Security allowed the captain to drive onto the tarmac. They were told the incoming plane was only five minutes away. As they waited, Wahab turned to the captain and said something in Tagalog; she figured that he was trying to get the captain's support. Despite her assurances and her best efforts, she couldn't see this ending well for the Brotherhood. Dulles could tell the CIA how important their co-operation had been, but it wouldn't matter if the government wanted to use the college as an excuse to run roughshod over the Brotherhood.

"There's a plane approaching," Reyes said.

Ava saw flashing lights against the black sky. It was just past eleven o'clock on the longest night after the longest day in her memory.

The plane landed smoothly and taxied in their general direction. It stopped about a hundred metres from them and Reyes eased the Jeep towards it. The door opened and a small, thin man bounced down the steps. Dulles left the car and walked towards him. They chatted while the pilot exited the plane, and then they joined him at the baggage hold. A moment later all three men walked towards the Jeep, carrying large leather boxes.

Reyes got out of the Jeep and opened the tailgate. Dulles introduced him to Alan Dawson. After the boxes were loaded, Dulles escorted Dawson to the rear passenger door. The technician seemed surprised to see Ava sitting in the back seat.

"We're a bit cramped, but it isn't a long trip," Dulles said.

He finished making introductions as they drove away from the airport. "So what am I doing here?" Dawson asked after everyone was acquainted.

"You don't know?" Ava said.

"I was told I might be looking for a body, but my boss was a bit vague about it."

"What do you normally look for?"

"We're a mining company. I look for metals, for ore, veins of ore."

"But you've looked for bodies before?" Wahab said, turning around.

"Sure I have, and I've done it for your government and for my own."

"You're American?"

"Yeah, I am."

"How does this radar thing work?" Reyes asked.

"Well, it doesn't matter if you're looking for a body or a vein of ore — it's the same process. I push my equipment, the radar, over whatever site you want examined. As I cross the ground, I send electromagnetic waves from the antenna. The waves reflect off whatever is in the ground and transmit the results back to a monitor I carry. The results are stored in the monitor's computer until I'm ready to display them."

"What are its limitations?" Reyes asked.

"What do you mean?"

"Can you work at night?"

"Of course, or I wouldn't be here now."

"What if there's more than one body?"

"We'll find them."

"What if there are twenty?"

"That wouldn't be a problem."

"How about two hundred?"

Dawson turned to Dulles. "Is he serious?"

"We're dealing with a lot of unknowns. You're here to give us a number."

Dawson nodded. "I'll find whatever is there."

Reyes sped through the empty streets until he reached the turnoff to the dirt road. As they bounced along the ruts, Dawson looked increasingly uncomfortable.

"Are you feeling okay?" Ava asked.

"I'm worried about my equipment."

"Captain Reyes, could you slow down please," Dulles said.

The police officer was at the gate when they arrived at the college. He saluted and swung it open. Reyes drove the Jeep to the back of the buildings and then eased over the ground to the pit. He stopped short of it and turned on his high beams.

They helped Dawson unpack his gear, then gathered around him while he assembled it in the light cast by the car. It didn't look particularly impressive, just a square box joined to a rod that led to a monitoring device. The three pieces were connected to a wheel that held the box off the ground.

"How long will this take?" Dulles asked.

"That depends on what's down there and how much detail you want."

"Be as thorough as possible, but try to finish before daylight."

"Yes, it's better to be sure," Reyes added.

"How wide an area should I be examining?"

Dulles took one of the flashlights. "The treeline marks the outer edges. We want all the ground between the trees to be examined."

"I'll work from the outside in," Dawson said. "I'll need light so I can keep track of my path. The headlights aren't bad, but it would be better if someone walked beside me with a flashlight."

"We'll take turns," Dulles said. "I'll go first."

Dawson rolled his equipment to the northwest corner. With Dulles alongside and the flashlight pointing down in front of them, he started walking at a steady moderate pace. Everyone watched his face, but it remained expressionless. He pursed his lips and retraced his steps from time to time. After fifteen minutes, Wahab replaced Dulles. Then Reyes and Ava took turns with the flashlight.

Dawson held the monitor in front of his chest. The

temptation to look at what he was recording was almost irresistible, but Dawson seemed to be aware of their interest and kept the screen angled so they couldn't see anything. His progress was slow. An hour turned into two and then three. The only time Dawson reacted visibly was when he reached the finger and the hand that were sticking out of the soil. He tiptoed around them.

When he finally reached the middle of the pit, almost five hours had elapsed and sunrise was closing in. Dawson stared at the monitor, looking up only briefly as the others approached.

"What did you find?" Wahab asked.

"Just a minute. I'm still doing the calculation," Dawson said.

"So you've found something other than the two body parts we can see?" Reyes asked.

"There are bodies in the ground."

"How many?" Wahab said.

"I'm having trouble getting an accurate count," Dawson said.

"Why?" Dulles said, his voice on edge.

"They're so tightly packed together in some places that it's hard to separate one from another."

"Can you give us an estimate?" Dulles said.

"More than 120 for sure, and I wouldn't be surprised if there were twenty or thirty more."

Even in the uneven light, Ava could see Wahab's face turn pale. Reyes shook his head.

Dulles turned and walked away, taking his phone from his pocket. "Where are you going?" Ava called after him.

"There's a call I have to make."

"We need to talk."

"After my call."

## 39

AVA STOOD NEXT TO WAHAB AND THE CAPTAIN. REYES
was speaking to Alan Dawson. He kept looking at the monitor, as if hopeful that the findings would change.

"Where's the American?" Wahab asked her.

"Making a call. He'll be back in a minute."

"I hope he's not phoning Manila without discussing it with
Captain Reyes and me."

"I expect he's talking to someone in the U.S. They'll be
anxious to know that the terrorist threat wasn't real."

"Are you one hundred percent sure that's the case?"

Ava touched him lightly on the arm. "Wahab, who do you
think is buried in the ground?"

"I know it appears obvious that it's the students, but that
doesn't mean it makes sense," he said. "Why would they
bring them all the way here and then spend three months
indoctrinating and training them before killing them?"

"I know it isn't logical," Ava said. The name *Murdoch* kept
resonating in her head.

Dulles emerged from the dark to rejoin them. He had a
grim look on his face. "Let's all talk," he said, and walked

past her and Wahab towards the captain and Dawson.

They followed him to the side of the pit. Just as they arrived, the first glint of morning sun appeared.

"It's been a long night and we've done the best we can under horrible circumstances," Dulles said. "I've just spoken to my people in the U.S. and given them a report on what we think we've found here. I've been told that unless there's evidence to the contrary, we're going to regard this as a Philippine domestic matter —"

"Did your people talk to the authorities in Manila?" Wahab interrupted.

"No, I haven't and they haven't. We believe that under these circumstances Captain Reyes should be the one to report these crimes. He'll obviously make his own decision about who to contact."

"You're just going to walk away from this?" Wahab said.

"As it stands, there's no reason for us to be involved. The deaths took place on Philippine soil. There is no U.S. interest at stake here."

"What about helping to identify and find the imam and his people?" Wahab said.

"I'm sure my government would respond appropriately to any request from the Philippine government."

"The brushes we sent to Manila?"

"I've just been told that the lab wasn't able to get a clean set of prints from either of them," Dulles said.

"There's no reason to question Mr. Dulles about what the Americans are going to do," Reyes said. "He's right — this is our problem and we're capable of handling it."

"And no one on our side doubts your capability," Dulles said.

Reyes nodded. "I'll make a call to the National Police headquarters in Manila. I wanted to do that last night, but I'm glad I waited for Mr. Dawson to conclude his work."

"Speaking of Mr. Dawson, we paid his way here. I've been instructed to tell you that, as a courtesy, we'll continue to pay him for as long as you think you need him," Dulles said.

"I'll pass that offer along to my superiors."

"Captain," Ava said, "I have some information that might also prove useful." She saw Dulles's eyes widen and his body stiffen. "I did some work with your Bureau of Immigration and I think we were able to identify most of the students. We have landing cards with their names and other particulars on them."

"That will make things easier," Reyes said.

"I can arrange to have them sent to you."

"Please wait until I get direction from Manila. I'll tell them what you have and then they can decide who they should be sent to."

"Thank you. Wahab knows how to get hold of me." The sun was partially above the horizon now, and its light was starting to find its way across the terrain. "Maybe we should go," she said to Dulles. "Unless there's something you want to clarify?"

"No, I think we're done here," he said.

"Just one moment," Captain Reyes said. "I think I need to make it clear that, if not me, someone on the force will have questions for you. Can I assume you'll both make yourselves available and be co-operative?"

"I don't have any objection, as long as I'm not required to stay in the Philippines," Ava said.

"When do you intend to leave?"

"As soon as possible."

"That shouldn't be a problem," Reyes said. "But you should expect someone to contact you within the next few days."

"You sound like a man who doesn't expect to be heading up this investigation," she said.

"I'm a realist, but not entirely a pessimist."

"And I won't be leaving the Philippines, although I can't give any assurances about availability or co-operation," Dulles said.

"I didn't expect that you could."

"Jurisdictional politics are my reality."

Ava shook her head. "But they aren't mine. Wahab, I want you to know that I'll continue to do everything I can for you and the Brotherhood. I have tremendous respect for the way you've handled all this."

"The respect is mutual. And that sentiment is shared by Juhar and the Brotherhood's other senior officials. We appreciate all that you've done."

The conversation stalled and Dulles filled the gap. "Thanks to all of you," he said briskly. "Ava and I have a plane waiting. Can we get a ride to the airport?"

"Sure," Reyes said, and turned to his officer. "Take them to the airport."

The first word that Ava and Dulles exchanged after leaving Zakat College was in the plane after takeoff, and it was only one word.

"Why?" she said.

"Why what?"

"Murdoch. Why didn't you tell them about Murdoch? Why did you lie about the fingerprints?"

He grimaced. "I need to thank you for not calling me out on that."

"Believe me, I wanted to, but I figured there has to be some kind of compelling reason."

"I don't know how compelling it is. I was simply told that we aren't ready to tell the Filipinos about him."

"But the Filipinos have no chance of capturing him unless they know his real identity."

"It appears that we don't want him caught, at least not just yet."

"Because you don't want anyone to know who he is?"

"That could be the case."

"Because he's an American and a former agent?"

"I think there's another reason at least as strong as that."

"What?"

"Tom Allison."

## 40

**AVA TURNED AWAY FROM DULLES. SHE WAS SURPRISED** but not shocked that Tom Allison's name had re-entered the conversation. However, her primary reaction was disgust.

She looked out the plane window and saw that they were crossing the northern tip of Tawi-Tawi and heading over the Sulu Sea. *What landmass will we see next?* she wondered, struggling to find a distraction while she gathered her emotions. She conjured up a mental map of the Philippines. It would be the southwestern tip of the island of Mindanao; then they'd continue northwest across Negros and Panay Islands. She'd done collection work in both places, in fact twice on Panay, in the less than enthralling cities of Iloilo and Roxas. Mindoro was next, she thought, and then they'd reach the island of Luzon and Manila. As Ava connected the islands that marked their progress, another part of her brain was connecting Tom Allison to Zakat College.

"Are you okay?" Dulles finally said.

"I was thinking about Allison's performance in his hotel suite," she said, without looking at him. "I thought it was contrived at the time. And then, of course, he didn't want to talk or meet with you yesterday morning."

"That's simply an opinion on your part, a reaction to a man who's not particularly likeable," Dulles said. "And he had an explanation for why he wouldn't talk to me."

"Are you making excuses for him?"

"Of course not. Besides, your opinion of him and my being snubbed by him don't matter very much. In fact, they don't matter at all," Dulles said. "What does matter is that Wallace Murdoch, Fileeb al-Touma, and the cast of characters that surrounded them are linked to a company called Glenda Investments."

"When did this Glenda Investments enter the picture?"

"Delvano mentioned it to me late last night. It came up during his initial chat with al-Touma."

"Al-Touma was co-operative?"

"He said he had done nothing wrong and had nothing to hide. Delvano didn't press him too hard on that. He thought it better to hear what he had to say first."

"Is this Glenda Investments an Allison company?"

"Officially it's an investment company based in Tel Aviv that is wholly owned by a woman named Glenda Marshall."

"And she is . . . ?"

"According to al-Touma she's a wealthy American busi-nesswoman with strong ties to the Middle East," Dulles said. "But we've discovered that she's actually a lawyer who works for Tom Allison. We're still waiting to confirm whether she's on his payroll as an employee or works for him on a retainer and fee basis."

"Either way, it connects him to al-Touma and Murdoch."

"Yes, we're sure it does."

"Which means you've got him connected to the college

through the casino and through Glenda Investments. Those aren't coincidences."

"We don't think so either."

"And how are al-Touma, Murdoch, and the others tied to Glenda?"

"Delvano said they're all employed by the company. Murdoch was the first hire and runs the show. He gradually recruited the others from various security organizations in the Middle East, including Israel, and in the U.S. It's logical to assume that Murdoch knew them all from his time in the field."

"What were they employed to do?"

"I'm glad you're sitting down. I wasn't when Delvano told me, and I damn near fell over," Dulles said. "According to al-Touma, their objective is to build and operate colleges for the purpose of training young Muslim men in providing security for their home communities."

"Colleges? In the plural?"

"The one in the Philippines was the first. There are long-term plans for others in Indonesia, Malaysia, and Pakistan. Indonesia is scheduled to be next. They've bought the land but are still accumulating the money they need from the casino to break ground and start construction."

"That's unbelievable."

"I wish it were," Dulles said.

"Did al-Touma ever visit the college in Tawi-Tawi?"

"No. He said he's the only one not based there."

"So he might not know what was really going on?"

"That's possible. He was insistent that his only job is to manage money. He said we'd have to speak to Murdoch for details on the curriculum — as funny as that word sounds."

"He referred to him as Murdoch and not as al-Bashir?"

"He said he's never heard of Tariq al-Bashir."

"Did Delvano believe him?" Ava asked.

"No. But again, as long as al-Touma was talking, he didn't want to put too much pressure on him. We can do that later."

"Did you tell Delvano what we found at the college?"

"I was instructed not to."

"By whom?"

"Brad Harrison."

"Does Harrison know you're telling me all this?"

Dulles leaned across the aisle towards her. "I told him that you've figured out all the essential parts already and that withholding a few details would be counterproductive if they want your co-operation."

"My co-operation or my silence?" she said, sensing his discomfort.

"There are some things that have to be left for Harrison to say."

Ava shook her head. She was exhausted and emotionally drained. The information that had just come to light was punishing her capacity to think. "Why would your boss have anything to say to me?"

"None of this would have come to light without you."

"Tell him he can send me a thank-you note," Ava said.

"Brad would prefer to thank you in person."

She looked at him. "This is becoming awkward."

"I apologize for that. It isn't my choice."

"So what the hell is going on?"

"There's a plane on its way from Washington to Manila. It will arrive late this afternoon. Brad is on it. I know that he has company but I don't have any details. All I've been told is that it's important that you be available to meet," Dulles said. "I've also been told that you aren't the only person they want to talk to."

"Allison?"

"Yes. He's been asked to fly to Manila, and evidently he agreed."

"So obviously you and your boss have discussed Allison's connections to the money funding Zakat College and Murdoch."

"We have, and I'm sure it's gone beyond him by now."

"If that's the case, why does anyone need to talk to me? I have nothing more to contribute."

Dulles shrugged. "I'm relaying a request. I'm not in a position to justify it."

"I don't react well when I think I'm being manipulated or pushed around," Ava said. "This has a definite feeling of manipulation, and I suspect that the pushing around will come hard on its heels."

"I wouldn't make either of those assumptions," Dulles said. "Brad isn't into playing games. He's normally straightforward."

"I'd appreciate it if you would be straightforward as well," she said. "Tell me, what would happen if I decided to hop on the first plane out of Manila that was headed for Hong Kong or Shanghai?"

"Don't even think about doing that."

"Why not?"

He pursed his lips, and for a second his eyes moved away from her. The sun was pouring in through the windows, highlighting the weary and troubled look on his face. "I suspect that they would find you and that they'd have their meeting whether you wanted it or not," he said. "I don't want it to come to that."

## 41

**AS SOON AS THEY LANDED AT AQUINO AIRPORT, AVA**
called the Peninsula Hotel and booked a suite. She and
Dulles hadn't talked on the plane after he insisted she meet
with Brad Harrison. There wasn't much more to be said, and
their discussion had seemed only to intensify their state of
exhaustion. He didn't say anything to her until they had
landed and were walking towards a taxi stand.

"I'm going to the office. I'll call you at the hotel as soon as
I know what the arrangements are," he said.

"Don't phone me too early. I have to sleep, and all I need
is an hour's notice."

"I'll wait until things are absolutely set," he said. "Do you
want to share a cab now?"

"No, I'd like to be alone, if that's okay with you," she said.
He nodded and stepped aside, and Ava climbed into the
waiting taxi.

It was the height of rush hour. Ava sat slumped in the back of
the taxi, absent-mindedly watching the jeepneys, buses, motorcycles, and cars crawl along Epifiano de los Santos Avenue. It
was mid-morning by the time she reached the Peninsula. To

her relief, the suite was immediately available. The second the door closed behind her, she began stripping off her clothes. Ten minutes later, naked and her hair damp from a quick shower, she crawled under the duvet and pulled it over her head.

She thought she'd fall asleep quickly, but her mind wasn't listening to her body. It kept dragging her back to Bongao and the college, and the patch of bare ground that had been turned into a graveyard. She couldn't shut out the images of young men like Jason Said. What had it been like on the day that they died? Did they walk to the back of the property? How many of them had gone at one time? Did Murdoch's assistants — his assassins — walk with them or were they waiting for them there? How much time would have elapsed between one group and the next? How much time would it have taken to shoot them, put them in the ground, and cover them with dirt? What did the students at the college think when their colleagues didn't return? Or were they segregated so they couldn't see and couldn't know? And how were they killed? A bullet to the back of the head was her guess; it was the quickest and surest way. Did they kill them one by one, or did four, five, or six guns fire at the same time?

Ben and Alcem had told her the local staff were given two days off at the end of each three-month term — the time of the killings. Had it taken two days to kill and bury the students? Or maybe they needed the time to make the ground look undisturbed. Maybe they needed to gather themselves as they waited for the next batch of students to arrive.

*It was so cruel*, Ava thought. The young men would have been full of enthusiasm, primed to set off on their own grand, horrific adventure. What would they have been thinking during the last seconds of their lives? Would they have realized what was happening or would they have thought it was a joke, or perhaps a last test, the final bit of training?

She understood rationally that these were not exactly innocent young men. They may have been naive but they had gone to the college for a reason. She couldn't help wondering what would have happened to them if they'd stayed home, if they hadn't been enticed to come to the Philippines. How many of them would have conceived the idea of killing Jews — of killing anyone — unless it was planted in their heads and then nurtured until it was their new reality? How many, like Jason Said, just wanted to create a Muslim state that reflected their community and values?

Ava felt tears well up and trickle down her cheeks. She wiped at them with the duvet and then shuddered — she felt unbelievably cold. She slipped out of bed, went to her carry-on bag, and put on a T-shirt, underwear, and her training pants and jacket. She started to walk back to the bed, then stopped. She reached for her phone and called a familiar Shanghai number.

"Hey, *mei mei*," Xu answered. "May Ling has been calling me, wondering where you are and what's going on."

"Well, I'm in Manila —" she said, her voice breaking.

"Is it as bad as you sound?"

"Yes."

"Do you want to tell me about it?"

"There's almost too much to tell."

"Do you want me to come to Manila?"

The offer was so spontaneous, Ava felt a surge of affection that prompted her tears to course once more. "I couldn't ask you to do that."

"You don't have to ask. I'll catch the first flight out in the morning."

"No, Xu, please don't come. I appreciate the offer, but the thing going on here is almost over, and all I want to do is leave."

"Come to Shanghai. Let us look after you."

"Yes, I'll do that."

"But tell me, Ava, what did Chang Wang drop you into?"

"Something he knew very little about, and if he does know now, it's because someone other than me told him about it," she said, beginning to gather herself. "There are about 150 young men buried at that goddamn college in Tawi-Tawi. All of them are Muslims who thought they were going to be trained to fight. Instead, they were recruited for the purpose of being killed."

"Who knows this?"

"No one. And Xu, you have to keep it that way until you hear it on the news... which should be soon enough."

"One hundred and fifty?"

"They're going to start excavating the bodies in the next day or two. That should confirm the number."

"What the hell happened? Who conceived of this? Who carried it out?"

"I can't talk about it right now."

"Okay. Do you want me to book your flight to Shanghai?"

"No, I'll look after it when I can."

"But you're coming?"

"Yes, I promise," she said, before saying goodbye.

She took several deep breaths; her chest felt lighter. Shanghai was a good idea, she told herself. Xu would listen to her and Auntie Grace would take care of her. She went back to bed and retreated beneath the covers.

## 42

**SHE WAS IN THE BATHROOM WHEN HER PHONE RANG.**
It was close to six o'clock in the evening and she'd been up for
half an hour. She hadn't missed any calls while she napped,
and a quick check of her computer didn't show much activity either.

"This is Ava Lee."

"It's Dulles."

"Where are you?"

"I'm at the office but we're getting ready to leave. Given
the time of day, it should take at least an hour to get to your
hotel."

"We're meeting here?"

"The idea is to keep things unofficial and informal. We've
booked the Reyes Room on the second floor."

"The Reyes Room?"

"I know it's the same name as the captain's, but that's
what it's called."

"How many of you are there?"

"Myself, Brad, Jeff Gilmour from the Office of National
Intelligence, and Charles Bentley, who works in the White

House," Dulles said. "Gilmour and Bentley will not tell you where they work, and you're not supposed to know. But Brad and I figured you should understand who you're dealing with. Bentley shares Allison's religious views and has a past association with him. He's a bit of a jerk but smart and tough, so don't underestimate him. Gilmour has his own ties to the White House. He's a heavy hitter in my field and as senior as Brad."

"Thanks."

"I've already given them a quick briefing."

"Have you spoken to Delvano?"

"He's been told to back off on al-Touma until decisions are made here. He's pissed about it but there's nothing he can do."

"Anything else?"

"Reyes has obviously reported the situation at the college. The National Police have called a news conference for seven o'clock tonight, and some friends over there said a task force has been mobilized. By tomorrow morning the college will be swarming with cops, military, pathologists, and any number of forensic and technical people."

"Do you know what's going to be said at the press conference?"

"They don't have any hard facts yet. All they have are bodies in the ground, but you can bet they'll squeeze as much drama as they can out of this."

"What about the Muslim connection?"

"It will be played up. They're going full out to try to locate al-Bashir, and they are emphasizing that he's an imam."

"Any al-Bashir sightings?"

"Nope."

"I feel badly for Wahab and the Brotherhood. They're going to get tarred with that brush."

"Well, he's got Captain Reyes to speak for him…assuming that the captain still has some role to play."

Ava's phone indicated another incoming call. It was Chang Wang. She hesitated and then said, "Alasdair, I have to take another call. Let me know when you get to the hotel." She switched lines. "Uncle Chang."

"Ava, I'm so sorry."

"I'm assuming that means you know what happened at the college?"

"Ramirez just told me. I can hardly believe it."

"He must be worried about the pineapple plantations," she said. "How does Tommy feel?"

"I haven't told him yet, but when I do, I'm going to remind him that he was the one who did the deal with Ramirez and he was the one who took on the risk. I'm also going to tell him that we owe you an apology for involving you in this mess."

"It's just awful," she said.

"I know."

"Just so it's clear, I did everything I could to protect the Brotherhood."

"I don't doubt that."

"And I plan to leave Manila tomorrow."

"I don't blame you," Chang said. "I thought about Uncle when I heard what happened. I thought how angry Uncle would have been at me for putting you in this situation. When he drank, he used to brag about how tough and smart you are, except he said you have trouble dealing with death."

"What kind of person is comfortable with death?"

"Those who accept that it is inevitable and who understand that all they're missing is the date," Chang said.

"Uncle was right. It isn't a subject I want to think or talk about."

"Neither do I. But then you look in the mirror one morning and a stranger is looking back at you." Then, sensing her discomfort, Chang said, "But you have many years ahead of you."

"Thank you, Uncle. I'll call you if something new comes up with regard to the college or the Brotherhood," she said, ending the conversation.

She looked at her reflection in the mirror. She closed her eyes and took a deep breath, then finished brushing her hair and coiled it back with the ivory chignon pin. She was wearing a white Brooks Brother shirt with a modified Italian collar and French cuffs, black slacks, and black pumps. Instead of the green jade cufflinks she normally wore, she chose a gold pair with blue enamel and Chinese lettering that read LUCK IS WITH YOU; she had bought them at the Shanghai Tang store in Hong Kong. She put on some red lipstick and a touch of black mascara and slipped her gold crucifix around her neck. She looked smart, professional, and — she thought as she fingered the crucifix — Christian.

Ava walked back into the living room and turned on the television to a local news channel. There was no mention of the press conference, Tawi-Tawi, or Bongao. She left the TV on and went to her computer. Starting with her mother, she wrote messages to her entire family and most of her close friends. She told them where she was and that she'd be heading to Shanghai the next day and would be back on the grid. She finished every email the same way: I love you and miss you.

At seven o'clock she looked at the television and saw there was a special news alert. She turned up the volume. An empty podium appeared on the screen; on the wall behind it was a seal with the words NATIONAL POLICE OF THE PHILIPPINES beneath. To either side of the podium Ava saw television cameras, with journalists seated in front of them.

At ten after seven the podium was still unattended, and there was no indication of why the news conference had been called. A moment later, what looked like a sound technician checked the microphones. When he left, she saw several uniformed officers begin to congregate in the background. As they started towards the podium, her phone rang. "Damn it," she said as she answered.

"It's Dulles. I'm downstairs in the hallway near the meeting room. We're ready to go."

"The press conference is just about to start."

"You'll have to skip it. Everyone is antsy, and making them wait will only make it worse."

"Five minutes, then," Ava said.

"One more thing: Tom Allison and his bodyguard George are definitely in Manila."

"How do you know that?"

"Allison phoned Bentley when he landed."

"Bentley is the one from the White House who knows him?"

"He is."

"Uncle used to say that the only thing more loathsome than politicians and crooked businessmen are the parasites who feed off them."

## 43

**AVA RODE THE ELEVATOR TO THE SECOND FLOOR AND** exited with some apprehension.

"Over here," Dulles said, standing about twenty metres from her in the empty corridor. She thought he looked even more agitated than when she'd left him in the morning. "Did you have a tough afternoon?" she asked as she approached.

"I'm tired, that's all. How about you?"

She nodded. "I slept."

"We'd better go in," he said.

She followed him down the hallway to a closed door. He knocked, waited a couple of seconds, and opened it. The room had one rectangular table with twelve seats around it. To the left was a small table with two white carafes, jugs of milk and cream, and cups and saucers. There were three men in the room. Two stood by the table with cups in their hands, while the third was seated.

"This is Ava Lee," Dulles said.

The man who was seated stood and walked towards her. He was short and wiry and had a fringe of grey hair that circled like a halo an otherwise bald head.

"Hello, I'm Brad Harrison," he said.

Ava had been expecting a slightly older version of Dulles. Instead, Harrison had to be in his sixties and was somewhat stooped, but he still moved with agility and exuded considerable energy. If his back were straighter, he would have been only a few inches taller than her. As it was, he looked her directly in the eyes. She blinked when he did. Not many people had that kind of confidence. The only other person she had known whose eyes were as penetrating was Uncle. And strangely, like Uncle, Harrison was wearing a black suit with a white shirt and no tie. The only difference was that Uncle had buttoned his shirt up to the collar, while Harrison's top button was undone.

"And Jeff Gilmour and Charles Bentley are the people getting coffee," Harrison said. "Charles is wearing the suit."

They nodded at her but didn't move away from the table. Gilmour was close to six feet, with thick blond hair and a pudgy face; he was wearing a white Nike polo shirt and brown khakis. Ava guessed he was in his forties and had spent his life sitting behind a desk. Bentley was about the same height but looked ten years younger and fifty pounds fitter; he had a receding hairline and, like the others, was clean-shaven. He wore a charcoal-grey suit, white shirt, and blue silk tie.

"We thought it would be best if you sat here at the end of the table," Harrison said, pointing to the chair they were standing next to. "Would you like coffee or tea before we start?"

"I'm fine, thank you," Ava said, taking the seat.

Harrison returned to his and Dulles sat beside him. Gilmour and Bentley sat across from them. They were sitting two seats down from Ava on either side. She didn't know if the seating arrangement was intended to intimidate her, but it certainly sent the message that she was there to be questioned.

"Ms. Lee, we would like to thank you for agreeing to talk to us. We know you're not under any obligation to do so," Harrison said.

Ava noticed that Bentley had taken what looked like a small tape recorder from his pocket and placed it in front of him, angled towards her. "I'm only here because Alasdair made the request." She looked at Bentley. "But I was told this was going to be unofficial and informal. If Mr. Bentley is going to tape our conversation, then I want to be extended the same courtesy."

"Charles, turn that off and put it away, please," Harrison said with a small, tight smile.

Bentley shrugged and did what Harrison had asked.

"Now, you know that we want to talk to you because of the goings-on at Zakat College," Harrison said. "Alasdair has explained how you came to be involved, how you brought him into the picture, and how your collective efforts resulted in your findings this morning. He has nothing but compliments about your contribution and we're appreciative of your work. But, unless you feel the need to review what he said, I'd like to move on."

"I'm certain that Alasdair gave an accurate rendering."

"Good. In that case what I'd like you to do is tell us exactly what you think happened at the college."

"You know what happened."

"Alasdair told us that you and he believe there is a multitude of bodies buried near the back of the college's property. If that's true — and no one is disputing that — how do you think they got there?"

"I believe that about 150 young men, maybe even more than that, were murdered in cold blood and their bodies were buried in a pit in the ground."

Bentley started to say something, but a glare from Harrison stopped him.

"And who do you think caused those deaths?"

"It certainly appears to be Imam Tariq al-Bashir, who we now know is Wallace Murdoch, and the staff that he hired away from several national security organizations — including, probably, your own."

"How do you know the name Wallace Murdoch?" Gilmour asked.

"Alasdair told me." She saw Bentley's mouth tighten. "We managed to acquire two of his brushes, which Alasdair sent to a lab in Manila. The lab found Murdoch's prints on them."

"We understand that you got the brushes through the Muslim Brotherhood."

"Are you implying that the Brotherhood acted improperly?"

"No."

"Good, because they deserve your thanks more than I do," Ava said. "Look, I fell into this because I was doing a favour for a friend. That led me to the Brotherhood, and I became a conduit for their concerns about Zakat College. They were worried that the school was turning young Muslims into jihadis. They wanted the training stopped. They wanted to prevent any attempts at terrorism."

"But is there any doubt in your mind that the men who were at the college were committed to becoming terrorists?" Bentley said.

"Or did the college turn them into that?" she said. "But either question is hypothetical because we'll never know."

"Charles, let's not leap ahead," Harrison said. "I'd like to go back and talk about Murdoch a bit more, if that's okay with you, Ms. Lee."

"Go ahead."

"If Murdoch and his people did indeed carry out these acts, what do you think their motivation was?"

"I don't know anything about him or them, so I can't speak to ideological bents or character defects," Ava said. "But we do know they were paid — and I'd guess very well paid, since they were willing to give up their jobs and live like monks in the middle of nowhere in the southern Philippines."

"They were just hired killers?"

"Why not? Money has been sufficient motivation for killers since money was invented."

"Murdoch left U.S. government employment four years ago. As al-Bashir he's been in the Philippines for a year," Harrison began.

"He most likely spent three years learning the Koran and developing his new persona so he would be able to pull this off. A lot of planning went into it. This wasn't some fly-by-night operation," Ava said.

"And undoubtedly you believe he was well paid for those three years as well."

"Of course."

"By whom?" Harrison said.

"This is ridiculous."

"Why?"

"Because you're asking me questions you already have answers for," Ava said. "Let me ask you one that's more to the point. Have you told the Philippine government who Tariq al-Bashir really is and who murdered all those young men?"

"No, we haven't."

"And why not?"

"The answer to that question is quite complicated. Among other things, it may be the same as the answer to the question about who paid Wallace Murdoch," Harrison said.

"I think you're going a bit too far there, Brad," Bentley said sharply.

"Gentlemen, we asked Ms. Lee to come here because we want her co-operation. I can tell you that, after talking to Alasdair and after listening to her here, I believe we're not going to get it if we keep circling around the main reason why she's here."

"And that reason is?" Ava said.

"Don't pretend you don't understand," Harrison said.

"I'd still like to hear it."

Harrison sighed and shook his head as if trying to deal with an obstinate child. "Ms. Lee, we want your silence," he said.

"We would appreciate it if you could forget the name Murdoch and leave things exactly as they are with regard to what the government of the Philippines knows," Gilmour added. "They'll be told what happened at some point in the future, but we have to insist on having control of the timing."

Ava stared across the table at Gilmour and Bentley. "I'm not convinced that you'll ever tell them, and you're not in a position to insist on anything," Ava said. "I knew you would want something like this. What I don't know is how any of you could convince me it's the right thing to do. I believe that Wallace Murdoch is a mass murderer, and by extension so is the man whose name no one has mentioned yet. You want me to forget the name Murdoch? What about Tom Allison?"

## 44

**CHARLES BENTLEY SLAMMED AN OPEN HAND ON THE** table. "Tom Allison is a great American patriot and a great friend to Israel!" he shouted. "I will not sit here and listen to him described in that manner."

"He financed Wallace Murdoch," Ava said. "He made Zakat College possible."

"I also find your characterization of Murdoch extreme," Bentley went on, as if he hadn't heard Ava's comment. "Many people would claim that Murdoch is the furthest thing from being a mass murderer. What he's done is identify and eliminate terrorists who were a threat to America and Israel and Jewish people living in every part of the world."

"The young men at the college hadn't terrorized anyone," she said.

"But they were committed. They all swore to participate in attacks on Americans. I'm told that every one of them was given two chances to leave that college, to walk away from their training without any repercussions, and they chose not to. These were not innocents. They had made a commitment to kill Americans."

Jeff Gilmour leaned towards Ava. "How can you argue that these people didn't know they were going to the college to be trained as terrorists?"

"They were enticed by Murdoch, by al-Bashir."

"If it hadn't been him, it would have been by some other imam or terrorist organization."

"How can anyone know that?" Ava said.

"It's no different in my mind from the kind of sting operations that our police forces use against pedophiles, drug dealers, and crooked politicians," Bentley said. "There is a predisposition to do the deed. Murdoch simply baited the trap."

"With one rather large difference," Ava said. "When the pedophiles and drug dealers are caught, they are turned over to the legal system. They're not summarily shot in the back of the head and tossed into a mass grave."

"They would have done the same to us if given half a chance," Bentley said. "Our president believes that while no one gets credit for disasters that are avoided, because they are never known to exist, it's still necessary to make those hard decisions. One question we need to ask is, how many disasters has Murdoch helped us avoid? How many bombings won't happen? Some of us are of the view that Murdoch has taken the fight against terrorism to a new and more refined level. The fact that his efforts were independent of any government is slightly troubling, but not when balanced against his results. The man should be thanked, not condemned."

"Are you telling me that this idea originated with Murdoch and that he went to Allison with it?"

"I thought that had already been made clear," Bentley said.

"If it wasn't, it is now. I guess that means you think Tom Allison should also be thanked for embracing the idea and financing Murdoch," Ava said.

"Perhaps he should."

"Maybe you can give him a presidential commendation," Ava said. "I'd like to see the wording of that, because I'm not sure what words you could substitute for 'mass murderer.'"

"That wasn't called for," Harrison said. "Charles has a point of view that others also share, but it's thorny and controversial enough that no one wants to publicly air it. And that brings us back to our problem."

"Tom Allison and Wallace Murdoch?" Ava said. "Or me keeping my mouth shut?"

"What we're facing runs deeper than them, although I would sound naive if I didn't acknowledge that Murdoch's ties to the agency and Allison's connections to the White House are a concern," Harrison said, sidestepping her latter remark. "But Ms. Lee, I genuinely believe this isn't about right or wrong. This isn't about our personal sense of morality. What's done is done and can't be undone. This is all about containment now. We do not want things to get worse."

"How can they get worse?"

"If the details of Allison's and Murdoch's involvement became public, the results could be catastrophic. The Muslim world would be enraged, and even our so-called moderate Muslim allies would not want to be associated with us. Our agency would be smeared because of Murdoch, and our ability to work affected. The White House, the office of the president, would be connected to Allison and all kinds of inferences would be made. No one would believe that a rogue agent and an overzealous billionaire had acted independently. This would become the big secret American plot to wipe out Muslims."

"So why am I a concern? What about Allison? What about Murdoch and his band of killers?"

"We'll handle them. All I can say is that they'll be out of this business."

"You know they intended to expand into other countries, like some franchise operation?"

"There will be no expansion. This experiment ends in Tawi-Tawi."

"But they're free to otherwise go on with their lives?"

"I wouldn't put it quite that way, but I don't want to lie to you."

"I appreciate that, but it doesn't change the facts, does it."

"No."

"This is all about keeping me quiet?"

"Yes, I'm afraid it is."

"Have you considered that my silence might make me feel like an accomplice?"

"If it made you an accomplice to anything, it would be helping to maintain stable relationships with our allies and making the world a safer place," Harrison said. "That's a worthwhile goal."

Ava looked at Dulles, but he had turned away. Gilmour and Bentley seemed disinterested, and that bothered Ava more than Dulles's avoiding her.

"We don't want to make things worse," Harrison repeated.

"Can we do some trading?" Ava asked.

"What do you have in mind?"

"The Muslim Brotherhood is afraid that the Philippine government will use Zakat College as an excuse to clamp down on them. Can you find a way to blunt that reaction?"

"That would be tricky. The Filipinos are sensitive to any outside interference in their domestic politics. But we could give it a try," Gilmour said.

"Can you get Allison removed from the presidential advisory group?"

"No," Bentley said sharply.

"Can you arrange for Murdoch and his group to be permanently sidelined?"

"I'll pretend I didn't hear that," Harrison said.

"No, I want you to respond to it."

"We don't have any control over private citizens, and even if we did, that's not how we operate," Harrison said.

"Are you saying that you never operate like that or that this case doesn't justify it?"

"Why are you trying to provoke us?" Harrison said.

"I'm not provoking. I'm testing."

"Fuck her," Bentley said to Harrison.

"No, fuck you," she said, standing up.

"Don't be rash," Harrison said.

"That is the last thing I am," Ava said.

"Then sit down, please."

"No. I need some time to think, and I'm going back to my room to do exactly that."

"We can't let this drag on. We need to know what you're going to do," Gilmour said.

Harrison leaned forward. "I believe that if you really think about this, you'll reach the conclusion that there are sound and humane reasons for not exacerbating an already horrible situation. And Jeff is correct about the timing. There are some constraints."

"I'm not typically indecisive," Ava said. "I will make up my mind and I'll communicate with Alasdair when I do."

She started towards the door, but before she got there, Jeff Gilmour spoke again. "Ms. Lee, I would like to add one more thing. I know you're Canadian, and I assume from your crucifix that you're also a Christian."

"You're correct on both counts," she said.

"So it seems to me that we're on the same team," he said. "And our team is involved in a war for hearts and minds. You can hurt us or you can help us. For the life of me I can't understand why you would choose to side with the opposition."

"I'm not sure what team you're referring to. I'm not aware of ever having been on one." She opened the door and stepped into the corridor. She paused for a few seconds, long enough to hear Bentley say, "What a fucking bitch. I blame you, Dulles, for making us have to deal with her. If you hadn't taken her to meet Tom Allison or told her about Murdoch, we wouldn't be in this situation."

Ava started walking towards the elevator. If Alasdair Dulles had come to Manila for redemption, she thought, he might have to have wait for a very long time.

## 45

**AVA TURNED ON THE TELEVISION WHEN SHE GOT TO** her room. The press conference was over and the host was now interviewing various government and academic experts about what they were referring to as the "Bongao Massacre." All that anyone seemed certain of was that more than a hundred people were dead and that the government's dispatch of a mixed military/police/civilian task force had been entirely appropriate. When asked to speculate about motives for the massacre, the experts were quick to say that the facts wouldn't be clear until the task force had completed its work, but they threw around words such as *cult*, *Muslim*, *terrorists*, and *jihad* in a constant, interchangeable stream.

She lowered the volume so that the program would be less of a distraction but loud enough that she could hear if something new was reported. She sat at the desk, opened her computer, and turned on her phone. She had missed two messages while she was meeting with the Americans. One was from Wahab and the other from Senator Miguel Ramirez. Both just said, "Call me."

She could imagine what Wahab wanted to say, and she

wasn't ready to listen. She phoned Ramirez instead. Elisha answered, with a weary "Senator Ramirez's office."

"Hi, this is Ava. I'm returning the senator's call."

"Are you okay? I've been thinking about you all day, ever since we got the news about the college," Elisha said.

"I haven't had time to think about being okay or not. How about you, and what is Zoey saying?"

"It's all very upsetting. That imam must be a madman. People around here are angry that he hasn't been caught yet."

"And how is the senator?"

"He was in emergency committee meetings all afternoon, and he's been bombarded with calls. He's on the phone now with Mr. Juhar, who's head of the Muslim Brotherhood in Mindanao."

"Well, tell him I called, and when —"

"No, Ava, don't hang up," Elisha said. "He told me to let him know the second you called. Stay on the line."

As she waited, Ava checked her emails. May Ling, Amanda, her mother, her sister Marian, and Mimi, her best friend in Toronto, had all replied to her cheery earlier missive. For not the first time, Ava felt that she was living in parallel worlds, and rarely had she felt so little control in either one.

"Ava," Ramirez finally said. "What a terrible, terrible day for all of us."

"How are you holding up?"

"I feel like a punching bag getting hit on all sides."

"I'm sorry."

"There's no reason to be — it's part of the job. This is just worse than usual," he said. "But I am worried about my friends in the south. This may not go well for them."

"Wahab called me but I haven't spoken to him yet."

"He'll want to ask you about the American who was with you. That's why Juhar called me."

"What about the American?" Ava asked, immediately on edge.

"They want you to talk to him."

"Why?"

"Truthfully, I may be the cause," he said. "When I was speaking with Juhar earlier this evening about the task force being sent to the south, I mentioned that there's a large number of SAF members in its ranks."

"That's to be expected, isn't it?"

"The problem is that they're not all identified as such. Some of them work within other organizations. I made the mistake of referring to them as our version of the Trojan horse. I don't know what I was thinking. I guess I wasn't thinking at all — I'd been in that damn committee for four hours listening to senior security advisors telling us that the college is the tip of the iceberg and that we have to get below the waterline to uncover the real danger in the south."

"The Brotherhood?"

"Not specifically. More like Muslims in general. But once that kind of thinking sets in, everyone is fair game."

"What does any of that have to do with the Americans?"

"Juhar and Wahab want them to be a presence in the south. They think that if they're physically there, they'll act as a moderating influence on the SAF."

"What makes them believe that?"

"The Americans are always talking about building bridges between themselves and moderate Muslim communities. Your American colleague knows how co-operative the Brotherhood has been. He might be prepared to recommend that they have an observer role in what's going on down there. I mean, he could maintain that they still have an interest until all those anti-American threats are disproved."

"I'll talk to him," Ava said.

"Just like that?"

"Yes."

"You don't have any questions?"

"None."

Ramirez paused and then said, "I'll tell Juhar. It may help a little. Who knows?"

"Yes, who knows?" Ava said.

"Stay in touch," he said.

Ava put down her phone. She thought about the four men in the boardroom. When she had asked them about providing a small measure of support for the Brotherhood, Gilmour had equivocated. What did that tell her?

She sat quietly at the desk and thought about the decision she had to make, and as she did, a memory of Uncle came to her. Early on in their partnership they had been offered two jobs, but they only ever did one at a time. One involved a large amount of money that looked like it would be easy to track. The other involved much less that would be harder to get back. She and Uncle had talked about their options over a bowl of congee at his regular breakfast restaurant in Kowloon. "I know there is less money in the second job, but the man and his family need it more," he said. "Besides, the wealthier man came to us and said, 'Get my money back,' while the other said, 'Please help me.' I know the job is more difficult, but that should give us a greater sense of satisfaction when we succeed. Over the years I have found that doing the hard thing is most often doing the right thing."

Ava had no doubt about what the easy thing was in this case. In fact, she'd already done it, when she asked the Americans to help the Brotherhood. But what was the right thing? She took her notebook from her bag, wrote *Tawi-Tawi* across the top, and then contemplated making lists of the positives and negatives attached to her decision. She started on the positive side and quickly wrote *a safer world*. Then she stopped. *What am I doing?* she thought.

She reopened her email and began to write a message to May Ling and Xu. It took her over an hour to compose a draft. The first draft turned into a second and then a third. When the third draft was done, she left the computer and went to the bathroom. Ten minutes later she returned, reviewed what she'd written with a clear eye, and thought that it still held together. She added Brenda Burgess, Three Sisters' Hong Kong–based lawyer, to the recipients line and sent the document.

She checked the time; it wasn't quite eight o'clock. She phoned Pang Fai.

"Hey," Fai said. "You caught me halfway out the door."

"I wanted to hear your voice," Ava said.

"Where are you?"

"I'm back in Manila, but I'm not sure for how long. With any luck I'll get out of here tomorrow morning."

"Where will you go?"

"Shanghai."

"Ava, I was thinking," Fai said. "Maybe I'm being silly about not seeing you during the entire film shoot. Let's talk tomorrow, after you've left Manila and we have more time to go over it."

"That would be wonderful," Ava said.

"Now I have to run. I love you."

Ava held the phone in her hand for several seconds after the line went dead. When she put it down, she returned to the computer and sent another email to May Ling. It read: If anything happens to me, please look after Pang Fai. You can tell her the details about what led to whatever does happen, but it's more important to me that you tell her she was the love of my life.

Then she phoned Ramirez again. They spoke for almost thirty minutes and then exchanged multiple phone calls for another half-hour. The time that passed seemed like a few heartbeats to Ava. When she had finished all her correspondence and calls, she felt twenty pounds lighter, as if she were floating in mid-air watching a passing parade. Now all she had to do was get safely back to earth.

## 46

**SHE WAITED FOR ANOTHER HALF-HOUR BEFORE CALL-**
ing Dulles. She guessed from the tone of his voice that he
wasn't alone, and when she said she was ready to talk, he
was quick to ask if Harrison could join them.

"I don't care who's there," Ava said. "Where do you want
to do it?"

"We've been with Tom Allison in the conference room.
Brad and I just left, but the others are still with him."

"Did Allison come clean?"

"Yes, but that's all I want to say right now. Where would
you like to meet?"

"Downstairs."

"How about in the Bar?"

"Sure. I'll be there in five minutes."

She didn't need to freshen up but she went into the bathroom anyway. She splashed cold water on her face and looked
into the mirror. She was paler than normal, and there were
dark circles under her eyes.

She was alone in the elevator. As it passed the second floor,
Tom Allison came to mind. What was going on in the Reyes

Room between him, Bentley, and Gilmour?

"Ava," Dulles said as she stepped out of the elevator. He and Harrison stood about ten metres from her. "The Bar is full, but there's an alcove in the lobby that will give us some privacy," he said.

"Let's go," she said.

She followed them across the lobby to a sofa and chair that were almost hidden from view. Harrison sat in the chair while she and Dulles took the sofa, each of them keeping as much distance as possible from the other.

Harrison leaned forward as soon as they were settled. It wasn't a threatening gesture, but his hands were tightly clasped and his face was clouded with doubt. "Are you going to disappoint us?" he said. "I told Alasdair I thought you were, but I like nothing better than being wrong on issues like this."

"I'm going to disappoint you," she said.

"Ah," he said, collapsing back into the chair. He placed his fingertips under his chin and looked quizzically at her. Then his eyes bored into hers. She didn't turn away. "Why?" he asked.

"You might have swayed me with your appeal to help make the world a safer place. But then again you might not have, because I found myself asking a question. A safer place for whom? And my answer was a safer place for you and others like you. Not so much for everyone else," she said.

"Don't exclude yourself from our company."

"That's another thing," she said. "I don't like being told that I'm part of a team that includes people like your associates Gilmour and Bentley. And I found Bentley's convoluted rationale for supporting a death squad to be completely repulsive."

"I share your sentiments when it comes to Bentley,"

Harrison said. "But he is beyond my jurisdiction. Part of my job is to limit the damage that he and others like him can do."

"And where does Gilmour fit into that spectrum?"

"He's in a less advantageous position than me; he has to deal with the White House on a regular basis. I don't envy him in the least, and I think he does a very good job under trying conditions. Don't judge him too harshly for his analogy. He truly is a team player."

"Even if that means covering up for Murdoch and Allison?"

"Especially if that means covering up for them," Harrison said.

Ava shook her head in disbelief.

"The reality is that if people like Gilmour and me don't focus on the bigger picture, then what are now skirmishes become battles, and battles become wars," Harrison said. "Sometimes that means we have to turn a blind eye to acts we find despicable, because there's a greater good we're pursuing and we need to protect the resources we have so we can continue to pursue that greater good. That's the vision I was trying to present to you. Obviously I did a poor job of it."

"No, actually you didn't," Ava said. "I do get it."

"Then is it too late for a change of mind?"

"I guess I'm not a big-picture person. I don't see much value in trying to save the world by hurting or destroying people you meet along the way. I can't stop Muslims and Jews and Christians and atheists or anyone else from hating one another and trying to kill each other over things I don't understand. But I don't have to condone it, and in my mind, that's what my silence would represent," Ava said. "Then there's the matter of respecting the people I deal with. The most important part of that for me is keeping my word and honouring my promises. I made a promise to the Muslim Brotherhood and I feel bound to keep that promise. So maybe I can't save the world and I can't bring those dead boys back to life, but I can keep my word."

"We'll do what we can for the Brotherhood," Harrison said.

"You're too late."

"What do you mean?"

"I pulled the plug," she said.

"How?"

"I've already spoken to the Philippine authorities."

"What did you tell them?"

"Everything."

"I thought you were going to talk to us first."

"I didn't agree to anything like that. I said I would make up my mind, and I did. Then I acted on it."

"Who did you actually talk to?"

"I imagine you'll find out soon enough," Ava said. "But there's one thing I need to say that you may think unnecessary and possibly objectionable."

Harrison hadn't changed his position or his expression since he'd sat back in the chair. He looked like a man engaged in casual conversation, and for the second time that day he reminded Ava of Uncle. "I'm listening," he said.

"I have written an account of everything that happened, everything I know, and everyone who was involved. I sent it to two close friends who have their own sets of powerful friends and contacts, and to a lawyer whom we trust. The lawyer has strong relationships with the media in the United Kingdom and the United States. If anything happens to me, they'll make sure that information gets into the right hands."

Harrison pursed his lips and then said, "You are

correct — it was unnecessary. Though I'll still have to let Gilmour know what you've done. And I'm sure you understand that I can't vouch for Bentley or fools like Allison."

Dulles's phone rang. He looked at the screen in annoyance, then quickly hit the Talk button. "Roberto. This is an unusually late call," he said.

Harrison's attention shifted to Dulles, and Ava followed suit. Dulles had the phone pressed tightly to his ear. She couldn't catch any of the incoming conversation but she knew who Roberto was, and she was impressed by the control that Dulles displayed as he listened. Several times he tried to say something but couldn't. Finally he did speak. "I will tell them, and I'm sure they'll be amenable to that suggestion."

Dulles hung up, looked at Harrison, and shook his head slowly. "That was General Roberto Mendez. He heads the intelligence service of the armed forces of the Philippines. He was inviting us to attend a meeting of the National Intelligence Advisory Committee, of which he's a key member. They want to see us tonight. He knows that you, Jeff, and Charles are here, and they expect everyone to attend."

"What have you done?" Harrison said to Ava.

"I told you, I pulled the plug."

"It was a rhetorical question," Harrison said as he pulled himself to his feet. "I'd better go and tell the others. We should get organized to meet with Mendez and his people."

Dulles drew several deep breaths as he watched Harrison leave. Then he looked at Ava. "I wish you hadn't done it that way," he said.

"What other way was there?"

"Harrison was on your side, and he might have brought the others around," Dulles said.

"It didn't seem like that in the meeting."

"He had to maintain his position."

"Which he did very well."

"I'm not saying that he agrees with your opinions, Ava, but his attitude towards you is more personal."

"What are you talking about?"

"Maybe I should have mentioned this earlier, but he ran our station in Hong Kong during the British handover to the Chinese. When I told him about your Hong Kong connections and the partner you called Uncle, he asked me if you meant a man named Chow Tung."

"Yes, he was my partner, the man I called Uncle."

"Harrison was convinced it was him, and that made him quite sympathetic to your situation."

"How could I have known that, and what good would sympathy have done? You were going to put off doing anything for as long as you could, in the hope that the problem in Bongao wouldn't be connected to the United States. I didn't think there was that much time to spare where the Brotherhood is concerned," Ava said.

"You're right. We were going to drag our feet, though I'm not convinced that doing that would have been successful."

"So what happens now?"

"We'll meet with the Philippine authorities. We'll come clean about Murdoch but we'll protect Allison as much as we can, because we have no other choice. We'll eat some shit. We'll try to talk them into keeping things under wraps, and they may do that if the right deal is put on the table. If, in the end, we have to give them their pound of flesh, it will be Murdoch, or more likely a couple of his colleagues and a pile of money."

"Where are Murdoch and his crew?"

"Allison's just told us they left the Philippines yesterday afternoon."

"How? Where?"

"What does it matter?"

"You sound as if you were prepared for my doing this."

"It was always a probability in Harrison's mind, and after we met with you it became likely. So Harrison did have a plan — you just beat him to it. But do you think you've done the Brotherhood any favours with this approach?"

"My contact thinks we have. He was the one who spoke to Mendez. There were SAF troops scheduled to go to Tawi-Tawi. Mendez has agreed to pull them out of the task force."

"Your contact is Senator Ramirez, right? You mentioned him to me and Ryan."

"He's the one."

"I didn't mention his name to the others," Dulles said, "but I would appreciate it if you could find a way to hook me up with him at some point. I'm going to need some allies when this is done, and he'd be a useful man for me to know."

"I can do that," Ava said.

Dulles stood up and looked across the lobby. "Here they come," he said.

She and Dulles left the alcove. He walked towards the others while she hung back, quite certain that she wasn't welcome. Bentley and Gilmour glanced in her direction, and even from a distance she felt their hostility.

Dulles moved to join his colleagues, but when he got close, Harrison slipped past him and went over to Ava. She felt herself tense.

"I need to say something before I go," Harrison said.

"Yes?"

He reached out, grasped her arms, and pulled her closer.

"Uncle would have been proud of you today," he whispered.

## 47

**AVA SLEPT BADLY. SHE KEPT REPLAYING HER CONVERSA-**
tion with Harrison in her mind. She didn't doubt that she'd
done the right thing. In fact, it was the only thing she could
have done and still live with herself. But his final whispered remark about Uncle had touched her. Despite Dulles's
praise of him, Ava had lumped in Harrison with the other
Americans in the boardroom. Now she felt she should tell
him how much she respected the calm and graceful way he
had received the news that she had done the exact opposite
of what he had asked of her.

Whenever she managed to put aside her thoughts about
Harrison, the space was immediately filled with speculation
about how the meeting with the Philippine government had
gone. What kind of deal had been struck? Would anyone
involved actually be held accountable? Or would the truth
about Zakat College and the imam become victim of a con-
venient collective amnesia?

She woke three or four times after shorts bursts of sleep
and finally got up at seven. She went to the bathroom, made
a coffee, and sat at her computer to figure out her day. All

she knew for certain was that she was going to leave Manila, but for the rest of it she would have no idea until she talked to Fai. She hit her number and prayed she'd answer.

"Good morning, baby," Fai answered.

"I was hoping I'd catch you."

"I've been up for half an hour and I'm almost ready to leave. We're starting a bit earlier today."

"I've completely finished what I had to do in Manila, and I was thinking about what you said last night about meeting you along the way."

"Do you mean in the next day or two?"

"I can leave here today if that works."

"It's perfect," Fai said. "We'll be in Qujing tonight and are staying there for close to a week. It's a big enough city that we can have some privacy. The crew is staying at the Guanfang Hotel. You should find a different one for us."

"I know this sounds silly, but where is Qujing?"

"About 150 kilometres east from Kunming. The best thing to do is fly into Kunming and take a train."

"There aren't any direct fights to Kunming from Manila. I'll have to go through Hong Kong, and with the connection it's about a six-hour flight in total. Add on the train ride and I won't get to Qujing until sometime this evening."

"Whenever you get there will be wonderful," Fai said. "Text me when you confirm your travel plans and have a hotel. This day won't go by fast enough."

Ava ended the call and felt herself flushing at the thought of being in bed with Fai that night. She immediately went online and found a late-morning Cathay Pacific flight to Hong Kong and a late-afternoon China Air flight from Hong Kong to Kunming. She booked business-class seats on both.

Her search for a hotel was slightly more problematic. Qujing didn't have enough tourist attractions to warrant an upscale international hotel. It did have one that rated five stars, but it was called Fairyland. The name was off-putting but the hotel was adjacent to an attractive park, and all its reviews were laudatory. She reserved a suite and then sent a text and an email to Fai.

She turned her attention to other people on her mind. Harrison was at the top of the list, but she didn't know how to reach him. She called Dulles.

"Hello?" he said, sounding tired.

"This is Ava. I hope I'm not waking you."

"I haven't slept yet. The Filipinos didn't want us to leave the meeting until they'd all taken turns verbally lacerating us. When I got back here, Harrison and I had to deal with Washington, and that wasn't much easier. "

"I'm sorry for contributing to that. I was actually phoning to say that I hope you both understand why I did what I did. I particularly want to thank Harrison for the considerate and professional way he handled it. Can you give me his phone number?"

"He's already on his way back to Washington. They went directly to the airport from the meeting," Dulles said. "But I can tell you that he does understand. In fact, it was one of the things that he specifically asked that I mention to you. He said it's the kind of thing he might have done thirty years ago, before the system swallowed him."

"One of the things he asked you to mention?"

"Yes. He also wanted to tell you that before he left he made a phone call," Dulles said. "Wallace Murdoch won't be taking any more contracts from Tom Allison or anyone else."

Ava's pulse skipped a beat and she felt her grip on the phone tighten. "Did Bentley and Gilmour agree to that?"

"He didn't ask them. It was his decision and he made it. He wanted me to tell you that Murdoch was the very worst of us, and he asked you not to judge the rest of us even though we were once colleagues."

"Aside from telling him I'd never do that, I don't know what else I can say."

"Brad expects that will you say nothing at all, not a single word. This is ultimately between you and him. I'm just a go-between."

"When did he —" she began and then stopped. "Was there anything else he wanted to pass along?"

"No, that's it."

"Then why don't you tell me how it went last night?" Ava said.

"About as well as could have been expected. The new president is no friend of America, but he appears to dislike and mistrust Muslims even more than us. There was no sympathy expressed for the dead men at the college, and only the most grudging acknowledgement that the Brotherhood — for all the right reasons — played a key role in exposing the danger we all thought the college represented."

"Was the president actually at the meeting?"

"No, but one of his key aides was, and he was communicating with him by phone during the meeting."

"So you cut a deal?"

"Yes. But, Ava, I can't give you any details."

"Just tell me, will the Brotherhood suffer as a result?"

"They should be okay, and by that I mean left alone. If you want details, you'll have to ask your friend Ramirez. He was at the meeting."

"I'll do that."

"Good. Now I really have to go. I need to catch some sleep."

"I'm leaving Manila today, so we probably won't have a chance to talk again," she said. "Please pass along my thanks to Harrison, and I want to say that I enjoyed working with you. We made a good team."

"I feel the same. Who knows, maybe we'll get a chance to work together some other time."

"I sure hope not," Ava said. She heard Dulles laugh before saying goodbye.

Ava stared at her phone and was debating if she should call Ramirez when a call came in from a private number. "Ava Lee."

"This is Chang."

"Good morning, Uncle."

"I just spoke to Ramirez. He told me that your project has ended," he said.

"It has."

"He was most complimentary about your contribution. He's grateful in the extreme. Favours will be owed."

"Owed to you or to me?" Ava said.

Chang laughed. "We should be able to manipulate it so that he owes both of us."

"I don't need any favours from him. You can have my proxy."

"Don't be rash. You never know what position he might hold in the future."

"Yes, Uncle," she said. "Tell me, did Ramirez mention how the Brotherhood will be treated in the aftermath?"

"He wouldn't be so grateful if they hadn't emerged relatively unscathed."

"That's good to hear. When I talked to him last night, he thought that was how things might end."

"How will they end for you?"

"I have an eleven-o'clock flight out of Manila this morning."

"I'll send my car."

"That isn't necessary."

"I'm sending the car anyway. It will be there at nine."

"Thank you."

"Ava, you have to excuse me now," he said. "I have a call scheduled with Tommy in a few minutes, and you know what he's like about punctuality. You and I can talk later this morning."

Ava put down her phone, thought about calling Ramirez, and then wondered to what end. Nothing seemed to have changed from the night before. She decided to shower and start packing.

She left the room at eight, checked her bag at the front desk, and went to the Lobby restaurant. She picked up copies of the *Manila Bulletin* and the *Manila Times* and carried them to her table. The headline TERRORIST THREAT dominated both front pages. Before Ava could read how each paper had added its own spin, a waitress arrived at the table. She ordered black coffee and smoked salmon on a bagel with cream cheese.

She began reading the articles. According to both papers, the combined efforts of the Philippine security service and the SAF had uncovered the illicit activities at Zakat College and brought them to an end. There was a vague passing reference to co-operation from the Muslim Brotherhood.

When she had finished her breakfast, she got up, collected her bag, and stood outside the hotel entrance. Ten minutes later a black BMW pulled up. Rodrigo, the driver who'd met her at Aquino Airport, sprang out, reached for her bag, and opened the back door.

"I thought I'd ride with you to the airport," Chang said from the back seat.

Ava smiled. "Uncle, this really isn't necessary," she said as she slid in next to him.

"I didn't get the opportunity to thank you properly for that previous job you did for us. I thought I should make up for it."

"The first time was a job. This was a favour."

"A point well made," he said. "But will you treat the favour owed in return as casually as you treated Ramirez's?"

"Not a chance."

He smiled. "Tommy sends his thanks as well. And although we never discussed money, he authorized me to offer you two million dollars in payment for your services."

"I'd rather you and Tommy owed me a favour."

Chang reached for her hand and squeezed it gently. "Uncle would have been really proud of that reply."

"That's the second time in less than twenty-four hours that I've been told Uncle would be proud of me."

"It won't be the last," Chang said.

**COMING SOON**
From House of Anansi Press
In January 2019

Read on for a preview of the next thrilling
Ava Lee novel, *The Goddess of Yantai*.

( 1 )

AVA LEE SAT NEAR THE REAR OF THE PACKED BEIJING cinema. She was there to watch the premiere of *Mao's Daughter*. The film was set in Yunnan province in 1959, a year after the launch of the Great Leap Forward — Mao Zedong's disastrous attempt to impose industrialization and collectivization on Chinese agrarian society. Many farms stopped producing crops, and more than twenty million people had died in the famine that resulted from Mao's misguided effort.

A fictional drama, the film followed a young woman who would defy Chairman Mao. The woman was the mother of one child, the wife of a rice farmer, and the caregiver for her aging parents. The land had been in her husband's family for generations before Mao's Great Leap Forward prohibited the private ownership of farms. When her husband resisted turning the land over to a collective, he was prosecuted, labelled as a counter-revolutionary, and sent hundreds of kilometres away to do forced labour. His wife was allowed to stay in their modest home, but any means she had to support her child and her parents was stripped away.

As the family's situation steadily deteriorated, the young woman's reaction morphed from submissiveness to fear, then to anger, and finally to an unbending determination to fight against the government. She confronted local Communist officials and they turned her away. Undeterred, she walked several hundred kilometres to the provincial capital of Kunming to petition senior officials for return of the farm, only to be turned away again. Those rejections strengthened her resolve, and she decided to take her case all the way to Beijing. She walked the entire distance, nearly 2,700 kilometres. To make her cause known, she hung a piece of cardboard around her neck that read I AM A DAUGHTER OF MAO. THIS IS MY LONG MARCH FOR JUSTICE.

As the film ended, a heavy silence filled the theatre. Ava took a deep breath, overcome by emotion. Pang Fai — her friend, her lover, the actress who portrayed "Mao's daughter" — had been luminescent. Her body language, her facial expressions, and her penetrating eyes had strikingly conveyed the woman's emotional and physical journey.

Fai was regarded as the finest actress in Chinese cinema and was building an international audience. Ava's involvement with her had started as a business venture — Fai was the public face of the PÖ fashion line, which Ava owned with her partners in Three Sisters Investments — and then had evolved into a full-blown romance.

"Pang Fai!" a man shouted as he rose to his feet several rows ahead. His voice seemed to liberate the rest of the crowd, and more than a thousand people stood as one, clapping and calling her name.

A man in a tuxedo walked onto the stage in front of the screen. He held up an arm in an attempt to quiet the crowd, but the cheering didn't die down. Finally he shrugged and spoke into a microphone. He was almost yelling, but Ava could still barely hear him. He looked into the wings and motioned for some people to come forward. Two men joined him; the only one Ava recognized was Tsang Min, the film's director.

When Tsang took the microphone, the crowd quieted. He introduced the other person on the stage as the film's producer. Then he spoke for a few minutes about how difficult it had been to shoot in so many parts of China, and how they'd felt at times like a travelling circus, putting up their tents in a different town or city every night. "But the truth is, if we had been rooted in one place or had even been limited to one room, as long as our cameras were capturing Fai's performance, the story could still have been told," he said.

He looked off to the right and nodded. Pang Fai stepped into view and glided towards him. She was wearing a pale blue cheongsam with a high slit that exposed her long legs. She was tall, about five foot ten, and in three-inch heels she towered over everyone else on stage. The audience erupted. She kissed Tsang and the others on each cheek and then turned to face the audience. She placed her palms together, raised them to just below her chin, lowered her head, and bowed. She held that position for at least a minute, and then for another as the cheering continued.

Tsang stepped beside her and handed her the microphone. She held it against her chest and said, "I want to thank you all for coming, for your support and your generosity. Without you, films like this could not be made." The audience exploded. Pang Fai bowed one more time and then left the stage. The others followed and the house lights came on.

Ava stood up, feeling something approaching awe. It was the first premiere she'd ever attended, and she'd had no idea what to expect. She saw Chen Jie, Fai's agent, standing in the aisle about twenty rows ahead. He was about sixty and had the rotund physique of a man who'd enjoyed a lifetime of good food and liquor. He had been Fai's agent since her early days in the business. He knew her intimately, including her true sexual orientation, which he had managed to keep secret. Public knowledge of it would severely damage, if not destroy, Fai's film career in China.

Her affair with Ava was the first real relationship that Fai had had with a woman, and Ava knew Fai had shared that information with Chen. He hadn't taken it well, and whenever Ava had met him at lunch or dinner, he made his dislike of her and the reason for it quite plain. Now, as she made her way down the aisle towards him, she wondered what kind of reception she would get. She thought he had seen her when she was ten metres away, but he either didn't recognize her or chose to ignore her. He was speaking to another man when she finally reached his side. He acknowledged her with a quick glance and then resumed his conversation.

Ava waited, her anger at his rudeness slowly building. Finally he turned to her. "You weren't supposed to be here," he said.

"I was invited," Ava said. "Besides, I was with Fai in Kunming the day before she started making this film. That was a year ago. I thought it fitting that I see the end product."

"I was told you couldn't make it."

"My plans changed."

"Does Fai know?"

"No. I thought I'd surprise her."

"She doesn't like surprises. And neither do I, where her career is concerned."

"I'm hardly a factor in her career."

"You are in her life, and the two things are not easily separated."

"Chen, will you take me to her?" Ava said sharply. "Or do I have to find her myself?"

He sighed. "Come with me."

He walked to the front of the theatre and turned right, to a small door that was blocked by two security guards. The guards moved to either side when they saw Chen, and one of them opened it for him. She felt the guards eyeing her. "She's with me," Chen said.

The door led into a small corridor. Chen walked briskly towards the far end. Ava trailed, her shoe heels almost making music on the tile floor. The corridor was lined with storage rooms, and Ava wondered where they were going until they reached a door that read MANAGER. Chen knocked and then opened it. Ava peered past him and saw Fai sitting in a chair by a desk, surrounded by Tsang, the movie's producer, and three others she didn't recognize.

"I brought you a visitor." Chen took a step to one side so that Ava could pass.

Fai stared at her with wide eyes. Then her mouth flew open and she leapt to her feet. In three strides she was in front of Ava, throwing her arms around her neck. Ava felt Fai's fingers digging into her shoulders, and she was pressed so hard against Fai's chest that she could hardly breathe. "I'm so happy you're here," Fai said in a rough whisper. Ava thought she could feel her body tremble.

"I wasn't sure I could make it until last night," Ava said. Fai clung to her, and Ava began to sense disquiet among the other people in the room.

"Perhaps we should leave you two alone for a moment," Tsang said.

"Please," Fai replied.

Ava didn't move until the men had filed out of the office and the door closed. She placed her hands on Fai's arms and gently pushed herself free of the embrace. "I didn't mean to shock you," Ava said. "I just thought you would be happy with the surprise — although Chen would probably disagree."

"I'm so happy you're here," Fai repeated.

"The film was wonderful, and you were fantastic," Ava said. "For the first ten minutes or so I felt I was watching you, but then I was drawn completely into the character. By the time the film ended, all I cared about was Mao's daughter."

"It was a good role, and Tsang is a great director," Fai said, her voice catching.

"Are you okay?" Ava asked. "Or are you always this emotional at premieres?"

Fai stepped back until she found the chair and sat down. "I've spent the past two days in hell," she said. "All I could think about was how much I wanted to see you and how much I needed you. I started to call you so many times, but then I always stopped."

"Why? You know I would want to hear from you."

"It was me, not you. I wanted to tell you what's going on, but I couldn't do it over the phone."

"Fai, what's the matter?" Ava said, moving next to her.

She looked up at Ava, her eyes brimming with tears. For a

second Ava thought of a scene from the film she'd just seen, except this time Fai wasn't acting.

"What happened?" she said.

"You may have just seen the last film I'll ever make."

## ACKNOWLEDGEMENTS

This story did not have an easy course, and it didn't fall naturally into the Ava Lee chronology. Indeed, it went through four different permutations — including two as a non–Ava Lee book — before becoming what it is. And what it is, I believe, is one of the very best Ava Lee novels.

I need to thank some early readers for their input. Among them are my daughter Jill, my wife, Lorraine, Farah Mohamed, Farzana Doctor, Robin Spano, and Steele Curry.

My agents, Carolyn Forde and Bruce Westwood, were particularly supportive, and there were days when their encouragement was really needed. My gratitude to them again.

My editor, Janie Yoon, and I had our disagreements about this book, but we finally resolved them over dinner at an American Library Association meeting in Orlando. The result fairly represents a melding of our views and reinforces for me the belief that it's hard to create a good book without a good editor. And I have a great one.

As always, Sarah MacLachlan, Barbara Howson, and the team at House of Anansi have been terrific. I'd like to give a special nod to Laura Meyer, head of publicity. Laura is capable and completely professional, but she's also a joy to work with, and that's a much less common attribute.

**IAN HAMILTON** is the author of the Ava Lee series. The books have been shortlisted for numerous prizes, including the Arthur Ellis Award, the Barry Award, and the Lambda Literary Prize, and are national bestsellers. *The Water Rat of Wanchai* was the winner of the Arthur Ellis Award for Best First Novel and was named a best book of the year by Amazon.ca, the *Toronto Star*, and *Quill & Quire*. BBC Culture named Hamilton "One of the Ten Mystery/Crime Writers from the Last Thirty Years That Should Be on Your Bookshelf." The series is being adapted for television.

# NOW AVAILABLE
## From House of Anansi Press

The Ava Lee series.

**Prequel and Book 1**

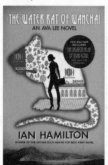

**Book 2**

**Book 3**

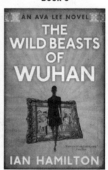

**Book 4**

**Book 5**

**Book 6**

**Book 7**

**Book 8**

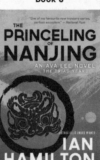

**Book 9**

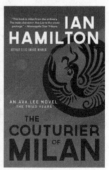

www.houseofanansi.com • www.facebook.com/avaleenovels
www.ianhamiltonbooks.com • www.twitter.com/avaleebooks